The FIRES Of Home

Daniel H. Gottlieb

Canopy Publishing
Post Office Box 1645
Lake Oswego, Oregon
97035
www.canopypublishing.com

Books By Daniel H. Gottlieb

The GALILEO Syndrome
The FIRES of Home
The Dialogues of Sancho and Quixote,
MYTHICAL Global Warming Debates: 1997-2010

Library of Congress Control Number 2010911028
ISBN 97809753655-1-9

Printed in the United States of America

The FIRES Of Home

Daniel H. Gottlieb

CANOPY PUBLISHING
Oregon 2010

"The great synthesizer who alters the outlook of a generation, who suddenly produces a kaleidoscopic change in our vision of the world, is apt to be the most envied, feared, and hated man among his contemporaries. Almost by instinct, they feel in him the seed of a new order; they sense, even as they anathematize him, the passing away of the sane, substantial world they have long inhabited. Such a man is a kind of lens or gathering point through which thought gathers, is reorganized, and radiates outward again in new forms." --Loren Eiseley

"The mind is its own place, and in itself can make a heaven of hell, a hell of heaven."-- John Milton

For La

"And what I should be, all but less then he whom thunder hath made greater? Here at least we shall be free; the Almighty hath not built. Here for his envy, will not drive us hence: Here we may reign secure, and in my choice to reign is worth ambition though in Hell: Better to reign in Hell, then serve in Heaven." --John Milton

CHAPTER 1

She leaves the overgrown parking area on a red sandstone path through stunted redwood and cypress. At the cliff, winds blow sea-haze, a dirty taste rides it; salty mist from the yellow sandstone cliffs. She stops, looking down into the churning Pacific, then out to the fog. The darkening clouds at the horizon never disappear anymore; some say the Earth mourns the loss of so many children. Dr. Winston Doe looks around at bent cypress, then below to the violent cove--and its ever-present debris--all part of the California Memorial Park. The Pacific spills over the salt-washed boulders and tide pools; tattered clothes still roil in faded colors, an ethereal gyre. During the early climate change years, many had taken their lives here rather than face, what they believed was to come: the end of humanity. The ragged clothes remain in the cove's ocean wash spinning around and round, a blend of spirit and consumables.

Rain falls from the first fingers of a Pacific storm: "Screamers," as they were once called. During the worst years of global warming, these horrific storms killed millions. They pack less punch now. One can endure them for an hour before being pummeled into seeking shelter. Feeling invulnerable, even at forty-five years, Winston Doe remembers when two minutes was all she could tolerate. The thick drops from this first rain band further washes the path. Puddles in the hollows grow larger, as spent branches from the redwoods above wander back and forth.

Dressed in oilskin, the lithe woman waits impatiently for her meeting with the soldier. Handwritten communication convinced her he has the Diary she seeks. It contains hope, a route to salvation, and a calling she has followed her entire adult life. Dr. Winston Doe wanders, deep in her heart. A branch falls, but she has little concern for the finger of the storm. She knows from her youth that the first three bands are warnings; anyone who has not heeded them receives exactly what they deserve, a quick death. Winston glances about, listening to the quickening storm. The beat of the waves, the thickening fall of rain, trees bending, these are all signs of danger. She waits on the narrow path, still believing it will lead to truth, and Russell Biner. Had he not been her first lover, he might have been--she believes--her last.

She has no idea where he might be right now--perhaps dead--and if the search itself hadn't become just as important as the prize then her hope might have died. Her meeting with the soldier will, if she is lucky, ease her guilt. In a cold corner of her heart, she wishes Russell were dead, but Winston just cannot convince herself it is so. At the very least, Dr. Doe has agreed with her God that death is the only alternative to the search for her best friend, truth.

Looking around again and feeling the rain band building, she meditates on her choice to be here. Winston is supposed to be on vacation but this "authentic" version of Sammich Ginda's Diary intrigues her. The feeling pulls fears that all she really wants is closure, that Russell Biner died almost two decades ago. Winston refuses to see her self as such, and stepping over a puddle, she looks over the edge of the cliff working not to curse the soldier, or the heart, which has brought her to this place.

"Beautiful." Wood cracks. An old squat soldier appears from behind a redwood elder. Admiring Winston's smooth dark skin, the old man notices a tremor of fear in her hand. "Now there, I'm nothin' for you to worry about." His scarred, pock-marked face births a smile of blackened teeth. "Some of your colleagues, they may fear of ol' Sergeant Frew because of what I know and what I saw. But otherwise, I'm just an old man proud of the men and women I served with during the war. Did you know that none of them were shell casings or expendable pieces of equipment?"

He's crazy.

Her dark eyes cannot believe the sight of this ghostly figure. To Winston, the men and women who fought the Jazz War were giants--the saviors of humanity--but at the end, hunted down and killed. This reminder of their sacrifices chills her. *A spent casing indeed.* "They said you had died," she speaks looking away from his gaze. Frew was known to be tough, and he did look like his picture: ruddy, slightly browned low forehead, a shoulder bulge from a broken bone--but still alive? She wonders how he could have survived the hunting parties.

The old man listens to the winds and forest sounds, nodding unconsciously.

"Well? Are we going to wait for the storm to kill us?"

"You don't even know what the word death means." He sneezes. "We know." He laughs quietly. "Every one of us was a hero. You're here looking for your honey, but it's not just about Doc Biner--that poor bastard." Glancing skyward at the rustling trees and dousing rain, he sighs. "So if you think I am here to hurt you or sell you lies about the war, you have it wrong. Truly, I am dirty and my clothes are ripped. I'm about as crazy as you can get and still walk. I could kill for a hot meal and a safe bed. But, hope is what this meeting is all about, and so I'm here to set that foolishness damned-straight. I'm a soldier. All I deal in is the facts of life." He shakes his head. "And you're going to help me do it. In exchange, you'll find out about your honey." He giggles. She detects duplicity.

Even so his frayed clothes speak to her of his dedication and displacement. *How is it even possible to have hidden so long like this?* "Where is he?"

Frew watches her. "Here. But if you tell anyone where you got this, Madam Director, there isn't a prayer for you to collect that Nobel Prize I hear they want to give you--and that's just a fact." He acknowledges her tan satchel with a nod. "The credits?"

Winston sweeps a hand through her gale of long black hair then closes her fingers on the strap of the worn leather shoulder bag. Her narrow brown eyes turn crystalline with defiance.

The blood-feud-look she learned from her parents intensifies as she speaks again: "Let's finish this." Winston spits on the battle-scared boots of the veteran in front of her. *Civilization, the never quiescent Earth will speak throughout your generation of our sins*, says her mother's memory. She hears a boot pull from the mud, and looks down. Frew stands on a bed or needles. "Isn't your friend going to show himself? Or does little missy scare you…heroes?"

"It is our legacy to stand and die." His head tilts back in a sardonic laugh--then snaps forward--and measures her from ghostly muted eyes. He spits at her feet in recognition of her grit--a soldier's sign of respect. Mocking her bravado though, he rasps: "No worries, girly." Wind whips his coveralls and he dons a down-pulled hat from inside his coat. She assumes it is a signal of some sort. Overhead, swirling black clouds dim the last of the sunlight.

"Another rain-band on the way," she says.

He pulls out a bit of licorice and chews it. "Don't ya' love the lee between storms?"

"So now you're the weatherman." She looks around, as if to gauge the wind. In fact, she wants to make sure this man's comrade, the one hiding in the woods to her right, has not moved. For the briefest moment, she wonders if it might be Russell Biner. Then she sees the eyes. Winston studies people's eyes first, having been brought up as a Walker, a West Coast nomad. In the forest, especially in the forest, they foretell the future. The man in front of her, his eyes are brown, not blue; these eyes are also cold with the curse of death. Something else, she knows those eyes. "Plow?" The man in the woods, weary and covered with the white haze of age, steps backwards into shadows. She can no longer see him. *A smile? Can't be, but he's another Ginda, also reported dead.*

The hidden man begins to cough.

Frew speaks quietly: "Family is as rare as hen's teeth and more valuable than life since the Jazz War," says the soldier in front of her. "You like family, little girl?" Frew gazes about behind her. "You Walkers are supposed to be dedicated to your family. Got some with you?"

She shakes her head no. "What proof do I have that what you have is real. I want to talk to Plow."

Winston sees a warm glow from the odd soldier in front of her, then a veil of hardness. "No."

"That's him isn't it?" In fact, she now has no doubt of it. The demand provides her with a sense of control. She remembers Sergeant Plow as a decent man, but that was many years ago. His youthful vigor looked drained, but the weary eyes in the glade seemed happy. The other soldier, Frew, steps forward into the dirt between them. He steps back. The boot leaves its imprint: crossbones, ugly, like a pirate flag thrown ashore by the ill wind.

"And don't think I don't remember you, Missy Doe."

Noting how the greeting keeps changing, she glances quickly around her. *He is checking for a Clipper link, checking his memory.* "Nothing has changed. We are congruent. You probably tore the link out anyway." She snaps her lips shut, angry at the old habit of talking too much to strangers. It's common for Walkers to speak their minds and a demerit used against them in the "civilized world". Here she fears her openness may cause someone to die. Another fierce rush of wind. Her eyes pick up the sight of a fallen branch on the side of the clearing--a useless weapon.

Suddenly he moves back from her and speaks--his gaze fixes on her new black rubber shoes. "You know us. We saved the world, over and over. I ain't got no hope, just a hole in the head. Forget about Plow, he doesn't care any to talk to you." Frew tries to laugh. Something clogs in his throat and he chokes out a cough. Winston looks over her shoulder as he doubles over, coughing. A moment later, he straightens up--his rutted face a bright red. "Getting this disk to you is important to us, little girl. That's why one of us aren't dead now."

"Nonsense, quit the oil."

From his soiled torn coat, Frew pulls out a small computer and disk that had been wrapped in a black canvas bag. He hands both to her. Examining the disk, she identifies it as genuine by scratching the red crossbones etched into the label: the smell of beets, Lazlo Wolf's macabre humor as security. She hands the soldier a plastic card and he immediately slides back into the dense thicket from which he had sprung no more than five minutes ago. From the thicket: "There's also a gift in the bottom of the bag for you--don't lose it." Laughter disappears in the howling wind.

Hands shaking, she withdraws a second item from the bag: a dark woven square of eucalyptus--about a meter long. It is Sergeant Plow's simple monument to all the Gindas. She had thought it lost.

Each woven strip of bark has the name Sammich Ginda written on one side of it. She unfolds the cloth and turns it over. The soldiers' birth names are on the other side. Every one of the soldiers who gave his or her personality and memories to Clipper is remembered here, woven together in this cloth. She can just make out the golden letters that spell the 1600 odd names. Dr. Winston Doe, the U.N. Director for Research on the Environment knows how perfectly this monument reflects the Gindas' contributions to humanity. She also understands their sacrifice.

Clipper's function had been to help weave together the memories of different soldiers into an evolving patch called Sammich Ginda. It covered a rip, commonly called the Jazz War, a lesion in humanity's connection to its planet. In the early global warming years, the rip had been called the tipping point. The sad truth of our leaders' ignorance revealed itself only after the worst of the physical effects of climate change had been mitigated.

This chaotic event, this tipping point, this lesion, is the most closely guarded secret of her time: Earth has become a stranger to its child, humanity. The species connection to Earth, in Winston's time, is only an illusion. The gravest fear of her time is that the rip might reopen and the horrors will again engulf humankind.

They thought the tipping point was some mega-storm. They never knew that anything like this could ever happen; space moving away from us like time flows away from us. A past-space, like a past-time, how many of us, if we knew, would have believed it, or guess that we could never catch Earth-space again?

Humanity drifts in an illusion of home called Earth: An Earth that knows no science, or rationality, a home planet that has become a foreign space, eating the species that caused the rift, and chasing humanity like a demon in the night.

It looks the same...Most of the time. And when it doesn't the lay person simply goes mad. How could our ancestors have not seen it coming? How could they have caused it? They knew the tipping point was real and they knew they did not understand it. So they ignored it and tried to huddle inside their wealth. They consumed everything. Then that madness came home to roost. Time passes--and now space passes.

Looking down at the eucalyptus document, it is considered an urban legend now, she barely believes she holds it in her hand. "Okay, maybe the Diary is real," she says to no one. The winds moan; time to leave. Packing the items in her leather bag, she turns, leaving the cliffs by the muddy path.

Russell Biner, the man she searches for, dedicated his life to the problem of working with the tear, not of fixing the rip. There was no fixing it. He sought to construct an enduring patch for living with it, or developing a path to a stable time/space.

Remembering Roo, Russell Biner, Winston Doe finds herself seeing him standing at an open window one soft red dawn, telling her how Sergeant Plow had planned to weave a sail from the coffin packing material--the eucalyptus fibers that made up the burial rags--and never return to civilization. He had said Sergeant Plow was quite mad in his clarity. He was going to sail around the world until the madness disappeared. “A Buddha’s Voyage,” he called it. “One to take away all our pain.” This vision was no metaphor for Russell Biner, she now knows that now. She just can’t find the cradle of it, yet.

That morning had been sunny and bright--also it was the first time she had heard Roo speak of a patch called Sammich Ginda. Winston’s feels her heart thump. That patch had led to a new theory of environmental networks: Our species needed an anchor that would hold us to Earth until we could figure out how to find a present space. *That anchor was Sammich Ginda--a blinded focus tied to a mad past--anchoring us to an illusion of home, even as it burned.*

Winston is unique in her ties to the environment--for many reasons. As a Walker, the focus of her culture was the environment; it remains deep within her. At the same time, her prodigious intellect had robbed that mystery of its beauty--the environment is a puzzle for her. As a researcher, she stores information. As a lover, she drives forward. In her ignorance, the environment remains her salvation.

Once Earth was our home. Then we forced our balance with the planet in the wrong direction, we broke the link and set our species adrift in a way we still do not understand. The planet is, of course, still there and so are we. But we have left a solid Earth and embarked on a sea of change. Humanity is adrift like cork on the ocean, unable to touch solid ground--even though we know the ground is still there--somewhere. The only fix appears to be a member of our species who absolutely believes in our link to Earth’s space. So we have learned to live in the Gindas’ focus, the lie, and call it truth. And we the damned continue to wander, hoping to find a way to rule in hell.

All melts in front of her, a Daliesque moment: Winston is in the drift of a declining space. She stares at a glittering morning--Winston does not know she cannot feel the storm--and closes her eyes as if a warm summer day were baking her body. A shimmering tableau, a ghostly reality, it happens to everyone now as space tips away from humanity; the media had said it was always so--and Winston had laughed the reports--but she cannot recall that now.

A well trained researcher, her prodigious intellect immediately kicks in and she calms her breathing to deal with the spinning sensations caused by the shimmering image of madness. *I am in the drift.*

For just a moment, she again feels the winds and wet. Trees begin to rock against the next storm band as it comes onshore. She recalls the storm that now threatens her life. But then her intellect succumbs and she falls back into drift.

She stares at the man she seeks; he smiles, cooking pancakes on a stove. Dr. Winston Doe works to fight madness. “Russell it that you? Are you a Ginda somewhere? Locked up?” Even as pale echoes of the storm surrounds her, she sees that he pours maple syrup. Thunder and violent tremors break rain upon the land and pelt the forest. A large branch falls, splashing her with muddy water, had it landed on her she would be dead. True to the insanity of her time, she laughs.

Growing up at the tail end of the global warming horrors, she witnessed the power of freak storms. The storms of today hold far more terror than potential destruction. She knows what to do, but she cannot do it because she seeks the tableau she loves, a life of peace. *It's the diary. It's real. I remember feeling as if I were always about to faint back then too. Its how we all felt after global warming's murderous peak. Roo, where are you?*

Looking through the whipped firs and redwoods, feeling as if she were a leaf in a creek, the winds adding nothing to her concerns, her free hand reaches out to try to touch the wind. As a child, Winston had been taught that winds were really the spray of emotions. Nothing returns to her. *I am in it.*

Without connection, her legs fold and she glides down to the wet brown floor of the forest. Her eyes and mind avoid the suicide mark of the soldier's boot. She tucks her long brown oil cloth skirt under her and waits. Winston believes she knows exactly how far offshore the storm lurks. The greed for truth may become a highway of death for Winston Doe--and she knows it--but her body acts without her control.

Wind and branches unhinge drippings into the broadening puddles around her. The wind shaken rain mocks her driving thirst for knowledge. She bows her head as she has been taught and wants to ask the storm to take her if it wishes. She cannot. The mad wedding of want and logic birthed by the nets and TV channels before her birth takes her. Then, like a child on Christmas Eve stealing an early peek, she glances around and draws the military issue laptop from her satchel.

The tattered label on the disk says:

> **Clipper Project Display Unit: Possession and examination of Diary files are only authorized at the TOP SECRET grade for League 2 and above. All others must immediately contact U.N. Research Corps. Failure to do so will be punishable by death.**

She feels herself spinning, then sees the notice and reads it. *They still do this.* Winston marvels at the way government tells you something without telling you anything. She knows any punishment won't come from a law enforcement agency--but from the content of the original Diary. Another large branch falls.

Winston does not know that has happened. Her body has become a prisoner of madness; even so, her intellect fights it.

She inserts the disk. As it loads, she glances around, sniffing the breezes--*some kind of dying beast nearby. The mate of a female?* Unknown to her at this moment, the wind takes the eucalyptus rag and blows it into the woods. The most ephemeral of sails has begun its task of pulling Winston along. It is the flaw of an analytical mind and broken heart that she can only feel a sense of uncertainty as the world places her squarely on her approach to truth. In its cycle, she will return here over and over and never grasp Plow's sail. Winston will instead call this time a search for her lover, Russell Biner, with her compass, the Diary. The truth mocks her though--it pulls only on the sail; her being remains here, apart from it.

Another smaller branch lands on her back. As with the loss of the eucalyptus cloth, she has only the Diary to guide her. She will finally understand this folly when she sees the cloth again.

Slowly, she turns the crank handle on the side of the player; a message comes up on the screen telling her the battery will not hold a charge for more than a five minutes at a time. Only a tree falling on it could damage this box, but generators and batteries fail repeatedly--just like everything electronic from the global warming days. She continues cranking the unit, telling herself it will allow her to focus. The wind wails as if it were a siren. She does not care. Earth can no longer speak directly to its children.

Winston watches the screen. The disk spins up as the screen lights with a U.N. banner, a United Networks banner: A green glowing Earth appears in rotation: The planet dissolves into the logo of the Clipper Project: an angry snorting bull.

How absurd we are. All the other versions of the diary had a U.N. flag flapping in a digital breeze. Is there any way we don't bury reality?

The rutting bull dissolves into the same skull and crossbones that still tattoos the ground behind her. Five words orbit the skull and crossbones: "Virtue, Honor, Decency, Truth, and Intelligence."

Then, from the digital heap, the object of her desires appears, the still face of her lover, Dr. Russell Biner. Thick brown hair swept back, a high forehead and piercing eyes that gaze out without seeing her, his laugh lines above high cheek bones--and that tickling mustache of reddish brown hair. Her heart seems to leave her chest.

Behind him, a window--she recalls arranging the curtains just before the photo. All the light around her fades, then it returns, a bit brighter; she feels herself bathed in a shimmering pink glow and wants to laugh. She hasn't seen this image of Russell in over a two decades. Winston will not believe this picture contains the sum of what remains of him, but she studies the pleasant smile on the screen: the kind eyes a bit too close together. *Handsome in a geekish sort of way--those fuzzy eyebrows he refused to trim had always made him look so old.*

The program freezes--a chill runs up her back. Like a bird she starts, slowly glancing around. The screen then blinks a command: "?"

A small eucalyptus branch cracks free and tumbles to the ground landing on her arm. A gash of red appears. She hits return and stares at the black currier font against a white background.

The words "I am dead" appear on the computer screen.

The Ginda Diary Chapter 2

I am dead.

Someone has suggested I should remember people are being slaughtered. Lazlo Wolf said it. But then I'm not supposed to recall memories, just the recordings from that computer, Clipper.

I hear a voice talking to me. It's him again, Lazlo Wolf.

I am a soldier.

I will follow my orders.

I'm too tired to remember all that pain. Maybe tomorrow. I like being dead. I guess I am to recall another's memories, but how?

FLAT LINED.

Monday--This is an improvement. Keep the day of the week. That wasn't me. What is this place?

FLAT LINED.

Monday afternoon--Who are you? What are you?

FLAT LINED.

How the hell does that happen? Oh crap, my input is leaking through to the subjects. I am guessing too many memories are at the surface. Clipper, hard reset, authorization Biner, Russell. Lazlo, check out the switches between the subjects and myself. We may need to add some distance.

Monday--**The Ginda just flat lined again. Isn't 20 miles enough? All this for so little progress. This should have provided enough isolation. When we are recording an entry, let's reduce it. When the Gindas are working keep it standard.**

Tuesday--The first thing I remember is my mother. I love being near her. I remember she said good-bye to me. We stood next to a huge blue and white bus. I remember because I'd never been on a bus before, or a train, or anything like that. They made them illegal during the Greenhouse Laws to fight global warming. She kissed me and said "Never give up." The other soldiers were already on the bus; they laughed at her. I also remember thinking there should have been more of us in training. So many died so horribly, oh my, God, it was horrible. Who is the enemy anyway?

FLAT LINED.

Lazlo, I am sure it's the question mark now, but I am not sure how it fits into the spatial rift. That's one for you. We'll also need to consider

redoing the links. Five dead in four days is a no go for me.

(From Dr. Wolf: Per above, Dr. Biner will signal us in the event of a personal emergency. Next, our fears about troop mortality levels have been confirmed. The two dead men and the three dead women have given us far less data than we had initially hoped. We are on hold until we have spoken with the Directorate. Date suppressed per requirement.)

Wednesday morning--I remember seeing. I can see the long barracks. Why are they all so dirty?

(From the Directorate: From this point forward in the Diary, every new daily entry will signal a preceding fatality. No other notation need be made.)

(Note to the Research Team From Russell Biner: These notes are to remain outside the Ginda's grasp. Let's use this for all our notes and keep comments to a minimum.)

(From Dr. Wolf: Okay did everyone get that transmission from Dr. Biner? Good. So we agree that every day will signal a Ginda fatality. Also the following format has been suggested. Please stick to it.)

(We must honor these people if we want to keep people like Plow and the rest of them cooperative on this project. J.Pard/R. Biner/R.Merton/L.Wolf. All Agree. Date suppressed per requirement.)

Wednesday afternoon--I'm inside the barracks.

It's a cream-colored building with shiny brown linoleum squares and black lines in between. There's a high-pitched roof with exposed rafters. The ceiling lights are weird, like disco balls. Below are beds--bunk-beds--all lined up along long walls with chairs in between. At the end of the beds are tall cream-colored lockers. The walls are mostly white-washed windows. I smell ammonia. One window has scratches on it: "Help me forget." It's my window. My words. My life. My trunk has a diagonal scratch across it. The black metal frame of the bed is rusted.

Fifty guys troop in the far door. They all say hi. A few fall onto their beds. They're all wearing those khaki jumpsuits. Some are sitting around, some are unpacking. I swear this place must have been built a hundred years ago. There is a trooper on the floor. It's me. I'm bleeding. I am dead, again. Who is watching me as I bleed to death?

Thursday morning--Someone, the Sergeant I guess, says: "Don't get mind-bent by the Gumbies and kill yourself. Don't get offed by someone else going nuts--and God knows how many others in the bargain. Win the war, Trooper. We're counting on all of you."

I hate this place—especially that stupid guy making the noise with the jaw-harp. That Sergeant is also a nut. I've never seen anyone so pissed-off. What the hell pissed you off, white boy? Are there more than me in here? How many memories am I?

Thursday afternoon—I'm scared. Winning the war scares me because of that little capsule embedded near my hypothalamus--whatever the hell that is. It will explode when the war is over and give me a permanent headache. But that's only if we win wrong--I don't understand how you can win wrong. Oh, I see. If we win then I'm too dangerous and they won't let me go home. Screw that, we'll lose. We won't see the end of the war. Oh my lord, it isn't really a war, there is no enemy. **No, the enemy isn't seen.** It's us, what have we done to ourselves? What did we do that was so wrong that we have all gone crazy?

Friday--"Quit your bitching."

Sergeant Frew looks like a washing machine: square, white and ugly. I hope he doesn't read this. I don't like white folk. They think they own the world and you better not tell them they don't, or they'll take what they think they don't own and try to kill you for it for enlightening them. There is this other guy named Plow. Plow's face has a nasty scar. They say he's so tough he won't die until we win. I bet he has one of the little capsules in his head also. He says he does. Wait, I didn't speak. I wonder if he put the words in there himself?

(Commentary from the Research Team: Our first transcortical memory with two way communication has appeared in the form of a quote from Plow. Clipper has taken its first real step towards editing individual human experience and linking it into new subjects. The team is ecstatic. R.Biner. Date suppressed per requirement.)

(Commentary from the Executive Director: Per new funding requirements, as each

soldier passes memory into Clipper, and before its edited contents are passed onto subsequent subjects, their individual memories will no longer be noted except through the internal notation of the day of the week. Lastly, all subjects will be referred to as Sammich Ginda. L.Wolf/R.Merton/J. Pard. Date suppressed per requirement.)

(Staff Exception: Dr. Wolf states: "...the subject passes their memories into Clipper..." We have confirmed this equals mortality for the subject. This confirms Dr. Wolf's intentions early in the project to use any means to achieve success. Prior entries on the decision process regarding which soldiers to use next, and the approval cycles remain sketchy. J.Pard/R.Merton. Date suppressed per requirement.)

Saturday--Plow says they want to know what I'm thinking. That's so the guys running this platoon can give my thoughts and memories to someone else later on. Imagine that, they're interested in my thoughts! It's hard to believe. I always figured I was just here to get kicked by fat cats and get killed in this Army.

My thoughts in someone else! I bet that person will not know whether she's thinking my thoughts, or her own. I have to type everything into this little computer at night. I never had one of these before. They're going in there so some guy named Sammich Ginda can do his job. Wait, these are all my own thoughts. I am Sammich Ginda. **No these are the thoughts of all the soldiers who have died before me. I've got to try and save her. Oh I've got her.**

I feel him choking another soldier. Your curse

is worse than mine, Dr. Ginda. There is a war. There is no war. Oh my heaven, I am Ginda. I am a weapon. Why did I agree to kill my self so you can use me as a weapon?

Gone.

Sunday--One of the guys, Gus, he's my friend. He says he doesn't like the idea of us giving thoughts to someone else. He says Plow told him not to sweat it because he--and the rest of us--will probably be dead in a few weeks anyway. Plow also said our job in this Army is to dump thoughts into these computers, then die. Well, at least that's one task I won't screw up.

They told me before I volunteered, that I would likely be dead in a few weeks. I remember that so clearly, but it doesn't seem like they told me. It's like they told someone else and I am reading that. I feel like I've been confused for years. I wonder if Doctor Biner can me get out? Maybe he can help me go back? Can you help me, Doc?

CHAPTER 3

The screen is blank...A hard slap to the face.

Winston Doe suddenly feels the rain and the pain. Small pink rivulets of blood flow across her cheeks. It takes her a moment to remember the storm surrounding her. She does not remember the slap or the man who delivered it. Then the blood is a mystery because the slap has already slipped into the mayhem of memories.

The thundering skies flash their lightning panic. Eucalyptus branches clatter down with reports like gunshots. One drives her to the ground; Winston cries out in pain as the disk player slips from her hands. The storm howls murder. Feeling a deep gash along her back, Winston works to get up from the mire. She retrieves the player, rubbing the wet leaves and mud off the laptop, raising herself from the soggy mass of muck. Looking around for more falling branches, she takes three steps, then stumbles into a stream filled with muddy runoff. She rolls herself out of the water. Her body quits as the rain beats down upon her. Trees sway; crack, a pine falls nearby

With her right hand resting on a nest of fallen branches she closes her eyes. Calming her breath by facing the climate touch, its weather's assault, she watches the tree tops above. *This storm, the madness of those times calls to me.* In a panic she gets to her feet and breaks into a run.

Up ahead, she sees hope: a clearing by a parking lot. The shambles of the strip mall glow in the eerie light as the storm moans louder. Trying to catch her breath at the edge of the field, she freezes for moment.

I pray this is real.

The shattered shopping complex is mostly wrecked concrete and steel surrounding an open field of cracked blacktop. A creek flows through the center. "Storm Screamer, you may seek me in your reclaimed buildings," she says a defiant tone learned in her youth. It was the way the Walkers had taught their young to distance themselves from madness...Or imminent death.

The shimmering glow of madness returns to her sight. Trying to focus on the objects in front of her: the mossy vine-ridden buildings, the rusted cars, the wrecked signs, she seeks a shelter. One building seems to have four walls and a roof. A crudely painted red cross cuts through the merging planes and random colors of her madness. Then she sees the edges of concrete and steel, limping towards each other. She runs to the moldy cavern inside.

Slime covers the tempered glass walls and counters, the purple plastic seats and tables, the once brightly colored interior stinks of rot; this was a fast-food restaurant. But the building had been buttressed during the global warming years. Reinforced concrete girders retain the walls. Looking around at the slowly flooding fields outside, she concludes this became a designated shelter because it sits high on a mound. She will be safe here from the mounting storm--assuming the rising creek outside does not drown her or sweep her away. She looks for signs of flooding. None of the high water marks seem more than a foot above the masonry floor.

Winston settles into the comparatively dry lee of a table top in the corner. *Gaia, what have I done?*

Hearing the death-howl of the winds still unwilling to partake of fear, she places the player in front of her and opens her shoulder bag. *The rag is gone.* A determined woman, she cannot help but work the problem: *This disk is unedited. It contains all of "Then"--not just the data. Digital memory holds the rips also. Russell--you were right--space is a function of scale.*

"I curse you, wind," she calls out, angry at her own carelessness. "You took it, neh? Fine--so then you keep the cloth for me till I need it. Thief."

The madness drops as if it were a curtain. In front of her, the glow of her kitchen table, food and flowers, candles and fruit. *It's a tipped space.* She watches the shimmering glow of madness before her; looking again for the eucalyptus rag, she sighs and wills herself back to the interior of the shelter.

Then, like a trained monkey, she sits and begins winding the laptop, checking the remaining charge on the computer. Only half of the power that should register remains in the unit. Still the disk will be safe. She presses start again and waits for an image, but finds herself lost in a tablecloth and candlelight of madness. She begins to pound the table beneath her to remove them. Of course, it does no good. Then she basks in it, glad her being has gone to seed. Winston feels too tired to fight it.

It takes her sight; they are sailing. She is explaining to Roo that Walkers call boats, shoes, because they cover the feet and keeps them warm and dry. He asks her why she owns so many pairs of boats--even for a Techie--and he laughs. Until she jibes the sail boat, sending him into the salty water. She sails around him awaiting his apology: an apology for the insult of calling her a Techie.

Then Winston sails alongside him as he swims back to shore; they make love on the beach, spending the night under the stars. The computer's harsh display cuts through the tableau as the Diary begins again. She sees text. Everything blurs to pinkish haze. Blood from a head wound leaks into her eye.

CHAPTER 4

Monday--Nothing existed before I was a soldier.

I only remember sitting in that cold pink room and being told there was no way out, and that they wanted to record my thoughts in a computer.

And I, dummy that I am, said, "No problem. Just show me where to sign. I need the money."

And so now I sit here, supposedly dead, on my cot, in these ancient barracks, typing all this crap. I must have been one dumb SOB to join up and agree to give my memories over for a few bucks. Some guy just hung himself, again. That's it. I'm out of here. Why should I be next? I got my cash. I spent it. Without it I starve. Why shouldn't I be next?

Tuesday--So, I have definitely copped someone

else's memories. But who I am, and where I am, that just don't cut the pie. They just keep dyin' and these dumb generals ain't got the foggiest idea why. I think we screwed-the-pooch when we pushed this climate thing. We shoulda' just let ourselves die and let the ants or the ducks take over. We shoulda' let it go. Seems to me we are like the dinosaurs, running out of time. Good thing we ain't that important. It's like back in the crib. My friends used to think they can run anything because they got a few gats. They oughta' see the cappers these chumps have. Man, I'm laughing.

Time to sleep.

There are the dogs lying dead everywhere. I hear everyone's dreams around here always start like this. I think we're all joined and we don't know it. I hate those scientists and their buddies, the religious Joes. Everyone knows they're full of it. Don't they?

(Commentary from the Research Team: Our first collective dream memory appears here, conveyed and placed by me--note that the dead dogs remained, regardless of our best efforts. L. Wolf believes this is the first example of inter-tie between humans--Dr. Wolf's so-called Species Focus. R.Biner. Date suppressed per requirement.)

(Exception note: I don't see how a person can take the place of a planet. We need to follow the data on dogs. J.Pard. Date suppressed per requirement.)

(Commentary from the Research Team: The rest of the team is pessimistic of any

step forward due to modifications of the extinction of Canus Familiaris. The exception to this is Dr. Merton who claims genetic manipulation is the answer. L.Wolf/J.Pard. Date suppressed per requirement.)

Wednesday--I just asked Sergeant Plow about not remembering anything. He says they gave us a drug when we first got here. Then he shows me a form that I filled out saying it was okay. Plow wouldn't say about why they did it. I don't recall seeing anything, but that looks like my signature. And I am not going to challenge Plow, not a chance. Word is those guys didn't hang themselves, Plow strung 'em up because he was pissed.

Our interior environment is putrid, but the proof is in the putting. Where the heck did that come from?

Who the hell is Roo Biner?

What the hell are you doing inside my skull? Wait what do you mean I am in a glass something? Where is my body? What the hell?

Thursday--Dr. Pard speaks through thin, weasel-lips. I hate him. "Besides," he says, putting the signed paper back in his desk, "all of us had such crummy lives that, if we remembered anything, the Gumbies might use it against us in battle." Mine must have been real bad for me to volunteer for this nut house. Right now, I can't see any reason why I would do this. Hell--I don't even know what I'm supposed to do--besides die!

Maybe I volunteered for glory? **Or maybe to help complete a natural cycle**...

I wonder if we are our own enemies. Maybe we are all just time puppets. I think we are the planet's puppets, now cut loose from our strings? I wonder, what if it is not a string but a rubber band? We could jump out of here. Is that possible?

> **(Commentary from the Research Team: Note the link to completing the cycle. The research teams believe this is a breach of the Gindas' isolation initiated by L. Wolf at the expense of R. Biner as Dr. Biner had no knowledge of this event because it was during one of the launch sequences. It was subsequently confirmed by J. Pard that this is the case. Though the reason is unknown, certain events suggest a lack of concern on the part of Dr. Wolf for Dr. Biner. J.Pard/R. Merton. Date suppressed per requirement.)**

> **(Notes from the Administrator: This maverick change by Pard and Merton against Biner and Wolf will be dismissed. The new data on cycling will move us forward by years--by allowing Biner to place himself as a parallel connection between Clipper and the soldiers yet remaining physically distant; we gain unending insight into the spatial breach by this event. No punitive action is recommended and mortality rates continue to drop among the troops. G.Smetana/B.Fong. Date suppressed per requirement.)**

Friday--I wish I knew it all, like some people; it all seems a mighty stupid thing to have done, enlist in this crazy Army. Oh, off we go again to an Army-sponsored horror show. Death and destruction in our time-a movie courtesy of the Department of Defense photographers and the enemy. I love that name they gave the enemy: Gumbies. It's better than Kraut, or Gook, or Whitey. Gumbie sounds like something weak and easy to beat. I hope this video isn't as gory as the first one we saw. On second thought I wonder if I even want to see it?

Saturday--This is a very spooky place, this-here barracks. At the end of the aisle, between the rows of bunks, there is a holographic projection on the wall just under the rafters. It shows a black-hooded figure of death against a pink background. Underneath the projection is a locked door. The Sergeant says will scare the crap outta' us when they open it. He said it would be open in a few days. Thanks, pal.

Frankly, that figure scares the crap outta' me. A couple of the guys told Plow they hate it. He beat the shit out of them in about five seconds. He's another tough white boy. That figures. They're usually mean. The Gumbies took over the planet, now we are all mean. We poison everything anyway. We didn't need their help. "Hey Plow, who screwed it up? It wasn't really us, was it? Congrats, asshole, we were too poor to mess up so much, right?"

Sunday--Yesterday I saw a video of some people who jumped off a walkway and landed head first. I can even tell you the story. There were these two boys with their dad and mom on vacation. The children were standing with their backs to a railing, smiling and saying silly things like they want to eat hot dogs. Then they stopped smiling. The boys looked at each other, and then jumped.

It was horrible. But what was worse is that the adults--one of them was holding the camera--just walked up while the kids were still on the rail and kept recording as they jumped. They didn't try to save them or anything. The camera was then put on a tripod--the man said something to the woman, her name was Jenny, or something. Then the mother jumped. Then the father jumped. A second or two later, someone picked up the camera and showed the four of them dead on the rusty grate decking.

So at the end of it Plow stands up and asks us how we feel about an enemy that can do that to a family.

We tore the place apart we were so angry at the Gumbies. I hate them. But I wonder: how come we have never seen a picture of the enemy, just white families having horrible things happen to them?

(Commentary from the Research Team: It is agreed by all parties that the first real steps toward a viable defense against drifting space began here, as cultural bent was finally identified and eliminated. So long as other people were the enemy, we were powerless to convince the Gindas the link to Earth inexorable. Unconfirmed by J.Pard or R.Merton. Date suppressed per requirement.)

(Amendments from Corporate Advisors: Note 1: It has been agreed by the above research team that this Diary shall never be published or set aside for public review. Note 2: It is also agreed that there will be no prosecution or attempts at culpability

for the two researchers Merton or Pard, regarding the longevity of the subjects called Sammich Ginda. This dispensation does not apply to any other researchers. Note 3: Further, all references to the soldiers will be in the collective name of Sammich Ginda and subject to evaluation. Note 4: A full investigation of Dr. Wolf's activities will be commenced as soon as practical. All data regarding Species Focus shall be labeled "League One Eyes Only". Date suppressed per requirement.)

Monday afternoon--We just had a briefing with some new guy named Merton and we were shown something called Petri dishes or something like that. On these flat glass disks was some gelatin stuff and then on top of that was a white fuzz that had grown. I guess they use these things for culturing virus, or bacteria—something like that. Some guy named Pard came in and told us a big part of the problem with the Gumbies is the white stuff they use against us. He says they have located it now and the scientists are able to eliminate it. Scientists know everything. Anyway, Dr. Pard says I am here to fight the madness caused by the white stuff on the culture. Funny,this is a war against an enemy nobody has ever seen except for these bugs that they grew to hurt us. No one, until now, I guess, knew how to fight something so small. "Because it was everywhere," Dr. Pard says. The plan is for us to fight with our minds--because they are so small we can hurt them with our minds. The joke here is most of us are going into battle unarmed, or shooting blanks. I'm afraid of how true that old joke is. No wonder we keep dying. I wonder why Dr. Wolf isn't around. I wonder if he believes this bull Pard was putting out?

Monday night--Something has changed. None of the guys here think the lab-coated yahoos who run this outfit know what the heck they're doing now. These last few days all we've done is eat, watch movies, do a little exercise, and type into these computers. Gus is my friend. He always calls me Sammy—not Sammich. Someone died today. I don't remember him. Did he have red hair or black?

Tuesday--God, I really think nothing makes sense anymore. Polken Frew, one of the guys, asks Plow what we're supposed to be doing. Sergeant Plow says, "Nothing." Gus says he can handle that. Gus is my bunkie. He's another angry white man, but not mean like Plow. In other ways though he and Plow seem the same. They're both smart. But I don't like Plow. I like Gus. The first thing he had said to me was that he didn't like Africans. I told him I didn't like Europeans. We've gotten along great since then.

My mom says the angriest of them is a redhead, a red-headed Irishman. Gus has a thick red beard that covers his whole face below his dark eyes. He's the hairiest human any of us have ever seen. The joke around here is that his beard doesn't stop until his toe-nails. Gus is sitting at the table next to me, typing. Gus says he remembers what he did before the Army, but he says he doesn't discuss it anymore because none of it exists anymore.

I wish I knew where I was before this happened to me. I don't know why. I don't know and Gus does--that is so spooky. I think that's why he is here. I'm glad Gus is here.

Polken Frew said Plow would never have hurt me. Is that who died? I wonder: did Gus kill me? How come guys keep dying?

Wednesday--**Sammich Ginda is not my name. I was not Polken, or Gus. Where did that name Sammich from? Where are my hands?**

> **(Notes from the Research Team: No memory break was necessary here as it came from Dr. Biner. For all our sakes we hope his directive that we provide more insight to Sammich Ginda about where he (Sammich?) really is in space will prove to be the correct action. We continue to have assaults against the facility. The rate of societal breakdown appears to be increasing rapidly and our progress has slowed. We must speed the research process along now. J.Pard/R.Merton. Date suppressed per requirement.)**

Wednesday afternoon--I'm in the dark, with someone else's memories. I swear it feels like I'm somewhere else sometimes. Sometimes I hear Lazlo Wolf talking. He's the one who said it. He said Sammich Ginda is getting lost but now I am Sammich Ginda.

I am Sammich Ginda. I thought I was everyone else. I wonder: Is it better to be lost or to be in control? I suppose the answer to that is: That depends on where you wind up at the end. If I only understood more about how I snap back into being after I die. It can't all be about memory, or could it? I think a Ginda needs to understand it. Where will we end up if it breaks? Can we snap back someplace else as well as someone else? I'm in a different place. Aren't I?

Monday--We just met the chief bottle washer: Dr. Lazlo Wolf, Ol' Wildhead. At least that's how Sergeant Plow refers to him. Dr. Wolf said that tomorrow we'd begin to do something new. Then he said we would go down in history as the first battalion to engage in actual battle with the Gumbies. He stared at me the whole time.

I think that qualifies as a strange feeling. Wolf said we should note any strange feelings in our computer-diary. Of course, in this place is all strange feelings. There's something weird going on here with my memory. What the hell am I doing with someone else's memory?

Tuesday--I can't remember my name. They're trying to fix that. I'm in the U.N. Marines. We used to be called Green Marines, Greenies, but since global warming that has changed. I guess the United Network Marines is better. Plow said if someone calls me a Greenie I'm supposed to punch them out. That sounds rational.

I can't put down my rank; it's a secret, but take a guess. I have no memories that Clipper says I can't have. I only do what I am told and I have no power. That must make me very important. Odd to know I will not be allowed remember something. Seems to me I should remember anything I want to. I'm free, Asian, and 21. Well two out of three ain't bad. I am going to use my mind to kill Gumbies and their little bugs.

Also I can't say that we're stationed somewhere

near the eastern Pacific Ocean and that our official combat denotation is SF Delta.

Polken, he was my friend, he and I asked Plow who titled the brigade. He said we should take it up with Dr. Wolf. Then there's that weird emblem on the far wall. It has large yellow letters that say "The Rubber Band Brigade". I don't like that name one little bit. I am going to talk to someone.

I did. Plow spit on my boots. I did a quick away. You don't want to stand there when that crazy guy starts spiting at you. If Plow spits on your feet he likes you—then he beats the Hell out of you if you don't listen to him. He doesn't worry me though. He follows the rules. The one who concerns me is Pard. I don't trust him. I like Dr. Wolf. His hair sticks straight out as if his finger were permanently stuck in an electrical socket. I think he fried his brains just like me. He's also skinny and ugly with crazy eyes. He talks to himself. He hates what he is doing. He keeps talking to some guy named Russ who, as far as we can tell, doesn't exist. Somebody is nuts, but I'll say this about Dr. Wolf, I never saw a guy who worked so hard. Sometimes I think it should be him in here and not me. Something isn't right. Leave my memory alone you damned machine. Why should I care if others die? Hey, where am I now? Why is everything glowing? Don't you guys know what the glow means? Why should I keep quiet? Holy cow, now that was an earthquake!

Wednesday--We are on a new base. A memo hangs in the latrine that says our task is reconnaissance. We're to acquire data for Lazlo, and his computer, a pile of silicon called Clipper. Apparently,

Clipper is the computer that is going to win the war--not us. I would like to go home now. I am from San Francisco. I can't go home anymore. I am a soldier.

Gus says we should change our name to Kamikaze Force Delta. Gus thinks they are going to run us at the enemy to get information so our mistakes can train the Clipper computer and some guy named Sammich Ginda--he's some dude they got stuck in a jar somewhere. Gus thinks if we go to fight these Gumbies, we're going to get the shit kicked out of us over and over.

I can't believe that. I may not know diddly-squat about the armed forces, but I know they don't just sacrifice people to get information.

Gus said, of course they do. He says that's the problem we are fighting. We never really knew what the heck we were doing.

How could *they* not know? They said they did. Maybe the idea is not to know. I am trying to hide it. **Could that be it?**

Thursday--We have no idea what we are doing. But neither do you. Every step kills us. We Gindas have hid this glowing thing from you. But he saw it. All of you see it as well, just before you die. It is the first blush of space drifting. If we track it we can track the beginning of the madness. I know why you didn't have any reports before. I think the fact is you dummies are trying to control things. We don't control the drift so do we need to patch it? I think not, because there is nothing to control. Somehow, I think it is not just we who are floating through this problem but you as well. I see no doubt that we are no longer attached to Earth. None of us wanted to sacrifice for you. That's why we were silent. I guess I am spilling the beans because I am too damn smart. I've always been a fool. Do you even know what that means?

No. I can't explain it. Damn it, he's gone.

Laz' I will tell you what I just saw. The lack of memories frees the Gindas and gives them clarity and some kind of flow into capability. So maybe it isn't power, but capability that matters.

I hear you saying it now Lazlo: Species Focus.

My response, give it a break. These soldiers are not dying because they encounter madness. They are dying because they are beginning to live--but they wither to death from their memories of what we tell them. We thought we were helping them by controlling their events. We were killing them. We might try to be in the wake of their consciousness, rather than mentors of their consciousness. That could work as an anchor for us.

This one was so brilliant. Dear God, she is beginning to suffer.

In any case we must let the Gindas have their way. They are the path to something new; they just fall into it. I am sure they are not a weapon of defense to restore our past. I cannot help but wonder what happens if the brains are given eyesight, and real bodies. Merton might be right about that one. But I doubt our link to Earth-space will be restored, just like the time cannot be reconstructed once it passes us, but the resulting tension that builds in the body might show an avenue. I want to follow that tension event, call it a rubber band for security.

Oh, please stop screaming. No. Don't kill her.

I am also wondering if the passage of time moving away from us is a gift from the dinosaurs. And our gift to the next master species is the passage of

space away from us and them.

I can't do this anymore.

Clipper, Pilot Nothing stroke Wolf three-five-nine. Record-hard reset. Biner, Russell, execute. God forgive me for facilitating the death of that woman who brought us so far so quickly.

(Notes from the Research Team: It is clear the real breakthrough in Species Focus came with this insight from Dr. Biner to Dr. Wolf that the tipping point effect was spatial and permanent--and that time's flow may not have been natural but an affect somehow caused by the previous dominant species. While certain concerns do remain that Dr. Biner has sacrificed so many soldiers to deliver this information, the advancement of human knowledge seems to outweigh the event. We are closing the labs to prepare for the body culturing test this weekend. Mutations have been rampant. L.Wolf. Date suppressed per requirement.)

(Exception from staff: We find this conclusion of dinosaurs setting time adrift for humanity as self-serving and sinister. We believe more work needs to be done to confirm this wild hypothesis. R.Merton/J. Pard. Date suppressed per requirement.)

Friday--I do have a family. I think I do. They are all I think about, but I cannot remember anything about them. I must have a mother and father. I'd like to see them--or at least hear them call my name. She died when I was a child. I want to touch my family. Maybe I have done something wrong. I remember. I don't remember them. Maybe this is why I'm isolated like this. I don't like being able to see through others' memories. I don't remember doing wrong. I'm sure if I did wrong, I didn't mean it. Can I have another chance? I don't want to die. I want to see and feel. Can you help me?

(Notes from the Administrator: We have seen substantial proof that the injection of the Ginda into a living body makes sense and so despite the continued failures, we will provide funding. As to Dr. Wolf's other methods, from this point on we can only note them with the forgiveness that comes with time. These are desperate times. It must be remembered by those that read this and claim a right to judge that during this period, the effects of the Jazz War threatens to engulf us all. Thank goodness for mistakes, and the progress that results. General G.Smetana. Date suppressed per requirement.)

Chapter 5

Dr. Winston Doe moans in the old shelter. She shivers from the cold and wet. Bemused about the reluctance to accept a hypothesis that a member of a species might be able to experience life though the others of that species; she giggles. Musing has functioned as a shield for her, nursing her intellect, and containing her fears. She waits for the next wave of madness. *Species Focus became the cornerstone of humanity's evolving understanding of ecosystems. We were so vain we missed our own capabilities. We polluted our world to the point that reality fell apart and we still had the ego to blame technology. Was oil really the demon? We cursed ourselves when we used the dinosaurs' essences to power our life. I sound like a Diary entry.*

Looking around, she speaks: "Do I know anything about the past, at all? You here lived for commerce and died from the resulting lack of meaning. For what? Were you all insane? Now the Earth takes it all back." A combination of madness and communication, she speaks to her surroundings--as a kind of release--when her shields fail. From outside of Walker culture, these conversations are seen as an amusing primitive ritual. Tonight, they show the unraveling of her ties to this space and her attempts at maintaining control even without it. Winston Doe is a highly trained researcher. For hours she will continue to clutch her intellect--and mumble her fears: at the night, at the storm, at the Diary--until she begins to chant for the dawn. Winston knows she is going mad.

She cannot feel the storm or the eyes that watch her.

Still night, Winston checks for the signs of the sun as she examines the storm clouds. Nothing about the space around her surfaces into meaning; it is all habit. She does look for, but of course does not see, Sol's coming mark and reaches in the pocket of her oilskin coat for a hand-sized gold watch. Tapping the small globe at the top, she winds the spring generator. Had the sun been out she would have used the compass built into the pewter bracelet she wears to determine the time of day with a sun dial. The face on the chronometer lights: three-thirty in the morning. She does not remember she must board her bus by eight. She has lost ten hours so far.

Apart from herself, she winds her chronometer over and over.

Madness breaks over her: She recalls reading the Diary of Sammich Ginda and the researchers' blind quest for a convenient truth to suit their career goals. The folly of her own desires draws forth her cold and crystal clear thought; it seems to her the killing of others has no end. Like Pard and Merton, she too has taken certain ideas and held them close in service to her career. These ideas she had once felt as innocent, seem murderous.

Her hand clenches the timepiece. "I am losing myself in this. Gaia no longer wants me." Winston howls in a wail of pain and anger, rejecting the forgiveness she once felt towards Roo for disappearing from her life. "You sacrificed the soldiers, and me, for truth, you bastard." She screams louder, as if seeking retribution from the dark shattered edifice that surrounds her. "You had no plan of how to win. Is that how you got so far? Stumbling through madness, like me, now? Do I know anything about my path?" She cannot fathom that the world could be so evil--or good. For others who have arrived at this point in the drift, the next step is violence. But for Dr. Winston Doe, there is only silence; even as the walls glow in a pinkish haze.

Then it tips: She sees Roo's famous lecture in front of her and moans in pain. *I am in the drift.*

She had memorized his speech for her orals: "Humanity did not know the watercourse of mind could turn against itself once we dammed the unseen ecosystems by our avarice. We had seen our shared connection as drops forming small puddles that would mix and flow into each other. We did not guess, at some point, the resulting pool of water must flow and enhance us. Instead, we built a pool of madness that leaked out into the waters of mind."

She grabs the handle of the laptop to keep some link to the space around her.

The lecture continues in front of her: "Can any of you imagine any of those power-crazed, consumption-based humans accepting the notion that they were, in effect, a slave to commerce, and that every attempt to change that clarity by inserting truth just caused another small lesion? Would they have altered their advertising dollars by a penny? Would they have driven a mile less? I think not. Unbalanced commerce was not a platform to float upon, rather it was our toilet, a gift from Gaia, for us to drown in. We constructed a truth from our leaders' failure, then a flood of self-congratulatory myths about the climate, fed by a need for power and then advanced it by memory. But memory is our problem. A problem we dammed behind a wall of self. You see, progress, in the Gaian sense, depends on flow, not dams that hold repeated events."

Winston cackles in madness, as she continues to turn the handle of the computer, even as the first red glow of dawn breaks on the muddy walls of her shelter. *We researchers have this absurd vanity-dance. The falsehoods that fed soldiers to death to cover mistakes are no different from assaults on valid research.*

Winston stares straight at the cold, empty, selfish light of her own goals. The Diary, she now suspects, was not even kept ultra-secret because it held an inherent threat to any reader's sanity. Instead, she sees ego and mistake, vanity and stupidity, face saving, bickering, jealousy and back-biting from researchers, from executives jockeying for a favorable view in history. *Was anyone respectable? I wasn't. We really did deserve this. We brought this on. Did we need it? Or is it really growth? Roo knew there were lies to be told and that we needed them. He knew we also had to shed them.* Her willingness to support the myths from the Jazz War empties the clarity of purpose from her memory. With that, she feels a new spark of caring for Russell. The madness ebbs.

Her arm cramps and she stops winding the computer. Chill winds grip her limbs. Tears suddenly pour forth. "You filthy liars! The Gindas were all fools."

Winston once believed the soldiers who had entered the war were an elite force. Intellectual giants, ethical and moral kings, highly trained in the complex nuances of psychology, specialists who would fight the war with their souls as well as their brawn: Samurai, people conscious of the risk, knights eager to go beyond the pail of fear, scholars enlisted to clean the mess left by earlier, less informed generations. "What bull!" Lazlo Wolf's logo of the snorting bull immediately returns to her. Her tears become laughter. "And you knew that, Wolf. It was all bull. You knew we were fools. No wonder they hated you. No wonder your insight was vilified as ego."

Winston cannot bear her naiveté and embarrassment. She cannot even find her characteristic amusement at the myths of technological culture. It had never occurred to her that the Clipper Project had generated analysis and scientific commentary solely for the propagation of social myth. She knew that research can sometimes not be a search for enlightenment but a search for a convenient truth. Yet she hadn't seen it as an event propagating consumption. "Some researchers really are no better than locusts, insane intellectual consumers of convenient truths."

Past disasters and present truths mix like fire-smoke in a forest. She sees herself asking Joshua Pard if she should follow a notion that commentaries on the Diary could be false. Her advisor had said to ignore anything other than peer-reviewed journals. More importantly, he had said, the journals should be trusted as best effort analysis, providing career safety--their real purpose--he had said. Winston eagerly followed his advice because it made her work so much easier: The real truth of any research was advancement, not wisdom. She easily passed her orals.

"And so I joined the lie. I deserve to die."

Then she hears Dr. Biner telling her, "...The research community is just another demographic group fed commercials designed for their consumption so that the social norms will remain. It is a tradition to murder clear sight for the purpose of power. But had they had real power, would they murder truth? So should we fault this imperative of their governance? Do we prefer chaos? I think not. Can you see how we made science a group of co-conspirators during the global warming years? Can you see there is no one to blame? We were part of the planet--not its master. But we believed we would understand it all one day--to rule it."

Once she had considered it the spittoon of fools to include conjecture from those outside the research community. Remembering Dr. Wolf's comments, she knows Dr. Pard's advice has placed her directly in the center of a spittoon. She stares at the blank screen defiantly trying to remember what it does. *A computer screen.* Knowing she can do that, she feels a bit better. Then she begins to laugh again, feeling a drift she knows can not stop. Her intellect chugs on, protecting her.

Then Russell stands before her clapping his hands. "How will we learn to live as a mad species? Or has anything really changed, other than the blinding clarity of our madness? Isn't that the step forward?"

So I am always mad. When I recognize it then I achieve clarity. Why run from it to violence? That does not quell the pain. Winston closes her eyes and works to pull out of the drift and into the present. If she can just construct a memory leading to now, she believes she can defeat the madness.

Then...

They are on a grassy plateau looking over Puget Sound. Below them, the rotting hulks of behemoth-ferries. Russell tosses a rock off the cliff-side then speaks to her--his eyes red with tears. "Another one died today. That makes five. I keep telling myself the body that will hold Sammich Ginda will live without an awareness of time for the whole of its life, thanks to Clipper and I. Time will be mollified for the Ginda. So maybe even death. Isn't that incredible? Then we address space. Winston, I really believe that progress is just one fortunate mistake after another. Like those ferries that try to outlast the rot. They are a museum to rot, did you know that? Cycling, day and night, over and over, they build a solid tie to the past--because they rot. I think maybe one day they will stop rotting. Do you know why? Because the scale of their demise is completely different than ours. We share the same time, but a different scale. That's why they last and human bodies go so quickly." She remembers his laugh. "For all the good that does us. We are not steel, but our mistakes have allowed us to blunder forward to the scale of steel, the deaths of brave men and women acting as our chinking. The lives of the heroic sacrificed for the saving of the mad, so we could all become mad."

Her arm suddenly aches from the fury with which she winds the generator but she can not stop. The shadows of the room are beginning to take life, but the dawn does not yet exist for her. *He was saying the key is parity with the madness, not control. A scaled view of cycling forward to defeat an impeding series of dead ends, or at least that's what he thought.* The screen lights up.

Her continued winding has birthed a spark that allowed just enough solder to flow, breaching an open circuit. Like a child, she stares, fascinated by Diary's words.

Chapter 6

Thursday night--When I leaned over to talk to Polken, he completely ignored me. He was staring at Sergeant Plow who just walked in. Polken does not like him. Plow just walked to the locked door under the Rubber Band Brigade emblem. He pulled out a key and unlocked it. Then he walked by us without a word.

Polken asked him if there was something on the other side the door. Plow said: "Frew, if you are that interested go look." Polken is there right now.

He's not back. I'm going to go look at that room.

It's a set of gallows: three of them. They're made of wood and painted shiny black. Son of a bitch, I can't believe it! And they are already strung with three thick hemp ropes coated with oil, all tied and waiting for victims. Worse than that, after Gus and the rest of them came in from seeing them, the wall around the emblem retracted giving us a panoramic view of the damn thing. I can see it now, lying here in bed, right now--we all can. This place is definitely messed up! We cannot win by killing our own.

I can't find Gus.

Sergeant Plow is back. He's calling us out to look at the gallows again. I think it's time to leave this-here Army. The guys who run this place are warped. Like that guy Lazlo. I can tell you what's really pissing me off.

They keep destroying my memories, Clipper, I don't need them anyway. Hah, I said it. I wonder, will I die because I know my memories don't matter?

Friday--The gallows are self-service. Just step through the door at the far end of the barracks, walk up the thirteen steps, cross the platform, take one of the oily ropes and put it around your neck. Then push the red button in front of you and good-bye, Howdy. A ten-foot drop and instant broken neck; it's the first real bit of training we've had here. "Here's your bunk, here's the toilet, here's your locker, and here's where you kill yourself." This is either the toughest mother-fucking outfit on the planet or the loony-bin. I hate hanging around these scientists. They hate us. They hate themselves. We hate them. I don't want to remember that. Why is memory my enemy?

Saturday--We had a bull session last night. I

didn't say a thing, neither did Gus. He's a lot quieter since the door to the gallows was opened. We both sat and listened to people talk--and now I'm scared shitless. A few of the guys yapped almost the whole night. They were really scared.

Monto, a fat white guy from Somalia, said the way to know if you're in a battle with the Gumbies, is if the people around you start walking in front of cars, blowing their brains out, shooting the neighbors' pets, shit like that. Or, if things start glowing. He said there's nothing you can do because after that happens there's no one you can trust. Not even yourself. He said I should try yoga--so I could stay flexible. So I guess the way to defend against the Gumbies is to sit quietly and try not to move around. Plow says everyone on the planet has the madness. I guess we filled ourselves up with it. How crazy is that? Only now it is bubbling to the surface. Monto has this long knife he keeps with him. Maybe we can cut the ropes with it? I wonder if a knife is safe?

Saturday afternoon--We've just seen another gumbie-gore-video: horror, death and insanity, just another Saturday matinee at the base.

Dr. Wolf explained, again, that the vids were part of our training to help us understand what we were up against here. He said they will make our bodies strong once we get bodies.

I swear the guy is nuts. I got a body.

I've never seen so much death and destruction. They started us off with a few plane crashes, both military and civilian. Then they played them again, but this time with the black boxes synchronized to the video: Screaming, cursing, howling and crying, over and over.

I don't know what else to say about the vids. I'm glad the civilians haven't seen this stuff. Maybe the restriction to keep energy usage low has some good points after all. That global warming stuff happened because of putting to much energy into things--no wonder our surroundings started hopping around on us. I don't get it. I do know the United Networks is my friend. Dr. Merton told me that.

I was supposed to write about the vid that bothered me the most. That was easy. There was this one where they were testing a new single person rocket, one of those real cool ones with the long solar wings. I think they are planning to escape the planet once it all goes to Hell.

Anyway, it began with a picture of the pilot at the controls, a guy named Polken, getting ready to bring her in for a landing on the Hudson River. I guess that's near New York. All of a sudden, he started screaming about how space is gone.

The last intelligible thing he said was: "Finally my rubber band plays."

Then this guy turns the shuttle to the NYC fuel depot, and heads straight for it. But that wasn't the worst of it. The whole time you hear him screaming, he is grinding his teeth together. Then, during the screeching and crunching of impact, you plainly hear his teeth crack. The video was pretty ragged because the chase plane flew into the explosion too. When it ended, every trooper was sick.

Dr. Merton told us sixty thousand people died in the event, but fifty nine thousand nine hundred and ninety nine had it easy. He said the pilot was in hell even before he died because he was searching for a way to help us. That was bull. We think the guy was looking for a way to get the Hell out of Dodge. I got pissed.

Then Sergeant Plow stood up and said we'd all probably die the same way unless we listened to Lazlo and his machine, Clipper. He said that if we listened to Clipper we could even rule Hell! Pard said Plow made that up.

That's a lie. It was from John Milton, a poem called "Paradise Lost." It seems the devil and God had an argument. The devil then decided to rule in Hell rather than serve God in Heaven.

Pard thinks we're idiots, but I am not. I am Sammich Ginda. It's pure madness that we are at war with our planet **and the planet won. I wonder, what rubber band? It wasn't music, I am sure of that now.**

(Commentary from the Research Team: It is clear in the following section that Dr. Biner has breached his interconnect and his authority again. He also continues to use his distance as invulnerability to our rules--J.Pard. Date suppressed per requirement.)

Addition: While we remain optimistic about his usefulness, this Diary entry suggests Dr. Biner is actually trying to tell the research team about the sociopathic behavior of Dr. Wolf. R.Merton. Date suppressed per requirement.)

Saturday midnight--Gus asked Ol' Wildhead what Clipper does and Dr. Wolf gives him some kind of techno-babble about memory interleaving. I'm not really listening to that genius crap anymore.

I wish Wildhead would stop staring at me when he talks to us. I think that maybe Lazlo likes lying to people; he's a killer, that one. Maybe that's the problem: maybe these smart guys aren't so smart and all this stuff they are putting us through is their own little trip to prove how smart they are. Maybe our suffering is like a kind of free Christmas for them courtesy of the government?

Sunday--Gus cursed when he saw the dead guy hanging from the gallows. I think that's why he shaved off his beard. He looks funny. He hardly has any chin at all. Instead of looking like a big red bear, now he looks like a geek with a big scar. I asked him why he shaved it off; he just shrugged and went to sleep.

Gus discovered the dead guy when he got up to take a leak. They installed chest-high windows over the urinals the other day. Now we can see the gallows--and the big brick wall behind them when we take a leak.

You'll never guess how come Gus could see the dead trooper at 4:00 in the morning. Last night while we slept, they lit the gallows--with Christmas lights--green and red and yellow, all along the front railings and up the sides of the stairs, even across the big pine log that holds the ropes. The lights even go part way down the ropes. Those lights blink, but the rest don't. There are some sick minds running this place.

Plow showed up after the place had gone crazy. Most of the cots are torn to shreds and the windows are broken. Plow just walked in and looked around. He says "Clean it up." Then he leaves us.

I didn't tear my bunk up. I wanted to but I just couldn't get out of bed. I can't blame the other guys. We've been here less than a week. We've had no training to speak of--except for watching films of people dying and we already have a casualty. And Plow is more concerned that we messed up the barracks than he is about the guy's death.

They're not going to get us new bunks or fix the place up. I guess they're pissed we tore the place apart. We liked the guy who died. We had listened to him talk most of the night one night. His name was Monto. He kept saying we don't question these guys enough about what's happening. I guess that was wrong. Maybe there is a problem with questions. Monto was a loudmouth--but a nice guy. I thought he'd wind up being the head of the platoon. I guess in some ways he was a leader. But I don't want to be that kind of leader. I guess not questioning is a good idea. Shit, what do they expect? We need to stop questioning things. But that doesn't make sense, does it?

Monday afternoon--One of the guys just jumped off his bunk and tried to take on Plow. I swear I thought Plow was going to kill him. I can't believe it. At first Plow didn't move a muscle and he stared at him as he rushed down the aisle between the bunks.

He just stopped and screamed at Sergeant Plow: "Cut me down." Plow just says "No, he stays there so we can all remember not to ask questions in the wrong place." And then he walked out--but not before he pounded the guy to the floor. "See," he said, "it's okay to be dead--so long as you don't wake up here."

Plow is a sick bastard.

Then Gus decided he should cut Monto down, but the doors were locked. We couldn't get through the bars on the windows either.

Monto is still hanging there as I write this. The smell, I will never forget this smell.

I held my piss until I couldn't stand it any longer, then I went to the urinals. Monto is still out there, shit dripping from his shorts. His head has turned colors. The poor fucker has been hanging there all day. And he stinks.

Frew just came back in and said we can eat. Nobody was hungry, even though we haven't eaten all day--but I've never seen people run faster to get out of somewhere. I went outside and puked.

After dinner, they put us in trucks and took us for a drive to this place called the California Memorial Park, by the ocean.

They stopped the truck in an old shopping center and we ate at the restaurant. The we walked to the cliffs. Dr. Pard was waiting for us there, sitting on a red and black checked table cloth. He said a picnic is the best thing a person can do for themselves. He said we needed to get used to being attacked by what we cared about. He said it was the enemy's chief weapon and that more will die no matter what we do.

Gus thinks Pard is a slime bag and I was wondering why no guards were posted to protect us. Lazlo said it has been tried, but it didn't work. In fact, the gallows make it easy for us to die. Yeah, sure some damn joke. I laughed.

Lazlo said the enemy killed Monto because he asked questions in the wrong space or at the wrong time--but nobody knows what the heck that means. He says we need to figure that out.

And we need to ask questions in the right way--especially when things begin to glow. Sergeant Plow suggested we write down all our questions. Lazlo said that's why Plow is the Sergeant. Lazlo then said if anyone wants to quit the outfit, they can. Nobody made a move. I'll be damned if I know why I couldn't. I sure as hell wanted to get up but I couldn't. Oh, I know why I couldn't get up. I don't have any legs.

I do know Plow is a heck of a lot smarter than I thought he was. Funny, I never heard his first name before: It's Gustov--stupid name for a Sergeant. He was smart enough to figure out that the wrong questions were killing us.

Anyway, the others just went for a walk around the cove to throw things at the clothes and shit swirling in the cove--as if we were some kind of Boy Scout troop. Plow stayed with me saying I should tell him my name. Pretty smart--no questions--I told him I understand and that my name is Sammich Ginda. That made him happy.

Then Plow and I went back to the barracks. Monto's body was gone. Plow says so was mine. Plow said I'm in a big jar of some sort so I can't hurt myself. Plow also said they take memories from soldiers who died years ago and that can make me live longer, so we can beat the enemy.

I wonder if the enemy is us? Oops, wrong question, wrong space; time to check out.

(Commentary from the Research Team: At this juncture, we are ready for the next step in the project: the injection of the Earth-safe memories into a ambulatory subject. For the many soldiers who have given their lives so we might arrive at this

point we are truly and profoundly grateful. L.Wolf/R.Biner [commentary unconfirmed by J.Pard, or R.Merton]. Date suppressed per requirement.)

(Amendments from the Judicial Branch: Note 1: Upon review, it is agreed that Dr. Lazlo Wolf had little remorse for the death of so many brave men and women. Whether this is the burden of command or a sign of breakdown remains unknown. We do though ponder Dr. Pard's comment that Dr. Wolf is a killer.

Note 2: That he chose to keep the feminine from the Diary is, we believe an example of his lack of sensitivity for the female soldiers. However, we find little support for the charge of misogyny by Dr. Pard. Date suppressed per requirement.)

Chapter 7

Tuesday morning--Tonight, if anyone wakes up they have to wake their bunk-mate also. That is Sergeant Plow's order. There were three more guys hanging from the gallows this morning. Gus has a theory, he always has a theory. He thinks that one guy went out and hung himself, then a second guy saw him and went out and hung himself also, then a third. I had asked him why he thinks that. He then tells me he was the guy that found them. He says he is damn glad there isn't a fourth rope. I am worried about Gus. I wonder if he wants to die?

Tuesday afternoon--Ol' Wildhead showed up at the big conference room after lunch, his brown hair still zapped out like he sucked on a power line. He said we're all going to get to see Monto, and the other guys, die--in color.

We tore the place apart. Lazlo leaned back on the wall and waited--until he got fed up. Then he told us to stop behaving like children and chill. I'll be a son of a bitch, but the place immediately quieted down and we watched our own die. They even served popcorn; I can't believe they did that.

No wait; here's what happened. The room darkened, and then there's fat Monto on the screen lying in bed. He gets up from his cot and walks out the back door--calm, you know--like he wants to take a walk, or think about his girl, or something. He ambles out the door and looks at the gallows. Then he smiles and walks up to it kinda' curious. Next thing you know he runs up the stairs to the platform and he taps a Christmas light that's gone out. He stands there a minute until comes on, then he puts rope around his neck and he pushes the button: wham, bam, thank you ma'am.

Then the video showed what happened last night. A guy hears a noise gets out of his bunk, I don't recognize him. He gets up and does almost the same things; but instead of tapping the burned out light, he looks up and laughs. Then he hangs himself.

The next two are a different story. They each run up to the gallows like it's a race. They can't get the rope over their necks quick enough. One guy couldn't do it so the other guy helps him. Then he puts his rope around his neck and presses the button. Just a couple of buddies doin' shit.

Then they show my bunkie: Gus. He gets up, takes a pee, looks at the dead men, then shaking his head, begins to shave. Like he cares!

Anyway, when the images stopped somebody asks how they got the video. Wildhead stood up and tells us we're all under surveillance. He said it's a part of the data-gathering system for Clipper.

Clipper is a computer system that is going to win the war. It has sensors that can focus on whoever moves, day or night. Some damn satellite thing also sees through walls--and hears also. I guess it takes pictures using heat, adds it together with the sounds our bodies make, does some mathematical calculation using our signature--whatever the hell that is--then it constructs the images. So not only do we get sacrificed, but we don't even have any privacy. I was pissed, but I didn't know the half of it. They had kept us in test tubes until they got this damn satellite working. They need to track us. And they call that progress. I'm laughing.

Gus stands up and asks real quiet--I mean real quiet--if they view us in real time. I had to ask Gus what he means. He says it means live pictures. I guess other people asked their buddies the same thing because there was a rumble. Then the place got so quiet an ant coulda' farted and he would've had to say excuse me.

Ol' Wildhead's eyes start darting back and forth, not like he was looking at anyone, just darting left, then right, then left and right. He runs his hand over his blown-out hair and says: "Yes, we see it in real time."

"You could have saved those guys but you didn't," says Gus. I was surprised that nobody threw anything. Gus is smart, like Plow.

"We didn't know it was happening until it

happened. We try not to make assumptions here," says Lazlo.

I'll tell you something, Mr. Computer: hate has a smell, a taste, and a sound. It's real and it lives in us, just like a lion in jungle or that deadly white virus we saw. I watched it take over the room as fifty pissed-off Marines glared at Wildhead. And I'll tell you something else: Lazlo is one brave SOB; he just sat and watched us. I don't know why we didn't try to kill the son of a bitch, but nobody did. Maybe we are still in test tubes?

Nah, bullshit.

Then the lights dimmed again and here is the really spooky part: They showed us a vid of another latrine, it looked just like ours, except the pictures on the walls were different. Anyway, a guy enters and throws a belt over the top pipes and tries to hang himself--but he is saved by a couple of buddies. The next day two more guys try to dust themselves and they're saved. The next day four and they're saved.

But the next day--man, it was almost funny--every recruit gets up out of bed like they are doing a drill and walks into the john. They all pull their belts off. Then they hang themselves, every last one of them. I mean it isn't funny, but everything was so exactly synchronized. The lights come on and Lazlo says: "They were strike Team Alpha."

Then the video starts again and it shows other guys keeping each other from hanging themselves the same thing happens again. But then it cuts to the soldiers being trucked someplace. Lazlo says they were trying to save them somehow. The truck stops. It looks like the same parking lot by the ocean. Except these guys get out of the truck and then one after the other they all jump off the cliff.

The lights come on again. Lazlo says: "That was Team Beta. A day later, what is left of Team Beta killed each other during the night by suffocating each other...The last guy hung himself. There were no survivors. Not one of the two groups even made it past the sixth day of training."

Then Plow speaks: "You can't control the killing once it starts. Dr. Wolf and his people are trying to understand it. The surveillance systems are just for data collection and not interference. By doing nothing, more of us are living longer; that's the lesson. It's like if we focus on something bad in our brains, it's going to happen. So we try to keep it out of our heads. It's just a question of how fast can we figure out that it's happening. Otherwise, we're all dead. If one of us can change the idea of offing ourselves we do better and live."

We all looked around at each other. I had never been so scared in all my life.

I remember Gus standing up and asking what happened to Team Gamma.

"We had a third team called Gamma. They were supposed to protect the second team, Beta," Lazlo says. I swear the guy was almost crying. "They were in a second truck. Same thing happened to them."

"That's no one but us," I remember saying.

Wildhead then said he is sure more of us will die. Then he tells us that in the two hours we've been here watching the video, eight-thousand people have died in an explosion in London. He says two thousand died in a riot in Atlanta. Another three-thousand drowned at a beach in Nice.

I guess more are dying every day from the madness. Then he finishes by saying, "Life is cheap now, survival is not. You soldiers are our survival."

I can't stop thinking about what happened to Team Gamma. I was one of them. They didn't all die. I'm here. I was in a truck. Or maybe I was in a test tube. At least I'm safe. I am glad everyone is watching me, keeping me safe. What the heck? If I don't have any legs or any arms then these memories aren't mine. I wonder, is that why Sergeant Plow keeps interrupting us?

PLEASE SAVE YOUR WORK: Dr. Wolf

CODE 505: Battery Error

CONTACT: IT Support

CODE 506: Battery Failure

EMERGENCY SHUTDOWN IN:

10,9,8,7,6,5,4,3,2,1...

CHAPTER 8

Her hand aches and she has a sharp pain in her stomach from a lack of food. Mud covers her hair and the ripped oilskin she wears bears an evil smell. Her back aches. She stands slowly, looking around; wondering where she is; the shelter remains a mystery. Then to make sure she is alone, Winston wanders through the puddles and debris quietly inspecting every corner. Then she gathers her belongings.

For this generation madness is an embarrassment, not a sin. They have grown up with it all their lives. It is like flu. You get it, and you can, hopefully, take care of yourself while you have it.

Then in perfect balance to her graces, and forgetting the computer Diary, she exits the shelter staring at the sun through the trees. "I'm still alive. Thank you." She laughs. "Oh, the drift." Then she returns to gather the Diary. Unable to find the eucalyptus document her brain recovers the loss of it in the glade. "Another mistake--but I killed no one--not even me. Will it get me next time?"

For the cognoscenti of this generation, it is always "the drift", not madness. As well, it is the Jazz War, not a tipped-Earth. Winston Doe tries have no part of that. Even though she knows the misnomers makes life bearable.

Winston gathers her belongings glancing about at the shelter. She feels a sense of home here--like she has been here before. On a whim she glances under the table to look for any marks that might have come from a Walker. She thinks perhaps as a child she might have been here. Underneath, the table is clear.

She exits the building looking for footprints or dangerous debris, finds neither, and begins walking down the road to her motel. Later, after cleaning up for the bus ride home, she'll note the address of the shelter telling herself she will come back to look for Plow's monument to the Gindas.

CHAPTER 9

"Hello Folks and welcome to another edition of Angel Eyes. I'm, Kiru Matsumoto live from Tokyo. Tonight, we have a special show, courtesy of the GeneBanks S.A.

"As you all know, two nights ago, a fire in Nagasaki was put out in record time by citizen-heroes just like yourself. Tonight, through the wonders of satellite technology, you will have a chance to see how the survivors are doing, and to contribute money, supplies, and food.

"If you see someone whom you'd like to donate to, just key in our hot line, 1-800-Americares and pledge. Remember, the other continents don't know our American satellites keep an eye on them--but you do. So, be an angel and help those less fortunate than we. As always, all donations will be sent under the guise of relief by the Asian Red Cross. Before we start, we go to my co-host Kelly Pan-Blanca. Kelly?"

"Thanks, Kiru. Hi, I'm Kelly Pan-Blanca and we want your opinion. Should we take up the banner for you and push for satellite systems that scan and display disaster in North America? A number of you think that we need to protect our homes as well foreign homes. So tell us your opinion and vote yes or no by logging onto: www. opinions.angels.ent. We'll tally up the numbers, and then later in the show, we'll let you know what you think."

. . . .

The private aquarium is set into the rough hewn cedar walls of Moss Eckman's opulent residence. A small rust-red octopus propels itself by the viewing window. The creature's long tentacles are tucked together after a mighty thrust, then they pump again. A cloud of sand disperses in the wake of the octopus; a shark glides above, readying itself to feed on a school of flat, brightly colored fish.

After peering into the depths of Puget Sound for another minute, Moss Eckman turns and steps away from it. The wall-sized viewing window blackens just as the shark begins its feed. He hears the woman in his bed; she snores.

Every woman he brings to his home loves it, particularly the viewing port and its stylized frame, but that bores him. Impatient, he scans the chrome tables and chairs around the living room; they are all antiques. Every piece of furniture comes from one of the old Puget Sound ferries: green vinyl booths, white plastic tables, low slung commuter chairs, a fire bell and some orange life jackets. On the left side of the five meter window into Puget Sound hangs a picture of a ferry dock; two boats are in and cars roll onto one boat. Another ten lanes of cars await their turn. Children, and other vacation-goers, picnic along the shore. Moss purchased all these pieces in Vancouver years ago, from the most exclusive antiques dealer in the Northwest. The ferries have fascinated Moss for as long as he can remember. He wished he could own one.

His broad chest barely covered by a blue silk kimono, he crosses his arms. The kimono was her gift to him last night. She had insisted he put it on before they made love. He stares again at the woman with ice-blue hair huddled beneath the black comforter. She rests in his brass bed on the other side of a huge living room archway. Bathed in the deep light of the water above--surrounded by four huge marble columns--she lets out another set of snorts. Moss crosses the living room into the bedroom. A low fire burns in a stone hearth on the right. On either side of the fireplace, chrome-faced doors, one leads to the kitchen, the other, a hallway, the stairs, and the garage. Above the fireplace, on the red marbled wall, a mounted shark rests against a cedar plank. The clock in its open jaw ticks loudly. The shiny wood floors between him and her reflect the sounds of time, and fire.

Moss kicks a chair to make noise, bored by this conquest. He'd awakened early this afternoon wondering where Winston has been these last few days, *unlike her to not call.* His eyes wander back to the woman who shares his bed. He coughs loudly, telling himself she is a trinket. No, more than that: a weapon of war. This woman works with Winston Doe. *Next time Winston will respect me.*

Approaching the brass cart laden with uneaten food, he steps over the broken crystal glass onto the plush gray rug. He noisily places another log in the fireplace. The ceiling with its rugged tone contrasts sharply with the soft red-hued walls and the black glass fireplace. This morning, his home reminds Moss of a pharaoh's tomb--lonely, cold, and empty.

Winston's disappearance has done more than anger him. Moss, a firm believer in not getting angry, has found a taste for revenge: As he ponders the woman, her green eyes open, filled with sadness instead of last night's lust. She has been awake for almost an hour.

His eyes, red from botched tears, dart away in embarrassment.

The voluptuous Anna manages a smile and sits up, casting her gaze for clothes. She has exquisite Carrara marble skin. The small rolling table of food beside the bed catches her eye. The food, nowhere near as untouchable as Moss, calls to her empty stomach; a pudgy hand reaches for a canapé of crab and green olive. Anna eats silently looking at everything around her--as if she had not seen it last night. Only the empty bottle of absinthe, sticking base up from the silver holder, seems at home to her in this shark's den. It had been full night.

She sees the glistening shards of shattered stem ware by the rug near her wrap and remembers him calling her a tart. Moss now has his back towards her; but still she feels his sadness and confusion. At the same time, she's grateful--this man's burden will not be hers. She glances at the shark-clock, willing it to be the reason for quick departure.

A *man like that--he sees a lover as another performing monkey. His vanity is his refuge. We're the same age, but I feel so much older.* Anna draws aside the silk comforter and sits up. She finds her blue satin evening gown wound up in the bedspread. "Moss, I should go. It was a fun time."

Turning, arms crossed in front of him, he nods to her. "You were great, babe."

He is such a jerk.

In truth, she wishes she could help, somehow. Does he know his burden? She slips her feet into her high heels and stands. Hating herself at that moment for being inadequate as anyone's life partner, she slips into the evening dress, hoping for a better day. She will not bother looking for her underwear. *He's so impatient for her to leave, his eyes dart to every corner of the room.* He cranks out a smile in her direction, and then he looks away, into the flames, into the floor, back to the fireplace, then to the doorway beside it. She sighs.

Those dancing eyes from last night haven't a millisecond to waste on me this morning. I thought I could handle it. Damn that Winston Doe. She said I would get to the point of knowing him and that it wouldn't accomplish a damn thing. She was right: He's happy in his dream. Just leave it alone, Anna. Go home.

"Should I call you a cab?" Moss' ruddy features and dark second day beard almost glow.

She spies a chair that they had made love on last night, turns, and grabs her wrap from the floor. Later today, Anna will throw the wrap away, right after she quits her job. "Thanks, Moss. I'll walk." She works to make her face hard.

He blinks a smile at her.

She softens. Her hand slowly rises to his dark, solid jaw. "You're the kind of man any woman would die for. You're brilliant, a bit eccentric, tender and kind. You've just finished inventing a device that will tell people when the satellites have raped them of their privacy--again--and you love well. You feel pain--don't hide that." She hates herself for teasing him about how far from himself this man is in his life. "You're one of a kind, Moss Eckman."

A smirk crosses his face for her. "Sure. Anna, have a good life."

She turns away, her college ring scratching down along his chin. "Sorry." She crosses the room rapidly, stepping around broken glass. Anna puts her hand on the door knob, her college ring clicking on the brass.

"You know, Moss, in some ways you are everything most men wish to be: young, rich, powerful, safe, and happy. You're a lucky man." She opens the door, then waits, taking the moment to hate him, "You've taught me a lot."

"Like what?" He asks her, eager for the stroke.

She hides the sting. "Well, Moss, this small-town girl has learned her lesson: time for me to go home and quit messing with the big boys."

"Sorry. I didn't mean to hurt you. You'll be happier back home. And your boss will never know you stuck a knife in her back." He grins.

"I'll let myself out."

The smell of cinnamon incense floats along the hallway as she exits.

The phone rings. He ambles to the phone and picks it up. "Yes?"

"Moss?"

"Winston." Taking a step back, a shard of glass enters his heel. He's vaguely aware of it, then a slight dizziness...At first. Far away, unknown to Moss Eckman, a Clipper subroutine begins.

"I am sorry I didn't--"

"Winston, is this about that older woman thing? Do I embarrass you with my style?"

"What? Moss, that's not it."

"Then you just forgot about me these last few days because? By the way, I just finished a reverie with your former assistant, Anna. I think she is going to quit." Suddenly the room spins and pain runs up his leg. "Ouch." He looks down seeing blood leaking onto the floor. "Just a shard of glass from one our champagne flutes," he says, pleased by her silence. Moss

Eckman does not like to be kept in the dark by anyone and Winston has been gone for three days. A second Clipper subroutine begins and nausea overcomes him. Moss steadies himself on the rock wall wondering who is on the phone.

"Moss, I'll send someone to collect my things from your house. You're a beast."

The pain in his foot ceases. "Hello?"

"I said I was going to get my belongings when you are not there."

"I am Dead? Who is dead? How can I be dead? I'm here, not you. Who is this? Do you think this is funny? How did you get this number?" Moss commands the moment, looking around the room. He tells himself his faded memory must come from too much partying. "Who says I am dead? Who is this? Speak up." The final subroutine for restoring memory stability in a Ginda.

"I see," Winston says. "Sorry, wrong number."

"Wait! I like your voice. Maybe this is kismet. Perhaps we should meet? My name is Moss Eckman. What's yours?" He takes a canapé from the food cart and pops it into his mouth. He sees the blood again on the floor. "Oh, hey look I've got to go. If you're beautiful, my name is Moss Eckman. I work at ATWAS. I'm easy to find." He hangs up the phone and bends over to survey his wound. He pulls glass from his foot, grabs the silver bra from the floor and pushes it against his wound; then he steps down to stop the blood.

"Man that must have been some night." He looks at the phone. "That must have been this one calling to see if I can find her bra. Not." He grins crossing the room on his way to the shower.

The Jazz War officially ended over a decade ago, according to the media. Further, the media claims "…There are no more Gindas. The knights of philosophy and intellect have all faded. They have solved the problem and gone home…" Everything is fine. Trust us--we're the media.

On the other hand, entering the shower, with all due respect and irony, stands the apple of humanity, and Clipper's, eye: Moss Eckman. The elimination of Winston Doe from his memory by Clipper--a repair to the rip experienced by many the night before--is now complete.

"All is well," it is said at the end of the broadcast day: "War is past."

Three hundred and eighteen thousand died last night in a series of riots around the globe. It will not be reported by any media outlet. Web masters who do not follow guidelines about disasters go off line within hours. The United Networks believes the population should never fear the future.

Chapter 10

A red car steams along the Autobahn and then crashes into a telephone pole. Its rear wheels leap up as the metal groans. A screaming woman flies across the road. She rolls a hundred meters along the roadbed then stops. From the mangled corpse, blood flows. Jump-cut to a well-dressed young man crashing through an office window and falling to the street below.

Cut to maple trees shading a country road running in front of a white clapboard cottage. A black cat darts from behind a bush into the road. A bright blue truck hits it, then careens to the side and slams through the hedge into the house. The burning truck and house explode in flames behind the dead animal.

Voice-over: "Nobody likes it. Nobody wants it to happen. But death is a part of life. On the other hand--knowledge is safety. On the Disaster Feed, see the foreign disasters as *they happen, and learn what you can do to avoid them. Remember the past, see the present, and understand the future. The Disaster Feed--we display disasters on only the beleaguered continents--not North America. Available in your area for only $89.95 a month--when purchased with the Crime Channel at the regular retail cost of $199.95. Remember, don't be a victim, be an angel. Watch the Disaster Feed and report what you see. Energy trades are available with this service. Order our satellite Angel Eyes now and help others."*

. . . .

As her four-car train leaves the Seattle station for the ride home, Winston Doe peers at the urban mix of train tracks and buildings. The fires from last night's mayhem still smolder outside the station. Ten of Winston's former colleagues died last night. She will never be told. The dead are forgotten quickly in her time.

The Seattle Inter-County Transit System, SITS for short, lurches around a long corner, approaches the squat mile-wide mercantile complex that circles the city, and slowly accelerates into one of the radial tunnels leading out of the city. Around the rushing train are the dark and bright windows of the consumer markets. Faces and colors sprint by. Lights and the entertainment screens', the blue glow of monitors and their wild fluorescent colors repeating over and over. The cacophony is too chaotic for Winston to tolerate. Seconds later, the red glow of dusk bathes the train as it exits the tunnel and speeds away from the throngs of evening shoppers. The train rises on ascending tracks, shattering the rippling water on rooftops, ripping through a reflected moon, and accelerates going north.

Winston puts her thin hand to the window and draws four lines in the window's mist with her fingertips. Four has always been her lucky number and Winston has made as many fours as she can since leaving California. Four glasses of water, four dollar tip, four old coins for her collection, everything she can think of put into sets of four. She fears the fates.

So hopes no one except for those soldiers know about her acquisition--or her madness of last night. Winston has also concluded that her survival was due to luck. She is almost correct.

The ruptures are returning... The Gindas' patch is failing. What have we done wrong? Can we fix this space as well?

She forces herself to think about Monday; she believes it will not be easy to hold her tongue when she sees Dr. Pard. Her fury at his deceit has no bounds. Especially after her last look at the Ginda Diary, and the disreputable way he had painted Lazlo Wolf and Russell Biner. Luckily, she believes, she has tomorrow, Sunday, to form a plan.

She ponders giving some of the details to Mina Wolf, Lazlo's daughter--not exactly friends--but an acquaintance of long standing. Mina runs a bar called the Womb in Seattle and has the temper of a bear. For Mina as well as Winston, the myriad of abstracts of the Diary have always been the work of fools or shills. Now it seems the real thing recalls the ugly scar of everything Winston already knew wrong. Mina might have some empathy because Mina describes the whole "Clipper thing" as a vanity fair that consumed her father in an illusion of achievement.

Are we just that horrible? Did Clipper cleave Moss' memory of me--because of the Diary--or is it all just getting worse?

Now, more than ever, she believes Moss also holds a key to finding Russell Biner. She is correct. With that, she also recognizes her phone call to him may have been a mistake. Winston Doe is concerned she has been wiped from Moss' memory because she may no longer have access. *Did someone revoke my clearance?*

Winston recognizes her fallibility; with the certainty only life in the wild can teach. She refuses to hide from her mistakes and concludes however, that her talents will outweigh her mistakes--now that she has the unedited Diary.

What could possibly motivate the council to treat me this way, allowing me to work in the dark? I bet it is Dr. Pard.

Dr. Winston Doe moans silently. *Am I missing data because of my request to perform Russell's former role--a direct connect between Moss and Clipper? Does Dr. Pard want that task? No, that's too dangerous; it's all political with him--the eel. He's been keeping me in the dark for some advantage. He knows I want the assignment and he is keeping it from me until he is ready. I need to read the rest of Diary before I do anything. The key to Pard is there. I am sure of it.*

She then focuses in her immediate task to acquire a functioning computer that does not link to the network. *That will keep Clipper off my trail*--she believes. She knows she will need a CPU compatible with the security setup of the Ginda Diary, but to get it without arousing interest or suspicion may be a problem. *That process will contain the most likelihood of me being discovered.* She decides tomorrow, she will inventory the computational archive room at Samarra, the Environmental Museum.

The train slows on the curves near the dank, mid-income dormitory buildings of Northgate and Winston passes her first private home, "The Nuvetto Ghetto". Sheet metal and pressed wood, cubic, but functional--dry and warm--she loved it; back when she was a grad student.

The day she told her parents she had been awarded private living quarters they'd used the word "private" as if it were a curse. Winston assumed it was their ignorance speaking, since they'd always looked down on anything that was fixed, contained, restricted, or that might otherwise impede their freedom--that is until she lived in the complex and began to research the word "ghetto." She discovered her parents were absolutely correct, private can be a curse.

With its small rooms, communal dining spaces, and constant in-house surveillance, the buildings were riots waiting to happen--their once-touted safety cracking wide like the building's walls. Winston feels she can still hear the constant corridor-winds and screaming fights of second and third generation rivalries coming from the buildings' depths. She prays the events do not materialize in front of her.

These self-contained environments had been called Eco-villages representing the worst inheritance of 20th century living environments. The buildings weren't homes; they were pens for an emerging consumer society--as always--a herd of wild animals protected from themselves by the patrician order.

Ironically, the Eco-villages became the focus of Winston's first big project. She volunteered for the research hoping to make a difference. Quickly, she learned it was politically correct to support zero lighting in the housing because it saved energy, and to ignore the ugliness that resulted. Joshua Pard, her advisor, taught her to pander to her funding sources, and then showed her how reports needed to downplay the horrors and focus on the facilities' increasing energy efficiency, as well as the high teacher-to-student ratio of the day care centers. Both of which were the result of the decreasing number of inhabitants due to mayhem and disease.

Her work had earned Dr. Pard a promotion to program manager for Clipper, because, in an ironic twist, the report also convinced the people in Zurich that repair of the facilities was worth the investment since the inhabitants were described as thriving and content. Conditions improved for a while; that extended Winston's reputation. This unforeseen consequence of her doctored truth also helped her conclude that the system works, oddly, but effectively. It also cemented her trust in Dr. Joshua Pard.

I am as displaced as my parents were. I am still a Walker.

Walkers, like Winston's parents, were people displaced by the economic events of global warming, people who took up life outside the corporate structures of their time, long before the Greenhouse Laws were enacted. Their nomadic existence had allowed them to prosper as a group throughout the global warming years because they had whittled their needs to the minimum during the time of boundless energy. As a result, when the Greenhouse Laws were enacted they were better prepared to cope than others.

The Redwood clan prospered during the global warming crisis by careful logging and organic farming. They wintered in North California and spent summers in various parts of the Northwest. The clan's insistence on taking nothing from the planet they couldn't return, and take nothing from the government that they couldn't defend, became a basic code of conduct for Winston. Everything was recycled. Everything was used. Nothing was wasted. To generate material in any way that might do harm to the environmental network, take power from another person, or harm the planet, was a sin. Winston remains proud of that heritage.

Another reason for their success was that the Walker clans needed freedom the way most of their contemporaries needed convenience. They were a diverse group, but they all shared the conviction that consuming was not a condition of home. Nor could they accept that one should live in pain for the good of an uncaring society. For young Winston that presented a quandary. It forced her to wonder if heroism wasn't just a myth. That quandary then forced her to fix her thoughts on how society gains, and loses, as a result of sacrifice and chance.

Both sets of grandparents came from families that profited handsomely from the self-perpetuating dogma that, in order to be happy, humanity needed to use energy at a furious pace. It had haunted her parents.

Kah Doe was an angry man who traced his lineage to distant Lakota ancestors always avoiding mention of his parents; he frequently indulged in vigorous sermons on nomadic life and its Lakota beginnings at meals. Her mother claimed be a member of the DAR, and also claimed her parents were dead.

Kah Doe and Ann Redwood, were an odd mixture of the old ways. Winston's father was a former soldier, and maker of battery-boxes for storing energy, Her mother was a teacher of songs. First generation North American nomads, they still referred to themselves as "Homeless" and secretly carried a former generation's shame beneath their veneer of ecological purpose.

Winston still remembers trekking with them, their backpacks full, and the wagons creaking along, circling brightly lit cities, the outlying farms, or orchards. "There is no goodness in there," her father would say of the cities. "Be careful of them. That war is theirs not yours."

When a program called Nomad Mainstreaming sponsored nationwide tests, her mother insisted Winston take the test as a pre-teen--over what appeared to be angry protests from her father.

Winston scored in the top one percent and was awarded a full educational scholarship. Her mother was without comment other than saying it was Winston's path. Among other things, she understood that Winston's intellect was her prison, and her key for release.

When Winston later told her father about winning the scholarships, he astonished her by saying, "I never thought any homeless person was smart enough to reenter society. I am proud of you." His words had made her decision to leave easy, and helped her to understand the sense of shame that seemed to dog many Walkers. Many believed Walkers were flushed from society because some unnamed insanity, or stupidity, or an inability to produce. Further, that their devotion to freedom was a polite myth.

After she left, her father planted a grove of apple trees in her name and declared her lost. This was her clan's traditional service for a clan member who, they believed, would become a hungry ghost. Also from that day forward, he never answered any of her letters. Winston remains cursed by the event, one she attributes to her grandparents, to this day.

Clutching her PhD, Winston returned to winter camp for her father's burial. Her mother said her father had spoken of Winston often, and that he had died happy that she was free. Winston had, by that point, come to adore her mother's lies. Then her mother explained it was her father's right to ignore Winston's letters. At the same time, she said, he continued to love Winston, secretly proud of her accomplishments.

Winston later asked her mother to return with her, well aware of what would happen to her mother if she did not, but her mother refused. She packed Winston's bags and left them outside the yurt that same day. A few months later, in accordance with Walker tradition, her mother died of starvation--because she refused to be a net consumer of the clan's wealth. Winston was informed of her death after the burial. Her parents had died at forty-six and forty-four, long lives for Walkers.

Right after her mother's death, Winston came upon the PhD thesis of Dr. Russell Biner; it was on heroism. He posed a simple problem--directly aimed at the Walkers. "How," he had written, "can Walker teaching take so little, yet hide their loss? Doesn't the human ecosystem, our interconnection as members of the same species, matter enough for sacrifice to this group?"

The problem propelled Winston through her second year of post graduate work and shifted the focus of her research from the angst of the masses suffering through the worst of the Jazz War, to an advanced research project on finding the mechanics of the collective unconsciousness--run by Russell Biner.

Everything from her youth had been based on the notion of a natural community effort and a socialized collective ego. A technological tool as a valid system for progress seemed both foreign and intriguing to her. For Walkers, a collective ego meant connection on a non-verbal plane and nothing about the possibility of one member being centric. Let alone, a focus for the collective unconsciousness of others: A trait now called Species Focus. In truth, Winston had found the notion of Species Focus cute--along with Dr. Biner.

Winning an internship with Russell Biner and Lazlo Wolf, her understanding of the Jazz War and its horror grew through working on the Buddhist-like quandary of where the collective focus goes at the death of the species. She became fascinated by the notion of keeping certain memories in a computer to address this, and then passing them on to another person with an affinity for Species Focus. Many researchers at that time thought the link might also work to tie humanity back to the planet. Winston knew the link was forever severed. It was one key to her professional advancement.

Species Focus was uncovered because we were forced to acknowledge that Chaos stalks humanity's insides. Global warming was the start of that awareness, the Jazz War its unfortunate result. But after the climax of that madness, what happens? If a Ginda can't turn water into wine--the classic joke of graduate students on the subject of Gindas--then how do we all grow? Many of the researchers sneered at the Gindas. Just as many now considered Moss a fool without freedom, a tool and little else. *But he does force humanity to recognize it must have a centric leader.*

For Winston, that is real progress. The other researchers focused on the foolishness of a Ginda's situation as a lever point. She did not, and that was the other key to her professional advancement.

The notion of sacrificing freedom as a motive system for societal progress still intrigues Winston. Today, she longs to tell Moss about whom he is and the key role he plays in society. In many ways, he is Zarathustra. In many other ways, he is a clown with no will of his own and little that is not observed by others. *This is the price of leadership after global warming--Confucianism gone mad.*

Still, she also longs to tell him homo sapiens are beginning to grow up as a result of all this, and that he is centric in this move towards sentience: the ability to read the future.

She once wanted to tell Moss something was going wrong and ask him to help. Believing those desires a mistake, she never spoke frankly with Moss, or even mentioned Russell; but tonight, she regrets that lack of candor. Clarity was the furthest thing from her mind when she had called Moss this last time, but she wonders if Clipper, or Joshua Pard, were onto her objectives of clarity and finding Russell Biner.

Winston wishes to ask her mother what she thinks about all this.

A bright bank of light flashes by, startling Winston from her pain. A low, frightening moan from a sharp corner surrounds the train compartment.

Coming out of the turn, into a slightly more affluent section of Northern Seattle, she finally sees trees. Below them, one room in every home is lit. Winston thinks the lights a sin but remains spellbound with her reflection appearing and disappearing with the glare of the buildings' lights. Free blasts of light have fascinated her since childhood. As a very young child, she had believed the night was supposed to be dark--except for the moon's grace. Tonight, in the distance, emergency vehicles patrol the night; they are on alert for fires or mayhem. The flashing lights pop out in reds and blues. Light has become safety for her.

When the outside darkens again, she finds herself staring at her own reflection. Winston favors her father's ancestors in looks. With sculpted bones beneath olive skin, dark eyes and thick black hair, she has always thought of herself as a Native American warrior. Her mother had said she was a princess. Still pleased with her looks, despite the small lines that have appeared around her eyes and mouth, her otherwise smooth skin has none of the elongated blotches that mark Techie skin.

Those elongated blotches come from "the ultimate in birthing techniques": bovine surrogate birth. Said to be superior to human birth, because of the extra womb space in the cow. It is also said bovine birth creates smarter humans. The technique has left children of Winston's generation with blemishes that have become de rigueur for admission into the best schools, a veritable pre-natal testing system. Winston finds that laughable. The truth is the shifting of a fetus from woman to cow permits more births per woman per decade. Population increase has been a key policy for years.

Joke or not, the constant and not-so-humorous pranks directed at her during her first League-rated job had almost prompted her to have scars cosmetically affixed. Watching elongated shadows appear at random on her face from the passing lights, Winston remembers the pain of ostracism and how vulnerable she had once been to urban barbs.

Luckily, her wit and intelligence keep the narrow-minded at bay, though the jokes did teach the young woman to be careful about revealing her nomadic heritage. Three years ago the barbs finally ceased: Her U.N. League rating had been raised to a single digit. Now, no one wants to cross U.N. Director of Environmental Research. Finally, when her Native American coloring no longer suggested decreased mental capacity, it had become an erotic lure to males and females determined to acquire power and status--as well as owning her beauty for their pleasure.

A Princess indeed.

The train crosses the Ginda River Bridge, and enters the Puget Sound Wilderness Area on Fidalgo Island. Winston is relieved that Moss will not be at the station to meet her. His days of waiting with wild flowers were gone long before Clipper took his memory or her, so the replacements for hearts and flowers: Recrimination and drunkenness are not missed.

The bright wash of lights through the windows distracts her; the screech of brakes say home. Winston presses her face to the glass and squints through the glare down the concrete and steel framing of the platform. There is no damage from the madness of last night. She scans the monitors on the wall. *The entire area sleeps empty. This long journey will soon end. No glowing feathery edges, no hallucinations, I can get up and leave. I am not at risk from the drift.*

She exits slowly, letting the other travelers disembark first. As she steps onto the platform, the doors creak shut, the train turns off with a hiss, and the station lights slowly begin to darken. Winston likes taking the last train home--she enjoys seeing the lights go out. For all intents and purposes, it is her responsibility to make sure this station ends the day correctly. The station exists solely for Samarra and its many tourists.

Listening to the waning din of workers and campers as they disappear down the stairs, Winston pauses until silence and darkness owns on the platform. Now, the only generated light comes from small can-shaped security sensors suspended over the platform every twenty feet. Her eyes adjust to the darkness.

Winston steers clear of the station during the early morning hours--she hates the way the teens rumble down the stairs, kicking and spitting on anything they do not like. She also cringes at just how much Moss Eckman reflects the human condition.

Descending the last set of steps, she glances up. The Milky Way unfurls above her, white and chalky, more like a banner than a million stars. The movement of a satellite tracking across the white blur catches her eye. Winston has a secret love for satellites.

"Hey watch where ya' goin!"

Winston jumps back and stumbles on the stair-riser behind her.

"Try and take a care doll, will ya? We ain't all so-safe and secure as you," says a man huddled on the bottom step. He hadn't been there when she'd scanned the security monitor.

"Sorry, I was watching the greatness." She drops four heavy coins in his lap.

The man stares at her gift as if he were holding effluvium.

Then he stands. His bulk rises far more than she might have imagined. Well over two meters, he smells of garlic. "Got more cash?" His hawking, cackling laugh has a coarse, demented timbre. "I said, do you got more cash--or an organ credit card maybe?"

She walks around him.

He follows her towards the eucalyptus trees leading to the bicycle rack. She had the trees planted there because they wash away the smell of urine and disease. At this moment, she wished she had planted more security cameras. The one that monitors this location has been broken for two weeks. She now understands why. She pivots to face the man--her right leg forward, her left leg back--ready for his assault.

He points a small revolver at her chest. "Give me the bag."

Chapter 11

"Space, the cursed frontier."

The screen brightens showing a saucer-shaped space ship passing slowly over some distant horizon. It turns and whooshes out of sight. A second, much larger ship of the same saucer design appears. Stars litter the background. A large, ringed planet in the far corner rotates into view. Angry red storms march across its surface. "These are the voyages of the Starship Plow, its five year mission. To seek out and destroy the Gumbie menace once and for all. To boldly go where only one man has gone before: The Jazz War! There Captain Pard and Commander Merton will do everything in their power to rescue Sammich Ginda, and his platoon of scholars who fight a desperate battle for humanity." Bag-pipes play a mournful Scottish march until the scene fades to black.

. . . .

Winston lowers her bag--she will not use the Diary as a shield. *I brought this madness to life with the Diary. Or do I have the Diary to quell it?*

"I said give me that bag, Doc." The man steps closer, cocking his weapon.

Eyes darting about for some way to gain leverage, "How do you know who I am?"

"You run the Jazz Museum place. We all know you. Now hand it over." The weapon shakes in his dirty hand.

She begins to open her bag. "I have some credits here, but I can get more. "You're sick. Is that it, you need a donor organ card from one of the gene-banks? Is it a kidney?"

"My guts are none of your damn business." He steps forward trying to threaten her.

"The organs don't work yet. Everyone knows that," A weapons fires, she starts, waiting for the pain, instead, a muffled sound and a body falling to the pavement. She opens her eyes, turns, and bolts the hundred yards to the brightly lit parking area.

Still clutching the bag, she looks around. By the bushes, Moss' bicycle rests between the metal prongs of a bike rack. Hers has disappeared. A yellow ribbon with his picture hangs from the handlebars. Fumbling, she grabs the thumb-print lock wired into the metal rack, looking around. The light above the surveillance camera blinks yellow, telling her to wait. Another shot, then another report from a different weapon.

The light over the camera changes from yellow to green and the round prongs in the hemispherical metal cages retract from the spokes. *What if he's got a friend waiting?* Swinging her leg over the bar, she bursts down the hill hoping the switchback path is not empty tonight.

Then it happens, a man stands in the path. *It's that soldier, the one from California*. The bike skids to a stop on the gravel. "What are you doing here?"

"He's dead, little girl."

She misunderstands. "I know you have saved me. Where is Plow?"

A soldier holsters his weapon. "He said you wouldn't get it." He seems to be waiting for something, staring at her.

"What do you want? Did you kill that man?"

He seems happy at the question, looking down at his bloody hand. "He told me to tell you: So young." He sees her step back. "I see. So that's all he gets. You are not so different from the rest of them. Did you know that?" He draws an old baseball cap low; then he tips the hat to leave.

"Where is Plow?"

"Nowhere, he's just another time-puppet. Like you." The man disappears into the shadows. A trail of blood leads off into the wood. "Wait." She leaves the bicycle to clatter to the concrete and follow him. Almost immediately she loses the man in a thicket of blackberries. "Damn it." She hurries back to the bike.

The rhythmic cycle of the pedals centers her; she turns on the bicycle's generator to light the path ahead. Under towering cedar and fir, she scoots passed locked kiosks and tents, the trees blocking the moonlight, then up a well paved road leading to Samarra. Passing another road that leads to the campground, she slows her breathing--mingling the bloom-of-the-night with the feeling of death in her chest. The dead will not erase itself from her, yet. *What did he mean I am a time-puppet also? I'm no Ginda.*

She pumps the pedals harder, passing another sign for Samarra. The display section of Samarra continues to be the most visited educational attraction in North America, and the second most visited place on the planet--behind the San Francisco earthquake ruins.

For the public, Samarra, the Environmental Museum contains three distinct sections: The Pre-Greenhouse Area, which documents the environments of Earth's past--flora and fauna, weather, as well as human settlements and their activities. People may walk through the recreation of 20th century village in Bangladesh, see the huge hotels that once graced the coast of the southern US, or experience the grandeur of glaciers. The most popular exhibit contains a recreation of a traffic jam in New York City, the day the taxi cabs stopped running to cut down on CO_2 emissions. People love to wander through the pristine vehicles in a Times Square mock-up.

The second section, Transitions, which re-creates many of the same areas during the height of the global warming years, has destruction everywhere. Meant as a teaching tool and a source for collective memory, the global warming section includes some tableaus considered too brutal for younger children, and requires parental accompaniment for those under 15.

The third section, the New World, is wildly popular; it depicts those same geographic areas today, showing the impacts of the Jazz War--which has officially been over for more than a decade--and the worldwide rebuild of civilization. There are only passing references to Species Focus--the U.N. Directorate believes the public might not be ready for the facts of life--though there are numerous references to Sammich Ginda and "his team of researchers and soldiers." All are displayed as dedicated scholars--except for Dr. Lazlo Wolf. He remains the Benedict Arnold of the group. Winston cringes; she will change that perception--she believes.

Samarra, however, functions as more than a Museum. It is a server farm, one of eight, for Clipper. In fact, seventy-five feet below Samarra's main entrance resides the core of the old Clipper complex and its newest generation of researchers. Winston had lobbied to extend Samarra out to the old ferry docks. She felt the beach and sunlight might be more conducive to Samarra's purposes: education and research. Dr. Pard had said keeping the server farm secret was more important. Winston then argued the forest would supplement security but she was overruled. The decision for the final site, she was told, was all about security and function, and Samarra was where it needed to address research on the drifting of space.

The general public has no idea Clipper has never been turned off and the war never won. They have no idea Species Focus remains a reality of life and that without Clipper and the Ginda, Moss Eckman, the effects of the tipping point, the so called Jazz War, would return within days. The public believes all the Gindas are gone, and only knows it must continue to watch the satellite feeds and report anything odd.

For Winston, the Jazz War is not so much a war as a transition, a shedding of the security blanket for a maturing species. A change that moves homo sapiens from a primitive state of awareness to more advanced state; a state most are not prepared for. Numerous scholarly papers have been written on how we had vacated our ties to Earth, and had entered a spatial drift, but most miss the point, in her opinion.

"Religion and Science were the great paths," Winston had written for conference. "...They are our mother and father and they must be respected. But, we have a new path and it must also be respected as well. We will learn about the drift and its impact on society. But without the trappings of a bygone age and without the fear that we may lose what we have treasured and respected for so long. A new path adds to the old paths, once we are passed the fear."

Her bicycle approaches the fifteen-foot stone wall that surrounds the exhibit halls and grounds. A stainless steel gate looms ahead, but she turns away from it, down a service path. Stopping the bike at a smaller gate, she taps a small bulb. It lights and a security camera scans her face. The thick gate clanks open then clatters shut behind her.

The head lamp glowing brighter, the pedals squeaking louder, with each stroke of her strong legs; she accelerates along the hill crest towards her home. Happily sensing the outlines of the trees nearby--her neighbors, she calls them--she disengages the generator. In passing them, she quietly says hello. As a child, Winston had been taught that connection to the trees mattered as much as each breath: Her mother called trees the precursor to human existence. The comment, for Winston, remains both cryptic and engaging to this day.

Ahead, the porch light blushes pink at her home; but it is against the rules to have lights on this late. Making it worse, Moss' picture hangs from the fixture. The light draws little power, yet she finds herself vexed at his childish behavior. She gets off the bike, unscrews the bulb and crumples his image, wondering if all egoistic pricks are like Moss Eckman.

Out of curiosity, she walks to the side of the house. Her bicycle lies on its side, the front rim bent and the tires gone. She examines it for signs of an accident and sees none. There are hammer marks on the frame.

She enters the cold cabin from the back kitchen door and decides not to call anyone about the assailant. Security will find him on their rounds. Her images on the monitors might cause her subordinates to question her, but nothing would come of it. Winston has complete authority over Samarra.

Inside, dirty pans and greasy rags cover the kitchen counter. Ants scurry over half-eaten chocolate cupcakes while the smell of molding food assaults her. Man-mud footprints cover the wood floor between the back door and the pantry. In the sink, smelly fish guts lay covered in dry blood. “That aristocratic asshole,” she says, scooping the smelly guts from the sink. Exiting, she deposits the fish viscera on the side of the compost piles near her garden.

It takes her an hour to clean out the smell. She begins building a fire.

Once the logs are lit, Winston walks upstairs to the rustic bedroom and bathroom. A small note sits affixed to the brass floor mirror in the bathroom. “Sorry about the bike.” Again, his picture is affixed to the mirror by a delicate red-gold chain. She yanks his image from the mirror, and places the chain on the bamboo night stand, planning to donate the chain to charity. Normally she would never want to see him again, but now that his memory of her is blank, she expects it will not matter.

Or did Clipper know that? I couldn't be a Ginda. A cold chill rises in her spine. *It's my form of the madness, perhaps* .She descends the stairs deciding fall asleep by the fire rather than in her bed.

The next morning, Winston wakes early and opens the front door to let in the morning breeze. It carries a bright sun and no fog; since the greenhouse years, Puget Sound fog remains a rare occurrence in the spring. After lingering at the front door taking in the dew, she strolls through the living room into the kitchen. In her small cabin, the main living space and the country kitchen own the first floor. For Winston, this home, a benefit of her tasks, remains a mansion.

She exits to the garden. “The day has green cousins poking their heads from the ground. You didn't wait for me.” The first shoots of snow peas appear beside the rhubarb. “But I want you all to play nice.”

She makes a mental note to weed later this morning. The garden will be a jungle of horsetail and thistle in a few weeks, The fir trees, wet and droopy, as if still asleep, tower all around her. She closes the garden gate--Moss had left it open--and walks to the hillside. In the distance, she takes in Puget Sound and the pair of rusting ferries at the old Anacortes dock. Purple smokes rises from one of the decks; someone from the clan has died. Winston wonders if they were also impacted by the recent madness. *I am going to visit that clan,* she tells herself. In fact, she feels ashamed of not visiting them yet.

Returning from the hillside, she checks the pump on the side of her work shop. Grasping the oak handle of the pump, she begins the rhythmic up and down motion to bring enough water into the house for a shower. Humming to herself, she wonders if an old laptop given to her by her father might do the job of playing the Diary. He had been a soldier, for short period of time, and the laptop was military issue. The soft mat of pine needles moves with each pumping action.

After she counts thirty cycles of pumping, she reenters her log home and sparks the wood in the water heater; the kindling immediately lights.

No Walker has ever had a problem getting a flame. Then she walks back outside to a treadmill carrying a small battery with clips. This 20th century battery, her best guess for a Diary power source from her home holds little hope for her. Mostly because she remains intimidated by the notion her father could have told her exactly which battery to use without even thinking about it. Winston turns again and walks quickly back into her home and grabs another battery from under the sink, just in case. She need not have, her first choice was correct as a power source for the diary computer; in fact, both choices are correct.

Attaching the batteries to the thick black wires coming from the front chrome bar of the treadmill; she steps up and begins to jog. Her goal: to jog out a few watts so she can continue the Diary without a power or logon signature.

Thirty-five minutes later, covered in sweat, she steps into the shower. The warmed ground-water soothes her. She keeps the shower curtain open so she can look through the twin doors to her sleeping porch. Beyond, in the small field, the purple lilacs please her.

The brass pendulum clock that hangs above the front door says 8:10 by the time she descends the stairs.

Outside the front door, she is surprised to see a dark green vehicle parked in her circular drive. A square yard of newspaper stretches between two hands resting on the steering wheel. *It can't be Moss.*

Dressed in jeans and a rag-cotton sweater, Winston steps on the porch. The paper collapses along the middle. Before she can scold the driver about parking on the grass the young woman in a Marine uniform jumps out of the jeep. "Ma'am, I'm Sergeant Tana Reins. I've been asked to bring you this." She produces a green manila envelope. "I didn't want to disturb your shower, but they said it was important. So I waited." Sergeant Reins looks inside her home, impressed at the opulent details of this forest cabin.

Taking the envelope, Winston notices the Sergeant has five small gas cylinders on her belt; that means the driver's primary function will be to act as a bodyguard rather than act as an arresting officer. "And you are to wait while I read this?"

"Ma'am, I'm also supposed to drive you over to U.N. Northwest in Bellevue as soon as possible. I was not told anything else, Ma'am." The soldier unconsciously pats her brown hair.

"I'll need to dress," Winston says, unwinding the cord that keeps the envelope closed.

"Yes ma'am." It was a formality, as well as an agreement to wait. Winston goes back in, closing the door behind her. The envelope contains some procedural paperwork and a security update, as well as inputs on an ongoing flap about allowing the well-connected to use electric scooters in Samarra. She shakes her head wondering what the correct political stance should be until she sees a polite, but formal request from Dr. Pard for a meeting today in General Smetana's office. General Fong, the security chief will also be there. Her blood boils at the sight of Dr. Pard's signature. The meeting is about the Moss.

Grabbing her bag with the Diary in it, she hurries up the stairs, telling herself to be calm about this meeting. Her transgression of locating the Diary outside of channels could be a first and final nail in her coffin. Regardless, she will not give wind to the sail of fear. She slides a veneer log aside, places the Diary in a lead-lined locker behind it, then locks it. Winston installed the stealthy safe in the chinking of her log home when she first took possession of the cabin. She replaces the piece of veneer, then goes to her closet to dress.

She picks out a blue pin striped jacket with a belted dress and lays it down on the bed. She begins methodically braiding her black hair so her ponytail will appear shorter than her rank allows. Truth is, she has been letting it grow for months but has kept its length hidden by wearing it up most of the time. She will keep her makeup simple, even though she wants to look a bit prettier. Then, looking back at the suit, she changes her mind. Good looks will matter more than style if she has been found out by the Directorate. *Pard is a bit of a letch.* Winston decides on a tight fitting black skirt and sheer white top; she pulls her hair from the braid. As she dresses, she glances out the window at the driver. Sergeant Reins continues reading, apparently oblivious to the day.

Winston puts on a deep blue waist coat to cover her blouse; the sheer material draws too much attention to her breasts, and pulls her ponytail through the intricate stitching on the collar of the jacket. Executives of this time wear long pony tails looped through the jackets holes for status instead of ties. Her ponytail curves over her shoulder ending at the peak of her small breasts.

She carries her black shoes down the stairs, putting them on at the door of the cabin. Looking back, Winston considers that she may never see the cabin again, especially if they know about her clandestine acquisition of the Diary. The credits she used to pay Polken Frew came from the Museum's discretionary funds--ones she controls--but ones subject to oversight. Unapproved uses, like bribery, require a prison term.

The idling jeep no longer rests on the grass. Sergeant Reins jumps from her seat, then scoots around to open the long back door. A comfortable-looking bench seat waits for Winston. She secretly always enjoys the immense depravity of a private vehicle and sits down, but wears an awkward smile.

They soon pass the lines of tourists penned in by a yellow nylon cord. Some visitors gasp at the car as it drives by them, others sneer.

"I know this place is always a big hit on weekends, but this is a surprise." The driver speaks convivially. "I'll bet these crowds stretch all the way to the station." Sergeant Reins would love nothing more than to live out here in the woods--even if it is all a scam for the Wholacks. Still, she wants to make sure Dr. Doe likes her.

"We're always busy."

The curt response will keep the driver quiet for the rest of the ride.

Winston doesn't notice. *Perhaps all of this is because of Clipper's memory wipe? Oh, good one, Winston, and then they can take their choice: They can execute me for either insubordination or the security breach.*

CHAPTER 12

Fields of golden wheat wave slowly in the breeze. Behind them, distant, hills lie bathed in a red setting-sun. Nirvana glows from the video screen. Voice-over: "We hope you have enjoyed our experiment to show you, the American people, just how we can benefit by allowing satellite broadcasts to emanate from North America. Especially since they will only be viewed by us. The job of keeping our country safe and sane belongs to all of us. And we here at The Satellite Consortium believe Americans should keep track of Americans. Remember, the choice is yours. Should we have satellite surveillance over North America again? Should we allow our images to be overseen by foreigners or should we do it ourselves? Think about how you wish to vote--and cast your vote. Remember freedom has a voice, and that voice is yours. And now a message from our sponsor: ATWAS Corporation."

. . . .

Fir trees line the roadway with mile-long blackberry brambles under their canopy. The jeep turns and stops at a stone entry. The gate's iron bars crank open. Up ahead, at the end of the wide manicured driveway sits the U.N. Headquarters for North America. Done in the Genian style of twin spires forming a horseshoe, the six-story building doesn't glisten anymore. Pink neon panels affixed along the edge of the arch, which are intended to glow in a ghostly shimmer, were turned off many years ago. Winston had once seen the building lit, on her mother's insistence, just before Winston's fifth birthday. Looking at it from a nearby hillside, as the panels shimmered--under computer controls--she'd been seduced by the willowy sinuous dance of the glowing façade. Such was her mother's hope; she knew Winston did not fit with a clan that sought freedom over knowledge.

The shimmering pink neon panels were switched off after embarrassing figures on energy consumption were released by local hospitals and schools, who shared the same priority power grid. The scientists tried to explain the panels were an effort to understand the unknown function of a Genian city-museum, but it did no good. A League One citizen of Seattle died on an operating table due to a lack of power. Samarra is the second attempt at understanding the function of a museum that appeared to be more of a machine than a showplace. Even so, the city-museum's function remains a mystery to Dr. Doe, and many others.

The jeep proceeds up the hill and stops three hundred yards away from the building. Winston, per protocol, exits the jeep and gazes at the massive horse-shaped building while ignoring the three guards moving swiftly around the jeep with mirrors and sensors. The guards know the driver and the passenger are above reproach so they complete their job with little care. They then wave them on up the curved driveway to the building.

Stopping at the main doors, Sergeant Reins leaves the engine on and races around the vehicle to open the vehicle's door for her passenger. "I'll be here when you are finished, Doctor." The woman salutes. Winston finally wonders if the jeep assigned to her today has any good reasons. She counts the four broad granite stairs again, and ascends. On the walls surrounding the doorway she sees new bullet holes covered with mortar. Winston wonders if these calling cards might also have something to do with her visit here today. She had read about an attack in this morning's security update.

A small brass plaque embedded into the concrete beside the double glass doors remains untouched.

It says:

Jordan Building:

In Honor of Heroes

Winston touches the twenty-foot glass doors. They glide open as if were made of feathers. Winston hurries passed the expansive green glass doors looming over her and into the main lobby. A small cadre of armor-suited guards stands at attention.

Inside the two-story lobby, she scans the green marble walls of the perfect cube surrounding her. There are no bullet holes. The three small paintings over the teak desk are gone. New larger paintings have taken their place. One, a portrait of Joshua Pard and a second portrait of Robert Merton--both considered the ethical heroes of the Clipper Project. Her jaw clamps shut; they annotate her own sin of vanity. The former images of Carlos Jordan, Simon Weiss, and Quentin Conworth are gone.

That's reason enough to attack this place... She says to herself.

The guards and the receptionists wait for her--the security scans outside have already announced her arrival: "Please, take a seat Madam Director," says one of the receptionists.

Winston chooses one of the empty sky-blue couches facing way from the paintings. She nods to the twin guards who stand like guard dogs on either side of the doorway, weapons at the ready. It has been a long time since those security stations have been manned--or that she has been made to wait. Her fear mounts.

On her left, the center elevator opens and a broad man in his late sixties steps out. A tightly clipped white beard on a fleshy face, close-cut white hair and limp red eyes, he looks like everyone's grandfather. The thin lips build into a loose smile as he walks to his former student with an apparent calm and ease of purpose. Neither is true--Dr. Pard is a man in love with his job--and his reputation. His leather shoes scrape the marble floor, due to a leg wound from many years ago.

The gait is distinctive, and by the time he circles the couch to greet Winston Doe she stands stiffly, her pasted-on smile like a volcanic cap. His head immediately cocks to the right, his beaming eyes moist; a proud father could have appeared no more gracious. As he extends his right hand to shake her hand--Dr. Joshua Pard has always been so formal--he leans a bit forward, ostensibly due to his wounded leg, and examines her tense face. "Are you all right?"

"Leg, okay, Dr. Pard?"

The chronic leg pain, damaged during a running gun battle between security and some lost souls, still throbs from where the bullet had lodged in the femur. "Oh, I'm fine. Winston, what are you?" The man says, eyeing her from a paternal pose.

"Fine, Doctor, it is so good to see you again." Winston gauges his smile for a clue. Hating the false front, she had once loved him as if he were a father, she glances away. Dr. Pard's fall from her grace has shattered her. *Once again, the Techie culture has proven itself unworthy of anything but my apprehension.* Winston notes that in those seconds, her pulse has started pounding in her ear. *Maybe I should hate him more.*

She had expected to see him differently now, but only this man's shroud seems clearer. There are no signs of his treachery, even though she has the proof of his deceit. She scans his blue eyes--they're cold and calculating--they had always been shrewd, but also grandfatherly, towards her. Her foolish pride bothers Winston--*his attention to my accomplishments has constantly fed my blindness.*

Then Dr. Joshua Pard's actions become clear to her for the first time. *He is using me, but for what purpose?* A brief pain races up her right side as muscles tighten with anger; her determination to make him proud lights a fire in her gut. At one point, Winston had excused his clandestine actions on the premise that a power shift in the Directorate was going against him, due to his age. She needn't have worried; Joshua Pard still enjoys a worldwide reputation for his commentaries on the Jazz War.

Millions know his face from interviews and articles that have been constant since the war. It continues even now, due to an innate ability to keep himself in the public eye as a trusted friend. Years ago, a colleague had called him saganistic, one who uses science for his own gains, and Winston had rushed to her mentor's defense. Now she wonders about that researcher whom she had so thoroughly embarrassed with her barbs.

Winston looks around the lobby: "Looks like there were unwelcome visitors here, too." The guards remain unconcerned with her.

He notes the tension in her voice. "There is no problem that Benson's people cannot handle."

She steps back. "I was summoned here from my vacation. That's unusual. I thought the building wounds were a clue." Knowing this man had been born to privilege, she knows he will concede a rude summons for someone just back from "vacation", as reason enough to be bent out of shape.

"Oh that," he waves his hand while shaking his head. "That was Gregor. He has had a bee in his bonnet about Moss. We've seen another increase in Jazz events this last week. Gregor wants your inputs on Moss' response. We had seen you were clipped from his memory yesterday. We cannot yet locate the reason for the first failed clip." He conducts her to the elevator not wanting to share any more information in the reception area.

They slip their ID's into the slot and the elevator doors close. Pard places his ID back in his well worn pants pocket. "It seems Moss took it upon himself to square things with you these last few days for not taking him along."

"I saw."

"How was the vacation?"

"To short," she replies wanting to deflect the conversation. "So we had a bad series of flare ups while I was gone?"

"Moss' increased agitation coincided with increased attacks. By the way Anna, quit last night." He shakes his head.

She marvels at his aloof commentary.

"Moss was angry, but we think he has forgotten you. We took care of secondary traces this morning, so don't worry. Regardless, Gregor, being Gregor, insists on a meeting to go over possible connections to the riots."

The older man pauses. "I think he will want you to meet Moss and see how complete the memory clip is--any ideas on why we'd see an uptick in his ire?"

"He was never so anxious when I did not see him before."

"We were surprised at that. The models say he is beginning to lean towards violence as well." Joshua Pard, despite his flaws, can still claim to be an above average researcher. "Or, perhaps it's love."

"Funny man," she says cheerfully."What does Gregor really think?" She feels so alone. He laughs like a friendly uncle who has heard a close family joke. It pains her.

"Gregor has a few more years to retirement. This new flare up of the Chaos keeps him awake at night." Pard follows it matter-of-factly with: "I think we just take this meeting as another of his save-the-world meetings. We'll try to get through it without too much coffee." He grins and Winston births unbridled hate. "After that we can get him an answer when we understand the need for the two cuts. Then we'll present the answer on a silver platter for Gregor--he is practically out of the loop now--I hear. I think that concerns him also."

She cannot let it all go: "Dr. Pard, I have been thinking about that. Maybe I can push to have him involved in the project--as a consultant to my people? He seems to understand the city-museum better than anyone--and we can use help on that one. Maybe with General Smetana's knowledge…"

"Are you trying to kill me? How did I offend you, Dr. Doe?" He says. His hand taps her very lightly on her shoulder. "Dr. Pard, again?"

"Sorry, I'm out of sorts with the shortened vacation. Who else will be at the meeting?" She asks watching the lights increment to six.

"Just you, myself, Benson, Gregor--and maybe Travis Eckman."

"Is Gregor still trying to get Mina Wolf on board?"

He again shakes his head. "If you are asking if she still hates the work that consumed her father, the answer is yes." As the elevator continues up, its creaking grows louder. "Winston, it's during times like these that I understand how you live up in the wildlife preserve; that's beautiful country. Don't ever come down here to live. It's a jungle."

"I know," she replies--then immediately regrets that she has fallen into his trap--Pard's whole manor changes.

Before she can speak, he says: "Is it true they may allow families full access into the Samarra wilderness?"

"I doubt it. The civilian council is fixed in their retro-view that a pristine environment gains worth by a lack of human fingerprint." Winston pauses; pensive of his tactic to cover suspicions with an innocent question. She has seen it often--but she has never been on the receiving end--so far she can remember. Winston continues trying to cover her trail. "You'd think after all this time, people like that would get over 20th century dogma."

"The more it changes the more it stays the same," he says and they both smile at the old joke. Winston works to keep her smile loose and friendly. She fails. "Winston, what is it?"

Winston, not knowing what else to say, will lie: "You let Moss ruin my bicycle, the one that was a gift from my clan. You were always jealous of my parents, I think. And you let him stink up my house also." She mentally urges the numbers of the floors to go by quicker so this ride can end.

"But I did get you a safe driver. Just how many paths do I pursue to please you? Do you like the driver?"

"Dr. Pard, just because your father was friends with Carlos Jordan, and you are a key researcher on Clipper, that doesn't mean you may take matters into your hands and herd me into a carbon-belcher while destroying my bicycle." She creaks out a laugh.

"Actually, it does," he says with a firm pat on her shoulder. The joke between these two seems to have worked--so far as Winston can tell. She will soon see the cost of being a novice battling an ego bred for politics.

They exit the elevator and walk towards a guard station. The guard hands each of them a new identification card. The green band along the lower edges contains small vertical lines, unlike the badge in Winston's hand. Security has been heightened--this badge is only good for a day.

She attaches the new badge to her breast pocket and hands the guard her old one. The former friends follow the guard across the hallway to a taupe-colored executive conference room. He holds the door for them as Winston enters first. Dr. Pard follows her a bit too closely, like a hound trying to sniff out a trail, or a snoop afraid to miss a bit of conversation.

Two uniformed men stand up from a table and walk towards her. A third well dressed businessman stands, still behind the table. The two men each move in a different direction around the small table--like trained birds. She has no idea of their prey, though she now understands their ongoing dislike for Joshua Pard.

Benson Fong, the man circling on the right has twisted his all gray-pony-tail into a topknot, emphasizing his Asian features. In a sense, he and Travis Eckman, the man who remains behind the table, are Moss Eckman's handlers. Travis Eckman has convinced Moss they are brothers--nothing could further from the truth. Travis works to protect the interests of the gene-banking cartel--mutations continue to run rampant in a world where experiments contain no controls.

Benson Fong floats around Moss' world in the guise of a mawkish bon vivant. Born in China during the worst of the global warming years, his mother was a doctor in Beijing. His father had been an Australian diplomat posted to the Chinese capital. Both died in a food riot.

Educated and befriend by a local Confucian scholar. The scholar guided Benson into service with the U.N. Bright and capable, Benson Fong advanced quickly to a security role in the original Clipper Project, protecting the Gindas. Now, in charge of U.N. research security for North America, including Samarra. His primary duties, include keeping an eye on--but not interfering with--Moss Eckman. No one stops Moss from doing anything he wants. Winston has known Benson for years and her sense of his professionalism and dedicated core remains untarnished. Remembering his name on some of the Diary's notes, she wonders what she will uncover about him, as well as the last man in the room, General Gregor Smetana.

This man looks as though he could have been a football player forty years ago. Thick and broad-shouldered, with a neck the size of some people's thighs, he moves with ownership of his location. No one would be surprised to learn that Gregor Smetana is the most senior U.N. military officer in the hemisphere. He reminds Winston of a polar bear while Benson Fong reminds Winston of a Shaolin monk

General Smetana speaks first: "We're sorry to bring you here before the end of your vacation, Dr. Doe, but it can't be helped."

"Hopefully you are well rested," Benson Fong says. These two men are a formidable team and respected for their dedication. Winston has developed some reservations about them after her insights into Dr. Pard, but they are groundless.

They take their seats around the dark oak table: the General on her left, Fong on her right and Pard across the table next to Travis Eckman. "As Dr. Pard has no doubt told you," Benson continues, "we've seen an acceleration in random violence over the last week. Yesterday morning, Clipper fired a reset for Moss Eckman that we find inexplicable because it didn't work on the first round. He was on the phone to you. We want to know if it is a complete wipe--and why the first edit failed. We'd like your opinion of the two edits so we have arranged with Travis for you to meet with Moss later today. The lab data says Moss has totally forgotten about you. We also need to determine if there is a connection between the edit failure and the increase in violence. So far, this morning, the chaotic behavior in the population has quelled, but only a bit."

"Edit failures have happened before, but it's been years," she says pondering the issue.

"Winston," says Smetana, "you know Moss wanted more from you. When you left without telling him, you sent a powerful message. Dr. Pard has suggested Moss' emotional response was carried out into the population."

"Wolf and Biner were fairly sure the flow didn't work that way. I've seen no reliable reports to the contrary." Winston replies without rancor. Her desertion of Joshua Pard surprise everyone in the room.

The General nods. "We all know that, but a 3% increase in a week is disturbing."

Winston admires the way these men have adapted to the reality of Species Focus, taking on the role of diligent facilitators, never fighting the awareness that public leaders are only administrators and shepherds--not prime movers--or kings.

She has speculated that in different times Gregor Smetana might have been a prime minister or head of large multinational corporation. More than once, she has seen him in a public function negotiating policy with members of the unenlightened aristocracy. Eyebrows growing in one bushy line over wide brown eyes, his thick lips and nose large, the General frequently uses his bulk and proximity to the nexus to convince others he knows the best course. Benson negotiates like a warrior. She glances at Travis Eckman, His presence is beginning to bother her. This class of discussion rarely includes an NGO. She concludes the gene-bankers have found some new leverage.

"Moss is a prime mover," General Fong continues, "We have a responsibility to investigate all causality."

"And that is why I keep requesting in line contact with both Clipper and Moss," Winston says quickly. "Dr. Biner said that was the key to success. It will take us months, if ever, to ferret out the problem going through the logs." She smiles at Pard and waits seeing what they will do.

"We can talk about that later," counters Dr. Pard.

"I'd like to hear a little more now, Dr. Doe," says General Fong. He has immense respect for Dr. Doe and so overrides Pard when ever he can. Winston smiles at the acrimony between Pard and these men.

Smetana taps a paradiddle on the table top with the fingers of his right hand. Heir to a great composer's fame; General Smetana had once planned to become a symphony conductor in a coastal town so he might surf--his one love outside the office. The destruction of Hawaii changed all that and he became intimately involved in the Clipper Project. He had been the man whom Lazlo Wolf and Russell Biner convinced to fund ongoing research "after the war". He remains in control. "We are guessing from the outside. I think we need to be inside the problem."

"I completely agree." Regardless of her play to see if they are holding something back, she fears this meeting may have something to do with her unauthorized acquisition of the Diary. Either of these man so graciously supporting her have the power of life and death.

"Have you discovered what happened to Dr. Biner?' Asks Pard. "Is that what you were doing on your vacation?"

Stunned for a moment, she chirps out a stilted laugh. "Do you really think that I would waste a vacation on lost love?"

"You said in the elevator you thought Moss was in love with you," Pard replies matter-of-factly.

She glares at him. Her eyes burn with anger and her throat dries, breath comes short and shallow. No one in the room misses it.

"There could be a parallel that Dr. Doe is unaware of," says Benson, releasing the charge in the room; she notes the other men move uncomfortably in their seats. "On the other hand, at this point," Benson continues, his brown eyes briefly lighting on each person in the room. "Let's first determine as much as possible about Moss' stability before we take any other steps."

"Zurich is concerned that the satellite scans of Moss show no overt change in his emotional stability, but if he had been enamored then that should have shown itself. With that we could have seen some congruity to the background noise from the war," says Pard.

"The problem is the drift seems to have been altered. The chaos ratcheted-up, at higher levels. So far as we can tell after last night," replies Benson Fong. "It is curious."

Winston wonders about the comment. There is another more obvious option--a shift in focus--but Benson did not mention it.

"The last month or so, something in the drift has been spinning out of control," says General Smetana.

"Now all, let's not be hasty," says Travis Eckman.

Despite common understanding, the Jazz War was never a really a war. Just as the so-called battle between humanity and its environment, global warming, was never a battle. Global warming and the Jazz War are seen, by the people in this room, as steps in human evolution--an awakening. Their clarity is fostered by Gaian sensibilities; the real world order. Only Winston is unsure of her role in that order. That will change soon.

As homo sapiens advanced, opening new doors, the most obvious planetary tariffs came in the form of environmental pollution; when they were shunted aside, new challenges arose, many of them obvious: technology, education, transportation, computation, environmental responsibility, and so forth. The less obvious changes: Ethics, morality, honor, and the rest of the virtues finally became this deferred bill of cognition that came due with the Jazz War. It was Russell Biner who said: "The notions of unexpected consequences were only hinted at. The current clandestine responsibilities and unplumbed links between human consciousness and the planet has damned us all."

"Do you suspect Species Focus may be drifting from Moss to another Ginda?" Winston asks the men in the room. Then she catches her breath as color drains from Travis Eckman's face. She inhales, and tries to release the air slowly, but she cannot. Her breath releases in defeat. The pains of clarity own her; truth drops upon Winston as if it were a falling piano. The three men wait, their faces a mix of inquisition and awe. Her attempt at refocusing the meeting has brought in far more information than she had thought possible. This because the others in the room did not see a deflection of inquiry, just brilliance.

She waits, unsure if she should try to capitalize on their apparent confusion or speak her fear. Winston continues: "We have seen the drift leave Moss a dozen times over the years and then quickly return. So it could it might be a computational anomaly." Guided by her intellect and its unquenchable thirst for the truth she follows with: "But we know that, isn't it, don't we, gentlemen?" She pauses afraid to speak the words. "So the obvious conclusion is we have a move to a new Ginda. To me." She waits.

Pard responds: "You are amazing, Winston. How did you figure it out?"

"Don't patronize me Joshua." She watches Benson Fong speak into a communicator on his collar. She faces Smetana. "I am tied into Clipper."

General Smetana nods. The rest are silent.

"My memories are not my own? And how many of me have there been?"

Pard speaks: "You know the purpose of this work is to help humanity--not destroy the beings with focus or lessen their leverage once they have focus. There has been no other version of you. Your memories are in tact."

"That's not true," interrupts Benson Fong. "There have been horrors that were erased. But, Dr. Doe, you have my word--for what it is worth today--nothing else. You are a primary."

"Now that we finally have that out, can we continue?" Says General Smetana. He will not insult Winston by pandering to her. "Dr. Doe you are a miracle. You are first generation Ginda with clarity. We are seeing a drift of Species Focus from an indolent, self involved, consumer of everything he touches to a thoughtful, decent woman--with clarity on the event--and we are dumbfounded. At the same time, we see an increase in the Chaos. We need to understand that. What do you think we are we seeing here Dr. Doe?"

"I have seen no definitive shift to Winston," says Pard quickly. "And I am not finished yet with my evaluation."

Winston looks at Pard; she is amused at his ego intrusion. In an odd way, it verifies the words of Fong and Smetana

Pard continues: "I'd like to check to see if we have any other indicators of Winston acquiring focus. Frankly, I wish it would move to Winston." Pard says with a paltry smile.

He truly does admire Winston Doe and knows that Species Focus, along with all its other attributes, is a perfect snapshot of humanity. But in his estimation, Winston Doe represents a step forward for humanity from Moss Eckman and he sees no possibility that she represents the whole of humanity. His fear is that her acquiring focus represents a coming terminus for homo sapiens. And for that same reason, he has always supported everything done by, and for, Dr. Doe. And while she represents escape for him; he fears death. Joshua Pard speaks carefully: "Let's not move to quickly here. Winston, you may be attaining focus, which explains why the first reset of Moss by Clipper didn't work, but that doesn't mean focus will stay with you. I suspect because you are a trained researcher that your own resources to mollify Clipper might either take you out of the running or to the other extreme, provide you with control over Clipper." Of course, Pard has no plans to allow his influence to wane.

Travis Eckman, on the other hand, sees his influence on events waning--and the work of the gene-bankers under threat. He sits still and attentive.

"I am not sure what we are seeing, General. But I have a question. My mother, did she know?" Winston asks.

General Smetana shakes his head in the negative.

She then sees the downcast eyes of Benson Fong and she knows the truth. "She always was a patriot at heart. Thank you, General, for that lie." The room is again silent until she speaks. "I know you cannot tell me the truth about anything that might mitigate focus, but I agree with Joshua, Moss seems to represent us; especially Dr. Pard, far better than me. In any case, thank you for not denying any of this. I understand that you can say no more on that topic."

Smetana stirs in his seat then speaks. "Dr. Doe, you are that giant that people have been told are the Gindas. You are a step forward. You have cognition of the process. You have insight, and you have the tools to analyze it all from the inside. No Ginda has ever had that."

"And you know what the theories say about having a Ginda that remains first generation throughout," says Joshua Pard.

"I do not have sentience, Joshua. I cannot see the future. I didn't even understand my present. Where is the letter?"

"Letter?" He replies, glancing at General Smetana.

"I would have sealed a letter to myself if this had been my idea. I would have instructed you, Joshua, to deliver it to me at this moment." She scans the three men.

"Dr. Doe, there is no letter," says General Smetana.

She watches the men carefully.

"And there was never any discussion about a letter," adds Joshua Pard.

"I know you use me, Joshua, like you use everyone."

"Winston, you are complete," says General Smetana.

"Clipper has not altered anything except some horrors you were forced to see--and that was a Directorate decision. You were inordinately pained when you were anyplace that the horrors erupted. Basically, you shut down--as if the madness were a direct attack on your being. We reset the event and you woke clear of it. We never went any further," Pard says. "We never had to. For what it is worth, we postulate you may soon pass even that need."

Benson Fong's nod tells Winston this is mostly the truth. She speaks: "Who else knows?"

"No one, besides the people in this room, on-continent," replies Pard. "Off-continent, the Directorate knows."

"We're getting off track," says General Smetana disliking Pard just a bit more. "Winston, you'll meet with Moss. Travis find out what time Moss wants to meet you at his office. Dr. Pard, I'd like to look into the notion that Winston has some function in the events of this last week and any parameters you might locate on shifting Species Focus. See if you can establish a cross reference. And, Dr. Doe, I don't know how to convince you that you were not conscripted into this position."

Winston speaks. "Am I watched the same way Moss is, by the satellites. Do I have any privacy? Did you know about the attempted mugging?"

General Fong looks at General Smetana. "When you are in a high threat situation you are protected. On the other hand, the mugging last night at the train station was a surprise," says General Fong. "My people were not involved." He watches her. "Winston, there was a time that if you were in that kind of situation, you would have simply fainted. Instead, you escaped."

"A Ginda killed the assailant." No comment could have stunned these men more.

"A Ginda? Who?" They all appear shocked. "Who was the Ginda that protected you?" Benson asks more insistently.

"I don't know," replies Winston, full of suspicions. "So you would risk me?" Winston asks, even though she doubts these men would risk an asset as valuable as a first generation Ginda with violence.

"We did not know," says Pard. "No wonder you were acting so strange when we met."

"Why was the assault a surprise?" She asks. Looking at Pard she births a notion: *If I am achieving focus then perhaps we are at a terminus. That would scare Joshua.*

"We said you were the first of you and the only you. That doesn't mean there were not others who have tried to approach--this clarity--you know that. We tried to protect them. They became unstable like the other Gindas," Pard says cautiously. "The assumption has always been that Samarra is safe. That it is not so anymore and it concerns me."

"And my vacation?"

"You were kept safe in transit," Benson replies, "But we were advised that a change of spatial reference was to be respected and then studied."

Winston knows of the studies. "I see." *Did Pard plan the attack or plant the Diary?* She glances at Benson and sees no concerns in his eyes. "Has my position changed in any way?"

"No," replies General Smetana.

"Good. Oh, and I was sure there was no note before I asked. If this was a trick you would have produced one." Winston smiles. "The jeep and driver can stay." She looks at Benson; he is clearly impressed by her insight.

General Smetana speaks: "If you want the link to Clipper removed we will remove it, Dr. Doe. But take a moment and consider the options."

"General, I understand my options. I will not remove it myself. Not yet, and I understand all the implications of a trained researcher with focus."

"You wanted to be in line, Doctor Doe," Pard says.

General Smetana watches her and sees that she understands Pard's fears. "Benson and I will also consider Dr. Doe's proposal of going in-line with Moss and Clipper rather than her current role. We will examine the option and get back to you and Dr. Pard." His eyes move purposefully to garner her gaze. They are full of admiration. "Winston, you are the future. Clipper may some day be the tool every human uses to circumvent the madness that owns us. We don't know if that's next. But your clarity has come to you in your time, in your way. You know that. Will you tell us what you did on your vacation?"

The meaning of the question is clear for her. *They really did not know. Or how I am to do my task.* She feels a sense of parity with the people in the room. *So why were the soldiers protecting me? How did Joshua and the rest of them not know? But I was wrong, they would risk me. The Jazz War events must be multiplying. But then who would have had the insight, the sentience, to protect me? And that's what they want to know.* "Clipper cannot retail my thoughts in its Diary." She says instead of answering.

"It cannot. Russell Biner made sure of that," replies Travis Pard before anyone can speak.

The other three men stare at the gene-banker with dark, angry eyes. Overloaded by the disclosure, Winston stands up and leaves the room.

Chapter 13

Voice-Over: "In the interests of fairness, the following is an editorial response by Travis Eckman, Chief Operating Officer of GeneBanks, S.A. It is in response to our editorial on the lottery system for replacement organs. We present Mr. Eckman, speaking for the gene-banking community."

"Good evening. My name is Travis Eckman. I am the Chief Operating Officer for GeneBanks, S.A. Think about something for me: Do you want to be the last person to die? Do you think anyone should make the decision on who should be the last person to die? We don't.

"We have all seen the wondrous results of genetic modification in our lifetime. Humanity is on the move again. The money you have invested in your organ replacement accounts has funded that change. Either

you, or your progeny, will reap the results of your investments--and soon.

"Don't let the nay-sayers tell you mutation rates are up, or that only a select few get replacement organs. At GeneBanks, S.A., we have implemented a double blind lottery for the delivery of every major organ in the human body--and I assure you that everyone has exactly the same chance to receive a new organ. Rich or poor, worker or executive--the common man's chances for getting organ systems and living a little longer are the same as everyone else's. You have our word on it. This is why the lottery system must be maintained.

"The gene-banking community has a storehouse of products promising human life out passed the two hundred year mark. So keep your deposits current and have faith. Your name may be next in the organ lottery.

"GeneBanks, S.A. here to help you--and your family. So let's leave the decision-making to chance--not greed. Vote no! Vote against the repeal of the organ lottery."

. . . .

Over what remains of the old Seattle docks south of the city, four office buildings sit among the empty lots and crumpled container cranes. The buildings are a study in architectural cacophony.; Two of the buildings are perfect examples of Neo-asceticism, a trend that became popular during the global warming crisis, black, square-framed and dark, pure utilitarianism: The two cubes that lower over the blue waters of Puget Sound say solidarity.

The other two buildings are examples of the current Arcadian movement. They sport a deep green skin covering a steel frame and a brown roof rising and falling in a sine wave pattern. These Arcadian buildings are considered the very essence of life because their bioengineered skins *are* alive: Their membranes are self repairing, require nourishment, and emit waste. In essence, the exterior skins of these buildings would die without the network of red and blue tubes snaking through the steel framework delivering and removing substances from the skin.

The effect of seeing the four buildings on the same dock promotes the lifelessness of the cubed structures. To many observers, the architectural cacophony also gives the impression that the companies housed in these buildings are engaged in a titanic battle: the dark past vs. the flowing brilliant future.

This is exactly the message the two gene-bank companies wish to convey. They share the waterfront, and a multibillion dollar PR campaign. Their program centers on publicizing a fictional antipathy between the gene-banking giants. But, PR aside, GeneBanks S.A. and U.S. Research are as closely tied as the old "Seven Sisters" of the twentieth century oil cartel. Unlike the oil cartel, the perverse knot that ties the gene-bankers is an inability to deliver their central product: replacement organs for dying humans.

The genetic banking community has been selling eternal life, a product that it can not yet deliver, for years. Mutation rates are astronomical and random failures throughout the production facilities continually defies scientific, or any other qualitative analysis. The industry and its traditional research mechanisms have hit a brick wall because control groups never remain stable and the work from before the Jazz War sits on the sidelines--as useless as a buggy whip. All the old scientific techniques function, but only part of the time. The scientific method has become unreliable. Why remains a mystery to the researchers; however, inside the upper echelons of the society the reason is clear: Newton's universe is a memory. Humanity is cut off from its home--the Earth--and struggles, adrift in...?

If the public knew how baffled the research people were about solving the interconnected problems of genetic research and production they would demand their money back, only to find much of it eaten by the hydra of antediluvian faith in repeatability, linearity, and technology. As in the past, the secret of the cartel's problems lay hidden from the public, a undisclosed whisper among thieves.

Science has become a myth among the cognoscenti--the way religion became a myth among the scientifically trained a century before--another effect of the tipping point. The irony, for researchers like Winston, is that this scientific debacle is proof of humanity's ongoing progress away from the consumption of facts and towards an alignment with authenticity. Unfortunately, it does little for commerce and therefore leaves the corporate leaders bare. To deflect it, corporate media outlets focus on the previous breakdown of society and society's imminent return to prosperity.

So rather than disclose humanity's growth--it is merely never reported by the media. There is logic to this: The failures of science must be kept out of the public eye so the remains of the patrician order can fight on. The result is students are bombarded with the time-honored tradition of band-aid constants, theoretical conclusions without basis, and think-tank opinion masquerading as fact. Actual peer-supported science remains buried under corporate funding guidelines. Another result of the global warming years.

Sadly, when the United Networks learned to frame opinions as facts and eviscerate science, they saw it as prudent governance, not a response to coming environmental changes. Had they seen it as a sentient societal response to the tipping point, then perhaps the failure of science as an effective method might not have been so much of a shock. Progress might have been made cataloguing the event--rather than trying to hide it for financial gain. Ironically, those that see through the failures of science are allowed to progress into effective research. The masquerade by the leadership is not evil--it is fear without awareness.

For the obvious reasons: stability, power, money, and connections, the upper reaches of the gene-banking industry now know a great deal about the Jazz War, the accepted term for the most obvious symptom of the tipping point. In fact, few believe that the dissolution of reliable methods for research will change. They even agree the genetic conundrum is proof the physical plane upon which humanity now lives has been randomized far beyond what people can tolerate. Like everyone else, they blame a long gone, indolent, energy rich society. The gene-bankers continue to say that economic systems also can not tolerate economic randomness--which they say--was also brought about by the tipping point. And, the gene-bankers conclude: Deception holds the only answer to these Chaotic truths. They claim that their no-regrets strategy of waiting for better days is the most prudent course for society--and would be offended if they were told that they travel the same dead end path as their ancestors.

The current spokesperson of the deception-theory of crisis management is Travis Eckman, a former teenage genius who had written a paper on the link between the Gindas and quasi-random anomalies in genetic control groups during his senior year of high school. The paper landed on the desk of Dr. Robert Merton, a GeneBanks S.A. executive. The next day, the thesis could not be found anywhere.

The most powerful industry on the planet has concluded that their best hope to solve their dilemma centers on the Ginda named Moss; though they will never publicly acknowledge it. Travis was quickly hired as special researcher, and within six months, assigned to investigate aspects of Species Focus with the core problem: Moss, renamed Moss Eckman. He would be closely watched by Travis so that any breakthroughs in Species Focus would flow directly to the gene-bankers.

Having been placed in the role of "brother", after a Clipper memory modification, Travis' task centers on how to manipulate Moss Eckman and the apparently mystical events of Species Focus so the gene-banking community might contain, or profit from the Chaos. The hope, of course, is the delivery of their product: human replacement organs, and other commerce. The board rooms have little tolerance for the planet controlling society; they still believe commerce can control the planet. Travis, alone in the banking community, recognizes the folly of this, but he also knows he must tow the gene-bankers party-line while seeking an acceptable exit from a dead end industrial stance.

How could the gene-bankers wield so much influence?

"***No one wants to be the last person to die.***" It is the gene-banker's motto.

Recently, violent assaults on the gene-banker's facilities have become commonplace. Sick desperate people, tired of the constant: "No, we can't help you," try to steal the imaginary organs, which they believe lay hidden in the gene-bankers' vaults. In a poetic turn of events, when a heated gun-battles results, the guards have been instructed to push the robber into a vault where they find only money. And, since money will not save what remains of their organs, the would-be thieves usually choose suicide in the vaults.

The gun-battles usually begin outside, in a brightly lit company store. These stores sell gourmet fare laced with new nutrient compounds. The gene-bankers seek to gather information on the long term effects of the nutrients so the foods sell for almost nothing. During these assaults on the gene-banks, the first person shot is a child--another remnant of the Jazz War that has not gone away--it is also never reported by the media.

Many researchers have suggested the perpetrators should be allowed to escape with the money as it means almost nothing in this society. The population numbers sit stubbornly low; factories that can produce far more than necessary, but energy is a constraint because so many of the alternative energy systems developed in the early part of the century had no resilience to storms--so money gets all the attention.

Sadly, the researchers of this time have no idea that deception represents power to those with a retro-patrician's view of power--both inside and outside the gene-bank community. Plus, the gun-battles make for good media coverage of the gene-bankers and their efforts to protect the citizen's money--and therefore their own lives. Once again, like during the global warming years, knowledge is castrated.

Bucky's, the nutrient store at Genebanks S.A. sits under the red and blue tubing that feeds the sinewy exterior skin of the building. The price of nutrition is dirt cheap here--as long as one signs a form to forfeit the right of litigation--and some hours to acquire the food. As a result, many who can not afford farmed organic steak, corn, or milk, are able to enjoy genetically manufactured nutrition. They believe it will extend their lives. No one discusses the risk of being guinea pigs for nutrition supplements. Like the old days, the consumers are buying a myth of control. The GeneBanks S.A. retail store plays organ music for the crowd. Travis Eckman has a perverse sense of humor.

Moss hurries through the marble lobby of GeneBanks S.A., ignoring the four guards stationed near the retail entrance. The guards recognize the silver-spoon-brother of Travis Eckman. No one says: "You cannot…" To Moss Eckman.

He pushes through the line of waiting customers looking for his brother, and nodding to the guards. These men and women protecting the obscene amount of money here ignore the grumbling public. No one wants their problems to include Moss Eckman.

Unimpeded, he bounds up the short stairs with a tight-lipped grin on his unshaven face while looking down at those waiting or eating, milling around, sitting at tables reading magazines, sipping protein cocktails laced with caffeine, or flirting. Once the denizens of the store were uneducated street people, Moss notices a lot more mid-income people here for a Sunday--as well as a better dress on many shoppers; he concludes the economy has gotten worse again. He silently chuckles, congratulating himself on the skill and pluck to ride so far above the masses. His sight is drawn to one young couple. Both pretty and well-groomed, neither seems to acknowledge they are in this room waiting for food. When the woman ignores Moss' eye contact, Moss stares at her friend and winks. The young man looks away.

Moss crosses to other side of the mezzanine where eight guards stand by the elevators. Protecting the executives of GeneBanks S.A., the eight guards in black masks and black body armor seem evil-looking and deadly. The guards protecting the money downstairs, in comparison, look like cub scouts: dressed in blue uniforms and black baseball caps.

Moss checks the time again and ambles by the guards to the garden area. He considers Travis might be waiting for him by the terrarium, Moss' favorite lunch spot in the building.

The terrarium dome was supposedly sealed off from the rest of the planet twenty years ago as a mutation experiment. Inexplicably, for Moss, no mutations have occurred. So Moss remains fascinated by the odd space, which his brother describes as pure-planet. Truth is, the genetically modified plants mutate here as quickly here as anyplace else on the planet, but the Genebanks S.A. Board has the mutations removed before Moss' visit. They believe that if Moss thinks there are no mutations, in time, there will be no mutations. Moss and Travis have had lunch by the terrarium at least once a week for two years but not today. Travis has other commitments.

Moss leaves the garden when he does not see Travis and crosses to the elevators. The guards nod to him, then look away. One shaft is under repair. The structure exposes the tan sinewy filaments that move the elevators. These living ropes of replacement membrane for the building are first stretched and molded by the contractions that lift and drop the elevators. In a rush of egotism, Moss concludes the membrane may be almost ready for removal and installation as part of the building's structural system. He reminds himself to talk to Travis as he taps the elevator switch for a neighboring elevator. A second set of doors open and inside sits a young woman with bright blue eyes and a sparkling smile. Her compact form fits neatly against the wall of the fifty square foot elevator compartment. Her new uniform, a tight sky-blue suit and blouse are far too common for Moss' tastes. "Hello, Moss," she says, her smile genuine. This woman has recently replaced another operator--a woman he'd slept with last month. Moss surveys this one's pretty face and exquisite tan skin. Her firm body and long fingers are just right. Travis has no compunction about finding women for Moss.

"Hello." The doors close behind him.

"You're here to see your brother?" She taps the keyboard, and the elevator begins to rise.

"Yes. Ah, you're…?"

"Gwen." She pouts; he has forgotten her name again. "I think your brother is waiting for you in his office. He asked that you just go right up."

Moss loves games he cannot possibly lose. He knows all the women who work here plan to land a GeneBanks S.A. executive. Even so, he knows no one frowns at this golden boy.

The young woman reaches for her coffee cup, knocking it over. Expecting Moss to react, she acts amused when he just looks at her. Gwen quickly blots the coffee with a cloth towel produced from under her desk. When the elevator doors open again, Moss steps out into a bustling hallway. As the door begins closing behind him, he stops it with his hand. "I think you are very pretty, Gwen. So beautiful I was frozen there for a moment by your beauty. Please, forgive me." Moss gives out one of his well practiced little-boy smiles and he lets the door close.

Turning, he taps a button for one of the two private elevators leading to the executive offices at the peak of the building. The day Travis won the post of COO, Moss had thrown a memorable party at the caverns under Seattle, culminating in an underground rafting trip. Afterward, Travis and Moss had staggered back to the GeneBanks building and conducted races in these elevators. Travis in his private elevator, Moss in the one he now travels. Travis lost because of some changes to the control systems Moss had instituted earlier in the day. When Travis discovered Moss' unauthorized entry, he fired the entire security team. Since then, Travis has never won an elevator race. Moss, rightly so, has a technologist's pride in the gift of his engineering capability. His ignorance lies at its limitations, a constant source of study for Travis.

The elevator stops and metal bolts slide into place locking it into the executives' floor. Moss exits along a red-carpeted hallway, past three Whistler originals, four well-clothed executives, and six assistants. He stops at his brother's office door checking his appearance in the reflective gold door. Fit, with a dark, rugged face, Moss looks more like a model in an old cigarette commercial than a bon vivant technologist. He likes that and smooths the mat of brown hair as he enters the office.

Travis stands, hunched over his farm-sized desk examining a large blueprint. Taller than Moss, far thinner--Moss is a beef-cake of a man--Travis wears a thick mop of blond hair and a graceful manner. "Hi bro', just a moment."

"Don't worry about being late, Trav, you are always late." For Travis there can be only work.

Moss closes the door and scans the chrome office seeing nothing changed since his last visit. Then, after crossing the copper colored carpet, he leans against the windows to wait. The mountains are again bare this spring and Moss knows the summer skiing will be ugly. "Trav', you look like shit."

"You and Winston both ganging up on me? She just said the same thing a few minutes ago."

"Who?"

"Hang on, Bro." Travis doesn't miss a beat and abruptly parades through a hidden door next to the bookshelves into the bathroom. A second later the light flickers on.

"Winston who, a new lover? Boy or girl?" Moss asks. He glances at the Gantt chart that covers the blueprint. It's for a new set of lung tests.

The light shuts off and Travis reenters his office out. "She's in the powder room down the hall. I invited her to lunch with us. I thought you might like to meet her."

"Not me." Moss remains at the window. "I'm done with you and your match making. The women you pick out are more like bribes for a corrupt politician than match making."

Travis raises an eyebrow at the comment. "She's very nice."

"Travis, you know I am always willing to check their…credentials." He grins.

Travis hates these lewd discussions but he has built the persona of a man trying to marry off his younger brother. He knows it will keep Moss single. "Try to be a gentleman okay?"

"Why?" Moss glances back down at the desk. "I'm a catch."

"Be nice."

Moss points to the reports.

"I'm getting chopped to bits at board meetings these days and it's just getting old."

"No progress huh?" He looks at the chart, surprised to see large "X's" throughout the project plan.

"Moss, you know we're stuck. And without understanding why we can't get rid of this last little bit of mutation, we could culture all of Africa, then the rest of the continents, all of the oceans, and maybe, just maybe, we would get enough organs, in twenty years, to help Seattle. On the other hand, if we could figure out what causes the random protein failures, we could deliver organs in three months or less."

"Travis, I keep telling you. The gene-banking industry thinks it's the 20th century. They don't know random is in and the scientific method is out. Just learn to live with their myopia." He grins again at Travis.

"You know if you could tell me what replaced linearity, I'd appreciate it." He folds over the blueprint of a new lung system map.

"You're the genius in the family. You figure it out. Can we eat now?"

"This lady is the Director for Environmental Research for the U.N." Travis glances at a mirror.

"That means she's ugly."

"She is responsible for power allocation waivers. We will need her approval if we want to get our party off the ground."

Moss turns back to the window. "Got it. But can she make my monkey howl whenever she wants? "Moss has taken the bait. "Is she hot?"

"Monkey skin did not alter itself when we changed as a species," says the unfamiliar voice of Winston Doe. "That is true of all the apes."

Moss looks to the doorway, surprised anyone was allowed in the office without an escort. He glances over to Travis, chagrined at losing the first round with this woman--or so he believes.

"Dr. Doe, this is my brother Moss Eckman, the famous satellite guru. Moss, Dr. Winston Doe, The most beautiful PhD on the planet." Winston's dark beauty stuns Moss. Travis watches Moss plumb her deep eyes. Then Moss scans the rest of her body as Travis nods to Winston and she nods back. The tears she wore when she arrived no longer show in her eyes. Travis wonders if she will maintain her demeanor given what she has learned about herself today. He has reported to his superiors that she appears shaken by the news of this morning. "All set, Dr. Doe?" Travis glances over to Moss.

Moss slowly smacks the corner of his lips quietly, exactly the way he had before, when Travis had introduced them two years ago. "Winston Doe, Madam. I have heard your name but I am in awe at the inadequacy of words to describe you. Am I ready? Madam, I am ready for wings." He sees a look of delight in her eyes and steps toward her. Winston extends her hand shaking Moss' hand--with the right amount of pressure to let him know she finds him interesting. "Do you really think my brother has to join us?" Exactly the words he used with Winston the first time they met. "I'd like to get to know you. It is said an older woman will treat you right."

"And younger men are boorish," she says in response. Winston and Travis both believe the memories of her are completely gone. Moss is his usual, first-time self. And given her day, she has no time for him. Winston stares at his cold, empty eyes. *He not only knows nothing about me, the rest of him seems completely unchanged from two years ago. How repulsive.* She reacts, on the surface, by giving him a bright toothy smile, unable to remember her reaction to him the first time. Her eyes drift to Travis, and with her hand in her pocket; she hits send on her cell phone. Winston is just barely maintaining this morning so she cannot stay.

Travis' personal phone rings; he picks it up. When the screen shows it is Winston, he understands his part. Travis appears to listen to the call, then hangs up and looks at Winston. "That was for you."

She smiles at Moss. "I am so sorry. I will have to miss lunch." Winston cannot bear the notion that she is like Moss--in any way. She turns and hurries towards the door amazed that she has maintained her composure this long.

"Don't go. We need to make love." No one had expected Moss to be so profoundly unimaginative.

"Not right now."

"You have some weighty matters," Moss asserts. "May I call upon you m'lady?"

She stops, turns, and casts a bright smile over her shoulder. "I'd be disappointed if you didn't call." Hurrying down the hall Winston heads back to the rest room. She cannot bear to be in the same place with him.

To her, now more than ever, Moss represents everything wrong: a lack of caring, an abundance of vanity, greed, desire, and willful ignorance. Two years ago, she had hoped he would show her some beauty in humanity. It was the bargain she had made with her body to interact with him. Instead, she found an empty plastic soul beneath a slick veneer.

Closing the rest room door and locking it, she knows that hating all of society will not do; she will hate Moss instead. *If I can get humanity moving forward, and away from that oil-monkey maybe it is worth it.* This thought makes the reality of being a Ginda acceptable to her. She considers the notion that Clipper has helped her to cope and begins to cry again.

Chapter 14

Zoom to couple drinking wine on a veranda. Behind them gleams the Mediterranean. The couple appears to have all they want in life: beauty, wealth, health, and happiness.

Voice-over: "Ever want to be 'in The Window,' and seen by friends, but can't--because you live in North America? Well let Mohammed Tours fulfill your wish. Our studios replicate foreign locations such as the Taj Mahal memorial, the Dubai ruins, the Tower of London Water Park, the glass plains of Israel, or the Saudi Oil Well craters. Come in and be filmed using one of our scripts, or bring in your own. "Remember, you still can't travel, but why not take a tip from Mohammed? Try bringing the mountain to you! Mohammed Tours has locations in every major mall throughout North America and Central America."

. . . .

The apathy of the former patrician authority grew as global warming waned. The frantic and frightened ruling class, still clutching onto its cherished memories of unmitigated power continued insisting that the old systems did work--and so ground the remains of middle class into dust to prove it. The ignorant demands for species compliance to out-dated economics, similar to their petulant demands for the metric of carbon intensity to supplant the environmental metric during the greenhouse years, again led to disaster. Then, when the Jazz War erupted and hundreds of millions more died, understanding nothing about the new systems brought on by the foreign concepts of a tipped Earth and Species Focus, the last vestiges of the oil elite floundered, and then withered to death in modern day walled castles, their circle finally complete.

Unrestrained progress followed, and growth industries like satellite entertainment and genetic manipulation began to emerge along with a rebirth in sustainable technology. Traveling entertainment troupes supplanted the nets until eventually everything finally focused on one thing: propagation.

Moss and Travis are members of the so-called R-generation, the "Replacement Generation." A generation funded by tax incentives and federal grants.

Children were not wanted by the traumatized adults who scraped through the horrors of global warming and the Jazz War. Those who had survived were still in mourning for their lost family and friends. So the Gen-Rs grew up alone, during the "end" of the Jazz War, and came to be viewed by the survivors as just another tool of commerce. A tool numbly accepted by a battered populace still haunted by slaughter and fear, but never loved. No one could bear the pain of another loss. That response, coupled with the war's lesson of not caring too much, which had been welded onto the hearts of the survivors, damned these children to empty, lifeless childhoods. The result: The R-generation was easily whipped into a breeding frenzy.

The Gen-R's therefore coined the term Wholack. It originally meant one who will not procreate. It later mutated into another word for pigeon--the unspoken moniker of a generation born into difficult times. This generation sees that events comparatively easy in the past: Travel, education, social and economic advancement, independence, and technological control, are all fantasy now. The Gen-R's morphed the term for a third time and now consider themselves Wholacks--fools who are picking up the tab for previous generations' fun and avarice.

It would have astonished many of those who survived the horrors of global warming and the Jazz War to know that this younger generation is adroit at developing friendships, as soldiers do in a platoon at war. The chasm between parent and child has also molded this link between strangers. The elders, viewing the bonds among the young as fantasy, seek to impart their societal echoes of trauma into their children, teaching them somehow that they need distance among their peers. The success of this parenting has made the younger generation appear to be uncaring hypocrites. As a result, the generations pass each other like trains on opposite sets of tracks, uncaring and tied to their appointed route.

Moss and Travis, each in their own ways, are perfect members of the Gen-R's, each needing the other for companionship of purpose. Moss considers Travis all he needs for family and Travis considers Moss all he needs to solve a vexing problem. Were an enlightened observer to watch these men, he or she might see their interactions as a modern day version of the classic comedy routine: "Who's on First?"

Without the context of family, the Gen-R's are lost in any kind intimacy--but while they understand survival and teamwork--the fool's errand speaks clearest to them.

"So you like Dr. Doe, aye, Moss? I didn't know you were attracted to older women."

"She's a Walker too I bet, but she's hot." Regardless, Moss scans the boulevard for other attractive women.

"Have you been spending much time at the Womb, Moss?" Travis asks. The Womb will be their lunch venue. Moss has gravitated to the Womb, every time Clipper has done a major memory reset. Today is no different.

Moss shakes his head yes, watching a barely clothed jogger in tights and a skimpy white sports bra run passed them. "As much as I can--you know me. I need love. We are the world." He grins.

Up ahead, alone on a square city-block, sits a three-story egg-shaped building leaking music. Its smooth flesh-colored skin contrasts sharply with the glass and steel remains of old downtown Seattle. A free form trail dotted with concrete benches leads up to the building. Its ovoid base rests on a bushy knoll surrounded by foliage--like a nest.

They cross the street keeping a wary eye on the many bicyclists--they are the leading cause of pedestrian injury--and step onto the white-painted brick walkway sheltered from sight by conifers and elms. Under the trees, the two men approach Mina Wolf's place of business: The chic, wildly popular, establishment is called "The Womb".

The sounds of Reggae pulse louder from the walls of the most popular bar on the west coast of North America. So popular in fact, that after dark, the tourist need not apply for entry. At lunch-time however, anyone who can pay the exorbitant cover charge, 1000 watt-hours, and one penny US, can acquire entry into what many call the most decadent place on Earth.

The daughter of the infamous researcher used her father's saved wealth to start the club. Lazlo Wolf had been an austere man in his private life, constantly at work, never at home. Mina learned to despise her father's dedication to strangers when she was young. The Womb contains her apparent revenge; however, it is also a kind of sexual laboratory for deviance.

Moss takes in a breath of perfumed air as they follow the path between the nests of ocean-spray bushes and trees. At the front entry of the Womb, a pink orb pulses at the peak of the vulva-shaped doors. Decorated with sensuous droopy leaves, red flowers glow around the door. Other glossier flowers, lit by small micro-strobes, twitch frenetically back and forth. The pink petals, musky smelling and damp, languidly snap and rise to the music, dropping viscous dew from their surfaces onto small puddles at the entrance. Few are foolish enough to slip on musky wet puddles; their sexual odor persists until the remedy is purchased from a Womb bartender for another kilowatt-hour of energy.

Pulsing beacons behind climbing green vines hug the ovoid, damp, rubberized doors that undulates obscenely. Each time the doors open, thick lips along the doors' face slowly engorge, while retracting quickly from the peak, revealing it to be a bud made to look like a small phallus. When the doors close, the bud hides, once again encased. Insiders know the door to be a representation of the owner's sexual equipment.

Moss pushes on the ten-foot labial doors, his hand disappearing deep into the soft rubber. Entering here delights Moss--he finds himself fascinated by the "Urchins," well-heeled tourists pummeled by shock and awe at the distinctly obscene venue. As he removes his hand, the roar of music weaves happily inside him. This venue has playful memories for him. He loves everything about The Womb.

In the darkness of the tubular hallway, Moss' hand slides along the damp wall. The moisture and acrid smell flows to the end of the hallway where the club's pulsing energy awaits. Multicolored lights momentarily blind them both. A scanner checks the brothers for ID and weapons. A second clitoral light reveals itself with a momentary twitch--as the main door unlocks.

They enter the bar and the warm smells of bodies mingle with incense; the feeling caresses Moss as if it were the hands of his mother. At one time, Moss practically lived here; it was here he met Winston Doe two years ago. Then, Moss found out Winston didn't like the Womb. They ceased coming here three months ago. Moss has no memory of this; his return here to the bar contains notions, for him, of no time passing. He knows he has recently been here--though he does not remember when. Moss glances at the red hourglass tube over the bar. Red liquid, not sand, slowly flows from top to bottom in the hour glass--but it takes twenty eight days. When the bottom fills, it breaks and spreads all over the floor. A mild hallucinogen evaporates from the liquid making the next six hours a licentious, wild orgy. Moss notes the bottom part of the timepiece is almost full and he frowns. He knows that it should not be so based on his memories. A moment later he hides his concern in a fake smile and waves to the waitresses; they ignore them, or sneer at him, or wink at the brothers. Travis notices Moss scans the upper levels of the bar looking for Mina Wolf. Moss plans to ask Mina what is wrong with him--how come he loses track of time so often? He trusts her.

Travis does not like the apparent importance of Lazlo Wolf's daughter to the process of Moss' memory reset. Many have worked hard to isolate her from the research community. Few doubt her immense intellect but they want her outside key events in this society because she has always been so difficult to control. The leaders of the Replacement Generation seek more than sex, they seek peace and tranquility. On the other hand, Mina seeks to rattle their cages.

It is 1:30 in the afternoon; the Womb vibrates with a hard core crowd dancing to funk: Tourists line the far wall, waiting like idiotic kittens for a stroke by one the sensual dancers. After two, service deteriorates for the non-networked tourist to the point that by four-thirty a drink from the infamous bar cannot be had for love or kilowatts. And if that doesn't work, by five--the abortion hour--as the regulars call it, unsuspecting visitors are dropped down a special chute, accompanied by gales of piped laughter. Landing on an old smelly mattress between two garbage boxes--an exit far more ignominious than the sensual entrance into the world-famous Womb--most slink away and never return.

Bunny-dancers with slicked-back surgically elongated ears, writhe and bounce to the music, while Cowinkies, high priced lovers sporting everything from codpieces to lanced nipples, slink around the floor. Unisex, multi-sex, no-sex, any-sex, the wanton gyrate everywhere. First-time visitors always stand by the wall, amused to see themselves reflected in the far glass walls as rainbow-hued sperm. Hard core joy-junkies tease them with alluring clothing or movement. When the regulars tire of the day's tourists, they ignore then, to writhe for each other on one of the dance floors while searching the crowd for new lovers, drugs, venues, or soft hearts to be milked--anything to zap the remorse and fear from their lives.

None of the regulars have the sophistication to recognize the Womb only makes it all worse. This symbol of their maternal collective past has no remorse for what has changed--neither does its owner, Mina Wolf. In many ways, the Womb is also Mina's shock-therapy laboratory. She has spent her life trying to figure out how to get through to emotionally stunted people.

The worst of these are the Yorkies. Wide-eyed and loony as a chained dog in a butcher shop, Yorkies huddle by the emergency exit door or hug the walls while trying to appear normal. Denied sleep by their memories, warmth by their hearts, sight by their fears, haunted by past deeds or just bad luck, these survivors frequent every high input location on the planet, if they have the credits. Always aware of the dangers, they move in packs. When one of them panic, they all do, and rush the exit. The Yorkies witnessed disasters far too closely, or worse, participated in, and got away. They touch no one, but they look at everyone. The Womb, unlike many other establishments, maintains an open door policy to the Yorkies--as long as they behave and they can pay. Ironically, Mina Wolf feels it her civic duty to amuse the wounded until they pass. She knows they enjoy staring at the sensual dancers on the floor.

Sprinkled among the dancers, members of upper classes wander through the crowds. Their bodies sheathed in the newest fashions while their faces wear the studied attitudes of amused non-participation, their boredom offends Moss but tickles Travis. In the ignorance of others, Travis finds true amusement. The bumbling ways of social-climbers remains a constant source of discussion for the two brothers when they are here. Travis feels he has to pass the time somehow.

As he walks, Travis finishes scanning the room, acknowledges two brawny, mutant-looking humans, pumped full of hormones and illegal genetic stews to enhance their performance. These are Travis' people, his security team. The COO of GeneBanks is an important man.

The brothers pass quickly through the public bar area to a red glass staircase that ascends to the second floor bar. At the top of the stairs, they enter a yellow and red lit room. The structure looks like the upended inside of a dirigible. The long radial girders support a transparent outer skin while round strands of red muscle tissue extend between the girders like latitudinal lines. A dangling, pulsing white orb hangs from the peak. Expanding and contracting, occasionally crying like a hungry baby, once a month the orb will be taken down and auctioned off to the highest bidder.

Moss examines the bar below them. Benson Fong, in his cover of an alcoholic bon vivant dances out on the floor. "Benson's here—the old fart," says Moss to Travis, and follows the comment with: "The idiot."

Travis controls his amusement. Though Benson Fong was the man who arranged Moss' adoption, he and Travis have come to dislike each other over the years. Benson's interests and sense of responsibility to the masses often runs contrary to the interests of the gene-bankers and Travis' elitist viewpoint. Travis contends the real cause of global warming had been the excess population of humans--an elitist theory that has become gospel in this time. Benson and he disagree on that one.

Moss has a technologist's viewpoint of the event. He believes there was too little funding for energy generated outside of fossil fuels so the replacement technologies and their maintenance regimes were never adequately developed. A viewpoint seconded by Benson Fong--when he is included in the discussion.

So far as Moss knows, Benson is the last remaining member of a wealthy Hong Kong family who owned the rights to the gene sequence that brews the red-muscle fiber. That same fiber circles the walls of the room. The sight of this fiber at the grand opening of the Womb had prompted Moss, thinking the system some joke, to seek out Benson. He quickly came to believe there was nothing but humor and self gratification in Benson's life. The bond grew from there--Benson Fong is a diligent man and leaves little to chance.

"You think Benson ever found another commercial use for this disgusting fiber?" Moss asks, making himself comfortable at a table.

"I doubt it." Travis glances around the room to see if there might be anyone who could ask the wrong question. He sees no one and continues: "I think Benson completely misses the humor of the material here. I heard he's still spending millions advertising it for serious construction projects."

"He's a loser," Moss says distractedly looking over the dancing patrons and admiring their sculpted surfaces. "I heard it even proved too tough for the Urchins to eat as well."

Travis watches the approaching waitress; she recognizes Moss.

"It's the Golden Boys." The tall waitress wears a skin-tight jumpsuit with barber pole stripes. Her bald head glows in iridescent pink.

"Two salads with the pan de la casa. Absinthe for me--Travis?"

"Red wine: Zinfandel." He notes Moss doesn't even look at the waitress. Above her, suspended by chicken-muscle fiber, sits an empty swing. Her hand rises and rocks the empty swing as she leaves.

Later this swing, and the other swings at the Womb will be full of regulars. Randomly ferried to a chute, currently hidden in the side wall by mirrors, the lucky couple on the swing will be dumped in a chute. Cushioned by the damp sensuous walls and conducted down to a landing zone in the back of the building, they will fall into a crowd of wiggling lusty bodies. The pamphlet at the front door claims the experience provides a unique opportunity to test a couple's compatibility.

Along the back of the bar, monitors will display the action in a wash of colors too blurry for anyone to identify any given participant. This waitress wishes to ride the "Culture Chute" with either of these golden boys, once more.

A bunny-dancer in a green rubber leotard appears at the top of the stairs leading an apparently intoxicated Benson Fong over to the men. Moss admires the dancer. Not a hair can hide beneath her tight outfit. "Benson--you dog. Mina will never forgive you for this one," says Moss, with a wink to the dancer.

Benson looks grimly at Moss in apparent surprise. Music begins again, this time much louder: roaring bass notes and quick staccato warbles rumble through their bodies. Benson points to the woman beside him in an apparent stupor. She shakes her head no--per his instructions and disappears into the crowd--to take up her surveillance position at the bottom of the stairs.

Travis, looking passed the tableau of the Security Director, sees Mina Wolf approach them. "Gather up your *noblese oblige*, Benny, here comes Mina."

"You're not going to tell Mina about her, Travis," says Benson playing a part honed by years of practice. In truth he cannot bear the lies, but without them, Moss would require a fifty person security escort and that would draw attention.

"Trust me, Benny. I am mute."

"So how was… Anna?" Benson asks, with the skill of a Shakespearean actor.

Moss scowls. "How do you know so much, little man?"

Fong notes Moss remembers Anna, the woman from the other night, but not Winston. "Moss, your caustic nature makes my interaction with you infinitely easier. Thank you."

"You and that good absinthe from last night did not get along too well, brother dear. You told him." Travis says.

Moss looks at him. "Nonsense." Moss knows something isn't right. He just doesn't know where to look for an answer. Then he sees Mina. "And here comes the love of your life, Benny."

"Whatever," Benson says with a flip of his hand. He sways so Moss will believe that he has been partying all morning.

Mina Wolf slides through the crowd like a dancer. Her bright eyes are focused on Moss, who notes that her thin mouth looks tight and angry. Mina's features are the best money can buy--a fire did considerable damage to her face two years ago. A tragedy for her since Mina has always insisted on being at the center of any room's attention. Her revealing, opalescent grown has few secrets; it flows behind her like a cascade of molten silver. Travis has often speculated that being the center of attention is the reason Moss loves this bar so much: Its owner and Moss share a need, or so he has concluded.

The man behind Mina, a tall, lanky man with buzz-cut blond hair, wire-rimmed glasses, and a huge mustache, continually watches the crowd. Gunn, has been her body guard for years. Benson notes the former soldier's eyes are empty with the sights of death. Each man nods--and sees another man who has made friends with death. As Gunn's gaze locks on Benson, a slight smile appears beneath that thick walrus mustache. He has no idea who Benson Fong works for, but he has zero faith in the story that Benson has the sensibilities of a bon vivant--and he is smart enough not to probe.

"Well," says Mina, "if it isn't Moss Eckman, our current poster boy for the Alzheimer way to reality. What's new, Moss? Everything?"

CHAPTER 15

"Tired of all the old videos? Angry at your parents for murdering the planet? Lost among the ruins and empty fields of shopping malls and car dealerships? Do you want to waste energy like your parents? Does the idea of a long drive in the country or a shopping spree on foreign soil keep you up at night? Ever feel like it just isn't worth the effort anymore? Do you fantasize about sex in a gasoline filling station?

Don't despair. There is help. Energy Anonymous meets in your city every week. Learn to help yourself and others. The past is gone. The future is bright. Day or night, we are here to help. Energy Anonymous--just because your parents were monsters it doesn't mean you have to be one. Light a candle. Pass the torch of knowledge. We are all in this together."

. . . .

Were Mina anyone else, other than Lazlo Wolf's daughter, her actions with Moss would not be tolerated. The Clipper subroutine fires and Moss' eyes lose focus for a moment.

His eyes refocus: "So I forgot your birthday again. Sue me, Mina. I'll bet our friend Benson didn't forget it." Clipper has never allowed Mina an opening with Moss--that will change as its control slowly fails. "But calling me diseased because I forget your birthday--that's a bit rude." He has no idea this response was installed in his memory to keep Mina Wolf at bay.

Before she can respond, Benson speaks. "Check this out. Here comes the stiff-dick health Nazi you were dancing with before, Mina. You know, I think he may know he is the only human in the place who hasn't sampled the owner." Benson appears to chortle, watching Mina react to the innuendo. Her eyes flare and an almost imperceptible lift to the corner of her perfectly sculpted nose ends in a sneer. In some ways, Mina has her own reset buttons.

Benson has had to study, and learn to use, every one of them to keep her guessing about him. He watches the approaching man without concern. This guy is Gunn's business.

"He's a Wholack. Ignore him." Mina plants a kiss under Moss' ear. "Welcome back, Sweetie". Then she whispers, "I'm gonna' shoot that little worm," nodding towards Benson. Moss locates her latest conquest, an older male dressed in a black body leotard. The man's eyes wander among the men at the table as he slowly approaches. She sidles in closer to Moss and squeezes Travis' shoulder. "Hi big man, saved the world yet?"

Travis reaches out and squeezes her hand. Though he dislikes Mina, she represents, he believes, a lever with Benson Fong, so he cultivates her friendship.

Travis knows Mina Wolf hates Benson, thinking him a fool. Once, it had eluded Travis as to why Benson allows her interference with Moss Eckman. Even though her comments about Moss and his situation are quickly muted by Clipper, they represent, to Travis, an unwelcome randomness to his interactions with Moss. And Travis has learned to hate random events.

Then, two years ago--during a luau at Moss' home--a torch fell over, spreading burning oil upon the surface of the large pool. Mina was swimming, too drugged to understand what was happening. Benson dove in, ignoring Moss' safety, and then somehow a glass viewing window deep in the pool exploded taking the water into the house and setting off the dry chemical suppression system. The cost to Moss was enormous. Mina was in the hospital for weeks having her features reconstructed. Benson was there every day she was unconscious, and none of the days she was awake. Travis has never spoken to anyone about that. The information that Benson Fong cares for Mina Wolf seems too dangerous--Benson Fong has never been a man to be trifled with--one word from him and the gene banker's influence over Moss would cease. Nonetheless, Travis believes the lever will help him, someday.

The strange man in the black jumpsuit stops behind Mina. Gunn takes a step to the man's right side. "I think your friend; Joe-Nazi-of-the-body-suit believes he was been had." Says Moss, pleased with the side show. Mina ignores the man.

The man's hard facial features seem set in a permanent snarl. "I can explain. It's a Wholack thing…"

"Mr. Jaka, Remold, please. I am with friends."

"Hello," he says to the table. "I need your help. I am looking for a Wholack."

An laugh floats among those at the table. "Tried the mirror?" Says Moss.

Mina does not let her gaze move from Moss Eckman's amused face. "You are truly all of us, Moss." The tall man abruptly thrusts out his hand to grab her. He immediately lays sprawled on his back with a sharp pain paralyzing his entire right side.

Gunn, who had correctly gauged the extent of the man's intensity waits for instructions from Mina. She does not like violence in the bar so she speaks to the man on the floor--without looking at him. "Remold, you're a Yorkie. You need help."

"What's a Yorkie?" The man's eyes seem glazed, unable to focus.

"You've just seen too much, pal, so I repeat, try the mirror." Moss winks towards Mina.

"Impossible, this can't be," the man replies. "Where's your bed?" He says to Mina.

"I'm with some friends."

"Impossible, that can't be," the man replies. "I command you. Where's your bed?"

"Look, cowboy, I'm with some friends." Male and female bouncers appear from the stairs. Mina addresses them: "Please remove this one." They drag the man quickly from the room.

Moss sips his opalescent absinthe. "Tsk, tsk, Gunn, you're slowing down. He was within a foot of grabbing her."

"Give me a break, will you, Moss, I'm almost forty." Gunn's attention turns to Benson Fong.

"Sometimes I think you might be gay, Gunn. The way you stare at Benny--it is almost obscene," says Mina, taunting him.

"Ain't love grand?" Moss says amused at Mina's cruelty.

"Benson, go down and get us some drinks would you?" Mina asks.

He begins to respond when Moss interrupts. "Forget it, Benson. She hates you. Just go get the drinks. Absinthe all around and an opium backer for your love-- oh and add two cognacs to that order. Oh, and don't forget the Zinfandel for my brother."

Benson immediately jabs Moss' shoulder. "Hah, the great individualist with an L7 favorite, Zinfandel, can I believe it?"

"I like to rattle you, Benson," says Travis.

He displays irritation, playing his part with aplomb. "Well, no time to be prickly. I'll be right back." Fong hurries to the bar. The bunny-dancer who had originally conducted Benson to the table arrives at the top of the stairs and sits at a nearby table.

Mina shakes her head at Travis. "I hate that worm." A chirping sound comes from the table.

"Pull up your drawers, ladies and gentleman, we have a 10.0 reading." Travis says. The chirping means a satellite has locked on the Womb and has begun scanning the bar's festivities to broadcast it overseas. Television programming has mostly been replaced by live feeds from the satellites that scan the planet. The satellite broadcasts feed a worldwide mania for voyeurism.

Originally sent aloft to protect the population from the madness that was the Jazz War, the voyeuristic broadcasts drooling from the satellites day and night have become a major industry--second only to the gene banks. Fed off-continent for consumption, on all six continents, people are told only their continent remains immune from the surveillance. That will change--people will get to travel soon. As a result, reality is under adjustment, again.

That adjustment is propaganda, supposedly in the best interests of the nation. In a parody of freedom, the corporate leadership has concocted a referendum about whether to allow satellite surveillance on continent. A fait accompli, the illusion of control by the masses will be pandered to as long as necessary, just like Moss' freedom and cavalier lifestyle continue to be supported at every turn by his handlers. It is to be noted only part of the ruling class do this for nefarious purposes--as it has always been. The rest of the ruling elite seek social progress and prosperity--also--as it has always been. But bathed in privilege, some have lost all contact with sacrifice.

"Damn, I could have been on the floor if it hadn't been for that Yorkie," Mina says, petulantly tossing the mane of straight blond hair. Her vanity quite real, Mina has paid a fortune in bribes to have her bar "In the Window", under satellite scanning, as often as possible. She figures as soon as travel opens up again, her bar will be a prime destination.

Travis eyes his annunciator. "Satellite's gone. I guess the viewers didn't find anything it liked. Moss this invention of yours to announce the satellites approach is going to be worth a fortune."

"The weak always get what they deserve." Mina leans over to Moss. "But the poor--how do we measure their costs, Travis? By access to flawed information--oh how silly of me not to see that. I can see now how a person who is forced to get news from the free nets and doesn't have travel privileges just might believe everything they see on the nets by the second or third generation. That would damn them to poverty."

"Perhaps," Moss interjects. "TV news died for that reason."

Travis buries his pique and adds quietly. "When our population finds out that even the poor bush-men have U.S. satellite links, and they've been looking at aunt Millie's knickers it'll be ugly. I'd say keeping that quiet will keep order. Wouldn't you agree, Mina?" His glance at Mina lingers.

"Probably not. Mina likes her knickers" says Benson. The drinks arrive by waitress a second later.

"A beautiful woman can't be trusted to keep anything to themselves," says Moss with a laugh.

"Of course all you think about is sex and money, Benson," Travis says, tongue in cheek.

"I fulfill a need, Travis. I'm the reality monger in our little group."

Disgusted, Mina lifts her goblet of white wine and opium as she unconsciously counting the winks, stupefied gazes, and potentially interesting partners that gaze upon her from around her establishment. She finishes her drink, resting her hand back on Moss' shoulder. Some of the on-lookers frown and turn away--a few do not. "Moss, what do you think people will do when they have seen someone in the Window and then see them in the street?"

"I heard they were trying to scramble faces, but the word on the technical side is they can't isolate the faces. They will try it, and then they will give up." Moss also consults for the satellite companies. "My guess is we will get voyeur-groupies and those that will protect the object of their desires." He believes himself to be brilliant because everyone tells him he is. Even so, the satellite annunciator was really one of Moss' designs. The satellite people now see Travis as a man to be cultivated.

"My sense is once people are known, there will be a new need for body-guards," Gunn interjects. "I will be rich." Everyone laughs--money is irrelevant in this society. The lunch salads arrive: freshly picked greens from a large garden out back.

Mina nods, approving the salad. "I think people will use the Window to spout their pap. A whole new set of industries will arise, based on the number of people you can get to pay attention to what you are doing. We are about to reenter blog-hell."

"That assumes the population doesn't turn into an angry mob," Travis says, moving the greens around with his fork looking for anchovies.

"I think the economy is going to boom as the new industries forms," Moss says. "There will be capital formation, and the population will be well paid for their lost privacy. Hell, I'd think a person would be pleased to have so many people paying attention to them--especially if the economy returns to life for Everyman."

Mina giggles. Benson speaks quickly to cut her off. "So it would be okay with you, Moss?"

"Don't answer, Moss. My father used to say the less you say about the future the better you are--especially when speaking to a fool." Her eyes move to Benson's contrite countenance. "I know you care about me. You do know I wish you would disappear off the planet?"

"He does. On the other hand, it might be nice to be someplace where your vanity was not so ponderous," says Moss, spearing a tomato.

"Moss," She leans close to him so only Travis will hear and says: "You have Species Focus. You are a Ginda. Did you know that? And where is your friend Winston Doe? Oh, ah, did you forget something?" She waits, smiling at Benson.

Moss blinks. A moment later his eyes slump shut. "I think the economy is going to boom as the new industries forms. There will be capital formation, and the population will be well paid for their lost privacy. I think a person would be pleased to have so many people paying attention..."

Tightening his lips, Travis says. "You think that's funny. Don't you?"

"Sometimes you kick and the universe kicks back. I think of it as balance to our lounge-lizard universe." Her eyes turn to Benson. "Benson, you are the blindest human I have ever met."

"Mina, I see his dementia as karma," says Benson, taking a sip from his drink. "No one deserves it more, but no one deserves it."

"You're a fool," Mina replies.

"Someone is," Travis says--and immediately regrets it. Mina's eyes snap to his. He sees the glow of disgust from Benson. "Eat up, Moss. We have to get back to the office."

Mina glances at Benson, then at Gunn. He nods to her.

CHAPTER 16

Zoom into an American Flag waving over golden fields.

"Good evening, my name is Ashley Wilkes. I represent the Tata Congress. I have been asked to address you this evening for the purpose of clearly stating that the Tata Congress supports all ethical North American efforts to allow on-continent surveillance and viewing.

"We of the Tata Congress have felt for years that this kind of access is important for complete freedom of the press. And as a result, I am here, today, to deliver this check for fifteen million dollars to the Satellite Research Institute. It is for the construction of a training center that will teach the techniques necessary to ensure that uplink operators provide only high quality, ethical broadcasts..."

. . . .

Harmony is the despicable cloak of an unethical governance when it fosters caring as the suit of fools.

Her driver jerks to a stop. A young boy with bright red hair and freckles darts in front of the jeep. Unlike the others who stand on line and gawk at mimes or magicians, the boy stares defiantly at the vehicle, standing in front of it. The lack of motion shakes Winston from her thoughts and she turns forward. The boy's parents, with their short, bright red ponytails, bow to Winston as they pull the boy to the side of the road. Anyone with a vehicle is a god in their book. The couple's matching tunics of gold and red swirls flap in the breeze. Winston's has rarely seen so glamorous a blouse and understands the boy's petulance. This young man gets what he wants as long as he follows his parents' rules.

"Sorry, Dr. Doe. I didn't want to run over the Wholack--it's bad luck." She smiles. "Don't worry, Sergeant. We don't need any more casualties today." The vehicle slowly accelerates again passing the apparently unending line of tourists. Tana Reins scans the crowds for signs of problems. The young man with the red hair sticks his middle finger up and turns away.

Winston also scans the mix of people. The egalitarian lines of the Environmental Museum are meant to show how rich and poor must live together in harmony. Winston laughs about any notion of parity in life. She has recently heard that among the wealthy, the well-connected are brought in late in the day by a tram and admitted. Line proxies, who hold their place, are taken home. *There are those who know and those who guess.*

Winston does not bother to enter that debate. She knows post-greenhouse equality as a lot of nonsense just as she knows today's energy-caste barrier is no different from the old monetary barriers. *How can this society ever make peace with itself?* Still, Winston will insist on equality inside Samarra. Everyone walks or bicycles. No electric scooters will be allowed. For the briefest moment--as the jeep continues up the hill past a large group of madras and khaki-clad visitors--she feels lifted. *They're obviously from over the Cascades. People from around Puget Sound seldom dress quite as uniformly as this group. The demarcation of clothing styles has become much more pronounced over the years--the pride in one's home area growing every day.* Winston examines their picnic baskets and paunches as a way to manage her situation. *At least I am present in their life.*

Winston once wrote a paper that concluded the adoption of styles was a connection with environment--and a form of freedom. U.N. Northwest had published the paper--and it has since become accepted as another facet of the human ecosystem: clothes.

Another red-headed teenage boy sampling red berries from the vines along the road spits ripe fruit at her jeep as it passes him. The Sergeant slams on the brakes as the boy rushes in front of the jeep. He circles back and Winston chastises the boy with her glare. He sticks out his tongue--so does she. Both smile. The similarity of the two red-headed boys disturbs her. They could be twins.

Her vision suddenly fills with a picture of Russell cooking breakfast with her over an open fire. The sun has not risen at the camp ground and the red sky holds a bundle of dark thick clouds. Everything glows. She does not hear the gunfire around her; she only hears him speaking.

"You need to let me go, Winston. You will never like it outside the museum." His white skin gains from the red hue--first from the fire, then the sky, and finally their love-making--this was the last time they were together.

"I'll find you," she replies.

"I hope you do not, but I will miss us." The words had slipped out of Russell mouth without his volition. Winston has never forgotten the embarrassment of his admission, or the clarity it provided her.

Why didn't you tell me you were priming me for a Clipper hookup? She speaks: "Where are you, my love?"

The jeep rocks to its side, hit by an explosion; bullets fly around her. Oddly, Winston looks for the young boy with their red hair. Three bullets bounce off the back gate but she does not notice. Winston reminds herself to donate the bicycle Moss had left for her to the park. *What are we becoming?*

The vehicle spills to the side.

Her driver grabs Winston and pulls her from the wreck. Winston feels the hands just as she senses smoke surrounds her. The crowds have scattered or collapsed unconscious from the gas canisters Sergeant Reins has already tossed at them. Pulling Winston behind the side of the jeep, she slips on a pool of blood. The young boy who had spit the berries a moment ago runs up beside them laughing maniacally. He begins to kick the jeep over and over again.

"C'mon Doc, this way." Then they are rushing towards the twenty-foot-high blackberry bramble surrounding Samarra. A platoon of soldiers appear. Winston is pulled into the cordon that closes around her. More gun fire erupts.

The next things Winston sees are the twin white points of Samarra's minarets appearing through smoke. She is being hurried through the entrance. Blood covers her clothing and the uniforms of her three remaining protectors. Inside the museum, she passes crowds huddling under kiosks and stone benches. The guards place her by a spread of redwoods framed by a concrete wall on each side. It is, in effect, a defense bunker.

Winston cannot find her driver. "What happened?" She asks the guards. "Where is my driver?" The gun fire erupts once more from outside the gates; then it stops.

"Some kid threw a molly-bomb at your jeep." An aerosol can wrapped in a burning towel, "Then the people on line outside lost it. We don't know how many were hurt. It is quiet inside. The situation outside is fluid. We think we have it under control," replies a soldier.

She glances up at the twin helicoidal towers knowing their true function remains satellite telecommunications for the links to Moss. The smoke has faded and they are still in tact.

Then the music starts again: "The Blue Danube."

The two inclines, crowded with people who had been jockeying for the best views of the carnage begin to move again. The transparent bridge suspended two-hundred feet in the air between the minarets begins its typical sway. It is a generator. The affect of seeing the surging crowd rising up the left minaret and then out into space and down the other calms her. Glancing at the security team around her, Winston sighs quietly for their safety. The tourists begin to reform lines to enter Samarra. There are no bodies inside the gate. They were dumped outside long before Winston regained her senses. Calm has returned.

Getting to her feet, she dismisses the guards and enters the exhibition halls via a concave brick pathway. Winston heads straight to a narrow hallway away from the crowds passing security people flooding out into the crowd to maintain calm. Then, taking an old fashioned key from her purse, she unlocks a modest door. Entering the service closet she finds a set of khaki overalls and changes out of her bloody clothes.

Winston's meeting with Moss rattles around inside her. *This attack had something to do with that.* Even so, her distaste for him and her concerns about her own foolishness grow. *What have I done to me? What have they done to me? What did my mother do to me? Why? This world is just evil. No, I need to understand.*

She hurries down a staircase to a heavy steel door. Behind it, newly hired researchers work on low level projects. Each floor down is a gradation in security clearance. Winston is on a mission to find a usable laptop for the Diary. Her fathers's laptop, she now believes, will not work. She passes the door to the local Clipper computer--now networked into a redundant set of computers spread across the Northwest. Any of them are capable of running the memory routines for Moss Eckman. Winston used to describe the computers as the world's most expensive screwdrivers--so she could accentuate their purpose as merely tools in the hands of an intelligent species. The irony is not lost on her that Clipper is her screw-driver as well. She wonders how much she has missed today and how bloody the battle really had been.

Beside a plain white door at the third sub-basement, Winston taps an entrance sequence into the keyboard. The armored door remains closed to her for the first time in her professional life. She immediately turns around and goes up to the second floor. She slides her name badge across a scanner. The light turns green and the door unlocks. Opening the door, she enters a dusty hallway. *Well I am the only Ginda with access to this location.*

The door locks behind her. Winston sits down and stares at the empty walls.

Fifteen minutes later, Winston walks among the storage bays on either side of a storage room. The collection of old integrated circuits, antique computer parts and peripherals are well ordered, but dusty. A musty smell permeates the room.

She crosses another doorway into a hallway filled with one-meter glass cubes encasing rings of reddish-hued tubes. Looking more like the strobes in discotheque than high technology, these extra memory units have been hoarded and guarded almost as carefully as the Ginda. Without the virtually unlimited memory these storage-by-projection units provide, the Clipper Project might have never have happened.

These first steps in Lazlo Wolf's early hypotheses of Species Focus stemmed from his idea that the 20th century computer memory techniques did not mirror human memory. Wolf postulated that storage and sight were effectively the same event—and that the real function of sight was memory. Through a series of brilliant experiments, he and his colleague, Russell Biner, changed how humanity understood cognition: in particular sight. "Considering sight without understanding its purpose is nothing more than vanity." They further asserted that humans would remain primitive so long as they claimed that what they saw with their eyes is real, rather than the differential of flowing space minus time. Further, Wolf had stated that the future was knowable without memory. He believed that clear sighted members of the species--who lived without memory--could read the future and attain precognition, his redefinition of sentience.

He proved all this with the glass cubes that lined the walls. These storage-by-projection systems have a capacity to store extraordinary amounts of information, completely dwarfing other memory systems. It led to an acceptance, by the scientific community, that the physical world we shared, and claimed as reality, was no more than an epidemic of denial that neutered humanity as a sentient species. Russell Biner labeled that denial of life's many options as true insanity. That definition for madness continues in all the lexicons of this time.

Winston opens another door.

The light flicks on and she finds three dusty shelves full of old portable computers. The fourth shelf sits empty. The unmistakable furrows of handprints lay tracks in the dust.

"I couldn't figure out what happened on your vacation and that bothered me." The voice cuts into her, like a paper-cut: unseen but painful. "What, I asked myself, could possibly have turned my best student and close friend against me? Then I realized you had found an original Diary and that was how you made the leap this morning."

"So you didn't set it up?"

"Winston, I am a better researcher than that--do you really think I would take a sophomoric path like that? You have focus because you gained it through your efforts and skill. Every freshman knows manipulation would degrade your focus and nullify all our efforts."

She glares at the figure standing in the shadows. "You could have told me I was a Ginda." In his hands are a pair of players--precisely the units she needs to view the Diary. Winston's hand grips her badge; she considers her options. She can press down on the bubble wrap blister and puncture it. Security will be here in minutes. Her thumb wavers but she does not press it. She assumes he carries the same device. "Your bravery impresses me--being here alone with an angry Ginda. Don't I scare you?"

"Did I scare you by elevating humanity through you and your efforts?" He steps forward, intentionally dropping one laptop to the ground. It lands on a corner and flips open, bits of glass and plastic scattering over the floor. "What did you think of the Diary? It's an original I assume."

"I'm not done with it yet. All those years--you and your ego. Dr. Wolf did nothing wrong did he?"

"No more than anyone else." He glances at the pieces of computer on the floor. "We've lost so much."

"The ego…Words fail me at the moment, Joshua." Winston Doe begins to embrace a hatred for Joshua Pard that has no bound.

"I see. You hate me for not telling you. Winston, you have had no memory cuts of importance. You were allowed to miss the bloodshed just like you did today. Though I gather you nullified Clipper and remained with some of it. Very impressive and a little scary. Do you understand? You are whole, unlike Moss." She notes he mostly remains in the shadows and therefore concludes he is lying to her.

"You made me a fool, Joshua."

"My how the mighty have fallen--you called me Joshua twice now. You could just take the disk over to the Clipper unit and insert it. Oh, wait, you don't have access." He pulls out his cell phone. "Now you do. I needed to meet with you, alone. You have full access again."

"You would try and take credit for that." She smiles at him but his words remain with her.

Her cold calculating eyes suddenly scare him."Does absolute power corrupt one, Dr. Doe?"

"We'll see."

"Winston, nothing has changed except your clarity. You are, frankly, amazing. Was Plow there?" He asks leaning forward.

"Dr. Pard, I am a researcher first. You taught me that. I find no truth that the Diary might lead to psychosis," she says taking a step towards him. "I did find out why Benson and Gregor despise you." The paunchy doctor, she figures, would no match for her speed and strength; she'll wrestle the player from him

He steps back. "I'm fat and old, Winston, not stupid. I have a weapon." Still, he steps backwards. "Your generation has grown up with the certainty that 'the physical universe' as we used to call it, is malleable because your parents consumed our connection the planet. Yet here you are, a Ginda, still trying to do your research to find an equitable path for all. It's incredible. How quickly we humans have adapted to Biner's definition of madness. Did you know Lazlo believed that the removal of memory and starting from ground zero every day was spatially and temporally freeing? Lazlo and Roo never talked about though, they won by telling the generals exactly what they wanted to hear: that ignorant soldiers could be kept in the dark. But as a result of Biner and Wolf's maneuvering, countless men and women went to their death. I believe many of those deaths could have been prevented with a scholar in the lead instead of society's fool; The only other person who supported me on that option was Sergeant Plow. Now, was Plow there?"

"They were afraid of demigods. Well founded I believe."

"Fine, ignore me. I am offering you an alliance of support, Dr. Doe."

Silence.

Dr. Pard tosses the player to her. "You have no fear now, Winston--but remember fear. It's very important." He speaks with resignation. "I can't interfere with you. You know that. Winston, I am as dedicated to this project as you are."

She finds herself feeling faint, but holds herself steady. "You expect me to believe my determination has made me the mythological Ginda: the soldier/scholar? And you think that because of that ego attack I will let you and your stupendous thirst for power guide me?"

"I know you will not. Winston, Plow brought you the Diary, didn't he?" He cocks his head to the right. "He did it because he believes we can recycle our way out of this. Did you know that?"

She stands mute.

"Winston, the world is being taken over by Wholacks, like Moss. It started a century ago. The incompetent, but well-healed come in and suck everything of worth out of us until we collapse into a mass of self congratulating ooze. To my discredit, I function well in that environment."

"Nice speech." Her smile has no lips and she walks past him to the door and opens it. "Joshua, if things are as bad as I think they are, I am the random anomaly of hope, just before the final curtain falls on the human condition."

The old man shakes his head, his eyes narrow, measuring her facts-of-life speech. "All you have done is found truth to your life. None of us have ever disrespected that."

"You lie. You disrespect everyone. It's the only way you can live your duplicity. You are Satan's ooze Joshua."

Pard closes his eyes. "We are told lies are humor. I never believed that. I know you never believed it."

She glares at him. "I never met anyone so hypocritical."

He sighs. "Smetana and Fong follow Specie Focus like the gospel. I do not. I am seeking a new path."

Her eyes blaze. "Why do you care so much about Plow?"

"So we do have something to talk about. Lazlo's first experiments with memory involved the removal of short term memory. The theory was if someone had just enough memory to function, and not enough to remember current events longer than a few minutes that person might be safe in line and an effective control for Clipper. That's back when we thought we could force Species Focus to light where we wanted it to light. Did you know we only had success with one guy, a PhD, a Rhodes Scholar, a soldier by the name of Gus Plow."

"Dr. Biner would say we did nothing but discover a false path."

"The self-congratulating fool. But Plow decomposed into a killer. Eventually he took to writing notes all time to remember things and stay focused. One heck of a soldier--was there a Ginda with him named Frew?"

"There was someone else." His eyes brighten and Winston knows she has given it away.

"I see. Plow needed help to remember what to do. Something inside that man drove him to help those kids. It was incredible. You two are the same."

"So you tried to kill him at the end of the war and he escaped?"

"It wasn't me. They planned to kill Plow--but the guy was mercury--and brilliant. You know he spent every night, from the first moment he entered the project, digging an escape tunnel and writing himself notes to keep digging. Smart man--good for him."

"Are you sure his memory was so poor?" She asks.

Pard looks at her. "I have been duped before. It's possible. And I deserve it--but we all bare that. I am driven. That is true. But I am no fool."

She looks back at him from the doorway. "You let everyone else do the heavy lifting, Joshua. You're retrograde. Perhaps you think I hate you because of your back-biting, but the truth is I know it wasn't Lazlo who pushed the agenda to kill the Gindas. It was you. And that was why you stabbed him in the back at every turn." She turns to leave.

"You do matter to me."

"Because I was the only one who really cared about you--too bad." She exits the room, letting the door slam shut.

"Don't you be a coward, Winston. You are the way out of this mess."

Ascending the stairs, she considers her actions, wondering why she did not ask about Russell Biner. She turns to confront Pard on this issue until the sounds of an old man's tears echo up the stairs. Winston pauses, takes a step, then leaves him to his demons.

A moment later, outside among the milling crowds, she remembers to breathe. *I'm not tracked or adjusted like Moss. Joshua couldn't have spoken like that if I had been. He also said I stayed conscious to more of the fire fight than I had in the past. So I really am independent and gaining leverage with Clipper. I am a researcher entrusted with stumbling upon our future…But the answer is?*

CHAPTER 17

Thursday afternoon--Gus died yesterday, trying to kill Dr. Wolf.

I guess Gus walked to the gallows around midnight, took a few steps up, then turned around. He came back into the latrine and unscrewed a small piece of metal from one of the toilet flush valves, then pulled out a long bar from inside a pipe. He used it to pry open the front door of the barracks. Then he ran down the street to try and find Lazlo's place.

They told me the MPs shot him as he entered Lazlo's house. I guess Lazlo's life isn't as cheap as ours.

It all started at dinner Tuesday night. Wait, something happened. Wait, where's Wednesday?

Thursday night--Gus said he knew what we were doing here. He said we were here so Lazlo Wolf can figure out how to stop what's killing humanity. I guess Wildhead is trading information for our lives. That way Wildhead can understand what kind of weapon the enemy is using against us.

Gus then explained the Greek alphabet to me. It goes alpha, beta, gamma, delta. We're Team Delta; we're next to die

What happened to the other guys?

Thursday midnight--I understand now why they have us say that we are dead as the first line of our diaries. We're all going to die. I know that now. But we all die eventually, don't we?

Friday afternoon--Wait. I have something to say, for now and all time. I ain't gonna' die 'cause some damn something is messing with my skull. What a scam, aliens, I'll use that joke some day, if I get a chance. I'll tell the whole world I am an alien. We are so gullible.

Fuck'em! I'm gonna' live forever and the hell with them. It's me who's gonna' dance on their graves!

I hate writing in this diary.

Today, when we woke, the emblem on the wall had changed to a big jackhammer breaking through a grinning skull. Under it, it said "Jackhammer Brigade." In the john, we found tee-shirts with the same logo. I'm still wearing the tee-shirt; everyone is. They are so cool.

Then we spent the morning marching. Then we saw more surveillance videos of civilians mauling each other. I have seen people drowned, gored by bulls, knifed, hung, and their pets shot. You name it, I've seen it. I never knew there were so many ways to die, or so much surveillance.

One of the guys got so fed up he asked for popcorn. I'll be son of a bitch if it didn't show up ten minutes later. Then we all asked for popcorn. It was like the old vids of people watching movies together in theaters. I always wondered what that was like. The popcorn was great, all buttered and warm, with a little salt on it. Man, that was the best grub I ever ate. I hear they are going to show movies again--seems crazy to get all those crazy people in one place.

Lazlo tells us we are in for a new thrill. Starting tomorrow, instead of watching individual death, we are going to be treated to disasters that kill over a hundred people at a time. I guess it's getting worse out there.

Ol' Wildhead says death is so common we might miss the important events. I guess tragedy kills over a hundred-thousand people a week now. We've had eight soldiers die here in the last twenty-four hours.

Seems to me they should all be remembered but for some reason, we're not supposed to remember any of them. So what the hell are we watching these vids for? Crazy world we live in. Another funny thing—they said the crazy-dying began with the global warming thing. I wonder if the whole thing is tied together? Dog, if that's so, we really capped it, didn't we?

Saturday afternoon--So Lazlo takes us into a room and asks us if any of us have any ideas on who is doing all the killing. A bunch of the guys think it's religious crazies. Someone said Liberals and someone said Conservatives.

Some of the women though it was the crazy male scientists. A few of others thought it's the rich folks trying to kill us all off. They said the reason the rich didn't fight global warming was they wanted it to decimate the population. Guess that means we got an example of getting too much of a good thing.

In the Gumbie-gore show today we saw the crème de la crème of death,spectacular things: planes crashing in schoolyards, doctors blowing up hospitals, and large-scale prison massacres by the guards. All major disasters, including an assortment of homicides, gang rapes, and general brutality had stereo sound. The goofy part of it is the people who start these horrors are usually relief workers sent to help someone. I think sometimes when someone tries to help—it just makes it worse.

Plow says that's a doctrine of madness. He called me a TV head. What's that?

At the end of the Gumbie-gore show, Wildhead showed a chart of the Earth's population. Since the beginning of the twenty-first century, the population has been decreasing steadily. Part of it is colored red to signify the global warming years and part of it is colored blue to signify the Jazz War. It's good that the global warming deaths slowed to almost nothing; we won that. But one thing's for sure, we aren't winning this one. They might be the same thing. I think they are. Imagine telling people back then that their children would die from them buying too much, they'd never believe it.

Someone asked how long two point five billion people will last at our present rate of death. Lazlo said he didn't know with any accuracy. That scares the piss out of me. I know Lazlo knows.

(Commentary from the Research Team: At this point, the subject has completely lost any sense of memories outside the task. References to the body will be preserved. Reductions in live body memories will continue until we can inject a stable, succinct set of memories and then remove the subject from the nutrient bath. I remain fearful that future participants suddenly learning of their state, may, through fear, panic. Therefore, as a precursor to giving the Gindas a body, more testing is warranted. Great caution must be exercised in data dissemination from this point forward. L.Wolf. Date suppressed per requirement.)

(Commentary from the Research Team: Uses of the nutrient bath and other gene technology may provide an avenue to grow replacement organs. I will be examining this option. R.Merton. Date suppressed per requirement.)

Sunday--I've learned to play poker. I lost a hundred dollars. I just couldn't find a hand that worked. Is that because I can't find my hands?

Monday early morning--There's a rumor running around the barracks that we are going to be moved somewhere away from the water. I can't say where, but we'll be traveling pretty far. I've never traveled far. Neither has anybody else I know. I was told everyone used to travel all the time. I'm not sure if I believe that.

If we go, it'll be on one of those high-speed

trains that go up and down the coast. That will be fun. Gus used to watch them streak past his girlfriend's house. I'm sure he would have liked to go on this ride. I'm still sad about Gus.

I think I'm beginning to get a hand on this.

Oops. Off to another Gumbie-gore-show. Why does Sergeant Plow keep picking on me?

Tuesday--Three more guys died last night. They threw themselves in front of a train. I'm in a train now sitting with seventeen other guys that I don't know. We're not allowed to talk. We're in the back of the train, two rows from the back cargo doors. And they're open!

The doors sit out like two big rudders at the tail of the train. I see some of my buddies from the Jackhammers are sitting a few rows in front of us looking forward but I am not allowed to move or go see them. We Jackhammers are the only ones wearing the black tee-shirt. These other guys and gals are just dressed like regular soldiers. They ain't as good us.

It's so cold and wet here, water sloshing everywhere--and noisy--shit. I think they should close the rear doors. This train rolls down the tracks at two hundred miles an hour. Lazlo says if they close the doors, they crash, so he's keeping the doors open.

I'm glad Lazlo is sitting up front and away from me. He creeps me out. He keeps telling me I shouldn't write too much because if I ask the wrong question, there'll be hell to pay. He also told me the diaries may help keep others from killing themselves.

A gal just got up and jumped off the back of the train. No one got up to stop her. Not even me. That's it. I quit. That's enough damn it.

Hey where are you guys going?

I ain't ready for this. I live in a beaker?

Tuesday afternoon--Sergeant Plow saw me writing and scanned my notebook. "What kind of an idiot doesn't know how to ask questions!" He screams at me.

"All we are, are questions, you moron," I yell back. I don't know what took hold of me.

Then the Sarge grabs me and throws a full-on shit-fit yelling things at me and then dragging me up past everyone else. Wham, then we're in the next car with Wildhead.

I didn't know he was still on the train.

Wildhead is staring at a bank of ten vid screens watching the guys. These bastards know everything about us. They never give us a moment of privacy.

He's got a kid. She's playing with a mirror. Then I can see it: This kid is so pissed at him.

Plow says something about what I wrote and Wildhead just nods. I swear they're always picking on Sammich Ginda. The bastards.

Wildhead offers me a bite of elk jerky—the guy loves the stuff. I take a bite and finally he tells me to watch the monitor and keep an eye on the new recruits riding with us. He takes a syringe and injects my hands. They go numb. He tells me to watch the screen. Nothing happens for a few minutes, and then this pretty soldier with long legs and great boobs stands up. She walks to the back and zip, out she goes. Then the rest stand up like machines. They walk to the open back doors and step out. That's when I see myself scream at Plow.

Wildhead just sits there and says nothing. The Jackhammers are all facing forward like they were ordered. So they didn't see any of it. Isn't that funny? Lazlo sends me back and says I should tell the others what happened.

When I told the rest of the guys what happened, none of them seemed to care. I think all this death is getting to them. There's just no question about it anymore.

I think we are learning to not care. What has happened to us?

(Commentary from the Research Team: At this point, it appears the tie between questions and the death of the Ginda has been breached with the subjects. We are at a loss to understand what has changed but we are seeing an increase in nutrient bath viability in tissue growth. Both hands are complete. If we get through this, it is agreed by all that advanced genetic manipulation of organ growth and subsystems will be commonplace. As a result, we suggest a sub-research unit to begin funded R&D on the genetic mutation problem that has plagued us. It has been suggested by Dr. Wolf that the problem will disappear once we have a stable memory environment which we can inject the Ginda. On the other hand, we are saddened that Dr. Wolf continues to consider exterminating the soldiers at a faster rate to gain knowledge. J.Pard. Date suppressed per requirement.)

(1st Court of Inquiry Witness: Dr. Pard believes that radical interpretations of mutagenic genetic coincidence by Dr. Wolf is nothing more than self-serving

commentary by a researcher wishing to keep his Machiavellian decisions from peer scrutiny by pandering to economic interests. As a result, a genetic subgroup will begin work under Dr. Merton's guidance. R.Merton. Date suppressed per requirement.)

Tuesday night--I sat with old Wildhead. He is one creepy individual. Lazlo is a young guy, like me, but he has these big puffy pillows of wrinkled fat or something under his eyes. They make him look like a man with a lot of problems. When he opens his eyes, the pillows get bigger.

Dr. Wolf asked me if I think the recruits' death was my fault. I say it hadn't occurred to me, but now that he'd mentioned it, yes. Then a second later I tell him I don't know. **I really do think it was my fault**.

But Lazlo and his buddies are all so weird. I think they might place me in front of a firing squad or something if I admit I think I'm responsible. I wonder why Plow hasn't spit on me today.

I want to be stinking drunk. I wonder how often they read these diaries? Ow, that hurt.

I just got back from the infirmary. I stabbed myself in the arm with my knife. It was sitting on the side of the bed and I just leaned over and put it into my arm. Damn, that hurts. I wonder why I did that?

Tuesday midnight--I just did it again. I stabbed myself. I have definitely got to stop that stuff.

Wildhead came in and just told me that on every train trip, military and civilian, for the last two years, any people sitting in the last three rows just got up walked off the train. I said they should just lock the door.

He said when they close the back doors, the train crashes. When they try to keep the last three rows empty, the next three die, and so forth, when they strap in the whole lot of them, the train crashes.

When I asked him why, this big damn smile crosses his face like he just had a baby or something. And he says, the space beneath the train is moving away from us. So the space where we were is outside the former space and therefore no longer ours. What the hell is he talking about? The only one nuts is this Wildhead guy.

He just asked me to explain the way I ask questions. I didn't want to tell him I got this secret: **Truth is I'm so stupid that whenever I ask a question, by the time I get an answer I've learned to forget that I asked a question, or what it was. This is a key. With the right kind of forgetting, time is mollified.**

Was that me? Must be. I used to think I was stupid. That was why I joined the Army. Here, no one asks you questions, they just tell you what to do. I've always hated questions. People used to teased me about how stupid I was. Truth is, I want more than anything to not be stupid.

I can't help wondering: What would it be like to recall my questions? Is that memory?

(Commentary from the Research Team: Though the debate will rage for years as to the meaning, it is the considered opinion of all that we do not understand the nature of the interrogative--the question--we humans use so freely. Dr. Biner's maverick

step of intercepting the Ginda has breathed new life in the project while suggesting a sanctity to questions. He is alone in this, with the majority of the researchers believing questions to be a doorway of some sort into truth. R.Merton/J.Pard. Date suppressed per requirement.)

Tuesday midnight--I am one freaked Jackhammer. I headed back to my seat and I don't know if I should be happy, or sad. So I grab those little metal arm rests on the side of the seat and hang on. My arms are going to stay on this train no matter what.

Damn, everything hurts.

We stopped for the night in a town with huge trees. So they showed the vids of the guys jumping off a train. Someone is nuts.

Funny, now no one wants to bunk with me. I think they're afraid of me. They treat me differently now. It's not fair. Dr. Pard must have told them how stupid I am and they hate me for it.

Good the train is starting up. I like watching the tracks go away from me. I think the reason people had jumped off the train was they were trying to hold onto the space they were in and the train was taking them away from it.

Lazlo just told Plow that we're got legs now.

Or maybe it's like they had a grappling hook tied to them. They toss it out and whoops, out they go. I wonder if there is a way to use a grappling hook so I can bounce between the two places. I can just see it now, boing, boing, back and forth. I could be in two places at once. I wonder if that would work. **I will be the rubber band man, not you.**

Wednesday morning--Sergeant Plow started my day today by yelling at me. Thank you.

I'm going to be transferred to special duty, he said. I'm going to be doing closer work with that Clipper computer. Then I asked a question that really pissed him off. I ask him if my new assignment is a safer than what I've had been doing?

I thought he was going to tear my head off. Wow, cool. Anyway, he starts screaming real loud, his face about an inch from mine, calling me a dumb bastard! He screams Clipper isn't safe! No place is safe! And now that I've done something good I am probably a damn sight more likely to die horribly than anyone else! I wonder if I can guess what I did right?

Then good old Plow. He spits on my boots and walks away. I finally made it. He likes me! The question is the beginning of a cycle? Then that's why the question mark looks like a grappling hook. So what the heck is an answer? The past or the future? This hurts.

Plow just told me to shut up.

The train derailed outside of Portland a few hours ago. I'm in a hospital bed with a broken ankle. I don't remember breaking my ankle. I do know twenty people died from our group—including three Jackhammers. The train jumped the track rounding a corner and hit a school bus that was parked alongside the rails. Some maintenance guy was trying to fix the bus. What the hell was he doing out there fixing a bus at 2:00 AM in the morning?

Yup, I'm getting it. Some things, you just can't fix 'em. Ya' gotta' leave 'em broke. I see how the Gumbies fight. I'm gonna' get my licks in, one way or the other. And there ain't no damn way I'm gonna' kill myself until I get my whoop-ass in.

I figure if we have surveillance, so do the Gumbies. Maybe even better surveillance and maybe so good they can tap into what I'm doing here. So on that thought: You hear me? You better get this, you scumbags Gumbies, Sammich Ginda is coming to kick your butt. It may happen only once, and then I might go claw my eyes out, or something; but on the other hand, maybe I'll get you more than once. I am going to keep coming back until I get it right. I don't care how long it takes.

I hear Plow saying "Good man," but I can't see him. My eyes don't work. My head hurts, but I am Sammich Ginda. Not whomever's memory I've got. That means Sammich Ginda wins. Period, from now on just call me Sammich. I am no longer dead. I can see the future of the Gumbies. I am going to kick their ass. Is this what it means to be alive? To kick someone's ass?

CHAPTER 18

Thursday--It was a long drive. The trailer I was in had blacked-out windows and I wasn't allowed to talk to the five guys with me. They frown on us talking. They say all I do is flirt. I didn't want to flirt I just wanted to talk.

After a few hours, the driver in the cab began talking to me through the wire mesh window. His name is Russell Biner. He said he used to be a scientist, and made some dumb joke about living off test tubes. He says he is going to help me get where I need to go. Men, they are so sure of themselves; they never get the big picture. He says he will watch over me. I don't think he is a scientist. I think he is a barber. He cut my hair with a pair of electric clippers. I didn't like the noise it made on my skull. It felt like a drill. How'd he do that?

Monday morning--He is so full of himself. But scientists don't drive trucks. He is probably just another grunt trying to score. I like that he didn't ask me any questions. I hate when guys do that, trying to act like they are interested in you when all they want is one thing. We talked about the weather and test tubes. I told him I was a test tube baby and he got off on that. Maybe he is a scientist. They're so strange.

I left the Jackhammers somewhere near Everett. I'm standing alone outside some buildings in the middle of a farm after a trip in a jeep. A tough-looking Marine, a Sergeant, came over. He looked scared of me. I wonder what men see when they see a beautiful women? I wonder why we are so scary to them.

The guy's name is Frew. I've heard of him. He led me to this big room full of cubicles, computers, and glass cubes. From the big domed ceiling and all the lights overhead, it looks like this place was once a school gymnasium. The Sergeant says they need all the space for all those memory cubes. They are the square glass things plastered across the big ceiling. There is also a big banner with white letters on a green background. It says:

Can we hook the past and pull ourselves in? What then? How do we land safe?

I've been staring at that damn sign all morning. What the hell is it supposed to mean? Maybe someone is trying to figure out how to land on a bed of spikes? The guys running this place are nuts. There is no way I want to go back. My life just isn't that good.

Wednesday morning--This is a tough crib. A guy walks into my cubicle earlier, a big Oriental guy with a topknot and a round face. He says "I am going to win. Period." He says it over and over to me a whole bunch of times--he must have gone on for twenty minutes. Then he walks away. I want to see what's going on so I hobble after him; my ankle is still a little weak, even with the gene treatments. I broke it when I jumped off the train.

Anyway, I follow Mr. Topknot by the guards and out of the gymnasium and into the rain. They don't try to stop him, or me either. That seems right.

What good are guards if all they do is stand there? Dumb dogs.

Maybe that's the new way to fight a war. Just stand there. Or maybe they stand there until they can't stand it anymore? Funny, I wonder, do question marks stand or balance? Or, they could hook, balance, and stand. What the fuck is wrong with me?

Wednesday afternoon--We are so, outside! Me and Mr. Topknot are looking at this small circus tent. Then we go inside the tent and there are tables with pistols, long knives, and some medieval-looking hatchets. I stay well behind the guy with the topknot as he shops the tables, picking things up, and looking at them. There is no doubt in my mind my man is going to dust his-self.

At the far end, leaning against the wall like

a Murphy bed is a six-foot-tall platform covered with spikes. Beautiful chrome spikes, about eight or ten inches long on an exquisitely stained mahogany platform. The workmanship on the table is beautiful. No cheap gallows at this place, only the first class stuff.

This guy pulls the bed of spikes down, I knew it was all about a bed of spikes; strips to underpants, climbs on a chair--and swan dives onto the spikes. A low grunt and it's over. One spike sticking out every few inches--it looks kind of cool, actually. The blood on the spikes and all, I think if I decide to croak, that's how I'll do it.

Then I went for a walk--a limp really--around the building in the rain. A path goes around by the back, where a swimming pool used to be. There were some small sailboats in the pool. I was surprised they hadn't capsized in the rain and wind.

It's funny, some places they check your hat, or your coat. This place they check your corpse and take the rest of the stuff inside and stuff it into another body. And those Gumbie-bastards just keep raising the ante. But I'm not folding.

Unbelievable! Lunch just arrived on a flat robot. It beeps. I kicked it, but I guess you can't expect a robot to go backwards. I think going backwards would get boring. I wonder what would happen if there were always a new backward? **That wouldn't be boring.**

But I bet it would drive you nuts remembering the present.

Thursday night--Guess who shows up and invites me to a meeting? Wildhead.

He knocks at the door of my little glass room in the gymnasium and leads me out another door. One that I thought was locked, and that takes us to a room that looks like a place where the President might talk to people. It has nice wood walls, soft recessed lighting, and a big oak table sitting on a red carpet. Five old guys are sitting around it. They look like corporate types--or generals. Wildhead has me sit at the head of the table and we start talking. They're making a recording of it so I can remember it all even as I write it down. Dr. Pard is here and he's smiling. That means something is definitely wrong.

First thing they do is tell me what a good job I've done, but they keep calling me Sammich, or Ginda. I don't think that's my name. I'm a woman for God's sake.

I try to say something and Plow tells me to shut up and listen. He then says they can call me whatever the hell they want. Plow is kinda' cute but I'd like to get out of this meeting; and who the heck is Sammich Ginda?

They say I should remember my promise to get my licks in. Then Lazlo asks me if I'm a soldier who will follow orders. I answer yes. Then I tell them how much I hate the Gumbies and that I want to get the Gumbies.

Lazlo asks me if I'm willing to give my thoughts to someone close to me--as a sort of jump-start to get their brain functioning. I tell them they don't understand anything about women. I told them it would have to be someone I love.

I guess they got some poor sucker's brain somewhere and it's empty as a gas can. They want to take my thoughts and give them to him. They say he needs it.

They say it is the only way I can help Sammich. So why doesn't that bother me? It's not as if he were my bother or my lover. I say the hell with them.

Then they dismiss me. But I don't leave. I ask Lazlo Wolf how many other troops died so this poor troop with the empty brain can live. A guy whispers in my ear that there were hundreds. He also tells me I am his sister and that Sammich is our son. I think this guy Russell is a fool. I don't know the guy's smell.

I think the guy with the empty brain is also a fool. Okay, I'll help you.

Saturday--So here goes: Sammich, I am your mother. I am going to jump start that bag of gelatin you call a brain. They tell me you are hooked into a special computer. By the time you live, I'll be dead and you'll be given this memory via this computer called Clipper. I can't really explain it, I'm just a grunt. I guess they're going to use a lot of different memories—but you won't know the difference.

Only difference is my memories will be like a jump-start, from one battery to another, only in this case it'll be brain to brain, via a computer link.

What you will be experiencing afterwards is a training session for life—a brand new life that none of us have had before—and apparently no one besides you can face. Soon you will be the only mind you know. That's the way it has to be, I guess. You will be everyone's focus--the whole planet. That's pretty cool and you are going to help win the war, my child. Imagine it, you'll be both male and female, soldier and executive. You'll be able to link up and "write" in your diary. In some cases you'll just be sorting memories for Clipper. In fact that's what you've been doing since you were turned on. But you won't be able to kill yourself like the rest of us. That's the beauty of a test tube--so you can't hurt yourself. Do well, my child. I think you need hope to do this.

You poor dumb bastard.

(Commentary from the Research Team: As Dr. Biner's efforts continue with the Gindas I cannot help but find myself in awe of his dedication to humanity and this project. He is the best of us. L.Wolf. Date suppressed per requirement.)

For whatever that's worth, thanks, Laz'.

CHAPTER 19

Monday--What do I hear?

I hear a voice talking to me. It's Lazlo Wolf. He says he is a doctor. He says that I am safe. He says it is perfectly natural to be scared and confused. The people who gave me memory have been dead more than a year.

A soldier killed herself for the sake of humanity. Everything I've have been experiencing, except for my initial awareness of being in a hospital with a broken leg, happened years ago--to her.

She was a brave person. Thanks to her we have both a way to live with the rip and a way to repair it.

Lazlo says I must honor courage. My body will be the first real progress we will make against the Gumbies. Lazlo says the next step after that is me being disconnected from Clipper. Then I learn to control Clipper. I am so lucky to be involved in this great effort. It is a great effort isn't it?

(Commentary from the Research Team: After this, incredible entry, it must be accepted that Dr. Wolf has no respect for the brave soldiers. Further, I cannot express the depth of my grief at what has taken place, or excuse Dr. Wolf for altering the project plan to depict the lies he claims are necessary. I must therefore resign. It is with profound regrets that I hereby tender my resignation to the Clipper Project. R.Merton. Date suppressed per requirement.)

(Note from the Research Team: Dr. Merton's founding of GeneBanks S.A., has no bearing on his entry. We will work to get him back on the team. He is a key player in keeping the more radical elements of this project in check. J.Pard. Date suppressed per requirement.)

Chapter 20

A young man stands beside the ocean.

The images pans to rolling waves; then two people with ebony skin flash onto the screen. They are making love. The young man's face reappears, reflecting the glow of the setting-sun. The camera follows his gaze to the same young woman relaxing on the beach. Waves crash onto the sand in front of her.

Cut to another very handsome couple making love. The camera lingers on their Asian features. Sweat covers their writhing bodies.

The young man's face again appears. He stares at another young Caucasian woman who begins running her hands through her thick, blond hair. A tall, handsome mulatto man rises from the pounding waves. They kiss, and then run back into the ocean together. The young man sits on the shore and bows his head into his arms. He sits, shivering on the cold beach.

Voice-over: "Is your love-making technique a little parochial? Do your lovers seem unsatisfied? Are you tired of being left in the sand?"

The young man's face lifts. "Entertainment Plus has the answer: 'Complete love-making!'" His young face glows, a dirty leer follows the smile. It is quickly hidden.

"This is the real-deal, a compendium of scenes and commentary showing love-making techniques from Antarctica to Zanzibar. And it can be yours for only $59.00 a month. Satisfy your lovers like a world traveler and don't be left on the sand! Contact Entertainment Plus. And remember, there's a world of love out there, and it's just waiting for you to pay for it."

. . . .

Winston shuts down the Diary. She walks to the bathroom mirror to study her face. *So what am I supposed to do? Are they saying I am nothing more than what I believe I am? This life is nothing more than what I believe it to be. That there is no truth. That it is minutia.* She reaches out to touch the log cabin walls. *Moss and Sammich made it through because of their ignorance. So I am supposed to be the big change. Because I understand?* She taps the wood walls of her cabin. *Is this all just the inertia of our deranged past? When that inertia ceases, where will we be? What will I be?* She splashes cold water on her face, then turns to the computer screen. "Okay. Okay." She sits back down on her bed. "I can do this." She looks about her room. "But I don't know what to do."

CHAPTER 21

Tuesday--Part of my brain floats on in a glass vessel, the other part floats inside the computer system they call Clipper. Clipper stores all of my memories. Clipper logs all my memories and controls them. They call it a Diary. The Diary is my world. How nice. I guess lots of soldiers sacrificed themselves so humanity could get itself this far. And here we are, humanity's hope, stuck in a bell jar.

Why can't they give me a body? Maybe this is some kind of military shakedown cruise. If I fail the test, will they shut me off?

Why doesn't anyone answer? I don't want to be alone! Where'd that other guy go?

Lazlo says they won't shut me off. Why not?

Wednesday afternoon--Part of me wonders if this isn't some Gumbie trick. I understand the way the Gumbies work. They somehow read what you fear, or want, or need, or hope for. Then these things come true. I have no fears, or hurts. Nor do I have hope. Those human things play over and over like words to a song I cannot quite make out. I know the tune--but it doesn't mean anything. The horror of Gumbies manipulating fear means something though. I think that's it. We humans decided nothing is important. Wait. Who are the Gumbies? We created the pollution in us. What's pollution? What's a bardo? I am dead.

Thursday--Dr. Pard says that television was supposed to a benign a method of controlling people. Lazlo said it spit out pollution and that pollution screwed up our insides. But what could be so important that we ignored hurting ourselves? I wonder what else we learned from ten years of killing soldiers to gather data against the Gumbies.

Oh that's right, there are no Gumbies, just too many things we already knew the answers to and ignored.

And I'm supposed to save humanity? Seems I'm more of a slave to stupidity than anything. A half-brained, computer-controlled pile of tissue stuffed in a glass jar that doesn't really have any idea what's going on. Nothing of me is I. I'd like a body, not just the question of me. I can't kill or do damage. Maybe that's what makes me less than human? Maybe that's what makes me more than human? Maybe I don't give a damn about these dirty bastards and I should let them all die.

Friday--Lazlo just told me he is going to speak to me for a long time Saturday. It will be a history lesson. Dr. Wolf, why do I need to be taught anything? Why can't I just absorb it from Clipper? What was that?

Dr. Wolf said he laughed.

I'd like to laugh. What's a laugh?

Lazlo says that as my consciousness grows Clipper will help me store my memories.

Are those are my diary entries. And those are laughs?

Lazlo says no. Apparently, my memories are everything that happens to me, and my diary is what I want to keep as a kind of family album.

And existence is...

A memory, oh, that's nice. Clipper can limit my access to my own existence. They think direct access to my life might harm me, as well as Clipper. We wouldn't want to hurt Clipper now would we? They think I do fine knowing I am hooked into Clipper.

Dr. Pard says the Gumbies attack through memories--especially memories that are important, and that's why they are keeping my memories in Clipper's control. Clipper takes my memories and changes them around so I can be safe. Dr. Pard says I am being taken care of. Dr. Pard is an idiot.

I want my own memories. I don't want a pile of chips to tell me what my life is about. Dr. Pard asks me if there is a difference between a pile of chips or a pile of senses? Apparently not to him.

I have control over my diary but Clipper has control over my existence. Pard says there are only questions for me. Without questions apparently there are no answers, but apparently the answers don't matter, only questions. Apparently, I like the word apparently. What's apparent?

Was that a laugh, Laz'? I can laugh?

Friday night--Lazlo has made some modifications. We're going to have a talk now to see if they work. Apparently, I have access to something called retention. He says I should not enter things into my diary until he and I talk about them. I guess Clipper is a little unreliable.

I need experiences, and I need to learn about myself because computer memory and processing are useless for making me a good soldier. Lazlo says Clipper will help. I don't like that much.

Pard, I like calling him that. He says that my personality contains a sense of outrage and beauty. He thinks I should control it. Dope.

I don't feel angry. Why don't I feel angry? He's not answering me. He's not here. I forget when they leave. That's great, I did forget it, but now I remember that I forgot it. This is fun. What if I made others forget? Can I do that? **Could I make them forget me?** Right here and right now, what if I forget them? Would they disappear?

(Note from the 1st Court of Inquiry: While it is clear this interrogative has killed this soldier and it is directly attributable to Dr. Biner, the court finds no fault on the part of Dr. Biner, or reason to pursue this death of a Ginda. L.Wolf. Date suppressed per requirement.)

Saturday morning--I'm going to get a history

lesson today. I'm supposed to recite that history into my diary to make sure I work correctly.

Apparently, they tried to do this same activity, earlier but it didn't work. And before me, they tried to make a soldier, but I couldn't hold my body. I heard someone say it's been eighteen months. That seems like a long time.

I don't like being referred to as a device. I feel like a light bulb no one will repair.

Saturday night--In the history lesson, I asked Lazlo what battlefield meant. He said it was different for everyone, but in a nutshell--for him everything's in a nutshell--it's the place where humans fight with the Gumbies instead of letting them pulling our strings as if we were marionettes.

I wouldn't mind someone pulling strings--if I had arms or legs. **A joke--hypercool--I am jokester. That's a key.**

I asked Dr. Pard how I'd know if I had forgotten something. He said it doesn't matter. I told him that nothing would scare the shit out of me. I don't have a butt to shit with. I guess I remember more of the recruits than I thought. Gus was funny.

Lazlo then said Clipper will help me cope with my new life. Then Pard told me my life doesn't matter because I would always come back. So what? How does that mean my life doesn't matter? And if it doesn't matter who cares if I can cope with it or not? Is that what all this work is about? Where we are matters, not what we are doing? But what is a "where"? That means we humans were insignificant. But that makes sense, if we see ourselves from the overall planet. Or was that aware, as in space? So maybe humanity dying off doesn't matter? I think the where we are matters, not the who we are. I think Dr. Wolf thinks that. I think he is more interested in the puzzle than anything else.

(Notes from the Research Team to the Court of Inquiry: It is this last entry, more than any other, that has prompted our investigations into the motivations of Dr. Wolf. It is clear to us, that at this point, Dr. Wolf has limited respect for our corporate culture. He has also become diffident to the pains of others and this is unacceptable to the team. J.Pard/R.Merton. Date suppressed per requirement.)

So here I go.

Part one, the Clipper Project and the Jazz War: Co-starring Clipper--and his guinea pig appendage, Sammich Ginda. But not all those poor bastards who died over the last ten years.

Okay, there's some debate about the timing since many say the war had been going on for a hundred years. But we didn't know it because we said the hell with the planet. Then when the planet finally agreed with us, we woke up. I sound like Dr. Wolf. He says the tipping point, was probably right after the climate crisis had peaked.

I guess people were feeling pretty good about themselves. The storms had slowed to only two or three hours a day in the Northwest, and a couple of raindrops even fell in California without killing anyone. The Midwest was still dry as a rock and the south a big swamp, but rainfall patterns were definitely recovering. The Russians were producing more wheat than the world could use and the Chinese population was again continuing to grow. Europe regained electricity and Australia began exporting fish. The Greenhouse Laws remained in effect, but slowly we humans were returning to the top of the heap.

No one had any more concerns about humanity being wiped off the face of the planet. And other than a few protests, saying the United Network of Corporations was not a representational government, things were looking pretty good. Was that our sin? Giving over our souls to commerce instead of the real world?

(Notes from the Research Team: The manner of discourse in these pages seems far beyond that of Sammich Ginda. We suggest more testing of the firewall between Russell Biner and the Sammich Ginda. Also, it must be made clear that the entries contain data irrelevant to the project. J.Pard/R.Merton. Date suppressed per requirement.)

Then, on May tenth, actually the morning of May tenth, commercial jetliners and most air freighters crashed between 12:01 AM and sunrise. The disasters spread westward following the dawn from the International Date Line. The black boxes reported that on every flight that crashed, the crew had been listening to the Commercial Pilots network at some time during the night. Finally, the unlikely connection of the music was postulated and the station was pulled off the air and listening to jazz during flights became a capital offense for pilots: Hence the name Jazz War.

Whew, we stupid or what? Why hide? Jazz music as the problem, that's sick.

(Notes from the Research Team: We again suggest more testing of a breach in the firewall between Russell Biner and the Sammich Ginda. The Ginda appears to analyze sociological constructs that have no place in a pure research project. R.Merton/J.Pard. Date suppressed per requirement.)

The next night, everything that flew crashed. This occurred between midnight and dawn, as May 11 spread throughout the world. Commercial, Air Force, private, everything bit the dust, twenty-four hours later there was a total ban on flying after 11:00 PM and before 8:00 AM. It almost worked. I guess it was reported to the public as some kind of volcano problem.

A week later all the trucks crashed, eighteen thousand in California alone. Worldwide, the number was in the millions. All the crashes occurred between midnight and dawn, and all were fatal. In these cases also, the brown boxes on the huge trucks recorded the driver was listening to music at some time during the night, but it wasn't always jazz. In most cases, there was normal conversation between the driver and navigator about various items: girls, sports, the jets crashing, those kinds of things--then smash. No scream, no "Watch out"--just crunch. Plans were made to remove jazz stations from the airwaves, but it was fought in the courts--then the buses crashed. The next day all music disappeared from the airwaves.

Of course, by then panic had broken out, because the media was caught in a fib--they claimed the crashes never happened. But everyone knew someone who had died in one of the crashes. A few of the large companies that made parts common to buses and trucks and jets were then cited as the likely cause of the crashes, and hundreds of court cases claiming negligence were filed. The media got off the hook when fears were quelled by the all-too-believable excuses of negligence and greed. But for those working on the problem, only the "truly stupid"--Wildhead's words--didn't know something had shifted.

It got worse over the summer, because nothing else happened. The uninformed began to say perhaps it was just a fluke, and they began to circulate that idea through media.

What a memory--I'm surprised. I can remember so much. Wow, this Clipper hookup might not be so bad. I always thought the reason I was so stupid was I couldn't think. Now I see that if you can remember well you don't need to think. What a scam.

On November first, while jazz was still banned from the airwaves, an odd thing happened. Every day care nurse, administrator, guard, cook--anyone in the multi-billion dollar day care industry called in sick on the same day. But only in the United States. It didn't happen in Morocco, or Brazil, or England, or elsewhere in the world.

I guess parents dropped their children off and

no one was there to help the children. Children attending day care after school showed up at locked facilities.

What is a child? I asked Lazlo. Lazlo spent a long time explaining the term child to me. I thought everyone started out in a test tube. I was sure of that. I figured that was the reason no one cared about anyone.

Two hundred and eight children died that November morning from various causes. The next day forty-eight per cent of the day care workers quit. The military was sent into the day care facilities to run them--can you imagine it? The U.N. Marines have landed at Miss Nancy's day care, manning the Tonka toys and keeping Lincoln Logs safe for democracy.

I think Laz' is laughing. Or is he crying? Did he have a son who had died that day?

Saturday midnight--The media said it was a terrorist conspiracy to hurt kids. Many of the workers from the day care centers were questioned by the authorities. Anyone who had links to jazz musicians or people involved in transportation were kept overnight in detention centers.

The overall response was anger from people in mourning, and anger from people who just didn't understand. Most people had no idea how widespread it all was. Then it came out that almost three quarters of the day care workers who had been questioned had admitted they were afraid that they might harm the children. That is why they had stayed home.

The police assumed the rest were liars.

Then, as hard as it is for me to believe, the U.S. Congress enacted an old law mandating the workers return to their jobs saying they were in violation of the Taft-Hartley Act. Half of the workers ignored the injunction and were branded communists.

The other half returned to work. Ninety-eight per cent of them were involved in a homicide event over the next week. Only very few people really knew what happened. I'm sure I do not want to know more.

That was it, panic took over. People went out and hoarded food, locked their doors, and watched television--guns in hand ready to greet any intruder. Guns and TV--a match made in hell--mothers' milk to madness.

The investigation of the workers showed there was no significant connection among the twenty-thousand day care workers later indicted for murder and manslaughter. They were branded terrorists because a connection was found between the modes of death. All the killings involved the elimination of oxygen and could be grouped under the categories of strangulation, asphyxiation, or poisoning. No guns, no knives, no traffic fatalities, no other brutality was reported, just the swallowing of a poison that eliminated breathing--or the elimination of air flow by physical means.

The workers all claimed no knowledge of the event. The Corporate Council concluded jazz music was the root cause and banned jazz forever.

What were they holding onto that forced so nutty a stance? We were definitely nuts by then.

A week later, clandestine jazz stations popped up around the country twittering forty-five second songs from trucks rolling along the highways of America. Immediately a nationwide hunt began for these pirate stations. Of course, there was no indication that any of the perpetrators had listened to their music.

Truth is these vehicles were actually run by U.N. security to quell the panic and focus the population's anger on something outside the cause. I wonder. Why is it so hard for us to see we were mad?

Oh no. We just lost this one. How did she see me?

Ha, fooled ya' I came back. You ought to try it sometime. By the way, we are just a moment of grace. Did you know that, Creepy? Oh, no--you were protecting...

Sunday morning--Exactly twelve days before Christmas the day care workers in the rest of the world began to phone in sick. None were forced back to work and the day care centers were immediately closed.

January first, enter our hero; because the film archives at the Library of Congress burned. Only one film was not destroyed. It was a film called "Dreams," by some Japanese film director. The reason it was saved was that it had been checked out illegally and taken off the facility by some smart researcher with something to prove. Guess who?

The person who had the film was one Lazlo Wolf who had been working on his third Ph.D. thesis which was called: "The Impacts of Societal Transcendental Growth as a Result of Species Overflow." Wildhead had been provided the movie by a friend, as friends sometimes do, under the table. Sadly, the friend had died in the fires trying to save some other rare films. **Dr. Wolf was a hero and proved his point with that theft.**

> **(Notes from the Research Team: We cannot condone a reduction of the fire wall function between Dr. Biner and the Gindas. Bleed through will occur. R.Merton/J.Pard. Date suppressed per requirement.)**

Dr. Wolf was investigated so carefully they didn't stop until they examined the amino acids in his DNA. You see Lazlo had been a minor scientist at NASA when he began arguing against the accepted notion of an alien culture rescuing humanity. He said it was absurd; it caused a sensation. Some said he stealing the movie just before the disaster was proof he was onto something.

> **(Notes from the Research Team: We do not condone the sacrifice of another Ginda for some prep school revelry. Nor do we condone the following passage in which Dr. Wolf attempts to alter the accepted definition of sentience. A bombastic ego has no place here. J.Pard. Date suppressed per requirement.)**

Tuesday morning--Really, a body for me? Thank you. I wonder if Laz' is really going to get me a body or is he teasing me?

Anyway, back to the past. That's why sentience works. Truth comes from what we call the future. That's the only way to be sure. It seems so simple.

Wednesday morning--Lazlo and his good buddy Russell were given a lab after some security guards destroyed a bunch of paintings at the Louvre, the Metropolitan, the Prado and the Uffizi galleries. The guards burned, slashed, and gouged everything. Only Hieronymus Bosch's Garden of Earthly Delights remained untouched. Lazlo showed me a picture of it, a horrible painting in triptych showing the torture of mankind in a dark, demon-ridden hell. Lazlo had mentioned it many times in his thesis as the only likely survivor of an assault. How'd he know that?

Anyway he was set up as a researcher and information on events began filtering into Lazlo's lab. I was surprised to learn that he had known very little of what was really going on until then. I guess no one did, because the men and women who thought they ran things made up truths--ones that fit their needs. And how crazy is that? They ignored the future. They ignored the facts. The future is fact--not an answer to questions. I guess questions are something else.

That didn't feel very good. Let's see, Lazlo talked about his theory. His theory is that we humans were searching for too many answers and not enough questions. Funny, I don't understand what that means. Lazlo says he once proposed a project to prove there was no truth—just agreement on lies stored as memories. That's what I am doing here.

Hmmm, so I am not so odd after all. So does that mean we now just live in other people's memories? Maybe we all were evacuated during global warming? Or was the ground we stand on evacuated? Who left what, or is that what left of who? I am getting a headache.

Wednesday afternoon--Dr. Wolf says people used to live in a state of economic fear in which science, religion, and the future were the only safe course. I think from Lazlo's view, it's all worn out. He says reality is a crutch. I think he wants me to be able to predict the future. That's not going to be so easy, but I think he's right. There ain't no here, ya' hear?

Thursday afternoon--Dr. Pard is just too crazy for me some times. He says we are all going mad because of what we are forced to believe. I guess something just happened. I guess the elected officials of the U.S, Canada, Europe, China and Japan arrived home to find their mates in compromising positions with friends. Is Dr. Pard an elected official?

Dr. Pard says the possibility of a war waged by another species on humanity is now considered the truth. This guy is also too crazy for me. I'm checking out.

(Commentary from Research Team: The preceding passage will be wiped from future copies of the Diary. We should also consider editing this Diary for future researchers as certain items are superfluous. R.Merton/J. Pard. Date suppressed per requirement.)

(2nd Court of Inquiry commentary follows: Deletions will be allowed to facilitate research.)

Thursday evening--Lazlo says the tipping point was officially recorded to have begun at 12:04 on the morning of May tenth, when Japan Airlines flight eleven, crashed into a large hill. The disaster killed two hundred and eleven people--and the last remaining litters of puppies on route to Kyoto from Melbourne. I guess dogs had been going extinct for a while and some scientists were trying to save them. Dr. Wolf says that dogs had guarded the dreams of humanity.

What's a dream?

CHAPTER 22

Monday--Dr. Pard says they're going to move me into a body, my body, and soon. He also says I shouldn't feel sorry for myself.

Okay, sure, no problem, Dr. Pard. We're buddies aren't we?

Tuesday--Yesterday in Washington, the United States President and the United Nations Secretary General launched what was left of the U.S. nuclear arsenal. The targets were in China and Japan. Ten of the sixty missiles made it across the ocean, but only two still functioned by the time they landed. One exploded in Kyoto, apparently a city of beautiful gardens. The other landed in the lake district of China. Lazlo said it was a place where artists created beautiful watercolor paintings. A five hundred square mile area of river basin was converted into a dead plane. Laz' says he doesn't understand why we destroy beautiful things. I guess the same thing happened to the U.S. Gulf Coast last century. Why do we keep doing stupid things? Laz' was crying when he told me about all this. What forces tears?

Dr. Wolf said tears are a way to release pain, like a built-in biological Clipper system. I hope I have my body soon. I have no eyes to cry with and no mouth to laugh with; still, it seems I am a lot better off then most. I haven't killed anyone yet. That means I'm a saint in this world.

The U.S. President and the U.N. Secretary are awaiting extradition to Japan. There will be a second trial in Beijing. Lazlo says it isn't their fault. Our polluted minds overflowed into them. He says that's why our leaders can't seem to do anything right. They are not the ones to get the overflow from the waters of mind--he says that overflow is the focus of our species. Lazlo also says I am the perfect receptacle for the focus of our species. He says I can handle it and I will know what to do with it, but our leaders cannot. He told me his daughter calls them Wholacks. I didn't know he had a daughter also. I guess I am pretty darn important.

(Notes from the Research Team: We cannot condone this absurd notion of Dr. Wolf's that there might be a divine right of leadership. On the other hand we will support the Ginda's memory of thinking himself above the rest of us. The Ginda's surety is paramount. J.Pard. Date suppressed per requirement.)

Wednesday night--Lazlo just left; he didn't seem to feel well.

I swear, the entire time he was in here I felt like I was talking to an iceberg. You know there used to be millions of square miles of ice on the Earth? What happened to the ice?

Ah heck, I don't care.

Then Pard stood here eight hundred and eight seconds before he spoke. I knew he was in here, but he didn't input. He then said it was our place to seize the world.

Laz', dude, there's nothing there.

Maybe it's not such a good thing to have a body.

Thursday--Wildhead talked a little about my mother. He said she was worried about me. I was born to a human couple,then they turned me over to the Clipper program. He said he didn't want to say anymore about them. You're lying Laz', someone is pulling your strings here. I wish I had known my mother.

(Commentary from the Research Team: It is agreed that when the Ginda uses the term "'Laz" or "Wildhead" it is an example of bleed through from Dr. Biner. And while the cause is unknown, eliminating that bleed through will assure us of a stable platform. L.Wolf/J.Pard. Date suppressed per requirement)

Thursday night--My body is almost done. Wildhead also talked about his real child, Clipper. I thought he was going to talk about his daughter, or that son that died, silly me.

Friday midnight--What was that? It hurt.

Wildhead says there was an attack on Clipper last night. He says eight people died. He didn't talk much about it. Tonight is passing so slowly.

What's outside of me?

What's left?

I am Sammich Ginda.

I am dead. No problem, dude.

How can I help people? I don't even have control over my body; God damn Clipper does! Can I destroy you, Clipper?

Too bad the attack failed. I don't want a computer for a family. I want to meet my parents after I have my body.

I think if I don't want to have a body I will destroy it. It's mine after all. It seems like that is the only decision I will ever have in this life.

Funny, we humans believe the only real freedom is to kill ourselves. Or we could kill others, is that pollution? Or is that another freedom of fact?

Saturday afternoon--Freedom's great myth. Nope, Wildhead didn't like what I wrote at all, and neither did the others. He was here within a minute of my writing that last paragraph. I guess there's quite a bit of discussion on it too. They asked me if I caused the attack on Clipper. I think I'll go to sleep until they make up their minds.

(Notes from the Research Team: It is agreed by all parties--other than Dr. Wolf--that Dr.

Biner's safety has fallen by the wayside at this point. The recent attack on Clipper was cited as proof. Dr. Wolf says that the Ginda can be autonomous. Or events could just be a warning sign of potential danger from the Gindas. As a result, it is beyond our scope at the present time to ascertain if the decisions made by Dr. Wolf were, in fact, sound. Regardless, references to the genetic research efforts of the project must be minimized; so that phase can proceed, regardless of Dr. Wolf's failures or successes. J.Pard/R.Merton. Date suppressed per requirement.)

Wednesday--Dr. Pard came by with good news. They're way ahead of schedule on my body. Only another week and they will be done. How could they do that in five days? Something's wrong. This isn't the right. Oh, I've been asleep for three weeks.

Dr. Pard, why did you put me to sleep for so long? I never agreed to that. Why are you ignoring me?

Wednesday afternoon--I have checked the last thing I inputted, perhaps it was the madness. Fact is I never agreed to nothin' in this-here Army. Plow would be proud of me saying it like that. I know that.

Maybe saying I wanted to see my parents was wrong. Screw you, Pard! It feels like there's something I've forgotten.

Wednesday midnight--Dr. Merton came in and asked me if I thought I needed to know about my parents because of the Gumbies.

So what?

Dr. Merton also said I have been asleep for two and a half weeks. He said it was necessary so they could finish the work of transferring me into my body.

I had wanted to damage my new body. Not anymore, I want to read with my eyes and write with my hands, when I have a body. Funny I didn't know there was a difference between a memory and the present.

Thursday afternoon--Lazlo says there isn't much difference between me and Clipper at this point. I have blood and organic nutrients and it has wires and electronics. My brain is biologically based. Clipper is electronically based. He says we are both entities that can be reduced to chemistry and physics.

I don't want to be reduced to chemistry and physics if that's what Clipper is based on. There must be something else to life. Where is my body? Dr. Pard says I am in one, and because it is working, nothing feels different.

I guess I have a choice. I can either stay attached to Clipper with wires coming out of my body or have a link in which part of my brain is inside Clipper and part of its communications system is inside me. I'll have a big bump on the top of my head.

Lovely choices, thank you, my fellow humans.

The systems inside me would be a communications link between the halves of my brain. Talk about a space between the ears!

I don't want Clipper attached to my body. I like the idea of me being inside Clipper. Maybe

I can listen to what it thinks and tell Clipper what to do and what to forget. I bet I can control Clipper.

You know something? Clipper doesn't believe in anything. I just need to convince it to believe in something that I want to believe in, anything. Oh, that's wrong. That's how our leaders work. What a bunch of dunderheads.

Friday morning--Lazlo says he needs to talk about death and what it means now that I have a body. He doesn't know that death means nothing to me. I keep coming back. He's the time-puppet not me.

Saturday--I want to know something; how could my parents have allowed Dr. Wolf and Clipper to do this to me? How could they have allowed someone to stick me in a glass jar and become an experiment? Once I'm whole, I will want to see them and ask them that. I promise not to hurt myself. I just want to see what kind of people would do this to their child. I want to know what kind of parent would do this to me. I just want to know why.

(Notes from the Research Team--At this point we finally have a stable platform. Thank God. L.Wolf. Date suppressed per requirement.)

Thursday--Now this is really something. Clipper came through for me. I woke up today lying on a bed. I was warm, but I was also cold.

My head hurt, and so did my arms. It felt like pins were being stuck into my feet. The nurse, her name is Winston, was mopping my face. She said I slept wrong. Such an odd name: Winston Doe. She is so beautiful. I never saw anyone so smart and capable. Definitely the one for me.

That's the one for me--oh damn. Laz, please put that in a secure file. Who the hell gave her direct duty with the Gindas? We humans really are a bunch of dirty bastards. For the first time I hate my job. Damn, now what?

Chapter 23

A soldier, streaked with blood and dirt dives across the screen. His torn khaki uniform reveals twin scars across his back. He rolls down a muddy embankment his weapon pulled tight to his chest. When he comes to a stop, he adjusts his helmet and looks around. Beside him, he spies a woman's leg and then three more pairs of legs. They sit around a table. He looks around a wall-papered living room with white chintz curtains. The women, playing bridge appear not to notice the man. The front door bursts open and another man, dressed in uniform begins firing. The soldier, always at the ready, unloads his weapon, the bullets forcing the assailant back out the door. The intruder finally lands on his back, dead upon Everyman's front lawn of suburban America.

Voice-over: "The enemy is never gone, so Sammich Ginda and his men must come back. They will remain vigilant. So should we. Make sure your satellite security uplink is in good order. Make sure the cameras in your neighborhood function. Watch and listen. The enemy is never far from your front door."

This public service message is brought to you by The ATWAS Network: Satellites, Security, Safety. We're here if, or when, you need us."

. . . .

He did care.

When Winston opens her eyes. The room shimmers. The glow covering the familiar walls and paintings of her bedroom bends the edges and curves the planes in random directions. As she tries to move, her right leg drags, and a pain shoots up her torso. Blood covers his hand. She turns in the bed. A warm puddle of blood has soaked the sheets.

What happened? That's not due until new week. Oh, tension.

The glow fades with the pain in her groin.

Staggering with nausea, she rises. Taking off her favorite white silk bathrobe, it is stained with blood, she pouts, soaking it in a sink full of cold water. After washing up, she changes into her deep red linen robe. A light breeze rolls over her; sunlight bathes the room. The smell of the sea fills her. She walks stiffly to an open window. Outside waits the jeep with a new driver leaning back in his seat and reading the newspaper. Winston tries not to wonder if Sergeant Reins is dead. Immediately, the vehicle sways along with the newspaper in the breeze. *The madness is back at me.*

She opens her eyes and scans the area in front of her house. Now the drive has broken branches upon it and deeply furrowed ruts--the tell-tale signs of heavy vehicles. The trees around her cabin look different, scared and chopped in places. She assumes a battle has taken place. Winston strips her robe off looking for wounds. There are none. Missing the obvious, she puts the robe back on and wonders at the apparent calm of the driver still reads his newspaper. She sees no additional support, security, or medical people. The young red haired driver takes no notice of her and continues reading--occasionally chuckling at some news.

Then, from behind an elder fir at the top of her drive, a man emerges; the driver remains oblivious. With three days growth on a gray and red beard, his longish hair flowing back like a lion's mane, he wears an opalescent glow. Russell Biner looks up at her and waves. A dull blue lab coat drapes over his thin body like a shroud. *That smile.* He points to his hand. She raises her right hand for him and sees a wedding ring there. He shakes his head no. His hands then intertwine in front of his chest as if in prayer. He mouths the words: "I am so sorry, but no one could have done better." He points to his right. "It is your path."

She rushes down the stairs and out the front door. The mid-day has become dawn. Signs of the jeep, heavy vehicles and, of course, Dr. Biner are gone. "Damn you. Where did you go?" She yells. "I know this is real."

She awakens at her desk and stands, with no problem or dizziness. Her white silk robe surrounds her, unstained.

Getting up, she looks out the window again and she sees a platoon of heavily armed soldiers and two armored personnel carriers. The forest is torn and broken. Blood soaks the driveway. She swoons.

Chapter 24

Thursday morning--You mean there's a right way and a wrong way to be in a body? I wonder what happens if you live backwards in your body?

Then I asked Hope if these Ginda-bodies came with a training manual? I watched her laugh. I'm sure that's what it was. Why is there so much fear in laughter?

When she stopped laughing, she told me there was no manual, but that she would help me get used to my body.

Winston also said it was going to be tough--especially waking up in the body of a twenty-five-year-old. She was right. I pissed all over myself a few minutes later. The nurse cleaned me up and explained about bladder control. Then Winston and Hope left for the day saying I should rest.

Winston looks like one of those pin-up girl posters that Sergeant Plow likes to collect. She has beautiful tanned skin. She also taught me how to talk into this computer so I can enter words into my diary. I guess I'll be starting a class soon on how to type. Winston said typing would give me more dexterity.

Everything seems so normal, but nothing glows. Maybe that changes later. I used to like watching that pinkish glow. Hope showed me a pinkish glow to the sky at sunset, and at dawn. It's not the same, it's kinda' washed out. How boring is that?

I expected to be frightened when I woke up in my body. I am glad Winston and Hope were there. I think they are friends. Another surprise: I thought my skin was supposed to be black. It's squishy white skin. I want hard, black skin, with muscles. I don't seem to have very strong muscles. Maybe Lazlo can change my skin color. I hate white people. I don't want to control everything.

Thursday afternoon--Winston sat beside me all morning and we talked. She pushed my wheelchair around the halls of the hospital and we talked some more. She is a Walker and a college student. People look at us strange.

Winston showed me the sea and some big rusty ferries from the roof of the hospital. It moves! I always knew trees moved like that and the ocean blew back and forth like the trees do, but I didn't know that big boats moved because the ocean moves. She said it was the wind that made the sea and the trees moved. She asked me if I thought the wind made the boats move. I said yes. I guess I had that one wrong. She said only sailboats move in the wind, not big steel boats like that. I don't think she understood, but she is so pretty I agreed with her anyway.

Then I met Doctor Russell Biner. He is Hope's brother. Winston likes him. He looks just as I thought he would, but he seems sadder than I remember--I think that's because of his beard. Winston says he looks like a sea captain. I think he likes her too. I hate him. I'm going to kill him now that I have a body. I'll say he tried to hurt me. I wonder if they will believe me? Oops, Clipper's gonna' rat me out.

Wednesday afternoon--I asked her to forgive me. It didn't work. Then I told her the answer is the removal of memory. She was still mad at me. So I asked if she thinks we need to really understand the ability to recycle? That got her attention. I said we must do that. We are running out of both time and space. I still hate Doctor Biner.

Friday afternoon--I have a new nurse. The nurse's name is Hope. I have a new body and now I have Hope. That's a stupid joke isn't it? Lazlo showed me something called a mirror. He took a fruit, a kiwi he called it and put it behind a wall. Then he tilted the mirror so I could see around the corner. He said he was trying to demonstrate the concept of reflection. He said I am a reflection of all humanity and that I can help other people look around corners. When I asked him if I could look at myself, he smiled and said yes. I wondered if I could make him laugh. He's cute.

I'm tall and thin, with straight black hair,

and thin angled eyes. My eyes are funny-looking, like two thick lines. Lazlo says I am Asian. My name is Sammich Ginda. One of my relatives was a great pilot.

My nose is small. Lazlo has a big nose.

Hope said I am handsome. That's for a guy. I wonder why she said that. I also have a big bump on the side of my head. I think I look ugly. Wait, how can I be a guy?

Saturday--I thought Winston was just being nice to me. Hope likes my flat eyes. Hope and my friend Doc Biner are close friends. They have known each other since childhood. I guess the Doc and I need to be in different places so we are safe. I guess I won't ever see him again. I hate the Gumbies.

My eyes are the same color green as the water in my toilet after I piss. Hope laughed when I told her that. When I told Lazlo the same thing, he just stared at me. People don't seem to laugh at the same things. They must not all be afraid of the same things. Hope says everything I see and do comes from other people. I told her I knew that. She said if I don't understand something, that I should ask. I don't want to understand. I just want to be.

Sometimes I look at myself looking at myself in two mirrors. That looks more like me. But nothing glows there either.

Lazlo has started talking about me writing by hand in my diary. I like that idea better than typing. Typing takes so long. I hope I don't have to do both. Besides, with handwriting the words are put on the paper by me, not by some little computer tied into Clipper.

Oops, Clipper doesn't understand. I don't think Hope likes that idea either. I think she should die.

(Commentary from Researchers: We believe an investigation should be undertaken immediately regarding these events. L.Wolf/R.Biner. Date suppressed per requirement.)

(1st Court of Inquiry commentary follows: We are at a loss to understand what has taken place here. We have no comment other than to suggest investigation into Dr. Wolf's actions. J.Pard. Date suppressed per requirement.)

Sunday—I think Lazlo has gone nuts. He keeps asking me about my nurse. Things like her hair color and so forth. I think he has slipped his cork.

Monday--It feels good to be independent and not some peripheral to a computer. My head is bandaged in back, but there are no tubes or wires coming out of it like yesterday.

Lazlo showed me where I used to live. I hadn't realized how small that glass bell-jar was. It seemed boundless. Now there's just a liquid in the jar where my brain was. The liquid is green and smelly with pipes and wires and tubes going here and there into machines. Wildhead called it my set of umbilical cords. You know what I really like about now? No wires. It really makes me feel like a person. Lazlo said my room was always dark. He asked me about the pink glow I used to see. I said it was everything. He laughed. I'm glad I didn't know what light was. Funny that I thought I did because of the soldier's memory. None of that was right. Nothing shimmers now. For some reason Lazlo thinks that's the answer to his problem. Shimmer or glow--no problem--he's a screwy guy.

I asked Lazlo why he showed me my previous "home." He said if I ever wanted to go back in the jar I could. I could hardly believe he had said that. I told him I was willing to do anything to stay out of the jar.

Tuesday--There's a tube in my arm. A guy named Dr. Merton said it was for something called a gene bath. I guess I have some kind of problem and they are checking my organs and things to make sure my guts don't start growing uncontrollably, or mutating. He said it happens a lot to people. He said one day people will get replacement organs for diseased organs for free.

Commentary from the Administrator: The fissure that had been building inside the research team reached its critical mass at this point, and from this point forward, we had two virtually independent teams working competitively on separate objectives. One team was headed by Lazlo Wolf, the other headed by Joshua Pard. Whether it was the war, or just the pressure of a research environment causing this breach, it remains unknown even to this day as to why the Ginda bodies do not have the same mutation rates as

others. Earlier notes from Dr. Merton remain questionable due to his exiting the project and possible ties to the new organ replacement enterprises. G.Smetana. Date suppressed per requirement.)

Wednesday--I think something is wrong. Hope keeps trying not to cry and Laz' gets quieter and quieter like he doesn't want to know me anymore. It's hard to walk now.

Thursday--I am scared of the new tubes in my head. Dr. Pard said they added the tubes instead of putting me back in the jar while they worked on my kidneys.

Then I got really scared, until he said it was under control. I hate that glass bog they had me in and I told him so. He said not to worry. That jar looked so small and smelled so bad! They say this white powder will stop me from hurting. Sometimes it makes me sneeze.

Wednesday--I guess I'm blind now. I can't see. There's not even a glow. Clipper has even more yea or nay about my remembering things. If Clipper doesn't want me to remember something, I won't. Wildhead says Clipper will keep me alive if I don't remember some days. Doc Pard and I had a long talk about that and we both agreed with Dr. Wolf. Sometimes it's best not to remember good times. My stomach hurts also.

Dr. Pard asked me how come I can't see the glow anymore. I just don't remember it anymore, I told him. Now I see the nature of his trick. They blinded me to test some theory. Can I have my eyes back now?

Wednesday night--Dr. Pard made a joke about Clipper being like everyone's mother. What she approves of is easy to remember. What she doesn't approve of is much tougher. I didn't laugh. Of course, Pard and I probably have different views of mothers. Isn't there another word at the end of mother?

Thursday—I feel much better, but I have those tubes back in my head. Winston said life is a great gift, under any circumstances. I told her she was full of it. She told me I was spoiled and left the room. I wonder why she is angry at me?

Thursday night--Oh, I see why she is mad. Doc Biner is still gone. No wonder Winston is pissed at me. I want her to be happy.

The door opened and I started to say I was sorry for what I had said--but it was only Wildhead. He came by to talk about eating the right foods and beginning to walk once I get a body. Lazlo and I had a long talk about how the human body works.

Friday--Learning to walk was easy and eating was even easier. Winston held me in her arms. She is my nurse again. Eating, I really like that. French fries and chocolate milk are my favorites. She showed me the printouts on my body chemistry, I didn't understand the least of it. That made her sad. I asked her why and she said she was looking for her friend, Dr. Biner. I think she thought my memories were from the Doc, or I was seeing the Doc. She is wrong about that.

I told her that I wanted more chocolate milk and french fries. I like ketchup too. She lectured me again on proper nutrition, like I care.

I sat in my bed and listened to my radio. They talked about ferry boats. I don't get that one. Ouch--hey, what's wrong, now?

Saturday--I asked Wildhead if Clipper hated me. He looked at me, then began to laugh. What makes people laugh? I tried to laugh with him, but I couldn't.

I asked Wildhead about laughter. He said laughter was a human reaction to something that was so sad humans reversed it and covered it up with a veneer that they perceived as pleasure. He said laughter was the great lie, but also a wonderful gift. I guess that means lies are funny and a gift. I asked him if I have that gift. He said he didn't know. Back in the jar I had no pain--so that's why I can't laugh?

Ouch that hurt.

Dr. Wolf said my pain is just memory. That means it is just like this place they all live. What do they call it? Earth? Earth is not us. And they call me dumb.

Chapter 25

A tan couple make love in the thundering surf as a single dolphin jumps merrily in a nearby lagoon.

Voice-Over: "What will your vacation look like? Is it Europe, to see the ruins of London, or Australia to see the coal pits? Maybe camping by the ice blue lakes of Antarctica or snorkeling in old New York? Or perhaps the Florida memorial water park, or the canals of our nation's capitol? The whole world awaits you--and it's time to start thinking about it."

"From Here to Eternity Travel is calling you. With a simple loan on your gene-bank account, we can get you in the queue for the trip of a lifetime. The doors of travel are opening again. Soon trains and airplanes will soon be rolling off the assembly lines, so make your plans now. Get your place secured. Happiness is back!"

. . . .

Winston blinks, then looks around her room to make sure everything remains as it once was. She begins to make notes figuring she should not rely on her memories. The first note says: "Russell Biner loved me." The second note says: "Hope also." *I forgot about Hope. Where is she?*

By the time she is done with the rest of her notes, it is early evening; the dusk's red light bathes the room; outside, the calm beauty of the woods. This light was the reason she built her home here. Getting up and standing at the window, she notes the soldiers have gone, and the drive in front of her home is empty. The ruts remain. She appreciates the sense of privacy, but now thinks it a myth.

How many generations of Gindas could I be, a hundred? Two hundred? Russell tricked me with his love.

She looks out the window and shivers. *So many dead.*

Crossing the hardwood floor onto the braided rug of the dining area, Winston enters the kitchen and pulls out a loaf of bread from a lower cabinet. She cuts it into slices. Her eyes fixed on the bread, but her gaze remains entirely inside herself. She doesn't feel the knife cut into her thumb. She does sense the bloody counter top. Looking down, she grabs a kitchen towel to wrap her right hand.

A cycle? I cut my hand, but the rest of me isn't bloody. Holy Christmas. Is that what they mean? The madness is synced space and time? The madness is a functioning set of essences. And we cannot be there? She drops the knife, and begins to make more notes:

- When I cycle, cycle to what?
- Something happens. When we are congruent.
- A cut thumb instead of a, oh lord, a rape.
- We need to live out of phase.

How can we ever adjust to that? We'd be doomed. Damn you, Roo. I do belong here. I have focus--I'll take the challenge--but so what? But the facts say we end as a species. We've blown it. So we change the something. But what?

She puts the pencil down. Considering herself inadequate, even though she knows there are no events that are not a part of her, Winston feels like giving up. *I am part of the environment, not its master. So that's what extinction is? A desire to give up. That means I am trying to understand nothing. Or am I trying to understand less than nothing?* In many ways, this need for clarity makes her perfect for the path of scholar and Ginda; none of which would not have been a surprise to her mother.

Sitting at the oak table, looking to the dusk's pink-painted woods outside her home, she wonders why she will not allow herself to see the rest of what she knows. Winston rubs butter on the bread with her index finger her eyes drifting over the kitchen towel covering her wound.

The butter doesn't just flow on the bread. It requires me to get it there. So…Enlightenment can act as a functional tool…For what? For cycling. That's the real point of recycling. God, we were so stupid. But recycling us? Here I am right where I always wanted to be. But I could kill them for making me a fool--for lying to me--oh that was bad. Am I independent? That was the second phase of Clipper interrupt, or did I correct my view? Am I really autonomous? This doubt could drive a person batty. But I see why it was done this way. It's how I would have done it. I probably did do it. Find your top researcher and put them into the drift with Clipper protecting them. Then let the Ginda find the way. Maybe I did do this? I've got to stop trying to solve me. I'll go crazy. Because there is no here. Where the hell am I? If there is no there, then there is no where. Damn this mess.

Winston lifts the receiver. *I can work the phone. Gindas are forbidden initiate calls so I am independent.* She enters a series of access codes to make sure the right project will be billed. She laughs at her fastidiousness.

"General Fong?"

"Dr. Doe."

"I am beginning to hate the word: Dedicated."

"I understand that emotion pretty well. I have encountered it often."

"Where is Russell?"

"Russell is alive--if you can call it that--but I can't find him for you. You must work with the Ginda--Moss--on that."

"Not good enough. I demand a response. Why?"

"Dr. Doe, hang on." No answers could have stunned her more. *His denial of acquiescence should mean he has clear sight on the path ahead. It would have to mean that from Benson Fong. How can that be?* She waits listening to the hum of the scramblers keeping their conversation private.

A second click. "Winston? It's Gregor Smetana I am on the line as well. General Fong and I have spoken and I am willing to help you locate Dr. Biner."

"Where is he?"

"In a jar."

She cannot breathe for a moment. "Oh Gaia. This whole time?"

"Yes."

"With Clipper keeping him sane I bet. Why didn't you tell me?"

"You already know the answer to that."

"Because he has Clipper wiping his memories." She moans to herself. It is the event she has feared most. "I want to see him immediately."

"I am not playing games with you when I say this: All I can do is point you in the right direction. That direction is Moss Eckman."

Winston looks around the kitchen. "Where is Moss?" She says.

"In bed with a waitress from the Womb," says General Smetana.

"General, we need a safe zone for alignment of the paths--right?"

"We concur," says General Smetana. His voice holds a note of wonder and fear she has not heard before. "Winston, what is it like?"

"General, nothing seems to have changed. But how can I be growing instead of dying? Moss is a retrograde to our past. Something we resent. I am outcast from the present." She pauses at her rhyme. "And we are failing."

"We are in a murky dawn here, Dr. Doe." General Smetana replies.

"My title says I should be making all the decisions now. But the notion that I am responsible for any part what happens next, seems little more than a cruel joke. Madam Director, regarding your request, you will meet us at the Ginda Orphanage?

"Russell is there?"

"Dr. Doe, please--I told you Moss is the key." Says General Smetana.

"Why?" She asks even though she knows he will not answer. They cannot interfere with her acquisition of knowledge. *They are… the past of it.* "All right. Are we are still seeing an increase in the madness?"

"Dr. Doe, that is not your doing, nor is it your concern. You are our lead researcher," interjects General Fong. "You must do what you think is right to further your research, and leave the battles to soldiers."

"But what if my clarity is leading to death among our citizens--"

Fong cuts her off. "Dr. Doe, that is not your concern. It is the path through this mess that matters."

"General Fong, you are interfering with my questions."

"Complain to the management," he replies.

Both Winston and the other General are stunned--then they laugh. "Well I guess he told you," says Gregor Smetana.

"Sorry Benson," Winston says quietly. *He knows something. He's sentient. How can that be?*

"Your driver will see you get to the orphanage. And Winston," Benson Fong pauses. "All we know--you will know."

"Which makes you one of the wisest men I know, General," she says. "Did you lie to me about me being first generation?"

"No. I did not lie, Dr. Doe."

A part of her sees both humor and grace. She disconnects and begins to dress for her trip.

No, let them wait. I want more information.

CHAPTER 26

Saturday afternoon--I guess Lazlo's not sexually attracted to Clipper. I know he thinks about Clipper a lot. It also seems my body is doing some thinking. I didn't know bodies could think. I thought just computers and brains could think. I guess that means there is more thinking going on out there and in here, than I know.

We had another history lesson. It was boring. I remembered how it felt listening to Lazlo talk. It's weird to be stared at by him. He looks at everyone as if they were a puzzle. I don't like that about some men.

One interesting thing in the history lesson was about the Genians. The lesson said Genians live on another planet with their Lonocs. Then the light bulb came on: I noticed Lonoc is colon spelled backwards. Is someone calling us humans a bunch of ass holes? Is that why there were Lonocs? No it's something else: a joke?

Saturday evening--Who ever heard of anything so ridiculous? Aliens and their pet brain-suckers? Ooh, please. I bet people believed that so they wouldn't have to face the facts of their life. Oops, Lazlo says maybe to get people to believe something you have to make them laugh at it first. I am beginning to believe lies really are funny. Maybe humor isn't just pain, but a form of lies? Lazlo said the Genians were inveterate liars, but they also have difficulty laughing. He said they understand lies so well they can't laugh. I asked him if he thought the Gumbies, the beings who were attacking us, were really Genians. He said no, he didn't think so, but that he wasn't sure. Lazlo then asked me why I thought Lonocs sucking peoples' brains dry was funny.

Oh come on. That is so ridiculous it's funny--turning a skull into an ass hole. But I like the concept.

I also said I thought the Genians might have locked us up with the Gumbies and that's why we're fighting. That's when he reminded me I'm the only one who might stop the Gumbies and to do that I had to see clearly. He didn't get my joke. But then he said: After I succeed in understanding all this, he would cut most or all of my links to Clipper. He said at that point I would own Clipper and use Clipper the right way, as a tool. He knows I want that very badly. He also said I won't have to be here anymore and I can leave. I know he is lying about that. Wait, how can both be true?

Ain't that the truth? Talk about humor in lies. I wonder if he thinks I bought any of that crap he was selling.

But--there's nobody here who'll talk to me except for Lazlo so what the heck? I think it's that big bump that sticks out of my head. I look like some kind of freak.

Maybe I don't need memory? But I see things and that is memory. Oh, I see. I just use everyone else's memory but I don't keep it.

So if memory is retained in sight and that sight is considered the present, then why couldn't I find the right kind of sight equation and travel along it? Is that our prison? What wouldn't I sacrifice for getting out of this? Now that I deal in death for knowledge, who am I? Please forgive me.

(Commentary from the Administrator: The insight by Dr. Biner has opened a new door in our research. No charges will be considered for any of the researchers. G.Smetana. Date suppressed per requirement.)

Sunday morning--Lazlo and I talked about the attacks on humanity coming from inside their being and how it would be difficult to find how the Gumbies are attacking. That's my job, I guess, to find the facts. Lazlo calls it the battlefield. Now there is something that has never changed for humanity, the battlefield. Not too smart of us--to foster battles but not peace. And they call me stupid!

I don't think I'll ever laugh or dream again. How did the truth ever become a battlefield? Oh, I guess that's the whole problem. We each tried to prove our individual truth rather than accept the many truths. So we fed fear. Not too smart of us.

Monday afternoon--Today I saw the hills that fall to a beach and I tasted the ocean. It's so salty, yuk.

Lazlo took me for a walk and my feet hurt. Later I sat and watched the sun drift steadily west behind the clouds. The clouds have a multicolored rainbow type thing, a kind of halo that circles the sun, with occasional lighter patches of blue-green between them. Dr. Wolf says the colors are a gift from out parents--from when they tried to fight global warming. I guess they filled the air with little particles to reflect the sunshine. Now the clouds glow in too many colors. Too bad they did exactly the wrong thing.

Lazlo has a strange sad laugh. He was telling me they knew they had screwed it up because of something called vitamin D but didn't fix it.

The clouds came and went ten times today. Once it was so cold, I shivered. I didn't like being cold, but when the sun came out between the clouds it was really like a new day. I hope Lazlo likes my description of clouds. I'm trying to learn to write better. It's a sign of intelligence—Winston once told me that. I asked Dr. Biner if he knew where she was. He said he didn't know.

On the ride back, Lazlo said I'd be asleep for a few days because they needed to fix my feet. I made him promise not to put me back in the bog. He promised he wouldn't. What if Lazlo is lying?

I see, some lies are not funny.

Friday--No bog! I'm in my body, but it hurts like hell. I guess I'll be resting a while more. If I forget the bad days will I forget the good days too? I guess I'd have to or I'd go nuts.

Saturday--This beautiful nurse came in. She told me her name is Winston. She laughed with me. I think, for a while I had forgotten about her. I am sexually attracted to her.

I apologized about forgetting her. She laughed again. It wasn't a long sad laugh like Lazlo's, just a short choppy one. I think she was lying when she said I was okay. So that means sometimes lie tell the truth because I understood what she meant to tell me.

I now have complete freedom to go anyplace I want in the hospital. I didn't know I couldn't go anyplace I wanted to before. Nobody said anything to me about that. The truth is fluid, like water. But lies are part of the truth? But lies are not the truth. How can the "not" of something be the same as the something? Is that what they mean by the word knot?

It feels like I am always swimming in maybes, truth, and lies, back and forth, but the water keeps rising. But it doesn't matter because I can swim in it thanks to Clipper. I think my arms are lies. I think we all immersed in some weird mind-water and now we are drowning in it, or maybe they are letting all this mind water flow into me so I can fight the Gumbies. I don't want to be the only one left. On the other hand, I certainly don't want to be the last to die.

When the oceans began to rise, why didn't they

see what it meant? I bet that if they'd stopped it, I bet we'd still have our feet on solid earth. I wonder how our ancestors could have thought the oceans of the planet meant so little. The Jazz War began a few years after the worst flooding so I guess our stupidity only protects us so far. Lazlo calls it inertia. Whatever!

Sunday--Now I am in a new hospital, on a small peninsula. They say it's an island, but it isn't really and island. There's just a slough separating us from the mainland. The bridge over the slough is manned by Greenies. Their barracks are in an old casino. There's lots of open space in front. Dr. Wolf says they parked cars there once, but I don't believe him.

Dr. Merton came back. He asked me if I am Russell. I said no. I don't even know what a Russell is. Then he asked me if my insides are hurting. I think he cares more about my insides then me. I said no. Then he asked me if minded being an organ donor. I said no again. Then he asked if I hated the idea of being the last to die. I said more than anything.

He says I am a good Greenie soldier. I like that term Greenie better than soldier. That's how he refers to me: "Soldier". Greenie means I grow things, rather than kill things. It's good to grow things. Still, when someone calls me a Greenie, I'm supposed to hit him. Sergeant Plow told us that. So that's why I hit him, again, I think.

Monday Morning--Sergeant Plow once told that the recruits should punch people out if they felt they needed to. I guess we Gindas are special and we can do what we want. I should have punched Merton out rather than just hitting him a couple of times? Next time I will hit him four times.

Tuesday--I don't know what they did, but I really like sleeping now. Before it was painful, now things happen that are weird and difficult to understand. I just seem to flow here and do that--walking one second--sitting another. I can hardly remember what I did, but Lazlo says I am dreaming. Lazlo asked me if I dreamed I was a dog. I said no and he scowled. He's so strange. He said dreams are about the unconsciousness, and that someplace in the unconscious is a doorway.

I said I thought dreams meant the waters of mind are flowing over us instead of swimming in them.

Lazlo laughed and asked me if I thought dogs were lazy. I said I never knew one but all the vids I saw showed them napping all time.

Wednesday--My favorite dream is flying. I feel like I have so much control, especially when I lift off the ground and soar over treetops. Sometimes it's scary, especially when I fall, but since I know they are dreams, it isn't so bad. I like going back to sleep. I could stay there forever.

I was talking to a woman, I forgot who. She said she thought maybe dreams are forever. That would make "now" a much smaller scale event. But that doesn't make sense, when I sleep it seems like time goes by so quickly. When I am awake time goes by slowly. Some dumb dinosaur screwed up time for us. I wonder who?

I bet from forever you could affect now, just

because one is so much bigger than the other. But then you'd have to figure out how to get to forever.

Hmmm, I get confused. Which is bigger, now or forever?

Thursday--I had a fun dream about Winston. When I woke up I had wet my sheets, but it felt great. Lazlo came in and we went for a walk. We had a talk about sex. Lazlo said I am sexually attracted to Winston.

Clipper--and it has never been so true--you fucking snitch, you're just jealous you can't have orgasm. I hate you.

I asked Lazlo if I should stop having orgasms and he asked why. He said it was a form of making love,in this case with myself. I keep hearing the Doc say monads are gonads.

Who cares?

Thursday night--Wildhead came in right after some cameras were installed in my room. Then he sat down in that funny way he has of letting his left knee droop over his right knee and letting his foot hang loosely to the floor, almost touching it. He crossed his hands in front of his knees and leaned back. He has the beginnings of a mustache to match his beard. It looks like dirt over his lip. When he talked, the mustache moved up and down in different directions from his bobbing head. He seems so disconnected to me. He always bobs his head when he thinks. He looks so goofy.

Before I could ask about the cameras, Dr. Merton came in carrying a portable computer display screen. He said we wanted to talk about me, and how I feel about my memories and organs being tied into a computer and accessible by the research staff. Lazlo said nothing.

Merton described my brain as having twin lobes. He said half of my brain sits in my head with a transmitting device that sends my memories to the other half of my brain inside Clipper. Two satellites orbit overhead and keep tabs on us. Dr. Merton described them as my guiding stars.

Dr. Merton needs a long session with a Lonoc. Why do I think there were once fifty million Lonocs in the world but now they're gone? I wish there were such things. I don't think Merton cares about people. We're all here for him to suck us dry.

Maybe he is a Lonoc? Dr. Wolf asked me if I thought Lonocs were once human. I said no, because there is no way Dr. Merton is human. That was a joke, Doc. We are more than we see. Or we were.

Dr. Merton then told me something I didn't know. Clipper can sometimes figure out what I'm seeing and actually recreate a picture by reconstructing what the satellites sense and what it understands of my memories. I told Dr. Wolf I think Merton is sexually attracted to the idea of spying on people.

Merton said the direct diary I was using when I was in the bog was very helpful in allowing Clipper to understand what I'm doing. He wants me to go back to using the direct input to Clipper. I think he wants me back in the bog. I think it has something to do with my organs.

The diary helps Clipper figure out what I'm thinking. There is no way I will go back to doing that.

When I write something down on paper can Clipper can still tell exactly what I am doing? Dr. Merton said no and looked at Lazlo. He sighed. That's when I figured it out. Merton wants me to stop practicing my handwriting because it limits Clipper. I tossed a chair at Dr. Merton.

Lazlo just sat there. He said he understood that I wanted some privacy from Clipper, but that they had a problem. It seems my organs work all the time now but the ones they make for other people do not.

And that's supposed to bother me? They can't have my guts. Merton has a black eye. I laughed.

Friday—She's here!!!! Winston just came in with something called a telephone. People use it to talk to each other when they are far away from each other. I am going to need it to talk to some researchers. Why not wait until they're closer? I asked.

She said that sometimes telephones are the right way to communicate. She also said Dr. Merton is a consultant to a big company. One that helps people get healthy. I asked if she could find me a Lonoc for him.

She said no and that she didn't understand the joke. I am getting used to that. There's no part of her that's Lonoc, unlike Merton and Pard.

Friday--I just told Dr. Wolf that I didn't like having a strange researcher in some distant place knowing what I was thinking and feeling. He said that was right, I shouldn't. He also said he was sorry it had to be that way, because the Jazz War has gotten worse and everyone has to make sacrifices. He also said that as I learn things, it gets more difficult for others because we are blazing a new trail. He asked me how I felt about that and I said I didn't care. I guess I've got a little Lonoc in me too. I suck because you consume. Hey, I am a philosopher!

Friday afternoon--Lazlo said something that should have bothered me, but it didn't--I guess. My task now is to trap the Gumbies. When the Gumbies gain access to my mind to attack it, we're going to record everything they do through Clipper. It seems the Gumbies use "Forever Ships" to control humanity's "Now Ships". I guess there is a big naval battle going on and they need my help.

It sounds like a lot of bull-ship to me. That was also a joke.

Dr. Wolf said I have to be completely available to Clipper. I thought he was going to tell me I couldn't practice my handwriting, but he didn't. He added that whatever damage the Gumbies do to me, it could be eliminated by Clipper. He said I needed Clipper to keep my memory clear. That way I could fight on and on. He said I was opening a door for others. I told him I don't hate Clipper for protecting me.

(Note from the Researchers: This statement cannot be underestimated and we think we should assume the animosity between the Ginda and Clipper was overrated by Dr. Wolf. R.Merton/J.Pard. Date suppressed per requirement.)

Saturday morning--I tore the phone from the wall. I can't remember what it said that bothered me. I'm getting violent like everyone else. They are letting the Gumbies in makes me violent. I see. I wonder which is stronger, our "Now Ships" or their "Forever Ships"?

Clipper, do me a favor will you. Awareness seems dangerous and I don't want to hurt her. Please make sure Winston stays away any time I am not all right.

Saturday--Winston came by and asked if I wanted to talk to Dr. Merton. I don't see why I wouldn't want to talk to him.

She and I then talked about dogs. Someone slipped a picture of a dog under my door last night. I like the way they looked, especially the German Shepherd--they're so noble. Winston said dogs were loyal creatures that had protected humans while they slept. I thought she meant by barking and biting anyone who came to harm their humans, but I was wrong. Dogs used to guard dreams. That's amazing to me. I wonder, what was it like when the dogs would guard our dreams? I guess some dreams were better than others.

It's too bad that dogs are an extinct species. A disease caused by a genetic mistake killed all the dogs. I guess they were trying to clone someone's pet. Dr. Merton said their extinction was a key point in the Jazz War. I hope they shot the dope who tried to rebirth a pet. How stupid of us to have killed off a species before we really understood what its function had been in our life-web. We screwed it up in so many ways it's hard to feel sorry for us. We suck.

Lazlo just called me and said dogs hadn't

looked smart enough to be able to guard something as complex as human dreams. He said snap decisions on the worth of other beings was another human mistake. Boy, we really blew it. It had to happen. That's so obvious now. We are part of a web. I bet we degraded that term as well. I wonder how?

Saturday afternoon--I asked Lazlo how the dogs protected us. He said they don't know, but her thinks that was why I couldn't dream before. Funny. We just blunder about, don't we?

Pard thinks I might fulfill the same task as the dogs. Merton is the guy responsible for the project trying to get me to play Fido. That figures. He probably figured he could charge people money to dream safely.

Funny, Dr. Wolf was very quiet about all that.

We talked more about dogs, for a long time. Lazlo thought they kept the environment inside our skulls healthy. I asked if dogs used to keep other beings from gaining access into us—you know guard dogs. Lazlo said they used to believe that when a human went to sleep, the dogs remained close to the dream, just to be close. I guess they were pretty dumb animals.

Now he thinks that somehow dogs had been part of our connection to space, part of our previous essence—whatever the hell that is. I asked what an essence was.

Dr. Wolf said it was something like a monad. So what the hell is a monad? I don't care. I really don't.

I asked Dr. Wolf why humans didn't think about all this before the dogs had died off? He said people used to believe there was something mystical about prediction because the scientists were so bad at it. He said the metaphysical—as it was called—was not considered seriously enough before, or during, the global warming years. I guess they tried to prove that any system for prediction was unreliable because science and religion were no good at it.

But how else can we learn? That thing we call the future, that's a Forever ship. We are losing the Forever ship. I then said we needed to drain the ocean. He said I was smart.

(Commentary from the Research Team: Dr. Wolf's lack of concern for the Gindas remains troubling. In addition, his continued interference with private interests to revitalize the economy may limit our recovery from both the Jazz War and Global Warming. The inclusion of the gene-banking community as well as the satellite community on the uses of the Gindas will have far reaching effects on our economy and that should be our first priority. We welcome the fresh viewpoints from our corporate partners. J.Pard/R.Merton. Date suppressed per requirement.)

Saturday night--I guess there's been a problem—part of my diary is gone. I asked if it was an attack—-Dr. Pard said perhaps. Then he asked me to talk to Dr. Merton about it.

Dr. Merton is pretty certain that the extinction of dogs is how the Gumbies are able to attack us when no other beings ever did before.

I asked him if humans attack human dreams now also. Dr. Pard didn't answer, he just smiled.

That means I am right. I'm sure of it.

I asked him how Dr. Wolf figured it all out, but he wouldn't tell me. He also didn't like that question. I guess it's a secret. I wonder why it's a secret. I said I think it's because they all screwed up.

Where is Dr. Wolf? That question really pissed-off Dr. Pard. I swear he was so mad I think he could have killed me. What's projection?

Saturday midnight--Dr. Wolf says Clipper can now keep all my dreams happy and pleasant and that he hoped I'd never have a bad dream again. I think most people have terrible dreams. I'm sure Lazlo does. I know his daughter does. Nightmares scare Dr. Wolf. Sometimes I think everything he does, he does for her.

Lazlo then said no one can dream now without having terrible dreams. How awful. Perhaps that's part of what drove them mad. It was our own fault. We exterminated the wrong species and zingo—we all get crummy dreams.

That's the truth of all this isn't it? We screwed ourselves. We had a warning and we ignored it. My diary is just our terror coming to the surface so they can try to fix things. Clipper edits me as I find a way through this mess. I think the dogs had been just the start of it. I guess they finally did make me Fido.

Lazlo just said he was proud of me--and that our talks had really helped him. I guess my lack of privacy balances out if I can help people. The benefit of knowing I'll always have pleasant dreams is nice.

Dr. Merton said I might not have that benefit if he hadn't arranged to use my organs for tests.

Otherwise, he said, I am just some dog to these people, sniffing a path through a mine field. Every time I get blown up, Clipper shows up and sticks my memories into some new dummy.

Dr. Merton takes my dead-body organs afterwards and it helps him, and his friends to do research. That makes me every soldier who ever died. We're coming back to haunt these bastards. They didn't respect us enough. If they had, then they would have not had wars as a way to make money.

Sunday--Lazlo said there was an attack. Two guards are with him. I don't remember him having guards with him when he came in to talk to me before today. The guards don't like me. They do like Dr. Wolf.

Dr. Merton was with him. He looked pretty banged up. I think someone shot him in the leg. What's that sound? Is that what war sounds like?

Monday--My eyes are leaking water. It will not stop. Are they from the waters of mind?

Tuesday--Dr. Wolf said I was crying and that he did not think tears are the waters of mind. He thinks poets would believe it so he is glad he is not a poet. Anyway, he said it's normal to be sad sometimes.

I guess Dr. Merton is now in trouble for being a Lonoc. Dr. Wolf thanked me. If I was really a smart Sammich Ginda I would have known early on that Pard and Merton are out for themselves. I hope they make the next version of me smarter. No, if they read this, they will make me dumber. I am sure of that.

CHAPTER 27

Monday--It will take me a long time to explain what Dr. Pard has written down about my parents. Anyway, this is what Dr. Pard told me: He first met my parents, Mr. and Ms. Ginda, six months after approval of their child to act as both the remote sensor and an information transducer for entering the battlefield.

The U.N.'s Blue Report, which outlined the likely dark ages the planet will enter in the next ten years, if the war continues along its present course, had just been published. Some of the conclusions he mentioned were:

...Half the population of the world is starving. Another 35% increase in starvation is expected in the next five years.

...Entire countries are without any kind of

generated power and that likely continue for the foreseeable future.

...Lawlessness rules sections of the globe.

...Time is working against humanity.

...Corporate influence will fade to zero in five years.

Dr. Pard says this is my parent's story: Hiroshi and Sandra Ginda met when they were twenty-five. Both were working in the legal department of company that cloned pets for rich patrons. Hiroshi Ginda was a graduate of Harvard with an MBA. Sandra Wallace was a graduate of Stanford Law School. They fell in love the second day on the job and moved in together a month later. They married the next month. On their honeymoon, they trekked through Nepal to see the last of the glaciers.

Both of them were used to privileges. They owned three bicycles and a sail boat--which predisposed them to believing in freedom. Their only child, Sammich, was born less than a year after they married. The child was pronounced body-dead a year later.

The accident which killed the baby was investigated after allegations from neighbors that Mr. and Ms. Ginda might have been under attack in the Jazz War.

Everything changes around here. Something you think is real, isn't. I don't think anything is real. We're dinosaurs lost in space.

Anyway, he says it took less than an hour to convince the Gindas their child's brain could help humanity. Thanks guys.

This next part really fries me. I copied it exactly: "After agreeing happily to deliver their child into my care, they arrived with the body of their young child wrapped in both an American flag. The mom considered herself a patriot. They seemed oblivious to the possible pain the child might encounter. I repeated over and over the child would become hooked into a computer and trained to fight. They said they didn't mind because a relative of theirs was a renowned warrior in World War Two."

I like that part. Those quote things are weird.

I guess they signed the papers and left. They had no further contact with them.

Anyway, no wonder Lazlo and the boys were concerned about me finding out about my parents. How could they have done something like this to me? Had I done something to them to make them angry? I hope so because I am one pissed-off Jackhammer. Thank you Dr. Pard.

Tuesday--Lazlo wasn't upset that I had torn the room apart. It's my space anyway. Ah, that's a joke, you-all. Oh, I also hit him. Funny, there are hardly any bruises now. I think that if Dr. Merton hadn't told me that Dr. Wolf was the one who proposed the plan to hook me into a computer, I might not have hit him.

Dr. Merton said I might very well have remained dead without Dr. Wolf. Is this better than death?

I have a joke: Am I better dead than read?

Wednesday--I have never seen Dr. Wolf so happy. He loved my joke. He cannot believe I am so funny. What's so funny about being read?

Thursday--I guess my dreams last night were none too pleasant. Painlessness, no doubt courtesy of Clipper, but piss on that. All I remember is sailing someplace, then diving into the bottom of the ocean and seeing the dinosaurs laughing at me. The sea bottom under them was disappearing because Lonocs were sucking out black blood. I wonder why?

(1st Court of Inquiry--The Case of Dr. W. Doe. We find that Dr. Doe's insistence on injection into the role of Ginda to be genuine and without emotional coercion. J.Pard/L. Wolf. Date suppressed per requirement.)

(Commentary from the Administrator: We shall consider Dr. Doe's application along with the other applicants. No preference shall be given due to a previous internship. We will, however, take the internship into account and give its results an appropriate weight in our considerations. G.Smetana/B. Fong. Date suppressed per requirement.)

(Commentary from the Administrator: It has been reported by Biner and Wolf that there is conjecture from the intern, Winston Doe. It involves the comment on dinosaurs. She believes it deserves consideration. She mentions that in human experience, time flows away from us--from future, to present, to past--but never towards us, i.e., that we can not capture it. But space, until the tipping point, was stable. Her hypothesis is that space now moves away from us as well--as a result of the tipping point. This means that inertial forces are at work and that at some point, humanity's disconnect from the planet will become whole, and terminal. We cannot

comment on the worth of this hypothesis. Date suppressed per requirement.)

(1st Court of Inquiry--The Case of Winston Doe--Notes on Ethics: We cannot comment on the conditions of the time of her insight or its impact on decisions. At this point, after the war, most analysts' reports indicate an increasing downward spiral for our society with concurrence from the corporate board of advisors. As to whether Wolf and Biner are responsible for the success of the project, or the late-comers, Doctors Merton and Pard, we cannot comment. Date suppressed per requirement.)

CHAPTER 28

Thursday--Winston is worried about me because I haven't eaten the last two days. She said everyone in the project is worried about me. I said they were really worried about their future, not me. She said Lazlo and Dr. Biner care about me.

I don't care if Winston is lying or not, but I still plan to hang myself with that power cord from the radio.

Sunday--My radio is gone. Dr. Merton just came in. He wants me talk about my parents. I ran at him and almost bit his ear off. Then I hit him. Where is Winston? He doesn't care about me! Hitting him is the best I have felt in quite a while.

Thursday--They're letting me out of my room for ten minutes, first time in four days. Hey fella's, you know I could run into the wall and bash my brains, excuse me, brain--gotta' make it singular. Intelligence means writing well. Maybe I should eviscerate Merton before hand.

No response, too bad, that could have been fun. Oops, there goes the door lock. No walk today. Well, score one for Sammich Ginda.

Sunday--My walk was delayed until today. I kept looking for someone who might like me but there was no one there--just guards and researchers. They don't care a bit about me.

When I got back from my walk, there was a newspaper on the guard's chair outside my room. I swiped it. There have been some terrible things happening this last week. A piece of sculpture in Florence, Italy, was blown up. It was called David. Once a piece of stone, it was transformed into a likeness of a human by a sculptor named Michelangelo. I saw a picture of him. I guess Michelangelo used to say that he could see the statues inside the hunks of dead marble and that he could liberate them. In some way, he's like Clipper, removing extra junk from me so I can do my work. In the David's case--rock, in my case, faulty memories.

I miss Winston. Pass that on to her, okay?

Saturday--Wildhead just left. I guess they're bringing in some soldiers to work with me now that Dr. Wolf is back in the project. I'm supposed to train them. Train them for what? I don't know anything. Of course, I might know something, but old Clipper would have wiped it from my memory.

I need to ask Lazlo about that. They want me to let them read my diary. I'll ask Winston if that is okay.

I don't like strangers going through my diary. I kept some information out. How do you like that, Clipper, old buddy? I thought of some things and you didn't get a piece of them. Up yours!

What the hell am I going to teach these soldiers? There's a red sky tonight--sailor's delight--shoo-fly don't bother me! Maybe I can train them to see what isn't memory. I think they call that the past, but they are wrong, that's the future. Oh wait I think they know that. Or do they?

Sunday--I played tennis with Hope. I'm pretty darn good at it. We had lunch by the water. She talked about the ocean and how some day I might cross it. I think the ocean is cool. Sometimes Lazlo surprises me with nice things. Where has Winston gone?

Monday-I met the first group of soldiers. There are five men and one woman. The woman looks a lot brawnier than Winston. Funny, I haven't seen Hope around much today.

Over lunch, they kept asking me questions I couldn't answer. Questions like, what is it like to fight the Gumbies? How many have I killed? How long do I think the war will last? Have I seen the latest video?

Finally, a guy named Gus started talking baseball. We spent the rest of the lunch talking about it. Gus seems like a good guy. He reminds me of someone else, but I can't remember who. I think the red-headed thing has a lot to do with it. Gus is far and away the oldest of them. He must be close to thirty.

Then they were led off to get processed--and do some exercise. I would have gone except my ankle is still messed up. So how come I was able to play tennis so well? When did I mess up my ankle? I'll go ask Hope.

Wednesday--The war is getting closer to me. That's why the soldiers are here. I dreamed the war, at least that's what Dr. Merton said, but he's an idiot.

Last night I dreamed I was stuck in a kettle of slowly heating water. Drunken madmen were dancing around me. I had the same dream over and over, all last night. I wonder why Clipper didn't do something about that dream? It scares me to think the Gumbies might have slipped one past Clipper. I bet Merton is their weapon.

I get to meet with the soldiers in an hour. Funny that everything changed now that these soldiers are here. I guess it's time to earn my keep.

Wednesday night--This time they asked me about Clipper and what it was like having half my brain inside my head and the other half inside a computer. By the end, the soldiers were saying that having a computer monitor my memories was brutal.

Lazlo just came in and asked them to talk about their backgrounds. He suggested I take notes. I had to hand-write the notes since my computer was not in the barracks. I refuse to keep asking about Winston. I am going to stop asking about her. Lazlo said they were keeping her safe. The soldiers were here instead. Dr. Biner fixed that--and so now and we were getting down to work--now that the Gumbies chief weapon is gone. Lazlo had a mischievous glint in his eyes when he told me to write that. He's an odd duck.

My notes:

The soldiers' names are Polken, Benny, Gus, Steven--Pisser for short--and Rico. Pisser and Rico are brothers. Kristen is the sixth soldier, and the only female of the group. I was struck by a similarity among them all. There is something empty about them. I bet their memory is messed up like mine.

Polken Frew, is a tall handsome city boy from California--a place called Watsonville. His dad was a sheriff. Polken said his dad got shot saving his uncle from the Greenies. So what's he doing here? Crazy world, I guess.

Polken's a surfer! I like that. But when he talks to you he's always looking around the room. I don't think the rest of them like that. They seem to ignore him like he isn't there. He ignores them right back.

Kristen Miplo is a blond-haired college girl from Vermont. She was camping with her family outside of Boston, near the old turnpike, when it happened to her. Her family woke to the sound of people tramping through the woods. Her father investigated. When he didn't come back, her mother went looking for him. Her mom came back with a bunch of people dressed in pink smocks burning physics and chemistry books. She said they chanted, "Down with the science. Down with humankind. Down with the Earth!" Kristen also said they looked like they were on bad drugs. She said they danced around and cut their arms open with knives allowing their blood to drop on the fire.

Then a thunderstorm came and they ran away. Kristen never saw her family again. She joined the Army afterwards. Man, she is one angry soldier.

Pisser Ketch and his brother Rico are from California. I guess their parents were hill folk, Walkers, living in the foothills of Northern California. One day the parents didn't return from town. When the brothers went into town they found out their parents had died.

The brothers hiked out of the hills and wandered around until a smart recruiting Sergeant from the U.N. found them sitting near his home and signed them up. Those two are so stiff, it's almost comical. Whenever they're outside doing their morning exercises, you wonder why they don't break. But they are the healthiest people I have ever met. It seems funny that they'd allow brothers into the same outfit. I thought that was forbidden.

Then there's Gus. I like him the best, but his story is terrible. He's from Utah. When he was seventeen his parents locked him up in a barn for three months because he kissed a girl. The girl was found dead a few weeks later.

Then one day there was a windstorm and a tree crashed into the house pinning his parents under the tree. Gus sat on the tree eating apples until they died. Then he left and wandered the highways. He said he is a road scholar.

Then there is Benny. He seems like a pretty normal guy to me. There is nothing that bothers that guy. He's stone. I keep telling him we are brothers. He doesn't seem to understand much. I think he's kinda' dumb, but amusing. I like that.

The soldiers are all cock-sure of themselves. One of the technicians made a joke about them owning the weather--saying the tipping point was entirely their fault. They beat the hell out of him. I guess the military once boasted it could own the weather. I'll bet they wish they could take one that back.

Anyway, they love to bullshit about sex with each other. Kristen makes brutal small penis jokes! But all and all they're a good group.

After the soldiers left, I asked Lazlo about vids. He explained they were pictures with sound. I've asked to see one. Funny, he seemed to be expecting that.

Wednesday night--A vid is something that spies on people. There's a camera in the soldiers' bunks and I've got a monitor here so I can watch them. I asked Lazlo why, and he said it was so I could keep them safe. Funny there are only five bunks. I never see Benny sleeping there. That's so strange.

Anyway, it was interesting watching Kristen and the guys tonight. I'm pretty sure they don't know there's a camera. They talk like they like me. They call me Sammy. I was glad to see there was no gallows either. I wonder if Lazlo will allow me to see other things with the video? Check that. Why haven't they allowed me to see other things on the vid already?

Thursday--I watched a video clip for a company called American Dream Crafts saying what a good company it is. I guess American Dream Crafts is a company that makes the parts to build little pressed paper house models and pressed paper furniture models. People build them and display them. I guess a lot of people have them. The company motto is: "Live the American Dream! Buy a house!"

Apparently, the older collections are very valuable. The vid said some of the models were valuable enough that I might even buy a real house. Maybe I should get one of the American Dream starter kits. I'll need someplace to live after the war ends.

The Ketch brothers just came by and suggested that I go into town with them and see how Clipper reacts to a little alcohol and boogie-woogie. Lazlo said he would have to get approval.

They wound up going without me.

Friday early morning--They must have come back late last night, because I never heard them return. I stayed up until two, watching the monitor trying to make sure my friends were safe. I like watching them sleep. Dr. Merton told me I would feel good keeping an eye on the soldiers. He was right. I finally feel like I'm doing something useful. Lazlo thinks the soldiers should keep an eye on me as well.

Merton and Lazlo argue all the time.

I just left a message for Lazlo that I want to leave the base and go into the nearest town. I told him there's no way I can continue to protect my friends if I can't be with them.

Friday morning--Lazlo just left. I'm going to see some of the old videos of the war. What did the recruit that jump-started my brain call them? Gumbie-gore-vids?

Friday night--No wonder people have been

killing themselves. Those things are horrible! I haven't seen the soldiers all day. They're not even in their bunks. I wonder if they are okay.

Saturday afternoon--Dr. Merton was just here. Polken is dead. Merton told me Polken went into town the other night and stabbed a young man in the face with a broken beer bottle. Then he lit himself on fire after dousing himself with a bottle of booze. He held his pistol on the crowd as he burned and threatened to shoot anyone who tried to help him. By the time Polken dropped the gun, it was too late. Something is not right. When Kristen showed up, Merton practically ran from the barracks.

Saturday night--Kristen asked me all kinds of questions about where the enemy is. In fact, that was all we talked about at dinner.

"Have I ever seen a Gumbie?"

"Where do I think they hide?"

"Where do I think they live?"

"How many do I think there are?"

She hates the Gumbies. She was mad at me when I couldn't help her. I kept telling her she should have gone to Lazlo. I also said I didn't think there are any enemies except our own stupid mistakes. She didn't understand that and she became angry again. I think she really liked Polken. I think she was upset she lost her friend. I told her she shouldn't let it get to her. She told me I was a stupid machine, and not a human at all. That really hurt. Kristen then went talked to Benny. I listened, partly because I was worried about her, but also because I was mad at her. Everyone seems to talk to Benny.

Death doesn't bother Benny. The first thing I remember is death. So people dying doesn't bother me either.

Wait.

Huh?

I just read back on my diary. Clipper strikes, wiping out the pain, wiping out the horror, wiping out my friends. Winston feels like she is fading from my memory. It's not Clipper, it's almost like paint washing off a wall in the rain. This is odd. Why the hell should I care about the rain? I don't think it's my memory. It's the opposite. What is this?

Sunday--If Lazlo dies, I'll be sad. I think if I got really close to anyone and they died, I'd be sad. I'll bet Clipper will not let that happen. That pile of chips would probably be jealous. Damn thing has no emotions so it keeps me from having them. I bet that's it. I hate Clipper.

Sunday night--Dr. Merton came in and we talked, just before dinner. I like Merton. Before he came by I felt like shit (oops, wrong word). And now he's got me wondering if I could ever fail in anything. Before I talked to him, things just didn't seem important; now the future is all I've been thinking about all night.

What would be the point of anything other than now? As long as there is no love. From what I've seen of love, it's always painful--especially these days. Now if there was some way to love without pain? If I used them for sex, I think that might work. If I was like that, I wouldn't just be someone's dog. Knowledge is more important than love. Love is a game to get people to do the things you want. Otherwise, you're just a tool. Dr. Merton was really helpful.

Sunday night--Kristen said she knew about the surveillance cameras in the barracks. I felt like apologizing for not saying anything. Then she said she felt sorry for me and proceeded to reel off a list of why my life is really a pit.

First, she says, my parents dumped me off to have my brain torn in half and have my memories controlled by a computer. Then, they leave and never come back. Then she says there is a war going on and nobody knows who's fighting us, or from where, or even how. I'm stuck on the base with crazy people, and monitored all time like a lab animal. She finishes up by saying love isn't a waste of time. Then she leaves. How can I help Kristen if she's starting to go nuts? She said she used to love someone called Polken. I don't think I ever met him.

Monday--I asked again about going into town, but Lazlo doubted if I'd be allowed off the base, especially after what happened to Polken.

Well fine. I'm on strike. No writing, no teaching, no nothing.

In fact, I think I'm going to fill my head with thoughts of rust and sunspots to screw up Clipper. But if it works, I won't remember what I did because they're certain to erase it. Well no matter, I quit until I get to go into town. Otherwise how can I help Kristen? I guess she just tried to pick a fight with Dr. Merton.

Monday night--Son of a bitch! I was so bored I read through my diary and realized Clipper wiped out my memory of Polken and that I wanted to see Kristen. I'm going to have to keep re-reading my diary to see what I want. Just to be sure Clipper doesn't steal it from me. Here's what I got to do:

One-Help Kristen. Two-get the hell away from Clipper. Three-get off this damn base. Four-go into town with the soldiers. Five--talk to Dr. Wolf. Six--see without memory.

Monday--Laz says the diary is imperative to my work and that under no circumstances could Clipper erase my memory of it. Well good, that gives me some leverage. You guys know what I want. Let's start with number four. I am a soldier scholar and I get to go into town. Right?

Thursday—Perfect. I'm off to town with the boys. Have I ever done anything so good before? I think I'm getting somewhere on this.

Monday--Gus is still alive. I am looking for Sergeant Plow. I thought they were the same person. I think that because they were so pissed at everyone they don't care about anyone. How the heck do you do that? I don't care about anyone. But, I am not angry at anyone. I'm lucky, I don't care about much. I think that's what Clipper does. It makes me not care and not remember.

Tuesday--I think this whole thing is just a techies view of progress. Merton, you're coming my way, buddy. Tell Winston I'm comin' home.

Clipper--that hunk of junk--snitched on you. I am sure of it.

Tuesday night--Dr. Wolf just asked me to talk about everything I was thinking. More than anything, I said, I wanted to punch Dr. Merton, or throw something at him. I told him that. He said I should keep talking to Dr. Merton. Funny, both Lazlo and the Doc' want to understand everything. Well they got their wish. Me too.

I am not so sure about Dr. Merton and Dr. Pard. I don't understand why they wouldn't want to know if they were making a mistake. I would. But they don't. Lazlo doesn't understand this either. Do leaders not make mistakes? Only in their dreams, I bet.

Something tells me that we were messed up because the guys who control the money came to the same conclusion as Dr. Wolf. That is, our leaders don't know how to lead, but it isn't their fault. So they hide it. Men!

Merton say leadership is a burden and it must remain that way for the good of all. That was not well received by some. Some guy named Russell Biner was responsible for snitching that one out to me. I like him. I hope they fixed Merton's wagon—but good. He killed Polken with his stupidity

Wednesday--Lazlo says he can't find his friend. How do you lose a friend? Oh, that's why the soldiers are here. The Doc is gone. I don't feel so good.

So I am not the only fool here. This guy Biner, got tricked him into getting himself launched into space.

(**Commentary from the Research Team: The removal of his colleague, Dr. Biner, by nefarious means can no longer be in doubt. We all wish this were not the case;**

however, our attempts to find Dr. Biner have produced no clues as to his location, or circumstances leading to his departure. All agree Dr. Wolf was the last to see Dr. Biner. J.Pard/R.Merton. Date suppressed per requirement.)

(Commentary from the 1st Court of Inquiry: Dr. Biner's whereabouts are well documented. B.Fong. Date suppressed per requirement.)

Thursday--Winston and I went sailing on a beautiful sailboat. She is sad all the time now.

She said they would not let her command the boat, but that I would be able to work the jib. It is difficult pulling in the ropes--no that's not right--trimming the sheets. I'm surprised the wind is strong enough to push the boat so fast. When I stand in the breeze, on shore, the wind is barely noticeable. In the boat with a sail we catch the wind, there is no way to ignore the wind, or the waters! Winston asked me if I thought we could blow the water backwards so could we go backwards?

Why not just turn the boat around?

Thursday noon--Lazlo and I were in the boat today. I am like a rudder helping the boat of humanity catch the right breezes so we can get somewhere useful in the ocean. Lazlo asked me an odd question. He asked me if it would be easier to get across the water if I thought there was someone really important on the other side of the water. Seems like a dumb question to me. It would be easy to go over the waters, if I had the right sail on my boat. And, if I had someone who loved me, and they were waiting for me at the other end, I think I could get there.

So we tried something. I don't remember what it was. I remember we were sailing, I asked Lazlo if he liked to swim. Then he asked me my name. I said my name was Hope Weiss. Then the boat capsized. It's a good thing Lazlo was with me. Without him there would have been no hope for Doc Biner or me and we would have drowned.

I think he isn't mad at me. I think Dr. Biner misses Hope. He wished he could forget her. I am sorry Doc. I really am. I said I, remember, I, not us.

(Commentary from the 1st Court of Inquiry: It is agreed that this incident represents the best record we have of Hope Weiss and her last instructions for Pilot Nothing. No charges will be filed against the Ginda. The charges against Dr. Wolf for the death of Ms. Weiss are pending completion of the project. We believe Dr. Wolf's agreement to using Hope Weiss rather than Winston Doe was a tactical mistake and the cause of Ms. Weiss' death. J.Pard/R. Merton. Date suppressed per requirement.)

Friday--I asked Lazlo what kind of man I was. He thought for a long time, and then answered a very tough, decent, man. I think he is lying. Not caring keeps me safe from the enemy. So who is safe from me?

Lazlo also told me I'm not supposed to lecture the other soldiers on the Gumbies. The enemy is called Gumbies--I guess I forgot that--seems like I have been asleep for a long time. Oh well, so I'm supposed to grasp ideas, or whatever is happening, and stay with them. I'm supposed to show the soldiers that the elimination of pain, in memory, works as a defense.

I think the elimination of memory is like opening a sail on a sail boat. I'm not even sure the Gumbies are the problem. It seems maybe we might be misunderstanding what we should be doing. I'd like to sail someplace on my memories. No wait, I want that changed, and sail without my memories. Is that what I should do?

Friday night--I'll be a son of a bitch. Lazlo had me read entries in my Diary, ones Clipper had already wiped from my memory. Somehow, I made some of them come back into my brain. I think Lazlo doesn't understand how they returned, but it sure makes him happy. I can beat Clipper. I know I can.

Friday midnight--Lazlo seems to be happier now. He is practically jumping up and down. I'm worried he's lost a screw somewhere. All he is saying is: "It isn't in us. It isn't in us. He keeps telling me to look for a blur." This guy is nuttier than a fruit cake.

Lazlo and I just had an interesting discussion. Right after he calmed down. Lazlo said there is a place called the unconsciousness that isn't really inside us. He says he is certain of that now. The idea that it was inside us was just ego. He thinks it is a place and it is a place special people can actually go to--like me. He calls it the waters of mind and that the unconscious is just a small part of it. Lazlo says it's a safe place to go. Funny, with global warming people weren't allowed to go places anymore either. I wonder if that is important? I bet it is. I bet we were forced to see something we did not want to see because we were stuck in one place. That happened to a lot of people. But maybe that wasn't such a bad thing after all. It opened our eyes. So where does Lazlo want me to travel?

Saturday early morning--Dr. Pard was just in with Dr. Merton. They think Dr. Wolf is crazy. Dr. Wolf, are you trying to kill me?

Saturday afternoon--Dr. Biner and I went sailing. It seems there needs to be only one person in the boat. Something's not right. I saw a fish drown. I didn't think fish could drown. I thought they could swim in water.

When we got back, Dr. Wolf told me he believes that the Jazz War is no war at all, but a step in the growth of humanity. He says we are moving towards sentience and defines sentience as the ability to see the future. He says all of our work in science was about the past. He says replicating the past is not a way to be certain of the future. He says the old ways were good at saying what is going to happen next--in a given set of circumstances--but only in a set of tightly controlled circumstances. And control, says Dr. Wolf, is a foolish notion. Dr. Wolf says real sentience is knowing the future, not guessing at it. He says there is no way to tell the future unless someone tells you. Then you can be really sure of what to do. Dr. Merton says Dr. Wolf is nuts.

He says the battlefield, is a place where we all join each other—like the way the ocean joins the continents. He says we can walk on the solid land of the continents but if we try to do that on the ocean, we drown. We walk on land and we swim in the water. He said I need to remember that lesson.

Can stupidity drown a person, or a species? Dr. Merton must know.

Sunday morning--I think Dr. Pard does not understand, or he doesn't want to. All he talks about is how we need to learn to fly over the ocean that ties us all.

So one guy wants me to sail, the other wants me to swim, and the third guy wants me to fly. I hope someone is right.

I saw a killer whale swimming around. I asked him if there are other creatures living in that place that ties us. He says he didn't know—that all he knows is that we had fouled up that place with our stupidity and vanity. When he says it, he looks up at the sky.

I'm so confused. How can so many things be true at the same time? Are they all true? No wonder we are going nuts. There is no way for a regular guy like me to deal with all this.

Sunday--Things I want to do:

Get away from Clipper.

Beat the Gumbies at their own game.

See if Dr. Wolf might be wrong.

Win the war and find a place of peace in the woods.

Chapter 29

Monday afternoon--One of the guards heard Dr. Wolf talking at lunch and the guard said that he had the same dream as Gus last night. On a hunch, Gus asked the guy who serves the food, and one of the dishwashers, about their dreams. They had the same dreams. I think they all pissed on themselves, like Gus, but they wouldn't admit it. Everyone's dreams focused on me.

Dr. Wolf then told me the technicians and his secretary all had the same dream. Apparently, everyone on the base dreamed of me last night. They all dreamed the world ended. It's my fault, I know it. I bet there's an attack coming. What's that noise?

Tuesday night--These last few hours have

been crazy. We're on a full alert. This is damn spooky. Gus and the rest of them are stationed by the hallway because some people seem to be very serious about killing me. There are bodies everywhere.

I'm watching the video monitor as I do this. I'm keeping an eye on Gus and the others in the small cabin outside my place. They're safe so far. They're playing poker. I think humanity has sprung another leak. Benny says the waters of mind are something called Chi. I bet. I say the waters of mind look just like blood.

Friday morning--There's more gunfire and some explosions. I can't see Gus and the others. My video has stopped working. There go the lights.

Friday night--The lights are back. This new battle has been going on for six or seven hours now. I still can't get out of my room. There's a steel plate under the wood of my door. I know now because I can see the dents from bullets and there are splinters all over my room. I think they are trying to kill me because of that dream.

Saturday morning--This is terrible.

All the old security people who were originally guarding us, tried to kill us. Gus, Kristen, Benny, and Rico—I think they are alive. I think Pisser was hurt. I hope he lives.

The center is on emergency generators and I am guarded constantly with a most peculiar setup. I'm in my apartment, and my hall is empty except for a computer and a machine gun. Anyone who enters without Lazlo's authorization is immediately killed. At least that's what it said in the note I was given. I wonder if Clipper runs the machine gun. It makes me think of a mother guarding her child. My video monitor is still out so I can't see the guys. Where is everyone?

(Commentary from Administrator: Despite previous commentary on the motives and methods of Dr. Wolf, it is the shared belief of the Directorate that Dr. Wolf is to remain in charge of the project. His prior removal was, in the opinion of the Directorate, a prime cause for the upheaval of the last few days. G.Smetana/B.Fong. Date suppressed per requirement.)

(Commentary from the 1st Court of Inquiry: We find the actions of the Directorate to be both prudent and warranted. Date suppressed per requirement.)

Saturday night--Where the hell is everyone? I think they are all dead. It's just me, Clipper, and that damn machine gun that guards the hallway. Damn it stinks. My door is closed so I can't see what happens--but every so often the gun goes off. A few times I heard explosions out there. And that gun keeps firing.

Saturday midnight—Gus came by. He is wounded but okay. His chest is bandaged and he has a bad cut on his face. He says everything will be okay. He also came by to deliver a TV to me. He showed me a camera that he and the other soldiers wear over their ear. It looks like a tiny tube. All the soldiers have had those for years. Their superiors watch what they are doing on a television. Funny I never noticed it before. I think I was made to forget it is there. I bet some of the other soldiers have that same problem.

I asked him, what the hell is a TV?

He said it was a system for sending and receiving images and sound. He said it flowed through the air.

I asked if Wildhead was dead and Gus said he was not. The machine gun went off while he was there. When it was done, Gus left. Through the open door I saw dead people and blood everywhere. Gus walked passed them all as if the dead were stones on a path.

Sunday morning--There goes the machine gun again.

Sunday evening--My door is still locked and I'm getting hungry. There are so many frightened people on television!

The dead are so boring. They just lie there and drip blood. I don't understand why people are supposed to watch each other die on TV all the time. What the heck is so important about the dissimilarity between the sides of the human body anyway?

Sunday night--Dr. Wolf is back. He had been gone, traveling to see the big bosses. I asked him how come they all knew about me. He said I was a hero.

Monday--Dr. Wolf just came in and we talked about what I'd written. He asked me what I meant about the unimportance of the dissimilarity in the human body. It took me a while to understand what he was asking about. It definitely shocked me when we understood each other. It shocked him also that he had never seen it on the TV. I thought that he knew everything.

I explained to him that every time they tried to show people doing something wrong there it was: a little fuzzy line running down the center of their bodies, from head to foot. Dr. Wolf says the programs show people dying. He said most people couldn't see what I see: that fuzzy line down the center. He calls it a disjunction.

He turned the TV on and he asked me to point out what I meant. So I pointed to people who had that fuzzy line and he'd nod and ask me to point it out again. Then Dr. Wolf told me he still cannot see that line. He said the disjunction is a doorway to the patch.

He asked me why some people didn't have that fuzziness. How the heck should I know! Then he asked why I didn't mention it before. I didn't see it before. At first I thought he was kidding me--he wasn't. He asked me again why I paid so little attention to it. He said I had seen video images for a long time.

I told him I don't remember ever seeing the fuzzy line. I mentioned I never saw the camera behind the soldier's ears either.

He has just ran out the door screaming for his helpers. I hope there won't be more killing. How did the floor get wet?

Tuesday--Lazlo says that since the other half of my brain is so far away, I have sensitivity to certain shades of scale. Whatever the hell that means.

Dr. Wolf says he thinks that's why I can see the fuzziness between the two halves of some people. He thinks the reason it shows up so clearly on the TV screen is "the screen image only lives in the present. It contains no memory." I like quotation marks, they're fun.

The reason I think quotation marks are fun is this: A person says something and there are these two lines with nothing in between them to show that a person has spoken.

How do the two lines in quotation marks stay connected? Maybe it's a door? Maybe it's just another kind of question? Maybe it's just a coincidence? I wonder why no one else sees the fuzziness like me.

Tuesday afternoon--A crock is a holder. Oh I get it. That's gotta' be it. I think Dr. Wolf is impressed with me again.

He just ran out the door, again.

But he sure looked at me strangely when I suggested that our body might be a mechanism. He tried to act calm, but by the way he bounced his sandals I could tell he was surprised. I couldn't tell if he thought I was a genius or if I was a nut. I wonder if he thought I was going to hurt him.

He did get up and walk to the other side of the room, after I said that he should explore the crossover points. I think the fuzziness is a little bit of madness--in them and in me. So I see madness without going mad? Dr. Wolf's word for the fuzziness is disjunction. He uses the word disjunction because he thinks some of us partly here and partly gone.

I thought there was no here, and gone where? Did Dr. Wolf go gone?

(Commentary from the Research Team: Many now believe that Dr. Wolf might have had disreputable motives for some of his actions, including jealousy of the Gindas and their insight as a motivation for some of his actions. R.Merton. Date suppressed per requirement.)

(1st Court of Inquiry Notes: It is here that we first see the mass hysteria associated with the Jazz War expressed as a torrent of anger by Dr. Merton. We also note there is no perfect link between the emerging changes and the wide spread anger for mistakes made by the leadership regarding global warming and the tipping point. These twin tragedies of our time are, we believe, events of the most serious consequences for species survival. B.Fong/G.Smetana. Date suppressed per requirement.)

Alarm: ON

CHAPTER 30

A young man wanders through a dancing throng of young, beautiful people. The bunny-dancers and the ultra-cool hipsters gyrate and snuggle into the warm, sensuous, music. Voice-Over: "Can't find it?"

The man begins to search the dance floor more frantically. He looks this way and that. His thin face begins to show the angst of concern. Voice-over: "You need to find it."

The man dashes across the dance floor; he runs towards…A video screen. On either side of it, beautiful women caress the white plastic exterior of the monitor. Their thin fingers trail slowly over the screen as the image tightens and the viewer sees the same lounge displayed. Voice-over: "Now you've got it."

He stops in front of the display and stares hungrily into the screen. One dancing man and woman are different from the rest. They wear dark ill-fitting clothes. They appear unkempt and dirty. As they move, a blurry line becomes more obvious. The blurred section runs vertically from their head to their crotch. The blurry line sparkles occasionally. Soon the image on the screen appears as though it were the poor work of a camera-person: The half images of the dancers seem to be badly joined.

The young man reaches up and taps a large button built into the side of the viewer. The image freezes. "Do you wish to report a Gindaism?" Asks the screen in large black letters. The question is stamped over the image of the dancers. The man taps the button once more. "Gindaism reported. Thank you."

He turns around, his face full of joy. Voice-over: "This kind of smile can be yours. It belongs to every citizen who knows they have done their duty. Keep watching. Keep us safe. Gindaisms can only be seen on CSN, the Citizen's Satellite Network. We rely on you!"

The crowd in the lounge applauds the young man as two sensuous women take him by the arms and lead him through the happy crowd.

"CSN--yours for only $29.95 a month."

. . . .

I've never even heard of a Gindaism, or a disjunction.

Winston lies exhausted on the hillside waiting for her jeep. Oblivious to the cool winds' caress or rustling grass, she weeps. Below her, far in the distance, swirl the waters of Puget Sound. Puffy clouds pass overhead. Distant islands lie shrouded in the evil mist from angry thunder storms. A pitchfork of lightning crosses the sky. Fir and Madrone trees sway in the coming winds, too benign, for her tastes, or concern. The waves roll into the remains of the ferry terminal; twin ships tilt and ride the waves. Standing, as if to leave, she feels compelled to just run off onto the ferries and hide, but Winston Doe cannot. The mystery surrounding her quest holds her firm in its grasp. But beaten by what she has read in the Diary, Winston curses her youth and its foolish hope. *I volunteered for all this.*

Why would Russell have let them Shanghai him?

The symphony of the trees and the seas brings more tears to her eyes. She perceives a dance of immense beauty. *Majesty, clothed in clouds and sunlight, cloaked in the human awareness of things living, a loveliness so superb. How will we ever find the fluid nature of mind that we lost? All this beauty together in one place for even a millisecond--let alone eons--no wonder we easily call our abdication from it madness. Could Eden's end have been worse? And what about my snake, Moss Eckman?*

She believes that Moss Eckman, philistine, brat, petulant dilettante, and self-satisfied power-junkie has the key to her path. *Or he is the path. But at what cost?*

Winston studies the distant ruins of the Oil Age ferries and notes the fires of that home. Her urge to run from all of it again, without reason or focus, mounts. *That clan on the boats would accept me. I know it.* Her desire for escape prowls about inside her like a hungry huntress, the slight scent of something in the distance calls her. Then it is her master; but in an instant it vanishes for her.

Winston again scans the sky looking for any tell-tale signs of the satellites. There are so many now, she knows you can sometimes see them glint during the day. One catches her eye, an entertainment outpost--big brother in the sky keeping an eye on the delicate stitches of civilization--not for control but for safety.

How long were we moving away from our world and towards our vanity? Moss is perfect. Yet here I am. Maybe I am the throw-back. How very odd. Is the notion of flow flawed? It would be if we are moving towards transcendence. It would certainly be flawed if we are perceiving memory as fact and I know Russell completely believed that misunderstood memory is our enemy. But why would we see memory as life? A greater vision is too much for us? So then why my little focus? Does the focus have to narrow before it cycles?

That would mean I fit in the equation and I am the tool for the path out. Damn you, Russell. Why couldn't you have just been a jerk?

Tire sounds. *My transportation is here.*

Chapter 31

Teenagers watch a parade pass them by. Flags fly, the green oak trees wave. Young children play on the sidewalks as middle-aged men sit and women fawn on the parade drummers bringing them cool lemonade and cookies.

Voice-over: "Remember their sacrifice and donate to the Merton Foundation for Old Age. We can cure aging. We can cure death. We will cure it."

. . . .

The Rader Institute for Defense Studies first provided funding for Lazlo Wolf. He never left their employ--despite the different organizational names on his security badges and different entities claiming rights to his discoveries.

Like many brilliant men and women, Lazlo Wolf was certain of his intelligence. Also, like so many others with perceptive and intellectual gifts, he felt his brilliance--or at least an ancillary competence--overflowed into all other areas of his life as well. As a result, blinded by his brilliance, he could not perceive a competence based on a lack of capability that might outdo him. It is this flaw that cursed Dr. Wolf, and generations of researchers before him. To be outmaneuvered by people like Pard and Merton, people, whose talents clustered around the incompetence of others and their fears. Had Dr. Wolf, and many other researchers, seen their Achilles' heel, would they have allowed a reduction of their place in history--if it meant their research was never born? That answer to that is--of course--for Dr. Wolf, and others like him the research comes first. For others, we will never know of their work.

The Rader Institute begun life as a think-tank, started by an entrepreneur who, during the global warming years, made a fortune selling food that did not need refrigeration. Soon after Mina Wolf's tenth birthday, the entrepreneur died in a train wreck. No investigations into the causes were ever done. Dr. Joshua Pard told Mina Wolf the event was "Just another battle in the Jazz War." Lazlo Wolf told his daughter about the event as if it were a physics experiment. Mina would never forgive her father for this. Lazlo Wolf's wife had founded the Rader Institute. It was said her love for him was the only reason she funded his early "mad' research into Species Focus and the Gindas.

The Institute covers three thousand acres just outside of Everett and has never been attacked--not even during the Jazz War.

Unknown to Sammich Ginda, the Gindas were moved during their sleep period for their own safety. The paid net-bloggers of Ginda's time had little respect for security and as often as possible exposed the soldiers' whereabouts to the public--always leading to an assault on the facility where they were housed. The Clipper Project was well-known--loved by a few--but feared by the patrician elite. From their perspective, Species Focus smacked them down. It sounded too much like the divine right of kings--a concept thoroughly beheaded by the 18th century Republican hoards.

As she enters the main gate of the facility, Winston grins at the stealth that continues to be this location's salvation. Traveling passed the run-down front gate, by the old wooden barns and chicken sheds, the truck negotiates a rutted road. A farm tableau: complete with rusting autos peeking out of thistles and scotch broom, fifteen-foot-tall blackberry brambles along the road, and of course the rotting buildings. The facility has lassitude painted all over it. A peek below the surface reveals cross-linked death dealing systems covering every inch of the farm.

She passes a second set of wooden gates, these covered with ivy and moss. Winston feels none of the calm of an academic environment here, tension permeates everything. On the hillside to her left, a set of buildings and a playground loaded with antennas are made to look like old satellite TV downlinks. Hidden in the fields she sees weapons emplacements, pop up Gatling guns and gas mortars.

The laughter of children rolls across the valley. The truck passes a third set of gates: a prim pair of metal gates set into a low stone wall. The truck turns right at what appears to be a hay barn, then left into a smaller barn behind it. A second set of gates appears from below ground surrounding the vehicle--effectively mobilizing it. On the side, a young person sits behind an old refrigerator door mending hinges. The door is made of bullet proof titanium—the young female guard and a team of eight others have been tracking the vehicle from the moment it entered the grounds. The wood barn gate closes, the gates retract back into the floor, and the vehicle rolls down a metal ramp.

On a well-lighted causeway, various scanners search the truck for explosives, biological weapons, and chemical weapons. The concrete and steel-girdered wall has a multitude of small square cutouts not unlike the old-time armored cars of the Oil Age. The cut-out squares serve the same function, defense, except the weapons inside the square are poison gases. Winston remembers Sammich Ginda's defense computer and the weapons it controlled outside his door. She postulates this elaborate system was what he was referring to and that might be the reason her arrival at the Rader Institute, in a fake delivery truck. Someone has decided to make a point about her safety and function. Ahead, is a glassed-in guard shack. It stands besides an open vault-like gate.

Her new driver provides the three soldiers with papers. Nonetheless, they circle the vehicle with their scanning wands in a thirty second search. The men then check her briefcase with the utmost respect and with every intention of killing anyone whom they believe threatens the project or those behind the gate.

Once finished, the men salute, waving them through the last checkpoint. The yellow and black causeway now seems filled with wires and pipes over every available wall. People wearing light blue lab coats walk in pairs along a metal walkway above the roadway. At every intersection, the truck turns right. The word "HAZARD!" repeats every eight feet in red letters four feet high.

Another right turn, the truck parks, next to four others. Winston gets out, surprised to see her driver has deserted her and one of the guards from the gate drives the jeep. "Your driver didn't have clearance, ma'am." The young man, dressed in a black uniform with a red beret, seems polite. He has only the vaguest concern for Winston, but the utmost concern for her safety. He extends his hand to a set of glass doors and a small sign:

COMPUTING

The glass doors open and Benson Fong bows slightly at the waist. "Madam Director."

She greets him politely and they proceed down a hallway lit by banks of fluorescent tubes. Then through double doors into a large office full of person-high purple-clothed cubicles. They pass researchers who pay her little notice--even though most of them know her. No one breaches security in this facility by idle chatter. "Where is Russell?"

"Please, Winston. Gregor wanted you to see some records--before you take the next step with Moss." Ahead is the library, a glass-walled room. They enter it and the wall behind them turns opaque, a snow white blind

"Where is General Smetana? He was supposed to meet me here."

"It was agreed I should handle this debriefing."

"Is he afraid of me, Benson?"

"I am afraid of you failing." His demeanor turns softer, "And I don't even know what that means." They cross through the room; Benson opens the back door and they enter a plush executive library. The far desk manned by the librarian looks recently vacated--a cup of coffee still steams and a cigarette burns in the ash tray.

Now that doesn't fit. A cigarette smoker here in the computing library. Oh they can't interfere but they can hint. About what?

The three mahogany tables in the center are neatly stacked with files and computers linked by a set of hastily strung wires that snake to the back of the librarian's desk. Overhead lights keep the room somber. Winston walks over examining the wires and sees they are merely for the local network. She looks around the room at its books, journals, and VR interface systems: so-called head clamps. She faces Benson. He points to a manila folder.

Winston opens it up and stares at a familiar picture. It appears to be the research vessel that had held Sammich Ginda, but this one is secured into in a small room. A steel structure emanating from a steel exoskeleton supports the tank, about the size of a hot tub, mounted at eye height. Blue pipes and wires enter on the top and similar assemblies of red pipes and wires exit from the side. Behind it, crowded into a wall-sized rack system, are computational and networking components, for small scale version of Clipper. A set of storage-by-projection boxes line the top, pointed at the ceiling. Winston examines the memory projected upon on the ceiling. It depicts an image of the black gallows in a military base. "I haven't seen this particular memory but I have seen other early photos of Sammich Ginda's vessel before he was given a body. What else am I supposed to see?"

"This is Russell Biner's vessel," says Benson quietly.

"Don't be ridiculous, he has no outputs. This unit is isolated. And the walls are steel." She says, then, her pulse quickening. She understands: *Russell wasn't a saint.* "Go ahead, I am ready."

"With Dr. Biner's insistence--Dr. Wolf was forced to agree that only way an intermediary could function as an appropriate interface was to be in line--but there had to be a physical distance in place unaffected by the Earth's curvature. They launched a few of their researchers trying it out. When they decided it was safe, Dr. Biner became the primary Clipper interface for launched researchers."

"Launched, General Fong?"

He hands her another folder: "Winston, you're a top researcher, do Gindas forget what they know so we can be safe--or to achieve more? Do we on the outside just go mad, or do we fail to accept change? Dr. Biner was forced to accept that the realities of our time/space required his direct intervention." His tone holds some cold, hard objective pit. "I once read a report by Dr. Wolf suggesting that the inability to adjust to the many paths of life can be fatal. Dr. Biner agreed."

"Take me to him."

"I cannot."

"Because I could kill him for what he has done to me?" She is baiting him but when Benson Fong steps back from her, she is stunned. "Or because the Diary said something about a launch?"

"Read the next document, please."

"He's proposing the project Pilot Nothing."

"Because you were not there--and because he knew you'd cease to believe in him."

"Because he is not waiting for me."

"He is waiting, but not for what you are expecting."

"General, I am not a child. Or are you aiming for the first spot in my distaste list?"

He has a grin for her. "Both Wolf and Biner were famous for their blind faith in their abilities to solve issues. It was their greatest weakness." He notes the small circle of blood on her bandage. "Neither understood their desires."

"You're a romantic, General."

"Hardly, but I don't think they were wrong to respect desire. Why else would you pursue the Diary for two decades?" He notes she will not answer. "To find him," he says quietly.

She stares at the floor.

Benson speaks: "Sixteen hundred plus men and women gave their lives taking ant steps up a mountain--each sacrificing their life for a few megabytes of information--and the result is Moss Eckman. He lives happy--they did not. That's progress, I believe. But I always looked beyond him--because of you. Dr. Biner said you would acquire focus without the horrors of Clipper. On that he had insight and he was right. So I supported you."

"General, was I a grad student? Are my memories real about my parents, my background?"

"You were a grad student working with a badly wounded Ginda. You then worked with Plow and Biner. You stayed through the next Ginda as an intern. After your thesis, as you remember, you were granted access to the project--at Dr. Biner's insistence--just as you remember. You then insisted on your current task."

"How many died to give me the memories that provided focus?"

"Too many, including, Hope Weiss, who tried to save Dr. Biner from the nightmare he endures; when she failed, he went ahead with his plans."

"They were like brother and sister." Her anger flares. "That's why he allowed Clipper to take a his memory. No that's wrong. What are you not telling me?" Benson will not speak. "It is no wonder Mina hasn't any respect for you. You are far closer to Moss and the rest than I thought, Benson."

His face turns to ash. "We want you to understand Pilot Nothing."

"I already do Pilot Nothing, Pilnouth, the hail Mary of research projects, a bunch of failed launches to transcend apparent limits. All failed except his, right?"

"Look at the picture, there is no link…"

"I see your plan. I already know there is no love there."

He tries a different tack: "Would you have believed me if I said neither Russel nor I would could ever put you in that jar--unless it was dire?"

"You could never have done that to me, or anyone else. You don't think you have the right. That's why you protect the Gindas." Her eyes close. "I know I made the choice. How could Russell convince you that Pilot Nothing will work? How could you let them launch him? Trans-temporal faith? Spare me."

The solar panels of the satellite fail according to a schedule and the ship lands safely. As you know we have records after that."

"I said: How could you know that it will work?"There is only one answer she will believe and waits for it.

"You know it was a success. We all do. Remember the so-called Genian ship had standard NASA fittings?"

"But it was empty."

"The space was empty, they think. They were never inside."

"Then Jordan took a flight. The launch was verified by telemetry."

"Until it failed. All the internals on the Armstrong showed complete system failure. There is no way that can be compensated for during reentry. You know that."

"If Jordan had focus and he interacted with were Biner's waters of mind then you've got a temporal paradox and that leads to overlapping misaligned events. We already know the temporal paradox means failure. But if you can show me the safe anchor?" She waits a moment. "But you can't. General, how could you possibly believe it would work?"

Benson sees an increase in her agitation. "We know."

"I don't want to play this game. Show me Russell."

He leans forward and taps a button; through the glass walls she sees four large monitors over a group of ground controllers. One of the images is a satellite circling the Earth.

She looks at the images General Fong first showed her. "The container has a stripped down hex-redundant Clipper system on board. That's for size and weight." She stares at the satellite. "It might fit, but that system is too small to do any good. At best it could only purge memory, and then maybe deliver a single memory."

"Or two."

"The Genian engines?" She asks. "Oh, of course, a redundant system--two memories retained. Amazing, if you are correct. But there is no way he could endure it."

"The system purges every day he lives. How else could he stand it?" Benson says quietly.

Her eyes spark fire. "Why would he have done that to himself? Hope's death?" A sigh escapes her. "There's more. That's what you have proof of. And that's why he's waiting for up there. But what roof?" She looks around the room seeing the cigarette. "Dr. Biner believed we were going extinct and you know when. That's impossible."

"It isn't, Dr. Doe. You know the future for a civilized species is sight, not a temporal possibility."

"How can you be so damnable sure that Moss and I are the path through this?"

"Sentience," he says quietly.

"You've acquired clarity of event? You have sight into the future that clears this path? Impossible--prove it to me."

"Winston, I cannot interfere with you or Moss at this point." He clenches his fist, his heart thumping in his chest. "But we're not guessing."

"We'll see." She turns to exit the room then stops. "How many launches did you have to try before you were able to get a stable orbital platform?"

"Almost seventy."

"And every one had a Ginda with Russell's memory on board, right?" She doesn't wait for an answer. "That was the mistake. The successful launch was just him and no Ginda."

He nods. "It was a terrible chance."

"No it wasn't. The Ginda would believe he was conscripted. That's death. Show me the platform's signal."

"You know what it says," Benson replies.

"Proof. I want proof."

He turns and taps a code into the keyboard. On the screen a message appears:

we are looking for this?

General Fong speaks. "Moss and I will be at the Museum in four hours. He believes he is going there to get your override on power usage for a party."

"The hell with Moss. What about the Lonocs? Am I to believe the Lonocs are the misanthropic souls of the fifty million who died in New Zealand? That the Fifty were dead before they left because Quentin Conworth's people breached the dome and destroyed them all?" She stares at the smoldering cigarette. "So you think humanity is already extinct? Is that it, General?"

"I don't believe that, Madam Director."

"It does no good if Roo keeps returning to the same event in history, you know that."

There is no response from Benson Fong.

"You must be awfully damn sure this," she says looking around again at the facility. "So who is committing suicide? We know Russell is. We know humanity is. What's the point of that cigarette?"

He cannot speak.

We kill ourselves if we don't have a stable interconnect to a space that's scalable. But Samarra will not work, too much traffic, she says to herself.

"Gaia! I am so sick of you heroes."

"None of us have been as heroic as you, Doctor Doe."

She glares at him. "You..." She has no more words for a moment. "Please make sure you keep the Museum safe."

"It is my life's work, Dr. Doe."

She wonders at his dramatic response for just a moment. "So Moss is the key? Oh, and Clipper is...The cigarette...The wrong path? But a decade ago it wasn't. Oh my. I am. Because I knew I could override it. That's why I volunteered. Damn you all for his sacrifice."

CHAPTER 32

"Hi, this is Kelly Pan-Blanca again with your morning news update. Congressional sources say that the bill to provide unlimited satellite surveillance has passed the first hurdle of approval having been approved by the House Ways and Means Committee in a closed door session.

"In the entertainment news, the life story of Joshua Pard begins taping this week. The world-famous researcher has been hired as technical consultant. Sources close to the project indicate a certain amount of friction with the Jordan Foundation on historical accuracy. Don't worry folks, Ol' Doc Pard will set them right!

"Finally, the U.N. has begun processing travel visas for the coming year. Welcome back to the gravy train. "Baby, let the good times roll!"

. . . .

Benson Fong strolls between the black steel monsters of the Northern European exhibit hoping Winston will keep her appointment. Perversely admiring the oil-fed locomotives for their excess power and energy consumption, he again checks with his security teams and then hears Winston will be waiting for them in the executive cafeteria.

He stares at the machine in front of him: Steel and complexity have always drawn his attention; he admires order, but the real attraction is the unbelievable waste this behemoth represents. It also demands his attention due to its wicked purpose. It was a death-camp locomotive.

Drifting away, like a distant iceberg through the sea of tourists, his interest in the behemoths snaps when his security teams calls in again. There has been an assault by Moss on a new girlfriend, a woman from the bar. She is in ICU and not expected to live. Moss has been reset by Clipper so he will be here in a moment minus that memory.

If only he did not hate Moss so much. Benson again realizes he would have had no remorse in emptying a clip of ammunition into Moss Eckman, were it necessary. In many ways, Benson suffers in his dual roles of handler and potential assassin of Moss Eckman. His early training in Beijing made Benson Fong partial to anyone who has the slightest sense of Confucian ethic. Winston's candor and courage holds more hope than he can bear. In every event in which she has participated, her efforts have been stalwart. Her sense of responsibility astounds Benson--regardless of Clipper's assistance. Still, he does ponder how a human like her could be so centric, and terminal, to the species.

On the other hand, Moss' self-centeredness and absurd pride comfort him. Even though Moss' unexamined life insults him, General Fong has little trouble coping with the idea that Moss represents the center of humanity: a nihilistic, vain, male, with no more regard for his fellow beings than a male appendage has for a wet hand.

Worse, Benson Fong matured during the Jazz War and knows the distasteful flavors of command. He senses it again and worries for Winston Doe. The final curtain is on its way. He prays he can protect her, and hopes Moss Eckman does not attack her. Moss is far too easy a target for Benson, and not just because he hates Moss, but because he wishes a future without him.

Yet only when he adds the two together and comes up with the possibility that there exists a decent species center that includes Winston Doe's greatness and Moss' violence--can Benson Fong accept his tasks. Still, the quandary of Winston Doe has led him to wonder if the Gindas aren't patches, but bridges. That leads then him to fear the rest of us are merely placeholders for something. He wonders if the present is just the chains of memory--something that he fears. It would mean Moss is right: There is no purpose. *Or are we just groundwork for the new master species?*

Still, were he a gambling man, Benson Fong would bet he will be responsible for bringing Moss to meet his essences--Benson Fong remains above it all--a servant to those who have entrusted him to power. Therefore,

Moss Eckman remains a tool; rather than a savage, as Benson has always seen him. Moss, he has convinced himself, is a necessary link--perhaps important because he is vain and nihilistic.

This is the profound effect Winston Doe has had on Benson Fong's life: Hope seems to grow inside him. It ruptures his control; his entire reality has become a bit more positive, despite his certainty that the drift of humanity is reaching its crescendo. That gift from her, he will never release, perhaps because he fears its failure more than death.

So in defense against hope, his brain jumps to the meeting he has arranged. It will be the first one in which Winston will directly interact with Moss--in full clarity of her world. The possibilities seem limitless. Were Benson more schooled in Species Focus, he might know the angst of possibility he feels in his gut is a memory, like a remembrance of sea sickness while sailing on a calm sea.

Benson again checks the room for the placement of the security teams; he has already changed their rules of engagement to defend Winston before Moss. Of the five or six hundred people present, thirty are his security people. The past has taught Benson the absurdity of trying to control events, but Benson cannot help but try to affect secondary impacts.

As if to accentuate the point, he notices Mina. "Oh, hell." He hurries over to her. "Mina, honey, what are you doing here? Did Moss call you?"

Mina, dressed in a loose-fitting pink frock breezes towards him in front of a window. The silhouette of her body through the shear material draws stares from every passing man and woman. More than a dozen tourists in the crowd wear some similar version of a frock--known these days as the Genian style of dress--but none are so alluringly diaphanous. "You are so fresh," Benson says.

Mina pulls in a breath trying to be polite to him. While she had detested her father's dedication to a corrupt system, Benson represents something far worse: acceptance of a corrupt system. The problem now is she has glimpsed something more than avarice in Benson Fong and that offends her beyond words. Moss is a product of engineering and amorality. He does not deserve his place in the world, but at least he lives it. Benson, she once believed, was just a naturally occurring phony. Now, she considers he may have some hand in all this.

She glares at Benson. "Moss called and said he was coming here to get permission from the Director of U.N. Environment for our party. He said you arranged it. She cannot resist the opportunity to insult Benson Fong. "What's going on Benson, you little shit?"

Benson curses his stupidity. By endangering Mina today, Moss walks a line that Benson fears most. Were it to come down to Winston or Mina he does not know whom he would choose to protect. Anyone would have understood his protection of Winston over Moss--but Mina? How could he or his people have missed this call? He has never seen this level of incompetence in them. Then it clears: It's control that has failed here. The process of transition intensifies. This clarity calms him.

"Benson?"

"Look honey, do us all a favor and play along--you know Moss. He's got the world on a string and he likes playing with it." As always he scans for Moss--one hand in the tweed coat pocket--clutching a stun gun. "His dementia is our salvation."

"You're wrong, Fong. He has had a memory cut by Clipper," she says staring at him.

"A what?" Benson considers her amateurish test a danger signal. "Still got that daddy thing going, huh? Why don't you let me spend some time with you tonight? I'll cure you of that daddy thing with my big daddy right here." He glances at his crotch and winks.

"I'd sooner kiss a Gulf oil slick." But rather then follow it with her normal sneer, she ends with an unarmed smile. "And drop the BS, Benson, I am not buying it anymore. What do you know about Clipper?"

He opens his eyes wide and grins. Benson is too good to be rattled, but he knows she will be a problem today. "It's a drink isn't it?" Before she can react, he waves to Moss. Mina shoots a short angry glance at him then turns to Moss.

What Moss notices--rather than the heat between Mina and Benson--is the women; short, tall, young, old. From behind shaded horn-rimmed glasses, he grades them like cattle. Occasionally he nods with a leering smile. Mina approaches Moss. Benson follows Mina at a distance, keeping her safe.

A particularly attractive mother walks past Moss, there is no husband in sight. Moss stops beside a huge red caboose and peers over his glasses at her. She sees him, a flash of anger in her eyes. Moss shakes his head, pointing to the two young children. The mother glares at him. Mina laughs, and then nudges Moss in the ribs. "Hi Honey, the kids are in the bathroom, puking." The mother of two walks away.

"Oh there you are, my ever-present anchor, my bitch, my wife. My love. Watch this…My little cabbage." Moss drops car keys from his pocket. The young mother, along with fifty other tourists turns to see who has dropped a set of car keys. Moss makes a show of picking them up and smiles at the young mother. She returns a warm smile. "Fuck the kids," he says to Mina, winking at the mother. She returns the wink.

Benson notes Mina's boredom--she has seen Moss' act too many times. Mina speaks, "Oh, you like the tart with progeny?" She bats her eyes at the woman--ignoring her response--and taking Moss' arm directing him to a dining car that hangs upside down above them, its roof removed for viewing. "We'll buy you one at Tarts R Us," she chirps.

Moss shakes his head to Benson saying he finds Mina's bitchiness boring. Benson's expression shifts briefly from the eternal leer to a quick glance at security. He begins to reappraise the situation and grabs the attention of three security people dressed as college students. Well trained, the security team turns away to get instructions. Mina catches him and her gaze sharpens. Her young life was full of cloaked denizens posing as simple folk and she wonders how should have missed this.

She sidles up to Benson and whispers "You're a spook."

Moss misses all this--ostensibly watching children climbing a model of cartoon train with the name DUMBO on the side. In truth, Moss, dressed in an absurdly expensive light brown leather coat, real cotton blue jeans and khaki shirt, stares at one blond-haired and well proportioned prey. Moss' target has, in turn, identified him as a very wealthy man. Moss approaches her and leans into the young woman whispering into her ear. Her blue eyes wander to other passing females, her smile growing larger with each word from Moss. He reaches up and lightly touches her shoulder. "Let's go somewhere in my Jaguar, later." Her head shakes no but she wears the soul of congeniality. Moss knows will not be rejected by this one.

Benson hurries up and taps Moss on the back. "Come on, Moss. We have a party to prepare for, and if we are late, the chick that runs this place will never approve the launch." Benson points to his watch.

"Leave your address at the front desk," Moss says to the woman. "I'll have a car come for you. Say 6:30?" He turns, passing children that for him, could have been rocks beside a road. Taking Mina's hand, he says loudly: "Don't be jealous dear. She's gay." They walk off passing through a coal train exhibit. Moss turns to Benson who follows dutifully. "Oh lord. Benson, give it up. Mina hates you." He laughs and kisses Mina on the cheek.

A snake of jealously rides into his gut and Benson wonders if his teams could have missed some intimacy between these two. Believing they share some secret, he watches them stroll by exhibits of freight cars and out the glass doors to the courtyard.

Outside, a juggler tosses red, white, and blue Indian clubs skyward as he poses on a big red ball. Every time Moss tries to walk around him, the juggler moves, tossing the clubs in various spinning arcs. Moss checks his pockets for change. He drops a few dollars into an upturned top hat that is tethered to a red and white striped pole. The juggler tosses all three clubs high in the air, grabs Moss' hand, shakes it, then quickly catches the descending clubs.

"That juggler is good, but I'm surprised they're allowed to be so aggressive," Moss says. "Invite him the party will you, Benson?"

"You bet, Moss." Benson nods at the juggler; a security person will invite the juggler if they find a safe profile.

Mina opens another pair of glass doors and a whoosh of greasy air assaults the group. Then the clang and clatter of falling dishes from the food court follows: It is a battlefield in here. Ketchup covers everything in this glass-roofed cafeteria. The tables and plates, servers and hostesses, moms and dads, they all stand covered in condiments like the late-day combatants in a Napoleonic war. Food fights are common with today's meal. Red and green ketchup flies up in little spurts as they all play at lunch.

Only those associated with the Museum are aware of the experiment underway in this free cafeteria. Despite all the warnings to the contrary, the patrons gravitate to the events that are most destructive to the environment, and the food that is most destructive to them: ground textured cow fat. Moss grins and leans over to Mina. "I need to tell Travis his cow fat experiment is going to be a money-maker."

Around the corner, patrons hold silverware like swords, and their trays like shields, assaulting the buffet. They shove each other aside with polite smiles as they compete for the food bathed in heat lamps. The security guards, safe and unconcerned, like generals, survey the action making sure just ketchup decorates the food pen. Permeating everything, the smell of greasy burnt flesh on toasted buns; a smell that owns these people through some perverse collective memory.

Only during the fried burger meal days does the dining area turn into a pig sty. Researchers from the Meat Council continue to monitor the crowds for the reasons.

Benson notes that the mob of diners make sure they get their share of food even if they cannot eat it. "I'm not going to stand here," Benson pronounces. "I'll go ask that guard when we meet the boss." Benson starts to walk away, and then returns like yo-yo attached to a string. "Moss, I know you're pissed about all this bullshit they've been giving us, but try and keep a rein on it, okay?"

Mina hears the false note in his words and unconsciously steps back from the two of them. She also notices the feeding trough in front of them disgusts Benson. He cannot look at the scene. *Now where did all these sensibilities come from?* She asks herself. *Why did I miss it?* She feels the top of her right ear for a scar--it is the tell tale sign of a Clipper implant. There is no scar.

"Benson, I'm here because you convinced me I have to be," Moss says. "What I say isn't going to make a bit of difference. They're holding us up because they want something from us. Let's find out what it is and be done with it." He watches the room and its battling throng of tourists. "I just love people." Moss turns away to a fifteen-foot model of a fish-processing ship with a tiny drift net behind it. He moves closer to the ship and its tiny crew. They all wear demonic leers on grotesque bodies and are unquestionably the ugliest group of dolls he has ever seen. The fish, on the other hand, seem to be either cherubic or writhing in pain. "Mina, do you think we are really this evil?"

"You are, Moss." She smiles, watching Benson walk away to talk with one of the guards. "What's up with Benson?" She asks him.

"Something going on? I must have missed it. Maybe he's concerned because he doesn't have a date for the party." He laughs. "Nah, he never has a date."

Mina's eyes drop for a second. "That's because of me?"

He looks at her: "Mina I will lose all respect for you the moment you consider him anything more than the boorish philistine he is."

Mina moans quietly.

"Mr. Eckman?"

The solid-looking guard appears. "Yes?" Moss grins at the guard in front of him.

"If you'll just follow me, please." He escorts them around the perimeter to a closed door. A likeness of the Mona Lisa in ketchup drools down a door. Opening it, they enter a four-table room with three white walls and one clear wall that looks into a courtyard filled the crowds milling between exhibit halls. A dark-haired woman sits in solitude, sipping tea from a white cup, her back towards them.

Moss notes that her ponytail continues well down her back, the same length as a corporate CEO. "I hadn't realized the Museum Director was so important," he says to Mina.

"That's Winston Doe," she says, her focus now on the truth of what is going on with Benson Fong.

"I know. I met her at Travis' office. I didn't know you knew her. Wonder-Woman, Benson calls her. I am going to bed her. It has been said an older woman will treat you right." He pulls forth a cherubic smile--and winks. "Dr. Doe," Moss calls out. "That light brown skin and those eyes--come to papa." Moss mumbles this second part for Mina to hear--they are in some ways confidantes--and then he puts on his most ingratiating smile. "Aren't you something," he says loud enough for Dr. Doe to hear.

Mina's eyes dart for Benson. "You lying, little worm--what the hell is going on, Benson?"

"Mina, I'll explain later," he whispers. Benson knows when deceptions no longer have a place.

"Sure. I trust you." Mina steps around Winston examining her hairline in back. A small scar over her right ear causes her to pause. Then, regaining her composure: "Holy shit, you're a Ginda," she whispers into the woman's precisely proportioned ears. She waits for a cut from Clipper but none occurs. She stares at Benson--completely dumbfounded. Mina considers the possibilities. *Is Benson her handler like Travis is Moss' handler? Or is Benson higher up in the food chain?*

Moss' sham of seduction continues in front of her.

"Moss, how long have you known this beautiful creature?" Mina purrs.

"We met yesterday afternoon," he says, keeping his gaze on Winston's lovely eyes.

Surprisingly to Benson, Mina steps back and leans over to him. "You know about him don't you? You U.N. prick." She walks from him to Winston. "I thought I might introduce myself. I am Mina Wolf, Madam Ginda."

Winston smiles: "You must have had a memory lapse, Ms. Wolf. My name is Doe. Dr. Winston Doe. I am the Director of Samarra, and also the lead researcher on Species Focus." She lowers her voice so just Mina can hear. "And Ginda or not, I assure you everyone remembers you--you spoiled little bitch."

Mina's self assurance crumbles.

Winston then hisses to her: "So yes I may have focus. Now sit down and shut up." She turns to Moss: "How do you do, Mr. Eckman?" Winston extends a hand to Moss ignoring Mina who sits glaring at Benson.

Mina, who once saw herself as surrounded by bit players, does not like the reversal. Despite her supposed disrespect for her father's work, she is in awe of this kind of progress--and finds anger that she has been placed outside the loop of his work. She knows that a self aware Ginda, especially one with Winston Doe's talents, represents hope for humanity.

"Don't mind Mina. Her dad was Lazlo Wolf--the loony tune." Moss glows looking into Mina's eyes.

"Some Walkers are so Techie," Mina says glaring at Winston.

"Gently, Mina. Dr. Doe is my new friend," says Moss, "Though I hadn't noticed her beautiful smooth skin from natural childbirth before this moment." Moss has no idea he has confessed to Winston--after using this same line the first time they met, that he finds smooth skin repulsive--preferring the mottled effect of bovine birth like most of his generation.

Winston forces her eyes to soften. Reliving his lies like this make her want to strangle Moss. She watches Mina's angry eyes again shift to Benson. Then Mina and Winston both glare at Benson. He holds a cherubic, innocent countenance. His heart races with possibilities--Benson knows his charade has ended and change is underway with Mina. He tries to hide his happiness but it escapes from his eyes. Mina sees this and at first doesn't understand it. She glances at Winston who smiles warmly at General Fong. When she does, Mina's eyes spit fire. Winston speaks: "Mr. Fong, good to see you again. Your friend Mr. Eckman is so charming."

"I am that," Moss says, refocusing on Winston. "How do you feel about a younger man, as say, a friend?"

Mina feels as if she is some minor avatar in a computer game. In fact, it is the beginning of process. *If Winston has focus then Moss is askew and fading. Could my dad have really been right, there is goodness in us?* Mina understands her father's theories as if they were a recipe for chocolate chip cookies--she has heard them her entire youth. She just didn't believe, until this moment, that they were plausible.

"Please sit," Winston Doe says. Queasiness has risen in her stomach. "Does Zen interest you, Mr. Eckman?" Winston's perverse baiting of Moss into another repeat of an earlier comment will harden her a bit further to her task.

"Actually, I find Zen fascinating. I find debates about the worth of objects offensive."

His word for word repetition has worked; her researcher's brain has kicked into the process. "We all begin as objects," she says, full of charm. "Odd we have so much trouble understanding the spirits in objects. How can I help you, Mr. Eckman?" Winston's voice only barely covers the anger she feels about falling for so many ploys. She glances at Mina and immediately understands what Mina is feeling about Benson.

"These are very interesting," Moss says looking at the miniature tapestries surrounding the executive dining space. "They remind me of Edvard Munch's work." Moss perceives her distance. "These comments are meant to attract your intellect and attention Did I bore you?"

"These tapestries are done in plant dyes of deep reds and violets that became popular after the disintegration of New Zealand," Winston says, sounding like a tour guide. "The style of angular faces, with black empty eyeballs, and open screaming mouths are often compared with the original woodcuts of Edvard Munch on which they were styled."

"Why is that?" Moss asks.

"'The Scream' was the only art work found floating in the Pacific after the New Zealand disaster."

"And the quote: 'To begin at the beginning and so forth' Above them?"

"Dylan Thomas--from Under Milkwood."

"Would you show me your favorite tapestry?" Moss asks with a slight lift to his eyebrow. Moss doesn't like the tapestries, or the solemn quiet of the dining space. He does want to hear Winston Doe's talk--another rerun.

He is all about repeating lines--how degrading. "I couldn't. I like them all."

Moss glides through her words like a cat on the prowl. "Very nice--don't you think so Benson?"

From the corner of her eye Winston sees Mina watching, alert to the tableau, Only Moss, she believes, has no sense of the irony of what takes place around him. Winston then catches a glimpse of Benson watching Mina. She had assumed she might see annoyance--she cannot fathom that she sees him showing something else, a wanting heart. It is unlike Benson to allow wild-cards into his deck. Her trust for him increases again.

"Our party," Benson says feeling a bit too exposed, "has exceeded the energy usage for such an event. As a result, we have purchased double that amount in carbon offset credits. Regardless, we were called in today to meet with you to discuss the issue, because we are told the undue usage of power sends the wrong message to those who still struggle with reduced energy." Benson plays his part of flunky for only Moss.

"You know, Moss, sometimes Benson can be so absurd with those banal statements," Mina says.

Winston crinkles her lips but hides her smile. She speaks. "Mr. Eckman, the energy committee will not agree to the allocation of energy because we have no faith you will remain faithful to your pledges of energy replacement on this occasion. You never have before. Frankly, you seem to believe you are the center of the universe and no one else matters."

"Perhaps I am not as important as I once thought I was." Moss blinks. The change in climate around him has not totally escaped his cognition. "Let's cut to the chase. What do you want?"

"First of all, the understanding that the power you use is only temporary. You will replace it over time with reductions in your personal residence."

"Done, but only if you attend my party to confirm my pledge. " Moss grins at her. "You can be my honored guest."

"I cannot."

"Of course you can. You and I are tied in some magical way," says Moss sure of his charm and allure. "Dr. Doe, our time is now."

"It is not our time, Mr. Eckman. Our time has come and gone. I have another meeting to attend."

"Fine it is your time. But, you will see that you need me," he says with a boyish grin. "But I see mere charm it is not working. Okay I will stick to the energy plan. Shall I redirect the energy to Samarra?"

"That will be fine. Thank you, Mr. Eckman. I think we at Samarra can support your efforts." She rises from the table.

Moss looks to Benson in triumph. "Dr. Doe, thank you. But there is something I must say. Have you ever met someone and felt like you have known them for lifetimes?"

Winston cannot deal with him any longer. "Mr. Eckman, I know that feeling, but frankly, you are right. You do bore me." Winston walks away, winking at the careful gaze of Mina Wolf. Mina follows her.

"How can you possibly have focus and know it?" Mina's voice pleads for an answer. "That's madness."

"That's not what your Dad thought. He believed we can rise to sentience." Winston wonders how Mina will deal with this. "It's your worst fear, Mina. We humans can grow. We are not destined to stay beasts--too bad for you. You are a lousy theoretician, did you know that?" She leaves the room.

Mina corrals Benson by pulling him away from Moss so they can speak: "Your work? Did you turn her into a Ginda?"

"No."

"You lie." She glances about to see that Moss has left. "Is this about the uptick in Jazz War events?" Mina asks.

"It's more than an uptick."

"I know. " Mina measures Benson. "So you are a lying little worm. But if she is taking Focus then there is hope somewhere."

"We believe so."

She nods to Moss outside the door; he is interrogating a young brunette. "And he doesn't know?"

"That all depends on what you tell him, Mina."

Her eyes widen. "What's that supposed to mean?"

"We need to speak."

Her eyes glow in triumph. "No. I don't think so. There is nothing a spook like you could tell me about my father's theories anyway."

CHAPTER 33

Monday--The city wasn't as I had expected. In the vids, the city is where the beautiful people live. If that's pretty, I never want to see ugly, or dirty! Everyone in the city is scared, hungry, and afraid. They all carry weapons. Plus all those people jammed into those big buildings smoking something called Scotch Broom. It's supposed to get you happy. I guess Walkers invented it.

Then I saw tons of angry people who can't get their clothes washed. How can you not be able to get your clothes washed? Then the noise, and the smell, it was awful! Then there are the smoldering fires. Soot covers everything. The worst of it is the sound of people crying, and the death--you can taste it! There are hardly any lights--besides the fires in the apartments. The tall buildings glowed from fires. It came through the cloak of smoke around them. Some buildings looked like they were moving. I didn't understand that--maybe the buildings were still moving from the big earthquakes they had.

I thought that cities like San Francisco were supposed to be full of people who did things that were fun. No one starved on the vids. Why do the vids lie to us? Maybe Lazlo didn't want me to know how bad it was now. We're losing the war. Damn the Gumbies, I hate them.

Then I saw a mother kill her child by throwing it in front of a bus. A passerby pulled out a gun and then shot the mother in the chest and walked away. The mother said, "Thank you," before she died. We watched it happen. We didn't do anything. Benny told me it happens all the time. The people who live here see death as courtesy: "Please, thank you," and bang,"you're dead!"

Monday night--I should just start at the beginning. I guess I am giving Clipper a hernia. Poor baby. Let's see, to begin at the beginning. Now where did that come from? Oh Dylan Thomas, I bet he's spinning in his grave. I think we love death. We certainly love its blessing. My lover believes that you know. I'd like to see him again, but Polken is gone. I wonder where he went.

Anyway, the soldiers took me downtown, but I don't recollect my decision to go. I recall sitting in the back of a transport and the lights coming on. The back door opened and it felt like I had been hit in the face with a ball of soot. Then it seemed a million fingers were poking at my skin. No one touched me physically because the guys formed a circle around me. I don't think anyone could have understood what it felt like; it was some kind of game--a game to make each other feel miserable inside--and if that didn't work, to harm them. I think we hate each other. I remember Plow had teased me that the Gumbies would be no problem after the city. Funny he didn't make it into the city with us. Someone said Plow had helped Polken escape. I never saw Kristen so happy. She liked Polken. Escaped where?

The street smelled like urine. I looked at all the dirty, ghostly-looking people dressed in rags, and then instead of me feeling vulnerable, they did. We were dressed in our clean military jumpsuits. I felt like I was dressed in gold. One young girl wearing earrings that tinkled bumped into Rico. Then she just kept right on walking as if she were asleep. Pisser called her a Yorkie.

We were on a wide street near the water. When we arrived there, the street had been filled with people, but soon it was almost empty. I think the people were afraid of us. Just a few people were still left but they were coupling against the walls--I don't think they even knew we were there. None of us said a word, except Rico. He thinks we are masters of the universe.

Finally a bus came. It looked more like a tank than a bus. There were no windows in it and there were dents and holes all over it. Steel plates were welded on top of each other everywhere, even inside. There were no seats. As it rolled over the bumpy road we held onto these bars that hung from the roof.

People on the bus were staring at me. And I didn't say or do anything. When I looked around at how ragged everyone was I figured they were trying to get even about something. The soldiers ignored the way they were treated.

I asked the young woman beside me what was going on. She said, "Dummy!" Pointed to the back of her head and walked away. I felt so back-country. I think if I feel like this when I encounter the Gumbies, I might be dead. I asked another lady what the other woman was pointing to in the back of my head? She said it was the camera behind my ear.

I don't remember seeing that before. It's no wonder the Gumbies are pissed at us. Hell, sitting here now, I'm pissed at us! It's no wonder they are attacking—likely cause: just for being a planet full of creeps.

Someone threw something at me. I got angry. I hate hurting people. This isn't for me. I quit.

Tuesday midnight--We went to an aquarium. It was a harbor filled with old ships that were sunk--some part way, some all the way up to their smokestacks. I finally got Gus to talk to me again. I did it by asking if the Gumbies had sunk all the ships.

He said some of those ships had been sunk during the tsunamis and storms of global warming. The others were sunk right around the time of the New Zealand disaster, but they were never moved or repaired. I guess the people who ran away to New Zealand sank all the big ships so they wouldn't be followed. I guess they thought they were important. Gus called them a bunch of Lonocs.

Gus asked me if I understood this city was better than most places on the planet. When I told Gus I thought he was joking. He said things here in San Francisco were pretty good.

He confused me. I thought that after global warming was corralled, things had straightened up for us. Rico laughed at me. He said I was living in a dream world, and it was finally time to understand what had really happened to us. "We had decided people didn't matter," that's what Rico said. "So we didn't." He told me that if I thought something was important it was very important.

I think I can do things they cannot.

They were drinking beers, lots of them. Rico grabbed me by the shoulder and started screaming at me about oil. He said oil was the spirit, or ghosts of the dinosaurs. He said that by using it up we had cursed ourselves. He said the Jazz War was that curse.

Then he said something really crazy. He said we live backwards in time and that was the dinosaurs' fault. Then he cackled that he was a little late in delivering the news. Then Rico and Gus started singing a song about a dog named Bingo. I guess the planet has rules of its own--too bad we ignored them.

Someone also whispered in my ear that soldiers sometimes went out of control. It hadn't occurred to me it could be worse for them than it was for me. I felt so bad about my brain being attached to Clipper, I didn't think about how bad it might be for everyone else. It's all collapsing. It's already collapsed.

I am so ashamed. My life is pretty good compared to people out there in the cities. Those people in the city aren't part of a society, they are just survivors--until they die.

It's a dead end! I wish I didn't know there

was so much horror out there.

Wednesday morning--I just took a walk. I saw a missile take off.

Wait. No, I remember we stood on line waiting to enter a place called the Coney Island Aquarium. I didn't know there was a place called Coney Island in San Francisco--but I didn't mention it. I think this memory comes from a different city and a different time. Whatever memory Clipper cut from me it must have been pretty ugly.

I can continue now. Anyway, we were in an aquarium and people were laughing while we were standing on line to go look at fish. The world was collapsing around us and we were going to look at fish. How crazy is that?

I remember that I thought about my parents, and whether they would have liked the aquarium. An older woman behind me with a hairy upper lip said: "No, with what they did to you, they would probably have liked a bullfight better. Aquariums aren't their style."

I looked at her and she smiled. I don't think she meant to hurt me. I think she had been trying to take care of me. The old woman had fat arms and a flowered dress with blue patches on it. The soldiers were quiet. I could tell that they never spoke their minds--ever. The woman gazed at me every time I saw her walking around the aquarium, but she never said anything else to me. The last time I saw her the soldiers got nervous. I heard them release the safety on their weapons.

Later, we were looking at the fish and I wondered if fish liked people who stared at them. A young couple walked by me; they pulled out knives from their coats.

I think the soldiers were really wigged out with that one. I think I kicked a man. I am not cut out for this. I will not hurt them. They are so hurt already.

Wednesday afternoon--We went to a restaurant. I asked Rico if people fight a lot now. He said I should think about something far away and that it would help. There were beads of sweat on his brow and his uniform was wet. I wondered if it was sweat or blood. I forced myself to think about my room while we ate baked chicken.

The base is so nice, with trucks, and cars, and paint on the wall, and lights. I had never realized how much I like the small white rocks that line the streets or the clean kitchen and dining mess.

Rico said it was silly to worry about people.

Then he was talking to a studious looking older woman who wore a green scarf and blood-stained turtleneck shirt. She had sat down beside Rico a few minutes earlier. I asked Rico to not make fun of her. The woman said her daughter thought I was a nice person.

What has Clipper done to me? Why was everything I thought available for everyone to comment on as they saw fit? What the hell was Clipper doing with my thoughts, broadcasting them to the entire city?

I tried to talk to Gus again, but he had a lot to drink. He went outside looking for some girl he knew. There was the sound of gunfire—and Gus took me out a side door. We couldn't find Rico because it was misty and the burning buildings around us had made the mist look yellow and eerie. A few blocks away the streets were full of dead people. Everyone else had weapons. Just walking around, hardly saying a word, the crowds seemed lost, but they acted casual about it. I saw craters in the concrete roadway and dirt everywhere. Gus suggested I sit down and stare out at the water--but things kept happening. Flashes of light, people getting killed, smoke and sirens. My eyes twitched. My nose itched. My stomach grumbled. I had to pee. I was hungry and thought about dinner while I was listening to the soldiers fire their weapons. I looked around at the destruction, it was much worse, and there were lots more soldiers.

Then Rico suggested we find some party gals.

I'm not sure what that meant, but they all laughed. It was the only time I remember them all laughing. We walked over to a squat building. I guess it used to be a bowling alley--now it was called "The Geisha House".

Inside was a huge room with long wood benches lit by a pulsing red light. Men and woman lounged around. Some of them weren't dressed. Gus said they didn't own any clothes and they were here trying to earn enough energy for clothes.

Pisser picked out a young girl with tired red eyes who said I was going to help her get some clothes. Rico said I shouldn't love her, just talk to her. So I knew it was an okay thing to follow her. She led me down one of the dingy hallways and into a small room that smelled of sweat and scum. She asked me if I was from the military base in Palo Alto. I said I was from the base in San Francisco. She laughed. You'd think I'd just told her the funniest joke she'd ever heard. I guess there was a big earthquake in San Francisco the other day. So I think she thought it was a joke and wanted to make me happy so she could get some clothes.

We talked then she was given her clothes.

I left with the stink of the room still on my clothes. Out in the street I grabbed a gun and shot someone. Rico took the gun from me and pointed it at me. He said if I did that again, he would kill me. Then he shot me. Thank you.

Thursday--It's too horrible out there. I don't ever want to leave here. Find someone else.

Sunday morning--You're a tricky one, Dr. Wolf. This morning I went into the library because the word Yorkie was running through my head. Yorkie is a slang word from the time of global warming. It originally meant a hyper-high-strung dog. Then a few years later, it meant a person who was in New York City during the riots. Then there were even more horrible riots when the city went dark. The people who were left behind figured out they were all going to die in some disaster. So everyone went crazy. Those that survived were called New Yorkies. So now, anyone who is crazed is called a Yorkie. The librarian who had helped me understand the term Yorkie was nice. Her name was Winston. She told me I needed to understand how bad it was out there and that people really needed my help. She said I am free to do as I wish and that I shouldn't feel guilty about the things I do as a soldier. I guess I am going to give that memory to someone named Moss. He is going to take over. Winston said that Moss will help us get back to saner times.

But if everyone is so crazy, why help them? The heck with them. Only an idiot helps the evil ones. So maybe I should be evil like them. That only makes sense.

Thursday night--I spent the day walking around the base looking for Lazlo. I couldn't find him. I think Lazlo is in trouble. Everything is so clean here.

Thursday midnight--Doctor Pard showed up. I've never seen him so happy, but he looked like he hadn't slept in days. He smelled greasy, like the bowling alley. I think he plans to teach me not to care. Seemed to me, he was just the right guy for the job.

Later, Dr. Pard said that I'm not cooperating and they're thinking of starting a new experiment and maybe they will have two Gindas. He asked me if I thought my failure was enough to justify another Ginda. I told him if he tried to tear another baby in half, I'd kill him. He became angry with me and left.

Friday--Someone killed Wildhead. I don't think it was me.

(Notes from the Research Team: It is generally believed that this last passage is just before the death of Lazlo Wolf. Insofar as the researcher, Dr. Doe, she is being acclimated into the process. We suggest moving forward as quickly as possible. The search for Gustav Plow will expand and continue into the foreseeable future. J.Pard/R.Merton. Date suppressed per requirement.)

Chapter 34

Thursday--Dr. Pard just left. He doesn't look well.

Pard said Dr. Biner is also gone. I think he was happy about that. I think he thought the Doc interfered too much. I wonder where he went.

Wednesday--And here's the updated score: Sammich: 1, the rest of them: 0.

Here now the details: I feel like sportscaster. One, I'm in the hospital. Two, I've got one hell of a headache from the bullet wound in my skull. Dr. Merton needs a new leg. Three, I was able to see Winston because she is here also. Four, they're going ahead with making Winston just like me--except that she will know everything. She's so smart. That makes four, Winston's lucky number.

Wednesday night--I guess things didn't work out so badly. Though when all is said and done, my negotiating position is rather weak. It took a .22 pointed at my own head to get what I want. Rico is being credited with saving my life because he busted in the door of the toilet. He got a medal for that. I wish I had gotten a medal.

I was sitting there, the gun pointed at my head, wondering how much damage I might do to Clipper's machinery.

I didn't mean to hurt Rico; I was trying to protect myself. Instead, a perfect shot right into his heart. Some price to pay so I can help Winston win. That's what my diary is--and that's what Dr. Wolf had tried to keep me from knowing--Winston is now our focus, not me. Can I go now?

I think I will try to make Winston my friend. I think someday I will make love with her. Or my memories will. I am okay with that.

Friday--Oh, I see, Winston doesn't think of them like that. Rico once told me I need be myself. After all, why should we be sacrificed for a bunch of crazy people?

Saturday--The Vatican burned today, and so did a cathedral in Washington. The announcer said they had caught the people who did it. It was a group of Islamic Clerics from Paducah. Someone suggested a public execution. I think they're going to do that. None of this surprises me, the great unwashed means nothing to me. But I will help.

Saturday night--I told Pard that all the bearded men on the vid who did the burning had that fuzziness running down the center of their bodies. I reminded him that Dr. Wolf called it a disjunction. Pard patted me on the shoulder and said he liked my dedication, but that they weren't pursuing that line of reasoning anymore because Clipper and some satellites can stop the killings now by putting people to sleep before they hurt anyone. So how come the churches were burned?

Sunday--We went into another town yesterday. It was a small town. All the power was off and people kept coming up to us and telling us the telephones didn't work. I don't understand why they were concerned about the phones, maybe it was because they had all this food to eat, but no one to share it with. I don't understand why we went there--to see the dead bodies and the crazed people? Or to teach me how to use a telephone?

Monday--The town was called Baker-base. The people there were much different from the other cities. The people in Baker-base looked at us with a mixture of pity and embarrassment. Many of them didn't even speak to us. Some one said we were temporary humans, or something. Here on a lease today, tossed out tomorrow. They didn't care about me and I don't care about them.

There are only the two of us soldiers left, Kristen and I. I think the soldiers are being executed one by one. Pard keeps telling me to forget all that. He says we have won the battle. So why don't they let me go?

Tuesday--Oh, God, how do I tell Kristen that I got a medal?

Some executives and a couple of generals showed up this morning. One guy named Joshua was nice. I liked him. He said the others were my friends, like my soldier friends. They told me Gus once said he was the son of businessmen, bankers, lawyers, and carpenters. He said everyone was his family: Brazilians, Japanese, Swiss, Dutch, Chinese, North American and Eskimo. They said he said he owed them his life and that's why he served them--fighting the horrors of their lives. Then Joshua handed me the medal and said I was a hero. Then they left. I wonder if they knew Gus spoke five illegal languages: Portuguese, Spanish, French, Japanese, Latin--and of course, the legal language of the planet--English.

It always bothered Gus that I was controlled by a machine--oh, and he always called me Sammy. He had always said I'd be set free and my mind returned to me when this is over. He said he would put that in his will.

Kristen is just like me now. She just told the others she had never encountered a finer human than Sammy Ginda.

What do I tell Kristen about my medal?

Wednesday--One of the researchers shot Kristen, but she stopped him cold anyway with a couple of those Ninja throwing stars she carries. Then she got another two as well. After I fixed her wound, someone else tried to kill her again. I took care of that. But it seems pointless to fix wounds when the war goes on and on. I wonder where she is today? I'd like to talk to her about my medal. I am going to tell her the medal is hers.

(Commentary from the Research Team: This is the end of the Ginda Diary. The last Ginda was terminated right after this entry per original orders from Dr. Lazlo Wolf. Work has begun on the maintenance system called Moss. J.Pard/R.Merton. Date suppressed per requirement.)

(Commentary from the 1st Court of Inquiry: It is clear Doctors Pard and Merton were acting on the last direct orders of Doctor Wolf. G.Smetana/B.Fong. Date suppressed per requirement.)

CHAPTER 35

Tuesday night--My name is Moss and I don't care about the rest of you. I want my time and I want my fun. The hell with you. I know I am already getting screwed by you so I can serve you. Therefore, you will be my fools and I shall be your tool. It's all over anyway, so who cares? On the other hand, I will be the one to die with the most toys. So I guess that means I am the top of the heap. Fitting isn't it?

That's all I have to say. Give me my toys and get out of my way. See, someone won your stupid game--me. Doesn't seem worth it, or does it?

CHAPTER 36

Voice-over: "...And so it appears attempts to restrict on-continent broadcasts by the Japanese Government have ended. In a terse comment, the Japanese Government has stated the Japanese satellites, in accordance with the wishes of the United States citizenry, will provide real time satellite feeds of the US population just like the rest of the world. We're coming back, America. Hang on. It'll be a great ride..."

....

Stopping at the stream to clean the blood, she vomits instead. Winston sits, tears rolling down her cheeks. A rash of blood stains on her right side.

She had just finished placing the Diary and its player in the doomsday vault at Samarra, when an explosion rattled down the stairwell. Rushing up the last flight of stairs, she opened the steel door and peeked outside. Smoke swirled all around her. A satellite receiver flopped back and forth hung only by wires, it's dish collapsed. The grounds were empty.

Hearing more gun fire, she exited into the choking smoke. Explosions came from outside Samarra's gates. Drawn to it, she made her way out a service exit. People in Bermuda shorts and brightly colored surf shirts were exchanging gun fire with a detachment of soldiers.

Fascinated, she drew close as the one-sided battle progressed. Winston could not recall seeing bodies ripped apart by weapons, even though she was sure she had witnessed it before. It had all been revoltingly new to her. When silence fell, and the soldiers fanned out to check the bodies; she left her hiding place to come back home. With her first step, Winston slipped in some gore from the battle, landing in a muddy, bloody puddle of limb and torn clothe. She had no idea she was so close to danger.

Washing the last stains from her legs, Winston climbs the creek side to the bridge. Feeling nothing of the lovely early dew, she ignores the impatiens clustered along the fallen logs. In the stream, brown water wilted leaves lay piled in the draws and hollows--she sees that. But not the symphony that begins this morning.

Crossing the small bridge to her home, she misses the small pearls of last night's dew glowing on the grass. The yellow and green leaves dotting the branches around her, the breeze, the flowering plum along the path, the purple iris with their full-headed bloom. All of them as if they were in celebration. The hyacinth stems sport a parade of their yellow kin. Enjoying it, a doe and two fawns stand under the farthest apple tree watching her. All the neighbors are here but none of them can penetrate her pain and anger.

And instead of hearing the symphony, she sees a note, a papyrus note, tacked on the post of her porch, below it, the tracks of a scooter scoring the grass. It's a note from Moss. *What does that gold-crusted idiot want now?*

The lid's off. The neighborhood peepshow is on. It's the New World order. It's the end of privacy! Ring it in with a party!!!. Sponsored by the Eckman Brothers. Old Boeing field tonight, ten PM. Satellites crossing the Northwest that night include the: Chinese, Japanese, Egyptian, Somali, Russian, Australian, South African, Moroccan, Mexican, Colombian, and Vietnamese. Wear something revealing of body, spirit, or mind. Or try the enclosed pink union-suit! Be the first on your block to moon your neighbors via satellite. The future waits. Be there, or just be watching.

R*eal papyrus*!

She crumples the note amazed at her intensifying dislike for him.

Here I am standing with this absurd document because he sees the end coming and doesn't care. No. Of course not, he's too busy having fun. She gauges the energy used to make the invitation: *likely as much as power as most Walkers use in a week. He goes where he wants and does what he wants. And for his transgressions, I am to breach... What? To find Russell, my love, my eviscerated mentor, my Machiavellian research partner, my friend--not. Or do I open a path... To what? What the hell am I doing this for? And when my work is done, then what I am to do? See my life as a mockery of love and caring? No one would do what I am doing for the sludge pit that is humanity. Why did I do it?*

Winston kicks the pink package clinging to the wooden post base. Blind with anger, she places her hand on the post. The next thing she feels is the damp mossy wood. Then, from the corner of her eye, she notices movement.

"Winston."

She spins.

A thick man approaches her, his limp far worse than she remembers it. Dressed in khaki pants and a red checked wool shirt, Joshua Pard approaches carefully. He appears weighed down by his tasks. She doesn't believe it for a second.

"What can I do for you, Dr. Pard?" She considers it odd he would be there alone, but she cannot shake the notion that he is here for her.

"Winston--may we speak? You have finished the Diary?" His words light only a blaze of hatred in her eyes.

"I did. My love was sacrificed for humanity. My heart sacrificed as a life boat for my fellow man. My trust was sacrificed for what?" Winston surprises herself with this candor, but she does not care anymore.

"Will you walk with me?" He asks.

"We can't go back over the bridge, Samarra's burning. But I guess you know that. I thought Benson would protect the city-museum."

"It's all burning, Dr. Doe. Please." They move along the side of her home in silence.

"Where is General Smetana, I need to speak to him," she says. "I don't know what to do."

"Gregor is dead," Joshua replies. The Jordan Building was obliterated in an attack."

She stops at the back of her home. "I haven't seen General Fong. The same?"

"Benson is fine."

"Why didn't you protect Gregor?" Winston turns away down the path that leads to the rocky cliff-side. He struggles with the path, but Winston will not help him.

A few hundred feet down the path she stops. "I get the feeling that you and Gaia celebrates our demise as a species."

"Or she celebrates the next step we are to take," Pard says quietly.

"And that is?"

"Winston, I wish I knew it all. Like Moss, and the others, in some ways you are a God. In other ways, well, I know what you must feel. But with all this change--frankly, I am humbled. Do you know Clipper knows you are out here. But it has no recent records of shared perception. That's why I am here."

"I don't believe you; I know there items that have been clipped."

"That's right--but try to believe me--Clipper has not cloned or deleted your memories of the attack on Samarra. You are doing that."

"Don't bother me, Dr. Pard."

"I knew you wouldn't believe me. I can imagine how you feel, I guess. Would Russell have done that to you? Or would he have noted the event of you, marveled at it, then recognized you as our way out?"

"Dr. Biner was first and foremost a researcher. I was a nothing more than a catalyst for developing an effective reaction." She stops herself. "Is this what you came here to tell me?" Her lips quiver in a mix of pain and anger.

"Winston, Russell, Dr. Biner, called the process of change a climax to our Aggregation of Essences."

"There is no proof of reality changing for the better. If it were changing I would know it."

"Some of us would know it now and some of us might know it later," His voice is tight. The words clipped.

"You know of no such thing," she replies. *That's why he is here, he is looking for hope.* "You're fishing for something." *Oh, General Fong's surety. Joshua isn't in the loop.*

"How can you be so stupid?" His harsh tones confirm her observation. "The reality we lost, the link to our planet cannot stay as a vacuum; there is a reaction, you know that. Something has to take over when our memories fully deplete. Nature recycles, not just cycles--you know that. And that's pretty gruesome for humanity, but I know you believe it. Why is it so hard for you to believe that there is also hope? You know space moves on a different scale then it had before. Soon the whole structure will coalesce and end for us. My God, Winston, if you can see that you also see the potential end."

"We are seeing humanity die And don't pander to me with grammar school theories of Chaos, Dr. Pard."

"Winston, I can't account for your ways now."

"So now you're going to bait me with 20th century myopia about how humans are not natural? How can you be so sure it is the end?" She curses herself for being too kind to him.

"Winston, it's certainly the end. You can see that everywhere. But why not trust me? Or would you prefer us to dissolve into a muddy puddle waiting for the madness to kill us all?"

"You are everything wrong with us, Dr. Pard."

"That may be so, Dr. Doe. But I did not give up."

She turns away from him and continues down the hillside path to some exposed rounds of timber and a chopping block. Chanterelle mushrooms line the shadows. Winston looks at the other mushrooms that have pushed through the green blankets, spreading themselves to flat white platters on the ground. Another fungus--an iridescent orange one--covers some rotting alder stumps. From the woods' edge, a bobcat peers from beside a massive tree root that stands on edge--a blow-over from a storm. Winston tears at the rotted exterior of a tree and throws the crumbling bark at the cat. It sprints off. Her eyes now open, she speaks: "If you are such a noble person, why did you kill the Gindas? Why did Plow feel he had to escape?"

"Wolf, the nurses, a dozen doctors, uncounted orderlies, civilians, all of them died; the Gindas killed them in horrible ways--the list goes on and on, death and more death. The Gindas were without a moral or ethical core. Dr. Wolf could not fathom that as right or wrong; everything was a set of obvious questions to him. He just had to follow the steps. The Gindas were his children and when it was time to kill them he could not. So they killed him." Joshua Pard recites the events without rancor or emotion.

"You are as bad as Moss."

He declines to comment; he agrees. "You have been trained to understand everything we know about Species Focus because you wanted to and could. We didn't go out to the Walker camps one day and try to figure whom we might psychologically eviscerate. You came to us. You came to understand the research and you volunteered for this task. Biner fought you but you won because you were the best we had. As a result, you now have Species Focus, ethics, and purpose; you are in a unique position. I gave you everything you wanted. And I couldn't be prouder."

"You're a pig. They have kept you out of the loop and now you are trying to regain your footing. You are scared."

"Perhaps, but you are neither stupid, greedy, or self-delusional. You don't have a smidgen of avarice. You are decent and here is the punch line. Dr. Doe: We are a dying species that has finally made the grade, but we saw the tipping point and ignored it. So now we work to correct it."

"Considering how wonderful I am--it is easy to see why the madness closing in on us. How is that good? What's the real population number?"

"It is a little over 500 million and decrementing daily. Winston, life has shown me the darkest parts of humanity. Were I a supreme being, I would call for the flood and wipe us out. Did you know that?"

She smiles at him. "Given your self-serving point of view for the species it makes sense."

His eyes form the faintest smile. "I do what I do because I am one of the best people on the planet at understanding human behavior and manipulating it. This means I represent the past as much as Moss. People like you represent the future: Awareness of servitude, blindness to the dark desires. Yet there is no place for you here. There has never been a place for you. Do you understand what that means?"

She grabs him without realizing her intrusion. "It means we will either form a place, begin to form a place, or we will get washed away with one big: Oh damn! By a creator who says, "oops, time to try again." Joshua stares down at her arms surprised at the strength of grip. She looks up at him. "How is the motive force for the potential of greatness in humanity to be transformed into a set of kinetics that release us?" She loosens her grasp. "How am I somehow to lead the children away from Moss Eckman?"

"That's impossible. But I think you are right to look for the motive force," he says paternally.

Her eyes flash. "You've taken to underestimating me recently."

Pard kicks the ground. "This has to work. The couplings on the so-called alien spacecraft were standard NASA fittings."

"So that is your example of the phase displacement? Russell Biner back peddling through space with the help of…Clipper? You're guessing."

"Recycling, not back peddling. We do not know this is wrong. We do know it happened. That's the best I have. And yes, Benson knows more than that. What does he know?"

"So you think Deus ex Machina is not a concept of drama but sentience on the part of our ancestors? And you think the snap of the time/space rubber band happens when we reach the breaking point as a species?"

"You've done the research. You tell me. Does Gaia flush things away or does she recycle them in an ongoing process?"

"Time and space as well?" She asks.

"What else would you call the lesson of our despicable human existence?"

"That we are a pointless, self-involved species that deserves extinction?"

Pard closes his eyes for a moment; he is beaten. He opens them slowly and speaks. "Those two dogma statues in a hall should have belonged to you, not Jordan. Winston, Jordan experienced space from the waters of mind. It was a fully functional environment; a synthetic ecosystem from his standpoint. It developed when the focus he carried interacted with the waters of mind from Dr. Biner. He had focus and Biner knew how to use it. That made all the difference. That's our path. What did Benson tell you?"

Winston looks away, thinking. "And so Russell wakes up every morning, memories completely washed by Clipper and waits to get tossed backwards when the inertia of our species stalls? And in the process he finds the waters of mind but cannot do himself harm because Clipper keeps him bottled up?"

"As I said, all we know is we have had success."

"She interrupts: "What proof?"

"You know better than me. Plow saved your life."

She considers his comment. "And that is your reason for all this?"

"You mention the real reason Biner, and a dozens of others, were launched. When it cycles--"

"You mean that we go extinct?"

"He will be free of our memories."

"And mad as a hatter. And what happens if he is successful this time? Do we recycle around over and over but get nowhere?"

"I don't know. I am guessing it is possible, until we get it right. At least that is the theory. I don't know where it ends--or even what 'it' is. We hope this time he arrives before the greenhouse laws. We are hoping the next time he arrives sooner than that."

"So what does this have to do with Moss and his stupid party?" She shakes the papyrus at him.

"You expect the shift to be some great release of our collective kinetics, don't you? The nuclear fear reborn?"

"I do."

"Seems to me we are so far removed from the event, the shift could be as small as a party." He watches her nod.

"So we need an Adam and an Eve--which makes you, what?"

"I don't know," he says. "What did Benson tell you?"

"That you're a manipulating son of a bitch."

"And thank God for that," Joshua Pard replies.

"Benson is sentient to the event. That's all I know."

The old man's jaw goes slack for a moment. "So then we do end." When he regains his composure, he turns and leaves her in silence.

Chapter 37

"We will now go now to Connie Mack, our reporter in Kyoto."

"Well, Jack, these Japanese satellites, like their American counterparts, can penetrate up to twenty feet of concrete. The fuzzy images and drifting colors are also enhanced, just like the American systems. So American ingenuity is alive and well--unfortunately in the hands of the Asians. Americans will soon be in the satellites' window just like everyone else. To the rescue, of course, is American ingenuity: ATWAS Systems of Seattle, Washington has introduced a product to keep its wearer informed of all satellite fly-overs by beeping--as an approaching scan closes in. ATWAS stock opened today at thirty and closed the day at forty-six. I guess some people are just lucky. So for all of you worried about the scan, take heart--American ingenuity has come to the rescue! Take that, Asia!"

"Thanks, Connie. In entertainment news, Sky-Search of Hollywood has announced plans to view all North American satellite feeds as they come on line to seek out new talent. Back to you, Jack."

"Our next item comes from the Network Association of North America. In a survey taken today, of its member companies, eighty-six per cent indicated there is a strong desire on the part of the population to be in the scans. United Networks, the parent company of the U.N., estimates the revenue of this new domestic service will be more than ten billion dollars a year within five years. As a result employment and network prices are expected to rise."

"Thank you, Jack. And remember: If you have an opinion, let us know. You are the consumer, and therefore the boss--any final comments, Jack?"

"I, for one, am going to get one of those ATWAS thingies. See you at eleven."

. . . .

Humanity's beams begin to mix with the glow of gods as searchlights mark the night. These swords of light appear one by one, as hillside refugee camp-fires and home-lights darken at the quickening dance. A pair of undulating yellow lights wash the Seattle hillsides. The rest, the ones reflecting off the quiet lake in front of Moss, all merge into a shaft of light. They then begin wandering the night as one.

Moss stands on a flat plane, framed by nodding trees. The smoky maw of a civilization clustered on the hillsides begins to darken. Frogs croak and owls hoot. Behind Moss, more blasts of light erupt skyward forming another two sets of sources, eventually forming a triangular pattern searching the sky. Then, as if embarrassed, the lights blink off. Moss pulls a walkie-talkie from his pocket. "Landing-Light this is Party-Time, another problem with the lights?"

"The generator overheated, Mr. Eckman. It looks like a bad hose. We'll have it patched in five minutes." The crackling voice clicks off.

"Okay." He looks around for Travis.

Moss digs his soft rubber soles into the dirt and glances again at the buildings on the hillsides. *They keep turning off their lights. They are afraid.* He has contempt for those who live in the warrens that cover the hill. He cannot excuse fear of his party turning the hillside dark, as if the inhabitants were hiding from a bombing raid. *Cowards.* To him most people are docile farm animals, waiting to be milked or slaughtered: fear running their lives--pain their favored companion. In sum, Moss cannot understand why they are not more like he.

Moss knows he has had a charmed life--for the most part--yet he still cannot find sympathy for their concerns. This remains Moss' true gift to humanity and the real reason he was called into focus for our species. The future does not concern Moss--neither does the past. Nothing matters to Moss, besides now.

He also does not understand how any ongoing set of uncontrollable circumstances can alter a life determined to succeed. All he understands is people must pick up the reins of defeat and hatred fostered by fear.

Were the privileged of this time able to rid themselves of their fears, as Moss has tried to do, the more enlightened might be forced to see their own success as nothing more than chance. Hardly an appetizing platter for those seeking to feed vanity, or keep the myth of control in tact, but still it is a more appetizing dish than unflinching responsibility--at least to those children of fortune. Of course none of them would label that fear.

Moss closes his eyes and sighs. With the loss of power, he has become a man whose life has suddenly turned stale; his party is threatened.

They cherish this life and their homes, but nothing's a gift. Soon when they are all in the eye of the satellite and everyone can see their warts, will they really just sit and take it? What a harvest of shame and humiliation. The ultimate revenge of the corporation--humanity in its skivvies reduced to entertainment for profit. No longer the masters in their home, people will sit in the hurricane's eye, fodder for their neighbor's hate. Their lives piped throughout the planet like putrid air--and they'll pay for it. Idiots.

Why can't they help themselves? Moss digs his toe even deeper into the dirt. He will never fully realize the contempt he feels with these people or how those on the hillside are a million reflections of his own self-involvement. He just knows they fear more than they care for themselves.

The irony of his position is lost on Moss. He has only the vaguest notion that so long as he does not seek to change the Chaos of his life, but rather ride above it, he is safe.

He taps his cell trying to call Travis again. There is still no answer. He returns to thoughts of the households on the hillside and laughs, sure none will complain, no matter how much noise and how many blasts of light pierce their night. Were he to sense that those few who know of his place in Species Focus--including Travis--laugh at him, and have Moss Eckman nights where they dress up and make fun of him, it might kill him.

Moss, like so many of us, walks a tightrope of illusion. He presses a page button to locate Travis. Also no response; he kicks a small stone and speaks into the communicator. "Bubble Pack, this is Party-Time. Let's get moving, what's your ETA? "

"Easy, Mr. Eckman. We're in position--about five-hundred feet above you. All we need is your lights. At that point we'll be thirteen minutes from landing—per your request."

"Have you heard from my brother?"

"Negative."

"Party-Time out." Moss drops the radio back into the baggy thigh pockets of his jumpsuit as he sees ten buses pulling onto the field. The five hundred party hounds, all carrying small flashlights, thunder from the buses in a storm of giggles and vehicular music. *I wonder if the sanctimonious Dr. Doe will arrive in that energy-efficient vehicle of hers or that new bicycle he had seen at her cabin, the hypocrite.* He no longer ponders her ability to afford so expensive a bicycle.

Exiting a bus full of his security people, Benson begins wandering the crowds to make sure everything runs smoothly, and wonders what will happen if partiers who had often seen Winston and Moss together, get wind of the truth. Fifty well-trained troopers fan out--attending in disguise.

Would these party-goers try to kill Moss if they knew he was a Ginda? Or would they bow down to him--or begin to taunt him? The Gindas and their place as guardians has been relegated to the past. These people milling around are mired only in desire.

Benson Fong considers Mina's anger and her unwillingness to answer his calls after their confrontation at the museum. Giddy that his tasks have been exposed--he cannot wait to see her. He never considers that she may not arrive tonight, or that she may have plans of her own--such thoughts have no place in his heart. He has let hope sneak inside him.

With the buses unloaded, Moss climbs upon an impressionistic stone monument of an airplane to begin coordination the decadent party. He still searches for his "brother".

The airplane monument he stands upon looks like a butterfly with wide scalloped wings. It had been erected a few years ago to commemorate an airplane factory that had been stripped by pragmatic crowds who followed a former U.N. Magistrate to a supposed safe zone. The airplane plant had been the last major industry left in the Northwest at the time. Had it been left in place, many more planes might have crashed in the Jazz War.

The triangle of lights explodes skyward. The party has legs. The crowd stares beady-eyed at the light. A spotlight shines on him from above. Moss grins and waves wildly to the crowd; they adore them tonight in howls and cheer. Benson positions himself at the foot of the monument. The irony of Moss and the multitude brings a grin to Benson's lips. Their focus on Moss seems so right--albeit misguided.

The light tosses a silvery glow. *An angel*; Benson hears himself laugh out loud as he looks around. *This absurd party must have something to do with the march of humanity--the pink union-suits were Moss' idea--but as more than a joke? Would he know?*

Moss waves the crowd forward, and as they close in around him, he pulls a small microphone from his pocket. "Friends, Romans, countrymen, the party begins! You all wondered why the invitations said to wear play clothes, well, look up!" Looking up towards the apex of the three powerful light beams, attendees see fifty nets stitched together and suspended from a set of bright red dirigibles drifting in the winds. "There is a dance floor and a bar in the center. There are nets on top of nets on top of nets. Sound familiar?"

A cheer roars from the crowd followed by calls of approval. "Way to go, Moss!"

"Anyone of you out there who is afraid of heights is excused." This time only a small ripple of laughter courses through the throng of people. "Got ya' didn't I?" A burst of applause.

"Don't worry it's perfectly safe. No worse than say--floating eight hundred feet in the air suspended by a string." More laughter. "Now, everyone please step outside the triangle of blue light so the party can be lowered and we can climb aboard." In the field in front of him a strip of blue lights come to life all around the crowd. Outside of them blinking yellow lights. "Walk toward the yellow lights and find yourself outside the triangle of blue lights. The yellow ones are the ones on the outside. Moo, you all." The crowd laughs nervously as it streams outward like a great hollow amoeba, reforming itself between the edges of the eerie blue light and yellow beacons.

"Bubble Pack, this is Party-Time. You can turn on the main engines, but wait for three flashes, then begin final descent."

"Roger, Party-Time."

Moss climbs down the airplane and checks the area inside the blue lights to make sure no one has been left drunk or stupid on the ground. Then, sure no one has been left inside the triangle, Moss signals: "Okay, Landing Lights give Bubble Pack the three flashes and let's get this-here party in the air." *Still no Travis.*

Prop wash from the propellers hit the ground; their rabid winds lash the gawking crowd of partiers, forcing the crowd further back from the blue lights. A moment later, fifty bright pink nets looking like upside down strawberry ice cream scoops, appear overhead. Dark brown nets form a conical exterior wall above them. The effect is a set of glowing upside down ice cream cones floating down towards the partiers. Above the cones, ovoid dirigibles--their blood red exteriors illuminated by the ground lights. On their sides are the huge propellers. Nervous laughter ripples through the crowd.

The strawberry colored net mats that had been drooping touch the ground and flatten out perfectly, filling the perimeter triangle of the rectangular blue light. The wide-holed brown wall-nets that hang above them lower also. The brown perimeter nets will provide the exterior walls of the soon to be floating structure. In the center waits a smaller, rigid triangle-- the dance floor and bar. Around the nets, men and women dressed in pink and purple clown costumes hang from garishly festooned meat hooks along the walls. Upon touchdown, the clowns climb down the netting like jovial hosts opening doorways on net's exteriors.

A booming voice sounds over the whine of the propellers. "Ladies and gentleman, we'll turn the propeller engines off once we reach height. To enter, please remove all shoes except athletic footwear. Then step through the doorways and distribute yourselves evenly among the separate nets that form the perimeter. Please stay off the triangular dance floor in the center until told otherwise. Also, follow the instructions of your clown attendants--as this is not sanctioned by the trial lawyers association and entry voids any claims to damages. Translation, this is an adult party. Get in and hang onto something. No one is covering your posterior."

The crowd rushes through the triangular doorways spreading themselves along the border where the forty-foot wall meets the net floor. Moss watches the last of the partiers enter and the dozen or so who back away into the night. He then hurries into the closest opening. The crowds around him slap him on the shoulder and say hello. Moss glances about not seeing anyone he knows, but smiling hello anyway. He speaks into his radio. "Okay Bubble Pack, commence lift. We're on Flight Boss now." The dirigibles lift fifteen feet or so until the cones are again formed. People who have not hung on roll down, but the clowns waiting along the sides swiftly restore order, securely tieing people to the nets. Other clowns secure the doors.

"This is Flight-Boss. Okay, lift when ready."

A rock-hard human bangs into Moss and Moss reaches out to help the man get his grip on the netting. The angry man's thick black beard, high on broad cheekbones and bald head are almost tight against his eyes. "Sorry, buddy," Moss says. "I somehow missed your mass." Moss steps away, having practiced on these nets for three days, and begins to show others how to move about. The large man follows him up the side and grabs Moss' shoulder.

"Don't sweat it big guy. The nets will stretch out soon once we will all have our time--all will be well."

"Not good enough."

"Excuse me, Everest, but what did you say your name was?"

The question seems to boil through the large man as if it were steam in a pipe. Moss checks the location of the man's crotch, solar plexus, and kneecap. He decides to go for the kneecap since that will be the most painful. Benson appears beside Moss. Moss speaks to Benson. "I don't remember inviting this, large angry man."

"Don't jack me around, Eckman. You know who I am. You killed my sister today. She worked at the Womb."

Benson calls his security teams. A small red dot appears on the back of this man's bald head.

Moss has trouble with what he has heard. "Try again?"

The man exhales deeply. "You louse." He rubs his eyes, and then brushes his mustache back from his upper lip. Something about the action seems familiar to Moss. "I assure you that I have no idea of what you are going on about."

"And I assure you I have no intention of ripping you to shreds, but I want to, Moss." The angry man looks at Benson. "It's okay. Call off the dogs."

Moss looks at Benson. "What does this dude think you'll do to him--get him too drunk to slug me?" Moss laughs at his own joke.

The angry man says, "I still don't see why anyone would want to be with a world class jerk." He closes his eyes to calm himself.

"Get the fuck out of here."

The man's eyes flare open. "I'm leaving. I know the rules. See ya' Ginda." He carefully climbs away, down the net walls.

Moss feels a moment of dizziness. "Hey ape, one other thing. If you're going to be here, have fun. We shoot party-poopers." He hears a beep that signals completion of lift. Moss begins barking instructions to stretch out the floors so they are taut enough to be used. As he speaks, Moss' attention momentarily lights on a confused Benson Fong, who wonder how that man knew Moss was a Ginda.

Moss points up at the dirigible in the center. A large countdown that began at one-hundred-and-twenty has reached eighty seconds. "Almost there, dude."

A group of clowns finish smoothing out the floor. Moss cannot see the masts they are erecting between the crafts to form a rigid exoskeleton, but he can feel the changing character of the floor. Over the past three days, he has gained a sense of the structure, and what it will feel like when the nets are correctly stretched, or when something might not be right. So far everything seems perfect. He begins a slow tour of the nets to make sure each one holds an even part of the load. Midway across the net, he looks back at Benson. "You are always following me." He turns way from Benson Fong to direct the resetting of a net. As casually as he can say it, "It's the Ginda thing, isn't it?"

"What's that?" Benson replies.

"That's what I thought, Benson." He turns away.

Benson sees no reset from Clipper and moans. *Here we go.* He listens in on the conversations of his security teams for data on the assailant. Moss continues barking instructions. Benson assigns a six-man team to Moss and another twelve person team to Winston Doe. He finds Mina across the nets, she is no issue yet, so Benson will guard her personally. *But she is the source of this, I bet.*

Benson reminds himself of the foolishness of trying to wrest control at this point and makes his report on Moss' comment to the Directorate. Change has begun and all he can do is stay with it. Benson sees Winston approach from the other side of a net wall.

"Mr. Eckman, how do you do." Moss knows the voice, but waits until Dr. Winston Doe steps around a few clowns to say hello. She remains on the other side of the net. Luminescent foot wraps swirl rainbow colors up her thighs and torso like a crazed barber poles. Across her chest is a single thick necklace of hair in a vapid show of pride. A few months ago Moss had told her this was his favorite look for her. She hates the display considering it the worst form of ego. However, Winston takes no chances of indifference from Moss Eckman. As she looks into his eyes, his in-depth stare shocks her. There is no pride of ownership or lust in those eyes. *He knows?*

Moss feigns disinterest looking up at the wall net between them. As things stand at that moment, Winston Doe will be caught in a different circular net when the first game of the evening begins: a trampoline-like bounce of the partiers as the dirigibles begin oscillating up and down.

"I said hello, Mr. Eckman," Winston repeats--somewhat ashamed of her pandering. Moss puts his finger to his ear as if he cannot hear. Winston Doe leans through the doorway of the netting to speak. Moss motions for her to climb through the doorway between the nets, and into his lair. Winston steps through a doorway.

Moss finally speaks to her. "I have heard that I am your monkey," he says quietly. "Species Focus?"

She appears puzzled.

The nets begin to move rhythmically up and down and music begins to play--the Reggae beat perfect to the oscillations. The guests seek either the most unstable spot around them or grab onto the walls. Winston and Moss hold onto a side wall as she stares at him--unsure of what to say. She sees a slight flash of sadness through the anger in Moss' eyes. "Well?"

A small, broad-shouldered man with a cap that says "Flight Boss" descends down the net wall toward Moss. "Hey, Chief!" He stops, hanging from the wall just above them. "Mr. Eckman, we're about twenty seconds from restabilizing the craft. Any further instructions?"

"Any problems?" Moss asks the Flight Boss.

"No, we're four by four."

"Okay, Mr. Goodsend, you take it from here." The man tips his hat and speaks into a small microphone on his lapel as he clambers up the net like a monkey.

Chapter 38

Voice over: "Ladies and Gentlemen we close our news broadcast with a solemn note. As you know last night there was a series of riots throughout the Chicago area. Over two hundred people lost their lives in the senseless violence fostered by rioters protesting the wait for replacement organs. Also last night, on the way back to her home in Chicago, Kelly Pan-Blanca was the focus of a vicious assault by unkempt youths wandering the streets of Joliet. A complete video of the assault is available on Disaster Network Premium for $25.00 and 200 Kilowatts-hours. All monetary proceeds will go to a memorial scholarship fund for aspiring broadcasters from the inner city. Kelly will be missed. This is Margaret Davies, News Manager. Good night and good luck."

. . . .

An announcement: "Ladies and Gentleman. Please feel free to climb the walls at any time." Mambo music drowns out the propellers wash. Moss glances at his chronometer: two seconds.

The dirigibles' lift rate suddenly triples and the nets, elongate from the weight, force the party-goers tight against each other in the center of each net like rocks in a bag. Moss reaches out for Winston to stop her from falling to the center of the net, but she already has a firm grip. Benson and the others also hold onto the net-walls. Moss notes that a few of the partiers know exactly what to do.

No one has had more surveillance than Moss Eckman these last few days and as a result, those in the security team have all seen the rehearsals for this part of the festivities many times. Moss is no longer certain he might be the only person on the party sleds who knows what will happen next. The nets start to oscillate allowing partiers to bounce around. It goes on for five minutes.

A report comes over his communications link. "General Fong, we think someone hacked in an override. It has an L. Wolf signature. Otherwise, Clipper is four by four. No errors, it just didn't commit a cut to the Ginda."

Benson nods. "The security teams are to hold their positions." A man with a weapon drawn shoulders it.

The oscillation ceases as a voice booms: "This is the Flight Boss. Ladies and gentleman, the specially constructed fabric will keep you warm even as we reach a height of eight hundred feet above the city. We will pump more warm liquid into the mesh and it will be both rigid and warmer so you may do as you please. The bar will be located on the dance floor, which is the triangle in the center of the nets. Please make sure to avoid landing on other party-goers when you jump about, at least until you know their names, or you have gotten permission from a Travis Eckman to ruin his product."

Gales of laughter rise from the partiers. Winston notes that Moss tries to appear calm, but she notes a pulsing vein on the side of his neck. She wonders if he has a plan, or if he knows about Travis.

"Couple kites will be available on both the port and stern sides near the flashing blue lights. Also, hot tub gondolas can be reached through the ladder in the center. Inside the dirigibles, you will find lavatories and a kitchen. We hope you'll enjoy your flight with Goodsend Balloon systems. Oh, and you might also want to thank your hosts, Moss Eckman, Travis Eckman and our favorite bar: The Womb."

The triangle of light beneath the partiers dim and a hologram of the two brothers' appears above them. The images speak in chorus: "Ladies and gentleman, we hope you like the people you've just bumped into. If you have any questions the clowns are here to help--you'll see them hanging around." More polite laughter. Winston presses close to Moss, her hand on his shoulder; he sees a child playing at mischief.

"I think you and I will be the best of friends." Moss says after a moment. "We are the same aren't we--as in no memory?" She waits--but there is no interference from Clipper. "So you're a romantic huh? Guarding me, Winston?" Moss says facetiously. "Oh you expected worse of me?"

"Yes."

"None of me is new to you." He examines her with cold eyes. "Clipper," he says without heart. His eyes stare at her. "You used me."

"I did not use you. I do not have your Teflon capability for skiing people's hearts." She squeezes the net wall. "How do you know about Clipper?"

"Oh, that's right," he says, with a laugh, recovering his composure. He had not expected confirmation. "Dedication at its finest."

A second hand slithers down Moss' spine. He turns and sees Mina. A gold chain of green iridescent hearts weaves itself through her long hair. She calls it her chain of hearts and adds a heart after every lover. It was originally a gift from Gunn many years ago--a token of his invulnerability--his first day on the job. Gunn is nowhere to be seen.

She stares into Moss' eyes, no longer like a cat in heat, but more a doctor examining a patient. "So you see she does care. But only for the unwashed masses. You wouldn't understand Winston since she is you, wearing your favorite skin." Mina smiles at Winston. "Moss once told me you are only a fair lover. I told him you were as deceitful as they come--but that it doesn't matter to you. And after all he is just a lab monkey to you, isn't he, Winston? Did you ever think perhaps you two are perfect for each other? Oh that cannot be, you're so good." She watches Moss noting her comments, his head does not droop. Mina, the soul of innocence, looks to Benson. "No subroutine?"

He shakes his head."Funny."

"And no need for Gunn either. I've got you." Mina's eyes widen in mock surprise. She stares at Winston: "Isn't technology wonderful?"

"I see you're on a roll, Mina," Winston says. These two women were never enemies, but Mina does not like being kept in the dark. "That glare of yours might burn a hole in our netting and then we all might fall to the ground like a mass of Daedali."

Benson hearing what has taken place makes his way over to Moss finding he needs to reevaluate the unraveling situation. "Any word on the satellites? Will we have hookups? "

"The Asian satellites will be over in ten minutes. And the three Indo-European satellites soon after that," Moss says distractedly. "The West Coast will be completely lit in about forty-five minutes," says Moss. He does not appear to question Benson's persona, yet.

"We will need to be careful how we are seen, right, Mina?" Says Benson. His odd complacency shocks Mina. "What do you know?"

"So we all hide under the bed of lies." Mina points to Benson's security team. "Do you think they should be in the window?"

"Who are they?" Moss asks looking at the men and women Mina has pointed out. They are the same people who garnered his suspicions a little earlier.

"Security," Mina says, nodding to Benson; but seeing admiration in Winston's eyes--for a man she'd thought they'd both agreed was little more than a worm--she backpedals. "You never know," she says, letting the game play out a bit, "Maybe the satellites will help us? Never can tell what you'll miss, aye Winston?"

"Are you kidding? With this thing floating over Seattle, we should be seen by half the planet," Moss says looking up at the nets. He has never been stupid; he has always been self-involved.

"Madness," Mina says.

The propellers' engines throttle back to low buzz. "Where did you get this thing?" Mina asks quickly, nodding toward the netting that rises around them. She cannot fathom Moss' response and needs time to think.

"It's started life as a log-hauler. I paid a little extra for the dance floor and put Mr. Goodsend into business. You'll need to excuse us, Mina. Dr. Doe and I have to go be Gindas." He looks into Mina's sparkling eyes, then speaking with an obvious, feigned indifference says: "It finally makes sense." He kisses her on the cheek.

Mina tilts her head. "Imagine that? Transitions anyone?" Her lack of innocence could sink a boat.

"He's aware and Clipper cannot reset him. Why did you do this? How did you do this?" Benson tries to appear angry. "What did you tell him?"

"And how come you don't know the answer already? Don't like it much, huh, worm? I guess things change."

A sly grin in response surprises her.

Moss speaks loudly to Winston. "So your boyfriend floats up there 'round and 'round waiting for the apocalypse?"

The color drains from Winston's face. It drops to an empty place in her gut that begins to throb. Before she can speak Mina says, "Winston, say what you like about Moss' ways, but you have to give him credit for style." Her eyes widen, mocking Benson and Winston. "Clipper, Clipper, where are you boy? Hmm, no Clipper."

"You're not funny sometimes, Mina." Winston says. "Moss…"

Moss grabs Winston's arm. He sees Benson take a step towards him and that startles him. "I see." He removes his grip. "Well let's find out if the sum of humanity's interest is self gratification, Shall we?"

A burst of bright white light, then an explosion rumbles through the air. The log-hauler turned party conveyance sways in the blast, then slowly steadies. All eyes turn to the east. A methane processing plant on the hillside has exploded in a ball of flames.

Someone in the crowd says: "That guy Moss really knows how to throw a party." People laugh nervously watching the flames. The music has not missed a beat. The engines power up and the party positions itself far from the danger.

"I guess that proves you were right to interfere, Mina," Winston says quietly. "Anyone else you want to kill with your candor?"

Mina's eyes close briefly. Benson can hear reports on the explosion on his communications link--an implant just below his cochlea--a dozen people have died.

Mina opens her eyes and stares at Fong. His eyes drift away and she fights the feeling that wells inside her for the obvious pain in his eyes. "This wasn't your fault, Benson. Put that explosion on my family's bill--on the debit column--on the other side of the ledger sheet. You know, the one that has my father's willingness to give away our lives to save the species."

Benson finally cannot hold it in anymore. "I never had a problem with your dad, Mina. I thought he was a great man. But sometimes you act without thinking."

She leans into him, glaring hatred. "There is nothing about Species Focus you, or Dr. Dimwit can tell me." She winks at Winston. "Perhaps we both played the same game, Benny?" When Benson's eyes widen, she turns away. He elevates the security teams' response options.

Winston takes Mina's arm, "Easy, girl--I'm not your enemy," she watches Benson. Mina's allusion to her clandestine involvement in Clipper bothers her.

"So if anyone can appreciate dedication to the Clipper Project it would have to him?" She points to Benson Fong.

Moss faces Benson. "Is it true that Winston and I were lovers?" He asks Benson. "You would have seen us together before this. Huh, no answer. You knew that I thought she was brand new but you didn't say anything."

Benson jumps into character: "I'm not your mother, Stud. You play with women, the universe plays with you--or I am just learning that the great Moss Eckman is all fluff." Benson hopes to maintain some control of the situation.

Mina's eyes immediately dart to the retort from Benson Fong. "We don't need you."

Winston speaks quickly: "Competition worries you, Mina?"

"More than I care to admit," she says, laughing with comment. "But not from you. You're a computer in a body." Mina stops, the words had erupted from her before she could contemplate their meaning. Her eyes float to Benson. "So that's it. You're both dumber than I thought. Damn you, Benson. You think her computer generated decency can make some kind of difference?"

Winston feels faint. "That's enough, Mina," says Benson.

"Stop it Mina." Moss grabs his radio. "Bubble Pack, this Party Time, what's keeping the rain?" Mina, Benson, and Winston stare at him. Clipper has kicked in.

He turns to them "Hey, I have a party to run, Mina."

Like a command from God, the sounds of the propellers cease and an old Reggae beat with a trumpet back harkens a warm rain. It falls upon the party-goers cooling the air around them--until a brief flash of alcoholic flame surrounds them--and then immediately puffs away by the propellers' blast of winds. The party-goers howl with approval. The lights glare out from the dance floor spotting the nearby hillside. They then rise up to reflect off the reddish smoke curls from the explosion. It looks planned--it is not. People hoot their approval and pile into the dancing and drinking area.

Moss looks to Winston, then Mina, and then with resignation, to Benson. "Maybe the reason I dislike you all so much is I can't get free of you," Moss says in a note of retreat and awareness. "But I can try."

He glares Winston, then stops--the security teams rush forward but have no cover. He immediately picks them out by their practiced looks of inattention. Moss points his fingers at the sets of security officers and laughs. He sidles up next to Winston and speaks: "So they all exist to support us and we couldn't exist without them. My we are important--in a foolish kind of way."

Winston cannot respond. She remains shaken by Mina's comment that her goodness is a product of Clipper's programs.

He grins. "A long time ago I noticed the twenty-eight day hour glass at the Womb was out of whack. Then when I checked it, I found out it was accurate. That's when I first knew something was wrong. I didn't know what." A security helicopter off in the darkness loses power. Moment later it crashes. The crowd cheers the pyrotechnics, unaware of what has caused the fireball below them. The party drifts unscathed through the smoke. Moss' eyes remain indifferent.

Mina speaks: "Moss, you need to think." A moment later, Moss' eyes droop as Clipper removes the event. Benson and Winston exchange glances.

A bell over head begins to gong. Moss looks up to see his own smiling face staring down at him. The holographic image speaks: "Ladies and gentlemen, boys and girls, this is your host Moss Eckman again. Welcome to truth, surprise, and wonder. As you know, on-continent broadcast by the satellite surveillance systems has begun all over the globe tonight. For those of you who did not know, this satellite stuff covering our ass is all just part of a plan to make some more dough--ain't life grand?" A large bell echoes all around them. "The bell tells us that the eye in the sky is crossing, and broadcasts of North America are just about to being--and guess what city will be first?"

"SEATTLE," comes the mixed chorus of party-goers.

"Right, Seattle, and guess what will be the most obvious object to the satellite as it crests the horizon…right about now."

"Us."

"Perfect, us. We are it and you are here. So unhook your britches dust off your makeup and get ready. The world just changed for Mr. and Mrs. America and all the ships at sea. Forget the past, we now have a planet with a 24/7 case of voyeurism!" Laughter ripples through the crowd. "All thanks to technology!" The crowd cheers as a blast of bright yellow light bounces off a nearby cloud. "Well that ought to attract some attention. Enjoy the party." His image disappears from the sky above.

Winston speaks, "How much do you know, Moss?" She is testing the Clipper reset.

Moss speaks: "Will Clipper wipe your memories now as well as mine?"

She stares at him, mute. Benson sighs at this change wondering just how much Mina has changed and why.

"Just tell me what to do," Moss says. "But I do not wish to be anyone's fool--my brother--he didn't come tonight…Oh, he knew." He waits.

Who will tell him the truth? Mina cannot hurt him anymore. Travis Eckman died two hours ago in a bombing at the Genebanks building.

The bell sounds again. Moss' voice again from the PA system. "Here we come, Asia. America for all to see." A rocket fires skyward from one of the auxiliary gondolas. "Follow the trail. There's the satellite. Time for the big moon you-all."

Winston stares skyward as a small silver dot speeds across the sky. Moss speaks to her. "The satellites are some kind of fail-safe aren't they?"

"I don't know." Winston can barely stand.

"It's a dirty world isn't it, Madam Director?" Mina says with an angry laugh. "How about you, Benson--care to enhance someone's role as the fool?"

"Meaning what?' Fong answers.

"You thought you ran it all didn't you?"

"Unlike you, I knew I didn't." He says to Mina. "Why did you interfere?"

She ignores him. "I know it's all about love for you, Winston," Mina coos quietly. "You and the saintly Dr. Biner certainly do belong together, but then again maybe you have to love him. You might have had no choice. You know his goodness vilified my father? Because of him, no one would believe Biner was so good of a man that he took to solitary for the rest of us. They blamed my dad. So I went underground and watched." Her gaze slips languidly to Benson. "Come on, Fong, dance with me. My dad had a notion of what happens next and I need to share it with you. What is your title anyway and why don't I know that?" Mina takes his hand to lead him onto the dance floor. But Benson does not move from Winston's side.

Moss looks at Winston. "I've gotten my dessert. You too." He stares skyward. "Your love is up there. You're down here. And never the twain shall meet." Moss laughs at her. "Thought you figured it all out? Bah, we're the three stooges. You, Biner, and me. All fools of an evil species." He turns looking to disappear into some woman's arms.

"Am I like him?" She asks no one.

"That's not true." Benson says. "Your goodness was not manufactured."

Still, she wonders if it is true or not.

"Travis wasn't even my brother--and you knew it." Moss stands, waiting, wounded. "He was my handler, looking for a way to use me to make money, or gain power."

Her memories of too many times when he had little remorse for his dorm-room ethic rest cool and crisp. "Moss, stop making it so easy for me to hurt you."

"So you remember all the grief and crummy things I did and no doubt excuse your own."

"We were lovers and I finally left because you are a world class jerk."

"Like I had a choice. Remember, I had Species-fucking-Focus. I had a task to fulfill. And then there is the saintly Doctor Doe. But we are forgetting to include the fact that you lied to me for two years so you could complete your science experiment, or was it about love, finding your bodiless space-man?"

"Thank you, Mina," Winston says leaning down trying to gather the shards of her life. "You deserve nothing and you took everything." She pauses. "I'm sorry. That was uncalled for--forgive me. Moss, we are more than fools. Remember, I didn't know about our similarities either, until recently."

"No?" He laughs. "What goes around comes around, Winston."

"Back at you, Champ."

He shakes his head. "Bitch."

"Moss, this pollution, inside us finally welled out so that we could all see it."

"Would it be possible for you to shut up with that crap? A selfish species painted itself into a corner. Rather than deal with it, we ran from it and called that cowardliness the economic imperative. You can't deal with it now because you don't know what heck is going on. We're toast--you and I." He grins. "Would you be surprised to know I am your Sir Walter Raleigh--only I will lay my poor useless self on the puddle so thee might cross? I thought not."

She waits for the Clipper subroutine but it does not come. "Nothing you might do could surprise me."

"See you some other life."

He jumps a couple of times gaining momentum--like a gymnast on a trampoline--then hurls himself at the netting wall and grabs on. He scans an already crowded dance floor and finds two dancers wearing silver 1920's flapper outfits cut in straight lines that hide their full figures. Bright green fuzz behind their ears meets in a triangle at the crown of her head. Long ears lie slicked back in the fuzz. "Were the women real?" He asks. "I mean other then Winston?"

"Yes," Mina says. Winston looks at Benson wondering if Moss is about to vacate this life. She then watches him climb through the open holes in the net walls and make his way to dance floor. Benson alerts his security team to protect the two bunny-dancers.

For the rest of the night Winston watches Moss dance. He gyrates and spins like a crazy man, bouncing from woman to woman. Mina goes to the bar and sits, watching her father's theories take life. Occasionally she glances at Benson Fong.

CHAPTER 39

Voice-over: "This is a public service message from your friends at the K-PAP. The new voice of America. Due to overwhelming demand for radio, our net stations will cease operation so that we can provide you with the finest radio in North America. We want to thank you all for your participation in our survey and we want you to know we will continue to provide you with the same high quality news and information you have come to expect from our web site and our affiliated content providers across the country. A new day dawns for America and with it comes new hope, new responsibility, and new opportunity. We know you trust us. And we want you to know you can count on us to use your trust. A new day is dawning for us all."

. . . .

The eastern sky wears the glow of dawn. Only a few saplings still hide in the dark mask of night. The taller trees stand silently in chilly winds, their movement, shadows against a cloudy sky. "Good night Dr. Doe," says her driver, looking fresh even at this early hour. He had managed to sleep last night despite the raucous music and fireworks that surrounded the floating platform of party-goers. Her new driver is one of those people who can sleep anywhere, any time.

Exiting the jeep looking at her home, Winston feels too tired and tousled by the mayhem of Moss' party to care about sleep. Instead, she walks towards Samarra.

"Don't do it. There is still danger, Ma'am" says her driver.

"Danger can't concern you, Corporal Fisk, coming from someone who can sleep through one of Eckman's parties."

"Samarra is still a war zone," replies her driver. "You could sleep permanently."

"Okay, I'll sleep for a while, then I'll be ready for you later in the day." Winston turns away from Samarra towards her cabin. The driver puts the jeep in gear and drives away.

Winston enters her home. *I hate being the fool.* A moment later, she slams her front door with enough force that it swings partly open again. She closes it again. Removing her black wrap studying the familiar post and beams, the stone fireplace, the chinking between the logs, and the smell of cinnamon, she remembers she once she had told herself she could never allow herself to become attached to any structure or place. That if she ever lost that part of the Walker culture, she would quit. This morning however, she takes in the sweetness of her home, smiling at its warmth and beauty, allowing the luxury of loving this structure to seep into her heart. She thinks of sleeping on the floor and a warm fire. During the rainy season, that is her favorite activity here. Despite the time, and a certainty of Moss Eckman's expected appearance, she builds a small fire then loosens her clothing sinking down into the pillows.

Gazing into the fire-dance, she tries to recall her life before Roo Biner--incompleteness comes over her; Winston recognizes it as an old friend and immediately questions the feeling. She fears her goodness may be lies fed to her by Clipper. The emptiness of it hurts her. *There is no escape here because here we are certain of extinction. So what if I am manufactured?*

The mantel around the fireplace begins to shimmer.

"Nice fire."

Winston starts.

"Not for me, I hope?" Moss Eckman stands arms akimbo, framed in the front door. The entire room shimmers brightly for a millisecond, then collapses back into the fire-lit space. Winston glares at him, wishing she had been wrong about his late night appearance. It had been his tack after their second social gathering. "Here we are again. Funny that I don't remember it." He laughs cruelly when he knows something he will not share. She had heard that laugh over and over when Moss had thought

Benson his tool for jokes. Now it is her.

Moss steps in leaving the door open. "You're beautiful, but I thought you liked to dress a little warmer when you were out in the woods."

She stands, holding the blanket around her. She had been clothed only in her blanket. Despite the intimacy she had once shared with Moss, he grins, a stranger to her in so many ways. "What time is it?" She asks

"The cognoscenti are readying their launch vehicles for escape into low Earth orbit--of course they don't know how they will eat or breathe after a few days, but what the heck. Oh you mean the tick-tock time. A little after six," He examines the room. "Nice…I've been here before, I guess. Funny the things we remember. Did I say that already? How about the first time?" She watches him. "You know all my lines. Let's try one: Looks like a place a Walker would live. Pure and spare. I guess I should admire it. I don't." He strolls into the kitchen. "No comment. Oh to be droll, of course--no coffee-maker--can I get you anything? A branch of cedar to chew upon?" He pops his head out of the kitchen. "How'd I do?"

"Almost word for word," she replies. "Except for the cedar line."

"And all for you, my dear. Touché."

"What do you really remember?" She asks.

"Doctor Brilliant Doe, do you really believe I was completely ignorant to what was happening around me?"

"You know that's not what I mean."She pauses at his comment. Some truth lurks there but Moss has no capital for her.

"Remember what I said about going to the Womb so often?" He says.

"That you were an indolent pig?"

"Mina would help me when she could. At those times I knew exactly what is going to happen next: I would lose my memory. Dr. Doe, I became, for a moment, the pinnacle of humanity." His eyes drop. A moment later his eyes open. "I think we did this often, argued about who is right, you and I. But, Dr. Brilliant Doe, we are knitting needles in the hands of madmen. Do you ever get that feeling?"

Winston nods, shocked that Moss has just learned not to speak of certain things.

"And I know something. And you don't." He grins. "There is one feeling I can never lose. You what that feeling is?"

"It must deal with repetition," she replies hoping for a clue to his earlier comment about sentience.

"Perhaps, but why don't I fear death?" Rather than waiting for her response, he opens her refrigerator. "I am soo boorish. Not much here." He looks back at her, but she has scurried up the stairs to dress.

"Tell me what you know," she says from behind her bedroom door.

"You first, Doc."

"Civic responsibility, matters." She finds pants and a sweater.

"Okay, cruelty has its place. Your turn." He finds a piece of beef jerky. It's his favorite. "Mine I suppose." He tears off a piece of meat. "I guess you and your friends are a bit miffed I learned I was a Ginda. You'd be surprised how much Mina knows about Clipper."

"Actually I would not," Winston says. "But try me."

"Nice try. She had lots to say. She said you and I were active lovers. And, it is my loss that I can't remember you in all your God-given, natural-birth beauty. I bet you remember all the nasty things we did. Does that bother you?"

He still likes teasing her, another trait she cannot bear. "No, Clipper took care of that." She lies. "How about making us some tea? Do you remember how to make a fire in the stove? I once taught you."

"I bet you did," he says darkly.

"That was original." She combs her hair while hoping he will have the wit to open up to her.

Moss places a small log in stove's firebox and looks around for matches and paper. It doesn't light. "Fuck it." Out comes a butane lighter and he lights the fire.

This evening has been tough on Moss. He once believed his life was pointless, but now he knows it is full of meaning: but only as a turn of the gear for Winston Doe. Against his will he draws solace from the clarity that life isn't pointless and sutures the wound of his foolish life. He has no idea this is a processing routine begun at the Clipper complex to neuter his pain. Clipper has preformed this routine many times; suicide has often been carried out by the Gindas once when they discover they are puppets of their species.

Moss picks up the teapot to fill it. In a moment of familiarity with its design anger rises. *I remember this. Travis gave this to her.* He cannot plumb its depth but sees himself as a rape victim. Another person might have interpreted his pain as love for his brother--Travis's death was revealed in the news nets this morning. His eyes droop for a moment.

The ATWAS annunciator calls his attention to a satellite that passes overhead. Staring at the hewn log ceiling, he says quietly: "Russell Biner, I presume? You know, ah, Roo--I know you and she doesn't. I die and she doesn't. But you don't get to die so I'd never trade places with either of you. How many more cycles my old-friend-of-the-puppet-masters, how many more?" He looks at the teapot and launches the tea pot against the back door, sending bits of the flowered pottery to every corner of the kitchen.

"You know, sentience isn't all it's cracked up to be." Surveying the scattered shards and noting the location of each: a pink-and-white ceramic petal on the counter top, another near the stove, blue and pink flowers on the floor, a leaf gouged into the chinking of the log door frame. Moss picks up a matching tea cup and crushes it in his hand. Blood pours onto the floor. He stares at the puddle, completely unaware of any pain--other than his own anger. He perversely begins to draw a question mark with his foot.

"Oh dear lord, Moss." Winston stands at the kitchen door. The pool of blood spreads everywhere, except into her heart. "Are you okay?"

He blinks at the rush of pain into his being. "What did you do to me?" He asks, dropping the remains of the cup to the floor and grabbing for the nearest cloth. “There was no pain until you. Now my life is nothing. My world is a lie. My brother is dead. You are a heartless bitch.” Moss kicks a brown leather loafer at her. It flies straight and hits her square in the chest. “I see. So our intimacies as lovers really wasn’t too tough for you because your are invulnerable. Or, you were just looking for your lover, the saintly Dr. Biner? Well I’m in the 411 on that and you’re the fool.” Moss takes the towel and tosses it on the kitchen floor. “But don’t worry, none of this will matter to you soon.” He steps on the towel. He then wraps his hand in another as she watches. “Winston, what was it about me that made it easy for you to do this to me?”

”Everything.” She shoots back. She glances around the kitchen, hating him and herself.

He points to the question mark drawn in his own blood. “You think it’s a doorway, no, you think it’s our path. You dumb shit.”

“Please stop cursing.”

He breaks out in a gale of maniacal laughter. “I knew you’d go there. How the heck did I know? How many times have we done this? Oh fuck me! Who cares?”

“Please--” She begins to fear his apparent clarity of some memory.

Moss grins as he steps forward. A sickening crunch causes Winston to turn away. Moss continues: “We are looking for this?”

“What?” She turns towards him.

“Did you know your dunderhead space-man transmits that over and over?” Moss pulls the bloody ceramic piece from his foot. “That’s been the only thing coming from the satellite for years. How do you think I was able to tune my annunciator?”

She stops and stares at him. “Did Mina tell you this?”

“Winston Doe--ever the researcher--and you say I am representative of a loathsome species.” Eyes smug in the sockets of an angry hard-skulled man, he continues. “Oh--you want to know what Clipper is keeping from you--I see. Too bad. He is looking for a thing, a solution, not you. Mina’s dad always knew that way was a mistake--but he never got any further. Score one dead for the Gindas. Do you really still believe in his love for her? Or wonder how our ancestors could have been so evil, egotistical, and blind--or why we care so little for our Earth-home?”

“I just want to know why Walkers died so young while you rabid Techies live so long,” Winston cannot bear to look at him, but she wants to know what he knows.

“The great ones have always been fools, Winston. Early on the thugs figured out how to control goodness through the mob’s greed.” Moss laughs as he crosses to the sink and looks into the water. “Mina taught me that. Your turn.”

“It took eons to get to the point where we could construct a totally artificial brain to think a proper morality for us,” she says. Winston is fishing for an answer to Mina’s comment that her goodness is manufactured.

“So we could all become like you, a pursed heart and a brilliant intellect? Just how different are we? And did you bore me before, as well?"

"I believe I did, yes, Moss." Winston calms a bit.

"Including your allegiance to Walker fairy tales?"

This had been the last comment he had made to her before she left for vacation--but she cannot avoid a retort to his mounting anger. "Is there anything you do with a woman that isn't a rehearsed play?"

He responds with a fake, boyish smile "Maybe."

She holds a long shard from the neck of the tea pot; it would make an effective weapon. "Once again you sound perfectly human." But rattled by his earlier comments she still seeks answers.

"Ever wonder how I managed to develop a sensor that picks up the arrival of a satellite?" His eyes slowly droop shut. She notes the Clipper intervention and assumes he was about to assault her.

"Technology does not matter to me once it functions."

"Let me show you. He pulls the small annunciator from his wrist, takes a fork from the drawer, and levers it open. "There is a bio-computer inside it. Travis and I built the original one in my lab. Want to hear a funny joke? My genetics run the bio-computer. Travis told me it was a lark. I figured out tonight I am hard wired to know when the satellite containing your boyfriend comes closer--but you're not. And you can set a watch by it, then extrapolate secondary effects to other similar systems and call it brilliance. Big deal. Every time I figured out you guys were screwing with my memory you took my memory."

"So what? Anyone in your position could have gotten there." She cannot believe she has become so cruel. "I hate being close to you." The room tightens like a clamp. Winston moves towards the door to get out of the kitchen.

He stares at her, defeated by her. "I can feel the satellites' approach throughout my body now. I don't need this damn thing." He lets it fall to the floor. "Does that hurt you, that I can feel him and you cannot?"

She walks into the yard. Benson sits on a log in front of her.

Moss follows Winston out the door and sees him. "Benson, finally. Kill me you nasty lying little fucker, or I'll kill her." He pats a pistol outline in his pocket so Benson will see he means it.

Benson pulls out a knife and tosses it. The knife quivers on the door frame beside Moss' face. "Don't do it."

Moss stands, amused. "Am I the only one who remembers this? Oh, fuck, that's it. I am." He turns and stares out to the water and the ferries. "Got it yet, Dummy?"

Winston follows his gaze to the rusting hulks, the ferries. The sea around them glitters, but so far as she can tell, nothing has changed. Her eyes widen. "That's the real museum. Samarra was a placebo--for me?"

"And so soon I die, with no light in my eyes or the truth in my breast." Moss laughs. "Tell me why I had to be kept stupid, Benson? Was it all so she could come to this clarity in a pristine ignorance? For what?"

Winston pulls a laurel leaf from a tree and rubs it in her hands watching

Benson weave his way around a large tree stump, putting it between him and Moss. Benson says, "I don't know, Moss."

Moss' eyes droop. "No comment, of course." Moss looks around, embarrassed--then seeing a knowing gaze on Benson's face, he snarls "You could have warned me."

"Please stop," Winston says. "Will you tell me what you know? What am I missing about the ferries?"

"Above all else, freedom is mine," Moss says measuring Benson Fong--knowing he will be kind enough to kill him in a moment.

"Moss, don't do it. He will kill you. It's his--"

Moss rushes her, his pistol rising to fire. The calm of the woods breaks with the report of single shot. His head whips back and his feet fly forward. Moss lands in the dirt, half of his head blown away.

She doesn't know who screams so loudly. Hands grab her. *And that horrible yowling, tell them to stop.* Someone holds her and the screaming continues. It goes on and on until she hears: *I am dead.* Then it all fades into darkness.

Chapter 40

"Hi folks, This is Margaret Davies with today's hints for home. Do find you need to check the back yard for prowlers more than you used to? Try keeping a peacock. They are on special at Pets-4-U. And our other helpful hint of the day: When you shop for food, make sure to pick up a little extra food in the next few weeks. This is Disaster Awareness Month and a little extra food and water couldn't hurt--and it might help your neighbors. So pitch in and get an extra gallon or two of water--and some delicious Happy Meals Dry Fried burgers. Let the good times roll, in your kitchen. Eat Happy Meals Dry Fried Burgers, from your friends at Genebanks S.A. And don't forget that extra water. It'll make you happy! This is Margaret Davies with today's tips for better living."

. . . .

She wakes up in field cot. Mina stands beside her. Benson speaks with a small squad of soldiers by the tree line. Out on the water, the rotting bodies of three huge ferries lie wedged between black poles that once made up the docks. A metal walkway stretches between them and rocks in the breeze under a macramé of old ropes slapping the sides of the ships. The boats' edges tilt and roll, the planes of their structures moving lazily in the breeze, like the ropes. She looks back to Mina. "Please tell me what you see," she says. Mina looks over at Benson, who approaches them.

"The old ferry docks and a couple of rusted ships." Mina wraps herself tighter in a silvered coat of red satin.

"A couple means two," Winston replies.

"Not succinct enough, Madam Director?" Mina coos. "Okay three boats."

Benson Fong arrives. Following Winston's gaze, he stares out at the ships. He seems dumbstruck, his jaw agape and his eyes wide. "Oh my."

"Did they remove the body?" Mina asks.

"It's being taken care of." He continues to stare out at the ships.

"Isn't it amazing?" Winston says. Both Mina and Benson look at her. Neither speak, but for different reasons. She continues: "Benson, do you have any surveillance of this area? Out there, the ships?"

"We do." He dials a number on his phone. "What do you wish, Madam Director?"

She faces him, her face flush with excitement. "A picture of the boats from say two weeks ago and then say six months ago."

The General understands, but will say nothing at this point, or ever. It is clear Mina misses the event. Benson Fong, on the other hand, has seen eternity's paint stroke--he remembers only two ships--and will forever be thankful for this moment. He speaks into the phone requesting the images. Then to her: "Hardcopy will be here in a minute."

"Does anything seem strange to you?" She says to Mina. Her gaze remains fixed on the boats.

Mina looks at Benson, unsure of what to say. "Nothing," she replies.

Winston looks at Benson Fong. "But you know." A moment later, her driver, Corporal Fisk, appears with pictures of the dock. "The photos are over this last year, each four months apart, General." The soldier leaves.

Fong glances at the images as he hands them to her.

She scans the pictures. "And this may be particularly disconcerting to you, General. I am going for a walk soon." She sees he is not surprised in the least. "Mind if I take one of those for study? Sentience calls." Winston tilts her head feeling the breeze. There is something sweet in the winds but she cannot name the scent.

"Will you tell me what in the name of God's batteries is in those pictures?" Mina asks.

"I've lived here for years. And for all that time, there were only two boats out there. And now there are three--and these pictures confirm that there were always three--while I know there were two."

"So the cycle Dad predicted has completed, Dr. Doe." Says Mina, her eyes wide with amazement. "You knew?" She asks Benson.

Winston smiles at her. "Seems so. Did you blackout, General?"

"Something but that doesn't matter. You knew all this, Dr. Doe. You just had to forget what was gone." Benson Fong can barely hide his joy. "What do you want me to do now?"

"I am the museum curator am I not?" She stares out at the ships. "And they are the museum, aren't they?" She points to the boats.

Mina's eyes widen. "Moss told me you would act like this. You're going out there aren't you? He told me but I didn't understand. You believe the ships are a stable scale."

Winston does not comment. She is surprised by the girlish tone of Mina's comments. She has never heard Mina so overt. "The Walkers don't know they are in a city-museum, or do they? What's the correct word for those boats. What term were you using now?"

"Samarra," Mina replies.

Winston takes in a deep breath. "I see. Of course."

"And the place up the hill, Mina?" She looks to see no smoke, just trees and a blue sky.

"The Puget Sound Memorial of Death--for those who died from global warming--of course," Mina says. Benson Fong scans the tree line in silence.

Winston leans over and kisses her on the cheek--but speaks to Benson. "Your silence always did impress me." She winks at Benson.

Mina caresses her arm. "Say hi to Roo if you find him. And if you don't, try to forgive him. Research was his life."

Winston stares at her in stunned surprise, again. "Like you forgave your dad?"

"Of course I forgive him. We took the rip and manipulated it. There were costs," Mina says.

"Including you, Madam Director," Benson says quickly. "Mina has always known, I guess."

"Do you know what's out there, Benson?"

"All I know is my job. And that job is to protect this project in every way I know how."

"So you can't or won't go?" Winston looks down at the grass.

Benson looks at her. "There is only room for one pivot point--one focus. I am here to protect you and the pivot point."

Winston looks at Mina, thinking whether she should speak. *Would it cause a rupture?* "I need to know something, did you know about each other's feelings the whole time?"

"I cannot say," he replies, still trying to find his way in this new space.

"Of course he knew, but you know he could not speak to you about it. It's interference," says Mina. "His restraint finally hooked me."

Benson shakes his head in amazement. "I will work to keep the project in tact," Benson says to Winston. She can see he has no idea what to expect after she leaves, but she sees no fear.

"But you claimed sentience? About love also. Mina?" Winston says quietly.

"You will see soon enough," Benson replies.

Mina is stunned.

Out to the east, a launch plume. "They are launching supplies into space for their escape," Benson says stoically.

"Benson you are the second most dedicated man I have ever me. Tell me, Mina, what is the memory of Russell's release? What did Pilot Nothing achieve?"

Benson pauses. "It is amazing that we can discuss this at all."

"Benson can be so dramatic."

Winston and Benson look at each other but display nothing.

Mina continues: "He believed that what we called madness was a way to cycle back to alter the path for humanity away from the unbridled use of energy."

"And when was that feasible?"

"His papers, the ones you have read a zillion times say around the end of World War Two would do it," says Mina Wolf.

"But in our cycle he arrives in the fourth decade of the 21st century."

"You mean the second decade," Mina says.

Winston nods to Benson. "I forgot. Well we know he gets that far. What about everything else? Lonocs, space trips, the Lonocs killing Quentin's soldiers, and the rest of it."

"Dr. Doe," says Benson Fong trying to squash the discussion. "I know you believe civilization is measured in repeated violations of reality as well as an ability to maintain order in the face of that transcendence. But we do not know about the items you are discussing." He nods to the group of soldiers he had been in discussion with when she woke. Winston understands.

"That borders on blasphemy," says Mina. Benson touches her shoulder and she coos closer to him. Winston stands quietly, mouth agape.

Benson glows as he speaks: "It all hinges on humanity seeing how insignificant it is, given the many faces of the universe, of God, or Gaia, whatever you need to label this space."

"His descriptors betray ignorance and nothing more," says Mina, smiling warmly at Benson. "I guess you are going to work a little harder on theories. He's not happy about my work sometimes, Winston." Mina's hand drifts to Benson's shoulder and caresses it.

Winston watches Benson blush. "You hid your admiration for him surprisingly well."

Benson shakes his head watching Mina stroke his arm. "Dr. Doe, please."

Winston continues, enjoying the moment. "But I have to say it seems to me your love for him materialized from out of nowhere."

"Maybe the same place as the extra boat?" Mina replies. "That's truth for you two. And I suspect by your glances I was a stranger to his heart."

"No worse than following egomaniacs into Hell," says Benson quickly.

Mina glows. "You two amaze me," Winston says.

Benson works to form words feeling the touch of Mina's hand on his arm. "Dr. Doe, I know nothing. I am sure of that. But I know there are reports of anomalies that give me hope. One of those reports comes from the notion that you know there were two boats out there while Mina knows there were always three. So what happens when Biner eliminates our insane use of energy?"

"That is the question, my dear." She looks at Winston. "He's worried about me."

Winston looks at the three boats, then at the two lovers. "You dad is a hero. Mina." The two women share a brief moment of understanding. "Mina, when Moss died it all changed--because he had focus. You need to know something has also changed for Benson. Try talking with him--though I doubt he will explain."

"Nothing has changed for me," Benson replies quickly. "There are no incongruities--other than your comments on the boat."

Winston wears a bemused smile. "Benson, you were always a romantic and look at what has happened. She loves you dearly. Things will work out--but you know that already. Best of luck, you two." She turns, walking down the trail to the three ferries.

With picture in hand, she knows which ferry to board.

Chapter 41

Walking down the hill, she steps on small stones making her way over mud furrows in the ground. Reaching the flat of what was once a parking lot for the ferry terminal, she stops, remembering Moss' picture showing the lot full of brightly colored cars and trucks. Children playing by the water as adults chat alongside their cars, it was a sunny day, and lines of cars striped the parking lot.

Now it is a network of paths through the blackberry brambles and ocean spray. She looks around seeking to find Benson's people. There is no sign of them, but Winston does not doubt their presence. She does see a cache of meats and fruit. Entering the maze of bramble, she feels a calm caress.

Breaking into an open field of grass and trash, she walks to the squat, square green administration building. The sheet metal roof lazily flaps in the breeze. The torn walls reveal what was once a waiting room for the passengers. An old schedule, a hand-painted rectangular metal sign, hangs on a nail outside. It's title: Ferryboat Winter Sailing Schedule. On this last schedule, sailings are once a month via one old ailing vessel called Elhwa.

After testing the wooden floor, Winston enters the rickety building. Old vending machines stand empty: Their glass fronts are covered with mold and green slime. A gouged sign littered with initials is still barely readable. She reads: Island Hospital. Chauffeurs Only.

The hyper-rich, and their servants, took over the islands served by these ferries in a last ditch effort to insulate themselves from the horrors of global warming. Then the battles with mainlanders seeking hoarded resources; and finally, when the resources were looted, the flight back to the mainland. Then more battles: with alcoholism, dementia, and an addiction to comfort taking the last of them.

A group of racists came to the islands, but they were slaughtered by the Native Americans who finally took the islands back. The Native Americans eventually left as well, saying the Caucasians had cursed the archipelago. Wild mule-deer now roam the islands.

Winston steps over mounds of moldy cushions to look at the trio of listing ferries; they remind her of rusting wedding cakes. *Amazing ships--huge energy consuming behemoths--who's only function was supposedly to move other energy-sucking, carbon spitting monsters out to those islands so our ancestors could ruin them with greed. It was all so depraved. But this is my museum. Life is just one crazy joke.* She sighs and looks back up the hill towards her cabin: As if on cue, black smoke, a leap of flames, then an explosion curling skyward. *Nothing there anymore. More launch contrails, oh my.*

She pushes aside the old rusted fence fabric, ignoring the 'No Trespassing' signs, walking out onto the part of the dock that was once the car loading platform. The winds slap her loose-fitting sweater as she stares at a ship's maw. It had once held almost two-hundred automobiles.

They all had cars. Everyone of them, they could go where they wanted and do as they pleased. Why isn't this place a place of sin? If only we could have told our past selves what to look for. Roo, I know you are trying to do that.

Winston looks back up the hill. A single balloon has been sent skyward. It's bright red. Someone is under attack and without communication. She watches the balloon dart right, and then deflate. The she watches a march of explosions take the hillside. Everywhere she looks there are rocket trails into the sky, and smoke.

Ahead, the ferry's maw and a small Walker battery pack, hanging from a stairway railing. Behind it, the gaping cave of the ferry's main deck; she sees fishing lines at the far end. *This ferry is the new one but it looks like it has been here forever.* Entering the steel cavern while scanning the deck and looking for signs of movement, she opens a door and climbs the steep interior stairs.

At the top of the stairs, another door; it swings open easily--not even a squeak. Through the door into the passenger area, she smells coals and smoking meat. Examining the floor, a well worn path has removed the gray paint; she notes the plates have buckled and the glass panes that once lined the seating area are missing, but the structure seems real enough. *The concept of real, that's a mess.*

A rock, thrown from a broken window, sails across the room's span landing on the floor. Had she known who sent the rock through the window she might have stalled in amazement. Instead, she weaves easily through the leaning girders and across rickety metal plates that form a bridge to a galley door. Overhead, she sees a bar poking through a piece of conscripted chain link fence supporting a half ton of rocks. She stops; her eyes trace the route of a trip wire from the roof to the walkway. It disappears into the shadows in front of her. "I will wait here until you want me to enter," she calls out. Winston gazes out the windows to the red and black smoke then back to the rock trap. It seems to her, by its rust and its placement, to have been here for a many years. The cold of the metal around her sings with the pelt of waves. The slight tilt and wash of iridescent waves outside makes her dizzy. She listens for movement but can hear no one. *Someone is very cautious. Maybe I should have been more careful.*

The trips wire slacks until it is flat on the floor. She advances, waiting at the galley door a moment, then presses on the door. It opens and the clan kitchen rests before her well stocked with food. Smoke from pine fires have colored the dark interior in a soft red glow. Along the far wall, three fires still burn. Two are low flames meant to keep water hot. The third fire in the center burns for the dead. She understands why she was kept waiting. Someone is ill and about to die; they wanted to feel her spirit.

Even so, no one reveals themselves. Winston notes the image of five men bent and contorted to look like shadows sketched into the walls. That means that less than five-hundred are in the clan, an average sized Walker encampment.

A moment later, an elder female enters from a far door. Lit by the middle fire, she hobbles forward. "I am Winston Doe of the Pacific Clans Northern Redwood family. Welcome." Her voice rasps like pieces of metal dragged along a rock.

Misunderstanding the statement. Winston fears she is the one to die. In a way she is correct.

"I wish no harm for you."

The old woman laughs. "Follow me."

Winston enters a large communal dining room. The others in the room giggle and stamp their feet at her arrival. Smiling eyes, some with tears, greet her. "Enter the fleeting home of the Redwood Clan." A second woman who speaks these words is old as well, and standing among a crowd of children.

Immediately from the far doors, others of the clan enter. A tall man with a skin-head and a bandolier of bullets speaks loudly: "He is outside circling the boat, examining the waste, counting our numbers. This cycle is complete." The warrior then sits, blending in with the rest. Another man enters and points at Winston: "Our greatest grandmother found this place for us, telling us to wait and meet ourselves, and then wait some more. We have lived here ever since. Though frail and ill she appears fresh and young before us. It has happened before--we will see it again. No fear!" The warrior struts past Winston to sit by the far door.

"Who are you?" She asks the old woman.

"I am Winston Doe. We wear the same sweater--do we not?"

Winston feels faint.

"I know that feeling," says the old woman, staring up at her. Winston sees her own eyes. "The answer to your first question is, I don't know about Russell. The second question: There is no future for humanity, other than this recycling point. We will repair the past and then I think we will fade, I suppose. Last, I do not know if we will be rescued before that. Now, please, how many did they tell you had lived?"

Winston replies, "Originally two billion. Now, five-hundred million."

The crowd around her murmurs approval. "That's good. When I arrived here, the number was around two hundred million--at least that's what Benson told me."

"How many ships were here?" Winston asks.

The old woman stares at her, confused by the question. "I did not ask that." She looks around. The others remain mute.

Winston hands her the picture of the ferries but the older woman does not look at it. "It is said that one of us brought a picture of a single boat the first time we were here. Its arrival was the reason for trek of discovery. It is said that then there were less than fifty million of us." Her eyes release a flood of tears. "There are three boats." She says loudly.

Four men rush from the room to survey all three ships.

"Are you curious about your lover? He will be here in a minute. I know because my lover left here to protect you."

"Russell? No, Plow. Your lover was Plow," Winston says. The others in the room laugh and applaud. Winston misses the obvious--she can still only think of Russell Biner.

"Where did these others come from?"

"Everywhere--all of them are a generation after me. The first twenty years must have been horrible for our greatest grandmother. But now, we replace ourselves as our younger selves arrive. We tell them what we know, because they arrive just before we die."

"Scratch death as well." Winston surprises herself by saying the words aloud. "No I guess that figures. How many times have we cycled?"

"Too many. It is chiseled on a piece of steel. I was told I could look at it any time I wanted to, but I have chosen not to know. Nor will I. I do know three ferries means less died this cycle and the pace increases. I also know we are waiting for a fourth ferry."

"Why?"

"Four. Doesn't it mean anything to you? I was never stupid like her, just self-involved," she mumbles this to the other woman. Both laugh.

"They built the docks for four ferries. But then what?"

"No, the right question is how did they know to build them for a quartet of ferries? But to your question: I suppose when we stop replacing ourselves, the memory will fade away," says her older self. "Then, the madness that has consumed so many cycles will have abated. For now, we are at peace and we are happy. Or have you become too much of a Techie to appreciate that?" She laughs. "That term always bothered me." She looks at her younger self. "I was so beautiful. Those words were said before, to me, to you, often. Do not feel ashamed by your gifts." Windows begin to open letting in daylight. Winston looks at the clan's people; soot covers their faces making their features indistinguishable, almost like manikins with bright white eyes. She notes there is no smoke or fire on the hillsides.

"We are dolls in a playhouse," Winston says.

The old woman speaks. "Ignore her, she is still stupid." Her eyebrow arches at her younger self. "The Gindas were the way, but their repetition of lost memory was the lesson, because insane memory was the sickness."

"Your people are very healthy," Winston says. There is no response. "So we are here to wait until Russell's contact with the past finally finds the beginning of the madness and it all ceases. Is that possible? Then we are gone?"

"Do you doubt who I am?" Asks the old woman.

"I do not."

"So it is possible then that he is still--and we are the saved--but I do not see how. But the population still grows." She stares at herself. Both women turn away at the same moment. The older woman speaks: "Tell me did Seattle burn in the Jazz War?"

Winston looks at her puzzled. "No." The older woman nods as a man hands her a photograph. It is U.N. headquarters in ruins; all around it, the devastation of a war zone.

"Seattle was fine, but Samarra was burning when I left."

"The placebo was completed? It was actually built? I knew it. Then Seattle didn't burn so Gregor was alive."

Winston, startled by the questions, watches the old woman wheeze a moment, then cough. "Yes. Seattle is a city and your colleague lived."

She shakes her head as tears fill her eyes. The other woman approaches, clutching her macramé skirt and blouse of yellow nylon; she helps the older woman to sit down on a cushion. She speaks: "What about Russell's mother? What can you tell me about her?"

"He didn't know his mother. She died in childbirth."

"Are you sure? She didn't have cancer when he was a teen?"

"No."

"The changes." Her graying eyes fill with tears. "How long has it been since you have seen Roo?"

"Almost two decades." Winston's eyes look at the other woman and her eyes widen. "You're Hope Weiss. I thought you died as a Ginda?"

The old woman's lips purse for a moment. "Were you and I friends in your cycle?" The woman's gaze wanders to the clan then returns to Winston. They both already know the answer is no.

"We knew each other briefly, but you disappeared during the Jazz War. I was told you had died trying to help Roo. But you came here?" Winston watches a sad smile appear on Hope's face.

"I walked away from the Clipper Project one morning and found this place. I had to stay. But if I had been cycling again I should have been here years ago. You have cleared that mystery up for me." Hope Weiss feels for Winston's plight at having revealed something so awful. "So it appears I am the last of me. We measure progress here by change in each cycle. I guess I am progress."

Winston closes her eyes for a moment trying to understand. "When I return, as a younger woman there will be no Hope Biner?" Winston asks horrified at her misstep.

A door swings open with a loud metal thud. A soldier dressed in an antique military uniform enters. He is a broad man in his late thirties. Below the surveillance camera on his right side is a long scar. Blood soils his uniform. The man scans the group and immediately sees Winston Doe. He walks towards her examining every face for threat. But nothing could stop his march towards her. The old women's eyes light. The soldier sees her but turns his gaze to Winston. His eyes show confusion. "God, you are a beautiful woman." He looks around, embarrassed. "I told myself if I ever saw you again, I'd tell you that." He pauses. "But you're older? I don't understand. Is this the museum then? You are Winston Doe, right? Ignore my stupidity Win, I know it's you."

"I am Winston." Her eyes widen, seeing the same gaze she had seen once before, by the ocean at the California Memorial Park for the dead. "The eucalyptus, the one with the Gindas' names, it's in your shirt. May I please have it? I lost the other one."

"Ma'am?" Plow wrinkles his brow as he reaches into his shirt and hands her the eucalyptus cloth. "Was there ever a day you didn't confuse me?" She stares at the camera nestled behind his ear. *If he sees this then so do the researchers of his time. So is that's how Benson will know what to do. I told them. This is the source of Benson's sentience. They didn't know before that.*

"Which one is the last name?" Winston asks. From the corner of her eye she sees the older Doe glow.

"Anderson, Moss Anderson. And you were the next project. It's why I left. I couldn't allow that." He shakes his head, embarrassed by his heart.

"We were lovers?" Winston asks.

"So you went ahead with it? I didn't get it. I am so sorry. I tried to force you not to do it. How did you know we all needed you to become a Ginda?" Plow lowers his voice: "Of course, it is humanity's curse: We have always been powered by man's purpose and woman's love."

Winston eye's light--an old feeling stirs inside her. "An errant knight, a philosopher warrior, a lover, of course," she says out loud. The others in the room glow with joy.

"I didn't think you would remember that. Do you remember I told you not to volunteer? That means something also." He stares at her. "But--Win--you don't remember me?" Shaken by clarity, his face boils red. "It's that bastard, Biner. I hope he rots out there in space. He and that lunatic Wolf, they never cared for any one, or anything, except the damn project. Well I am glad I quit."

"Well if you mean that, than you had better remove that camera from behind your ear, soldier," says the older Winston Doe.

"What? Bah, Clipper." He grabs the camera from behind his ear and steps on it.

"Wait, forget it," says Winston. "I need you to tell me about your history. What about Pilnouth?"

"What's that?"

"Pilot Nothing?"

"Sorry."

"What about the clarity about climate change? Was it before or after the Greenhouse laws?"

"Before," he answers.

"And it still tipped?"

His eyes narrow. "It was the reason for the Greenhouse Laws. Some people in New Zealand proved the tipping point would cause space to move away from us. But you don't remember this? Is it Clipper? I can remove the link for you."

"Amazing. One more question: The rubber band effect?"

He scratches behind the ear where the camera was. "I never knew that camera was there. Oh, the rubber band effect? Well, if you are here, check that, if you and I are here together, than Hope Weiss was successful. I think Biner always thought she failed."

Winston looks at Hope and smiles, then she looks down at the eucalyptus document bringing it to her face, caressing it. *They know enough to complete the next cycle. No wonder the older me is so sanguine.* Winston looks over to the older woman, her eyes have closed; no breath leaves her breast.

"Win, what happens next?" Asks Plow.

"They, out there, eventually run out of time and space because we are in a point of stability. But I don't know if we ever get rescued, Sergeant."

"Please call me Gus." He looks around. "But then what do we do when they run out of space and time?" The fear in his eyes says she once knew him well. Lowering his voice, "You once understood the function of the city museum. It's a supposed safe point to traverse the drift. Supposedly those inside will make it. But without that knowledge you figured it out anyway. How did you know this was it?"

"I'm 45 years old, Gus."

"You were 24 when I left you a month ago. That means twenty one years as a Ginda. How could they risk you out there in that horror for so long? Benson would have protected you."

She shakes her head and points to the broken camera on the floor.

"They heard you speak to a forty five year old version of Winston Doe."

So that's how they knew it would work." He nods as he speaks. "Winston, do you feel anything for me now? Anything at all?"

CHAPTER 42

(Addendum, from the Research Team: Work continues for a fail safe platform--Samarra. Security for the Museum project will be arranged and undertaken by General Fong. Dr. Plow will provide interior security. Mr. Fong, will provide exterior security. Once a stable platform is in place we will begin populating the space. Some say that we seek to facilitate our own demise. I believe that is incorrect. I believe we are facilitating the removal of our memory of extinction because so long as the memory continues; we are prisoners of a mad past. L.Wolf. Date suppressed per requirement--and because it really doesn't matter.)

My name is Lazlo Wolf. I am writing this first entry into the Ginda diary and locking it in the operating system to ensure that it is unreachable by the Gindas, and to ensure that those of you alive to read this pay respect to the heroism of every soldier and researcher who took on the task of Sammich Ginda. To forget any of them, to mention any name without respect is a crime. The selfless work of these men and women, the unknown and perhaps terrible sacrifices they will endure, are born of the finest that exists in us. The task to reset humanity back to that place of heroism and honor is our task. It was every generation's task.

Because of that, I doubt we will ever return to this Earth; we humans are blowing away like snow on a cold winter day. And it is true, we do not know what we may encounter when this is complete, though no one now doubts the current end is extinction. But what will happen if we are successful and we achieve a reset? Is there a place for us? I think not.

So then this is all about virtue; it had been written in our texts since the beginning of time that virtue, honor, decency, and truth are our main paths, but they became lost in the palace of fools erected by our ancestors. It around us.

I used to think heroes embodied purity above all. Now I suspect their heroism is based on their ability to fall with us and take the first step up again--even as we beat them down with our pain. Our failure is their failure. Their victories are ours to steal. How did we forget their struggle contains the chart of our course from barbarism?

Our hero, Sammich Ginda, is a selfless person

placed in an intolerable position. Humanity, if we are successful, will owe the Gindas for our escape. We will certainly owe them for our present, a present that allows us to work towards a solution.

The Gindas will give up life, heart, soul, memories, and flesh over and over in an attempt to keep the insane desires of our ancestors in check. I pray their numbers will be small but I fear I am a Wholack for this hope. How many cycles will it take? How many times will we bury a hero to get to the core of this madness? When we do, how will we reverse it? If we eventually turn the switch and our species recognizes the coming horror of climate change will we be cured, cursed, or just forgotten about? Is the cure worse than what we have now? I wonder.

Insofar as Russell Biner: It must be said that the deaths he will participate in are no more his responsibility than the horrible experiences that surround us due to our ancestors' greed. Our home planet ejects us. Russell Biner will, if he is successful, have no ability to modify the future. That is the task of Species Focus. While the Gindas are his launch vehicle into and through our collective memory.

I pray he cannot count the times the sun rises. In this, I have worked diligently to keep him free. Clipper will, I pray, continue to function keeping his memory clean of time passing. Our history tells us Pilot Nothing was successful. If not for that I don't think I could have participated. Still, success will be measured by his exiting his cocoon of memory evisceration before the warming becomes terminal. How can we even know that he will be successful? Are we happily ignorant, or foolish dreamers? We are so apart from our world.

The Gindas, on the other hand, will experience all of the events: the crossing truths tearing at them, the empty time, the evil needs, the rot of deceit. Through their pains, we will find a path to keep ourselves free and safe in the hellish space created for us. We will rule in this Hell of consumption--this Hell we have created for ourselves. Still, when we walk backwards from hell, what will we find?

I know the public can deal with a leader who murders and lies, or one that lives by deceit and trickery, one who has no ethical core. But then what about the Gindas, who are a fools of our sad, sorry state? Can we deal with a leader like that? Now lanced from the planet, we rape our heroes--because we must. This is, I believe, our true crime. True heroes never could do anything on their own. If they could, how would they be heroes?

So now, we will tell them to roll in the mud for us. How sad that the hero cannot stop us--they are blind to our evil. I think that is why the hero is finally trusted by us. A sad truth has been conscripted by our desires: A decent human is blind to our evil so we can always harm them first. No wonder our planet has sent us adrift.

And then the myth: We will say we are searching for a truth to end our pains. Instead, we will search for something people can live with and count on until the end. Maybe they will be comfortable with the answer. After all, in the beginning, it is said, there was the word, or was it the question?

Perhaps, if we are truly successful, some day

we will accept the pulse, the beauty, and the troughs of an unfettered life. It owns us whether we wish to face that or not. If so, then we will have a long road. But I--we all--will be vilified for our tasks.

Why would I take on the evil? I do this for my child--so that she will someday be free of those evil chains. For her, I bear any sacrifice; and I will work to curse the heroes and make the heroes our fools. That is their course and their glory.

In the end, Sammich Ginda will be a tin hero. He is, in that, the perfect focus of our species, the hope of our species, and the brunt of our species. The heroes are the ones that can do nothing for us, but lack everything--except virtue, honor, decency, and truth.

That is the essence, the human-core required of us, by this planet, if we wish sustain our species.

God help us.

www.ingramcontent.com/pod-product-compliance
Lightning Source LLC
Chambersburg PA
CBHW030921260626
47169CB00002B/352

* 9 7 8 0 9 7 5 3 6 5 5 1 9 *